Joanna Rees grew up in Chelmsford before getting an English and drama degree at Goldsmiths College. After several bizarre jobs, including running her own sandwich-delivery business and writing promotions for the back of Sugar Puffs boxes, *It Could Be You* was published in 1997 under her maiden name, Josie Lloyd, and enabled her to meet fellow novelist Emlyn Rees. Together they wrote *Come Together*, a twenty-something rom-com, which became a number-one *Sunday Times* bestseller and was translated into twenty-six languages. They went on to co-write six more successful novels, and along the way got married and had three kids. In 2007 Joanna went solo and wrote *Platinum*, followed by *Forbidden Pleasures* in 2010. Joanna also writes a light-hearted blog about her life as a novelist and mother in Brighton called mumwritesbooks.com, which was in the top ten *Times* mummy blogs. *The Key to It All* is her twelfth novel.

The Key to It All

JOANNA REES

PAN BOOKS

First published 2014 by Pan Books
an imprint of Pan Macmillan, a division of Macmillan Publishers Limited
Pan Macmillan, 20 New Wharf Road, London N1 9RR
Basingstoke and Oxford
Associated companies throughout the world
www.panmacmillan.com

ISBN 978-0-230-75828-5

1 3 5 7 9 8 6 4 2

A CIP catalogue record for this book is available from the British Library.

Typeset by Ellipsis Digital, Glasgow
Printed and bound by CPI Group (UK) Ltd, Croydon, CR0 4YY

Visit www.panmacmillan.com to read more about all our books
and to buy them. You will also find features, author interviews and
news of any author events, and you can sign up for e-newsletters
so that you're always first to hear about our new releases.

For Liz Murphy

Acknowledgements

I find that the spark of inspiration for any novel always happens in the most unexpected of places and the idea for this one came from hearing a story a mate told in a pub, so many thanks to Sara Elman for that. I must say here that any similarity to real-life events is accidental as this is entirely a work of fiction.

Once again, thanks to the team at Pan Macmillan for making this book happen. It's been a lovely experience to write and edit, knowing that my book has such a great home. My heartfelt thanks to the most incisive and supportive editor a girl could have, my brilliant publisher, Wayne Brookes. Thanks also to everyone at Curtis Brown, especially Vivienne Schuster and Felicity Blunt. You two are simply the best.

I feel very blessed to have lots of people who support me through the whole process of writing a novel. First of these – and peerless – is my wonderful husband, Emlyn Rees, who gets me through the highs and lows with countless cups of tea, words of encouragement and the odd eureka-moment plot fix. My girls, Tallulah, Roxie and Minty who leave notes on my desk before they go to school, urging me to carry on and 'write well' and who never mind being hauled out of bed by their tearful mother to type the words 'The End'.

Acknowledgements

Then there's my treasured girl friends – Dawn Howarth, Katy Whelan, Toni Savage, Harriet Rees, Ruth Hasnip, Anna Christoforou, Ali Gunn, Laurel Lelkow, Clare Willis and Bronwin Wheatley who hold my hand in various ways and generally make me feel fab. Particular thanks to Katy and Toni for being my early readers and giving their honest feedback. Thanks, too, to David Verity who gave me great information about Iguazu Falls.

As well as my parents and sister, my extended family are supportive of my literary exploits and for years have flown the flag, telling their friends when I have a new book out. That said, right from when my first novel *It Could Be You* was published and my scandalized Nanna said it was 'worse than *Forever Amber*' I've had a certain reputation! One person in particular, however – my very glamorous Aunty Liz – has always been on my side, and it is to her that this book is dedicated, with my love.

Lastly, I'd like to thank anyone who has bought this book. I really hope you enjoy it. Please feel free to get in touch with me on twitter @joannareesbooks

What do you desire?

August 1985

'Where are you?' muttered Mack Moncrief, adjusting his grip on the night-vision binoculars. The hard eyepieces pressed painfully against the swollen skin on his cheekbones, but he forced away the discomfort. He concentrated, slowly caressing the grooves on the dial, so that the distant hills on the other side of the valley came into sharp relief, the eerie green of the night vision making everything seem charged with danger.

An owl hooted in the forest behind him and he felt rivulets of sweat on his temples. He'd thought there'd be some let-up in the temperature tonight, but the summer here in France had been a scorcher and the air felt close and still. Mack knew the weather would break, that a thunderstorm was imminent; it was just a matter of when.

Another mosquito screeched past his ear. The high-pitched whine stopped. He slapped his neck where he sensed the insect had landed. Had he got it? He was too tense to tell. It wouldn't be the first or the last tonight. He thought of the midges he used to endure while night-fishing on the loch back home. He'd take Scottish midges over these rude French mozzies any day.

He swallowed, annoyed that Hackett had lit up another one of his filthy Gauloises cigarettes in the truck. A puff of acrid smoke filled his nostrils and he resisted the urge to cough. He glanced over to the truck, to where Hackett was preening the curly fringe of his mullet in the visor mirror. The guy was such a philistine. When he'd finished, he'd probably flick the cigarette into this tinderbox and send the whole mountainside up. That sure would be one way to cover their tracks, Mack thought wryly to himself.

There was a faint beeping sound from the new digital watch on his wrist and Mack gripped the binoculars tighter, his gold wedding ring tapping the casing.

Then . . . he held his breath . . . *There it was*. Right on time.

The express train burst from the tunnel in the far-off hillside. Mack glanced up, away from the binoculars, his eyes adjusting to the mauve of the night, his feet crunching quickly over the bed of pine needles on the forest floor as he stepped towards the truck.

'Now,' he told Hackett.

Hackett, in the driver's seat, put the headlights on full beam, then turned them off. Then twice more.

Mack stood on tiptoes, his eyes straining across the valley. Two reply signals from headlights there. Two pinpricks of light to tell him that the job was on.

'Move it,' Mack told Hackett, getting in the driver's door. Even before Hackett had fully clambered over to the passenger's side, Mack had revved the truck into reverse. It handled strangely now that the axles had been reinforced, but Mack's army training was already kicking in, a silent stopwatch playing in his head. All he had to do was get to the train, do the job and then . . . ?

He didn't dare think about then.

Twelve minutes, fifty seconds. That's all they had, he realized, checking his watch as he drove the truck down the final part of the path towards the all-important stretch of disused railway track.

He thought of the insane amount of preparation that had gone into making sure that the train would be resting in the siding at the end of this track. Would Vincent, who'd hidden overnight in the train, have successfully managed to subdue the driver and slow the train exactly as planned? Would Eddie – also on board – have got to the guard? Would Anton – most crucially of all – have got into place in the control centre, so that nobody could raise the alarm until the job was over?

Mack thought about the safe house on the outskirts of the ugly French village and the board on the wall in the rough kitchen where he'd drawn endless plans. Drumming the details into the crew.

Voss's ugly, argumentative crew.

None of the men had been Mack's choice. He just had to trust that after all these months of training, each man was a cog in the wheel of this operation. A wheel that was hopefully still turning. Gathering momentum.

It better be.

Voss was relying on Mack Moncrief. He'd told him so. Right before he'd shown Mack exactly what would happen if he got ahead of himself or didn't follow the plan to the letter. The memory of it made Mack's beaten face ache and his heart rage with anger.

They clattered over the rotten tracks, the tyres bumping over the ruts. He drove quickly and precisely. Round the bend. And there, right at the end, was the sight he wanted to see. On a track at right angles to this one, intersecting it, was the high-speed express mail train to Paris – at a very definite stop.

Vincent was standing by the exposed carriage – the one nearest to the track they'd travelled along. The door was open, a yawning square of black behind him. He stood nervously, his gun at his waist, his baseball cap pulled down low, as he looked along the track.

Hackett was up in his seat.

'He's done it. He's done it!'

'He's done nothing . . . yet,' Mack reminded him.

In a moment they were out of the truck, Mack grabbing his heavy holdall from the back.

'Turn and reverse it up,' he told Hackett, 'then check the driver.' Mack strode towards Vincent and, without saying anything to him, jumped on board.

It was dark in the carriage. Two feet inside were thick steel bars – a cage to protect what was on the other side. The bank had been taking no chances when they'd built the safe for this train. They just hadn't figured on Mack having helped with the designs for it at the security company he'd worked for. A job that had made him come to the attention of gangland criminal Voss – and brought about the whole sorry chain of events that had led to today.

But there was no point in being bitter. Not now. Not now that this was finally happening, Mack thought, reaching out to grasp the metal bars. What looked like a fortress to anyone else was a simple puzzle to Mack. A puzzle he'd spent months solving. He clicked on his headlamp.

Now he delved into his holdall, firing up the industrial steel saw. As the blue sparks flew, the noise seemed to rip through the fabric of the night, but Mack knew that there wasn't a house around here for miles, and no way of getting to this part of the train from either end of the track.

He made four neat cuts and two sections of the bars fell away. Then Mack crawled through and wasted no time in checking the safe was the same one he knew had been ordered at the bank in Edinburgh for the train transfers.

Semtex. That was all he'd need, Mack thought, his fingers feeling expertly around the edges of the black steel safe. Semtex and luck.

He checked his watch again, then carefully took from his bag the state-of-the-art plastic explosives that the army were beginning to trial, working out where to attach them to the safe, all his years of training as an army bomb-disposal expert giving him a confident hand. Vincent watched him anxiously from the bars.

After a few minutes Mack was satisfied. Coming back out through the hole in the cage, he dragged Vincent with him. 'Keep down,' he said, as he set the detonator.

He waited.

Three . . . two . . . one.

The blast made the whole track shake.

Suddenly, Eddie jumped down from the train and Mack saw that a man in a dark blue jacket was behind him, holding a gun to his head. Eddie had his hands up next to his skinny neck. He had a tough-guy crew cut and an ugly spiderweb tattoo, but he was the youngest member of Voss's crew. Mack had been an idiot to trust him.

'For fuck's sake,' Mack swore at Eddie, before he could help himself.

The man, clearly the train guard, started babbling in French, his eyes wide as he realized what Mack was doing.

Hackett was out of the train in a moment, stealthily jumping down behind the guard. In a second he'd fired at his back. The guard fell face first onto the track as Eddie jumped out of the way. The sound of the gun ricocheted up the valley wall.

'Why d'you shoot him?' Mack said. 'Idiot. Nobody was to get hurt.'

'He's too dangerous to keep alive.' Hackett reached into his jacket for another cigarette. As he lit it, he punched Eddie in the back of the head, annoyed with him. Eddie shook as he wiped the guard's blood from his jacket. The bullet that had killed the guard could have gone right through him. It could have killed Eddie too and Hackett clearly wouldn't have cared.

Mack fought down his rising nausea as the Frenchman bled out on the hard ground. He had no stomach for the kind of violence towards civilians Voss's men were so unbearably blasé about and now panic was rising. Nobody was supposed to get hurt. Let alone cold-bloodedly murdered. This was a robbery. Just a robbery. Of a passenger-less mail train. That was what he'd signed up for. Not this.

He jumped back up inside the carriage, forcing himself to focus, and waved the smoke aside. He was all too aware of the seconds ticking past.

The blast had worked. Mack kicked the back off the safe and it clattered onto the reinforced boards of the train carriage. He knelt down and looked inside. The sight of the gold blocks made a dull disappointment creep into his guts. A sinking sensation at the inevitability of it all. That men like Voss, with his mahogany tan, ugly gold chains and fat, cigar-clenching fingers, always got what they wanted.

'Holy sweet Mary, mother of Jesus!' Vincent exclaimed, wiping his cap away from his head in awe as Mack reached in and grabbed two of the gold bars. They were heavier than he'd expected, even though he'd fortified the truck for the purpose. He handed them through the cage to Vincent without a word. Vincent kissed the gold, then quickly passed them to Eddie, who loaded them into the back of the truck.

Mack checked his watch. Four minutes left.

He picked up the pace, sweating now, his back aching in the cramped space, as he swivelled to get more of the gold. Then behind them, the bags of cash. And there – in the secret compartment in the bottom – the case.

His ticket to freedom.

Mack popped the clips. Inside was a large velvet bag, but he didn't have to pick it up to know it held the diamonds. They were the reason they'd chosen this train. It would only have taken one person to change their mind and not put the diamonds in with the gold for the plan to fail. Mack felt the enormity of his fate as he stuffed the bag inside his jacket, feeling the soft velvet against his heart.

'That it?' Vincent said, turning back from the truck to Mack.

'Yep. Let's go,' Mack said, squeezing through the bars.

The truck was slower going the other way. This time, they were travelling along the old railway track for a straight five miles. Mack and Eddie had cleared it yesterday, so they knew the path would be good, although the trees at the side of the track were overgrown and branches slapped the top of the truck, looming out of the shadows like ghostly fingers.

In the back, Eddie was laughing, weightlifting the gold bars.

'Cut it out,' Mack said, trying to concentrate on what lay ahead. As well as the shot guard, Mack had a horrible feeling there might be another hitch sooner or later. The Presbyterian pessimist in him told him so.

He couldn't wait to drop that goon off in a minute, when they reached the end of the cutting. Then Eddie would drop down into the field and make it cross-country to the safe house, where Mack and Hackett would meet the others later on.

As soon as they were at the safe house, they'd split up the gold bullion and load it into the false bottoms of the small Fiats Mack had worked on. Dressed as holidaymakers, they'd take the cars down to the *costa*, to where Voss would reward them for a job well done. And fulfil his promise to Mack.

Please, God, let him be true to his word, Mack prayed. Please let him get back the thing that was most precious to him. The one thing that Voss knew would make Mack complete the job.

In the front seat next to Mack, Hackett was fiddling with the dials of the radio transmitter. The aerial stretched out of the top of the window. He was trying to find the police channel, but the static and hiss were making Mack feel nervous.

The radio was just a precaution. They'd secured the train and Vincent was already driving it onwards to Paris. By the time he got there, he'd be hundreds of miles away from the scene of the robbery. He'd stop the train at the signals outside Gare du Nord and leave before the tunnel. Dufont would be waiting in a car for Vincent.

The plan that Mack had finessed was happening. Events were rolling out ahead into the future like a carpet and yet . . . yet with each passing moment, Mack felt more and more uneasy. Could it really be this simple? Could they really have got away with such a heist? All his nerve endings jangled with adrenalin. He should be feeling euphoric like the others, but instead he felt sick with dread.

Mack stopped for a moment and Eddie jumped down from the back of the truck.

'Go quickly,' Mack told him. 'Stick to the path we agreed.'

'Nice job,' Eddie said.

Mack scowled at him. It was Eddie's fault that the guard had been shot. Eddie who'd got himself overpowered. He had no right to take any credit.

Mack watched Eddie scramble down the siding, through the farmer's gate and onto the small country road.

'Wait a moment. I need to piss bad,' Hackett said, dumping the radio on Mack's lap.

'Jesus,' Mack said. 'Hurry up. It's like a fucking kids' outing. We are trying to get out of here.'

'One minute,' Hackett said, already out of the door.

Mack watched him walk behind the truck in the wing mirror and unzip his flies. He felt tension rising in his shoulders. What the fuck did Hackett think he was doing? They'd just robbed a bank train and now he was taking a piss? Anton would only be able to cover up the unscheduled stop for so long. They may have already raised the alarm when the train was late into Toulouse. Despite all of Anton's intel, it wasn't clear how many people would be monitoring the bank train on its journey through France.

He stared ahead. He should just go, he thought. Leave Hackett. Take the whole goddamned lot and see how far he got. If Voss had taught him one thing, it was that money could buy anything. And Mack had millions in the back of this truck.

Hundreds of millions. Enough to disappear and make a totally new life out of the one he'd messed up so badly.

But he couldn't. Voss had made sure that such an urge was impossible for Mack. He'd taken out the best insurance policy possible to ensure Mack finished the job. Because it wasn't just *his* future at stake.

Just then the police channel crackled into life on the radio and there was the unmistakable panicky sound of a report . . .

Mack gripped the radio set, holding it in both hands and staring at it. It couldn't be, could it? They couldn't be on to them already?

Panic swept over him, goosebumps erupting like a Mexican wave over his skin.

He looked in the wing mirror. If the police were called, it wouldn't be long before they discovered Mack's getaway route and a net closed in on the safe house.

'Hackett, come on,' he shouted. 'Now.'

But Hackett was whistling, his back turned to Mack.

Mack snarled with frustration, dumping the radio on the passenger seat.

'We've got to go,' he said, the hairs on the back of his neck standing up as he climbed out of the truck.

There was still no response from Hackett. Mack took three strides towards him, away from the truck.

It was only then that he saw Hackett wasn't taking a piss. He was holding a gun.

He turned and aimed it at Mack's head.

'What the fuck are you doing?' Mack stared at him.

Hackett didn't look so dim-witted now. His eyes had a steely glint in them as he walked right up beside Mack, his nonchalant manner all gone.

'Voss says, "Keep your mouth shut in jail,"' he said, his breath stinking of cigarettes. He aimed at Mack's leg and pulled the trigger.

Pain exploded in Mack's knee. He collapsed to the ground, gasping, as Hackett strode to the driver's door and got in. Without a backwards glance, he revved the engine and was gone.

In the stillness that followed, Mack heard a distant clap of thunder.

CHAPTER ONE

Julia Pires walked into her classroom through a shower of paper missiles. It was noisy and hot, the kids hyper at this time in the morning. She glanced across the mass of bustling children and saw that nobody had bothered to open the windows. Through them she could see the slum rising up the mountain on the south side of Rio de Janeiro, like the contents of an overturned rubbish skip. Rocinha was said to be the largest slum in Latin America and she was tasked with educating the children from it – or at least those who bothered to come to school. This lot were, apparently, the good ones.

'Hey,' she shouted, but there was no response. Over in the corner, there was a scuffle going on. She noticed an arm flailing out, knocking over one of the pots of pink orchids she'd been growing with the class to celebrate the national holiday.

'Hey!' she shouted again, striding over and pulling two of the boys off the top of Eduardo. 'Sit down, all of you.'

She looped two fingers in her mouth and emitted a shrill whistle – the only useful thing Uncle Marcello had ever taught her. Reluctantly, the crowd dispersed to sit on the neat rows of desks. Above them, pictures and photographs were looped on strings across the classroom, the walls decorated with brightly coloured maps and photographs. Julia's effort to make a pleasant environment for the kids had taken several weekends of her time.

Julia helped Eduardo to his feet and put her hand on the boy's bony shoulder, checking he was OK. He was a bright kid. That was why he was a trouble-maker, but he was small and she knew Paulo and his gang picked on him.

'He's being a pain in the ass, miss,' Paulo shouted, dusting himself down. Julia ignored him. He already had the arrogance and swagger of a street pimp. Julia knew his occasional visits to her classroom were merely a distraction from his real education on the streets. She dreaded to think what went on in his domain – in that warren of lanes in the top reaches of the favela – where she'd never dare to go for fear of her life. Even the BOPE were cautious up there.

'What's up?' she asked Eduardo, ignoring Paulo and picking up the orchid pot and returning it to the side, gently pressing down the warm earth with her fingertips.

He shrugged, not meeting her gaze, wiping his nose on his sleeve.

Eduardo came from a broken home with a mother who never fed him. What chance did the poor kid have? Surely he wasn't high, she thought, registering his vacant gaze. Or was it something worse? She knew how many of these kids ended up as child prostitutes on the streets, selling their emaciated bodies for a few reals. When she looked again, she could see that Eduardo's grubby cheeks were pale . . . too pale. She put her hand on his shoulder and felt his light body swoon against her.

'When was the last time you ate anything?' she asked him quietly.

Again he shrugged, but as his eyes met hers, she saw the truth in them. She turned him by his shoulder and led him towards the door, as the rest of the class whooped and catcalled Eduardo for being in trouble with Julia.

Outside the door, away from the prying eyes of the class, she reached into her handbag and pulled out her purse. She saw the pile of change in it, remembering that Vovo, her grandmother, had given her money for a lottery ticket this morning and had made Julia solemnly swear she'd buy one. Vovo's belief that one day her luck would come in was unshakeable. But now Julia handed the coins to Eduardo. She'd have to work out the lottery ticket later.

'Go on,' she urged him with a gentle smile. 'And, Eduardo, try and drink some water too, OK?'

Julia stared after him, then was distracted by her phone ringing. The beautiful strains of the bossa nova track 'Ela e Carioca', which was everywhere thanks to a mobile phone ad, were coming from the deepest part of her bag. She remembered now that her nephew Fredo had changed her ringtone last night – a task that had kept him occupied in their cramped apartment whilst she'd marked her books. She dug it out, checked the screen and saw that it was her best friend, Natalia.

'Hey. What's up?' Julia said, lowering her voice. It was against the rules to take calls in school time. She glanced along the empty corridor.

'I have tickets to the party in that bar tomorrow night. You know, that new one I told you about, down near Cinelandia,' Nat said.

Julia pictured Nat in her air-conditioned bedroom in her high-rise apartment, trailing her hand along the clean windowsill in her short robe. Today was her day off from the travel agency where she worked.

'Tomorrow? I can't,' Julia said. 'Vovo is bad. Her heart is

playing up. And I've got school work to do.' The thought of actually being out in downtown Rio seemed impossible. Nat might as well have suggested that they go for a drink on the moon.

'Julia!' her friend protested. 'How are you expecting to ever meet a man if you won't come out and meet one? And me too? We always work better in a pair. And I got two tickets from a client. It was a really big favour. Some of my colleagues are going, but there's an extra ticket for you and me . . .'

From the way she said it, Julia knew that Nat had already rehearsed this answer – had already assumed that Julia was going to say no. She knew her better than anyone, but that wasn't surprising, as they'd been best friends since school.

'Besides, it's a Thursday night,' Nat went on. 'You'll only have one day to get through afterwards, then it'll be the weekend. Come on, girlfriend. Let's party, party, party,' she sing-songed, making Julia smile.

In her heart of hearts, Julia knew Nat was right and that she should be biting her hand off for the opportunity. The problem was that, whilst Nat was looking more and more like a good prospect these days, who would ever want Julia? A twenty-nine-year-old, living in a dingy apartment – albeit in one of the better parts of the favela, who looked after her uncle and grandmother, not to mention nine-year-old Fredo, with a demanding job that was her first priority. She was hardly baggage-free, or the kind of girl to pamper a man's ego. Which, in a macho city like Rio, was generally a prerequisite for getting a guy. The rich men that Natalia wanted to go after in the bar she had tickets for went for an altogether different sort of woman to Julia – who looked different, dressed different, *was* different. In every way.

Julia looked down at her shabby dress and cheap sandals

which were the smartest she could muster. She didn't own any clothes that could get her into the type of bar Nat was talking about, even if she wanted to go. She thought about the slick women with their perfect hair and toned bodies. What chance did Julia have of being noticed when they were the competition?

'I can't think about this now, Nat. I've really got to go. My class are waiting. I'll call you later. I promise.'

'But you *will* think about it?' Nat sounded forceful and Julia knew the face she would be pulling all too well. 'If you come early, I'll do your hair . . .'

'Okay, okay, okay,' Julia said, glancing up to check that there was still nobody in the corridor. 'I've got to go. You'll get me in trouble.'

The morning's lessons passed by in a blur and Julia barely had time to sit down. There was a staff meeting at lunchtime, during which the police took yet more statements about the stabbing in the canteen last month. She was about to go to the scene of the crime itself and grab a coffee when Senhora Azevedo, the tough headmistress, came out of her office and fixed Julia with her hawklike gaze.

'Can I have a minute?' she asked, taking off her red-framed glasses.

'Sure,' Julia said, already dreading what Azevedo might say. She'd already roped Julia into far more extracurricular activities than she could possibly manage with her workload, but the businesslike headmistress was difficult to say no to. Julia, like most of the staff, was terrified of her and tried to keep below her radar.

Today, Maria Azevedo was wearing a dark green linen trouser suit. She stared at Julia's skirt as she came into the office, making Julia self-conscious about her legs. Then she closed the door softly, muting the sound of the kids in the corridor and the slam of the metal lockers. She walked to her desk, while Julia perched on the low leather sofa. The staff all knew that the diminutive Azevedo did her hiring and firing standing up and now Julia tensed as she towered above her.

Behind the headmistress was a glass cabinet filled with two pitifully tarnished trophies, and behind that, the wall was covered with a scuffed tile mosaic of Copacabana Beach. Several tiles were missing.

'Julia, you can't personally finance these kids. It's favouritism. How are you going to stop Eduardo wanting you to pay for his food every day from now on?' Senhora Azevedo asked, dispensing with any social chit-chat. It was her trademark to be so abrupt, but it immediately caught Julia off guard and she felt herself bristling. How did the headmistress know about Eduardo already?

'It was just a one-off. I couldn't teach him. He was almost fainting with hunger,' she explained.

Maria Azevedo rolled her eyes and pointed the frame of her glasses at Julia. 'All the kids in your class are hungry. Your job is to give them knowledge. Not food.'

Julia stared at her boss, knowing that she was right, but hating her for it too.

'I'll let it go this time,' she said, 'but don't do it again.'

Julia nodded and stood up. She started backing towards the open door.

'And, Julia?' Senhora Azevedo said, making Julia freeze in her tracks.

'Yes?'

'I'd like to go over your lesson plans.' She put on her glasses again.

'Lesson plans? Why?'

Yet, as Senhora Azevedo picked up a pen, Julia already knew the answer. She'd obviously found out how much time Julia had spent on the off-curriculum class project – a look at all the tourist attractions of Brazil – and how enthusiastically the kids had thrown themselves into the creative-writing project she'd set, asking them to write an account of an imaginary school trip round Rio.

'Julia, I don't think you understand . . . This school is about getting the kids a basic education. We're not trying to give them ideas.'

'Ideas?' Julia couldn't help the tone of her voice. Surely the whole *point* of school was ideas.

'Most of these children will never leave the favela, or their kids either, but that doesn't mean to say they won't or can't be happy. Don't fill their heads with dreams they'll never fulfil.'

She smiled sadly at Julia over the top of her glasses, and shook her head briefly, before returning to the stacks of paper-work on her desk.

'Oh, and Julia,' she said, 'I take it you're aware of the rules regarding personal calls in school hours?'

Julia's head was aching by the end of the day. It had rained in the early afternoon, so she'd had to supervise a deafening basket-ball lesson indoors, which she always dreaded; then she'd had to fill out more paperwork.

By the time she had a chance to leave school, the sun had broken through, but it was that biting-hot afternoon heat, Julia noticed, as she stepped back out through the yellow doors. With the humidity still high, Julia squinted through the glare and walked past the corrugated-iron panels that had a spray-painted scene of a voluptuous black woman in a vivid green, yellow and blue bikini – a street-art project she'd instigated – towards the car park. A gang of kids bounced a football between them, and the traffic roared in the distance.

As she reached her moped on the scrubby patch of grass beneath the trees, she considered driving straight to Nat's apartment. She could borrow a bikini and they could swim in the complex's pool, or even hit the beach. How long had it been since she'd been to the beach? Months and months, she realized.

And she would go to the bar with Nat tomorrow too. Who cared if she had a hangover? Why shouldn't she enjoy herself? It wasn't as if Senhora Azevedo expected her teaching standards to be high.

Not trying to give them ideas – Julia had never heard anything so ridiculous. She was still smarting from their encounter this morning. Why shouldn't the kids have dreams? Why shouldn't they aspire to a better life? To see the world they lived in? That was why Julia had trained as a teacher: because she was passionate about giving these kids a better future. It infuriated her that her headmistress, of all people, didn't share her vision.

But now she remembered the lottery ticket and her promise to her grandmother and cursed. She'd have to stop in town to buy one, and the traffic would be hell at this time of day. She reached into the pannier to get her helmet. Which is when she saw the black wallet.

The glossy black leather rectangle was wedged underneath the back wheel of her moped as if it had been put there deliberately. Julia stooped to pick it up. She examined the wallet, confused. None of the kids could possibly own a wallet like this.

Which meant that it had to have been stolen. Had somebody deliberately planted it on her, or had one of the kids found it and put it under her wheel so that Julia would hand it in?

She opened the wallet. Inside were crisp banknotes. It was unheard of for a wallet to have money in it around here. Especially this much. As Julia pulled out the notes, she gasped, counting 2,000 reals. More than a whole month's salary, she realized. Enough to buy Fredo his football strip, and a new TV for Marcello. More importantly, it might even be enough to get Vovo into a private clinic, where they might be able to treat her heart condition before it was too late.

This must be drug money, she thought, her mind immediately going to Paulo, the thug in her class. This must be connected to him, or his relatives. Was he setting her up for some kind of sting? Just because she'd taken Eduardo's side this morning?

But something still nagged at her. Gang money was dirty, surely. Clandestine and illicit. If it was drug money, it would be in grubby low-denomination notes. Not pristine and smart, like these.

She quickly looked through the rest of the wallet, but apart from the cash, there was only a single card inside. She pulled it out to examine it.

It, too, was glossy and black – the kind she imagined only the most classy of businesses might commission. On it, embossed in silver, was a picture of what looked like a key. Beneath it in neat silver letters was a number.

She should go and report this to Senhora Azevedo, Julia told herself. She should go straight to the school office – even report the wallet to the police, who'd only just that morning counselled the staff to look out for anything suspicious and out of the ordinary.

But as Julia put the card back in the wallet, a peculiar feeling spread through her and she remembered Vovo's words this morning: *I have a feeling today is a lucky day. That something good will happen.*

Without giving herself time to think, she slipped the wallet into her backpack.

CHAPTER TWO

Christian Erickson hung on to the rusty bar in the back of the truck as it jolted over the bumps in the dirt track. Behind the truck, dust billowed up in an ochre cloud, and a small child dressed in a brightly coloured tie-dyed shirt ran after it, waving. Christian waved back and the kid stopped and smiled, his crooked teeth white in his black face. In a second he was obscured by the dust.

Christian knew seeing such a kid was a rare sight. And that he was one of the lucky ones. He was still able to stand – and to smile. Here, in central Somalia, where the drought and fighting were the worst Christian had ever seen in Africa, thousands of children like that little boy were dying of starvation every day.

And thousands more made the dangerous journey with their entire village on foot to the camps in neighbouring Kenya and Ethiopia. Places like Dadaab, where Christian had come from, where half a million Somalian refugees crowded into the make-shift shelters that were built for a tenth of the capacity and where many would be living for generations. There seemed to be no end to this hellish mess.

He rearranged his checked scarf over his nose as they passed the rotting corpse of a camel on the side of the track, vultures picking at its flesh. The camels had been an Oxfam initiative, but Christian knew that most of them in this region had been slaughtered by the offshoot of the militant Islamist al-Shabaab group who ruled this area with senseless violence.

In every direction, the earth was a scorched, dry brown. Ahead, through the mirage, Christian could see ruined roof-less farm buildings, overturned burnt-out vehicles scattered next to them. He stared up for a moment at the sun through his shades and saw the relentless yellow eye staring back at him. He wondered how many times he'd looked at that sun with scorn. You couldn't help but let it get personal here in Africa.

'So, how long you been out here?' Dan shouted over the noise of the truck's clanking engine.

Christian stared across at the new recruit he'd just picked up, sitting on the bench in the back of the truck. He had dark curly hair and bright blue eyes and a freshness to him, an eagerness that made Christian nostalgic. Like remembering the scent of a flower.

Had Christian really been that green himself? he wondered. He must have been. Back when he hadn't seen death and famine and bloodshed and experienced all the horrifying heartbreak of life as a front-line doctor.

Why on earth they'd sent him this guy, fresh off the plane in Mogadishu, God only knew. He'd been expecting an experienced nurse to replace Kali, although it would be impossible ever to replace Kali, with her mad hair and infectious smile. He fought away images of his trusted, treasured colleague and the way she'd stared at Christian for that fleeting last moment, even though the bullet had taken off half her skull. But Kali – barely twenty-five – had been gone for over three months, Christian reminded himself, and he could no longer work alone. When he'd got a message out that he wanted backup, he'd hoped for someone from his old team, not someone who looked like he was barely old enough to shave, let alone to have qualified as a doctor.

He hated to be cynical, but Christian wanted to tell Dan to get out right now, before he was suckered in, like he had been. He wanted to tell him to take his fresh face elsewhere while he had the chance. Because if he didn't . . . well, he'd become like Christian, and before he knew it, death and famine and bloodshed would become his way of life too. And *that*, Christian wanted to tell him, was a dangerous way to live. Because it meant you couldn't ever give it up. Couldn't ever stop.

But something in Dan's eyes made Christian refrain from spouting his cynicism.

'I've been here too long,' he replied. 'Way too long, in fact. I was a surgeon in a hospital in Norway, but after my mother died, I took a sabbatical to go travelling and stopped here on the way. Somehow I never left.'

'Hey, man, they say that you're, like, the *best*,' Dan said enthusiastically, his American accent full of sincerity. 'They said I'll learn everything from you.'

Christian was both flattered and dismayed by Dan's open reverence. How he'd achieved such status baffled him, but looking at Dan, Christian realized that his fearless attitude had probably been noticed back at HQ after all these years. Christian was their main Afri-Aid man on the ground, the doctor who went right to the heart of the conflict, where the help was needed most. It seemed like the only logical way to be to Christian, but to his superiors, behind their desks in their air-conditioned offices back in Nairobi, he guessed he must seem brave.

It wasn't bravery, though. Not in Christian's book. The women who held their starving children were brave. The villagers who endured torture at the hands of the rebel militia, they were brave. The elderly women dying from Aids . . . The list went on.

But yes, he thought, smiling wearily at Dan, he had once had that enthusiasm, that belief that he was helping, that he could solve problems and mend lives. Back before he realized that as far as saving this country was concerned, most of the time their efforts were as effective as putting a Band-Aid on a fresh amputee.

'I forgot,' Dan shouted, grinning. He opened his heavy bag and pulled out a small white padded envelope. 'I've got mail for you.'

He passed the package across to Christian, who held it in his tanned, dirty hands. He stared at the postmark and the Norwegian stamps. It must be from Kenneth, he thought, realizing with a stab of guilt how long it had been since he'd been in touch with his brother back home. Or his father, Teis, persevering as a lonely, belligerent minister in an empty church up in Senja. Their sterile white and grey snow-bound world seemed so far away from this scorched brown land.

'Thanks,' Christian said, putting the package inside the front of his jacket. For a moment he felt a pang of real homesickness, remembering the smell of his father's pipe-smoke on a snowy day and the Northern Lights above their holiday cabin in the hills.

But home wasn't the home of his dreams. Not any more, he reminded himself. He often thought about the old days just before he went to sleep under the stars, wondering if his mum was up there, watching over him. Wondering if she'd be proud of the direction he'd taken. Wondering if she found it comforting that he'd followed in her footsteps. She'd been one of the first aid workers to get to parts of Rwanda back in the 1970s. It had been her love of Africa that had led him here.

'It's up here,' Olu, the driver, shouted, interrupting his thoughts.

The truck slowed. Using the bars for support, Christian negotiated his way round the boxes of medical supplies and the tank of fresh water under the tarp, so that he could talk to Olu. He'd stopped by a fork in the road, shaded by a scrappy baobab tree. A rusty signpost had bags of litter scattered around it.

'What do you think?' he asked, putting his hand on the driver's shoulder. Olu was in his late thirties and exuded a competence Christian admired. They'd been together now for several years and he trusted him completely.

'It's dangerous,' Olu said, staring at Christian.

'Too dangerous?' Christian asked.

Olu shrugged. 'Your call,' he said. 'I'm not sure if it's clear. And the radio is still dead,' he said, picking up the radio and clicking the button.

Christian ran his tongue round his teeth, looking at the barren road ahead, knowing it would lead to the village he'd heard was in trouble. Knowing, too, that the rebels who had killed Kali would almost certainly be nearby. This was the heartland of Colonel Adid's militia, a brutal guerrilla guard who had drained the region of all its resources through taxes and draconian rule. Their group was said to have links to al-Qaeda, and their morals were non-existent. Christian thought back to the children he'd treated last week who'd had their hands chopped off – supposedly for stealing.

Christian knew how dangerous this was. The tyrannical colonel had eyes and ears everywhere, and if Christian's truck was spotted, they'd be in deep shit, especially without radio backup.

'What are we waiting for?'

Christian turned to see Dan standing in the back of the truck. His eyes shone, eager to get to some action.

OK, well, if it is action the guy wants to see, then I'd better show him the way, Christian thought, burying his misgivings. After all, he'd gone in where angels feared to tread plenty of times before. This wasn't the moment to start being cowed.

'Let's go,' he told Olu, slapping his shoulder.

Christian had the kind of gut feeling he knew he shouldn't ignore, but even so, he didn't turn back, cajoling Olu to drive further into the village. The further they went, the more the hair on the back of his neck stood up. Several of the huts were still smoking. A dog limped among the debris. The silence was the most frightening thing of all.

As they came into the centre of the village, rather than little children running after the truck, as he was so used to, they sat at the side of the road, their wide eyes accusing him through the flies.

Too late, their shocked looks said.

In the centre of the village, in the clearing where the well was, Olu slowed the truck to a stop. The ground was strewn with bodies – women and children mostly; the men were gone. All except the elderly leader, who was hanging from the hook above the well, blood dripping from his severed toes. His eyes were closed with bruising, congealed blood like dark jewels on his naked torso.

As Olu cut the engine, Christian heard the all-too-familiar wailing of the women break the silence. They came then, out of nowhere – from behind the smoking huts, women with haunted looks in their eyes, on stick legs, starving. They came with their hands outstretched, too parched to speak, desperate only for water.

'Get the tank,' Christian said, springing into action. 'You OK?' he asked Dan, who shook his head. Christian could see the disbelief and shock in his eyes.

'This is where things start to get better,' Christian said, trying to sound reassuring. He instructed Dan how to manhandle the tank, and in a moment they were bailing out water to the crowd, who clamoured for more.

Christian jumped down from the truck and with Olu started to talk to the chief's wife. His grasp of the dialect was basic, but Christian could pick up what she was saying. The rebels came and rounded up all the men before beating them. The chief was tortured. They fired shots. Lots of shots. Then they put the men in their jeeps and left.

Christian followed her as she led them away from the main square along a blood-spattered path, the colourful cloths hanging to dry in the sun smeared with blood and mud.

'Get my box, Dan,' Christian shouted.

The chief's wife led them to the largest of the huts and pushed open the woven door.

Christian swallowed hard. Of all the makeshift hospitals he'd seen, this had to be one of the most grizzly. Inside, the sick and wounded covered the whole floor, lying where they could, bleeding and crying. The air was filled with the metallic stench of damaged flesh and the low-pitched resonance of despair.

He nodded to the old woman, stunned by her courage, determined to help whoever he could, his medical training kicking in. He began firing out orders to Dan, barely managing to avoid tripping over bodies as he tried to find enough space to erect a simple workstation.

Soon they were both covered in blood, their foreheads drenched in sweat as they helped each child in turn. Christian glanced at Dan, seeing the horror on his face, the disbelief that this scene could be possible in the modern world. But whoever had trained this new rookie had done a good job, Christian thought, watching him bandage up a kid's arm with calm proficiency.

Christian hardly noticed the door opening and Olu coming in and waving to him to come. He was too busy setting up an IV drip for a five-year-old boy who'd been shot in the leg. If they didn't get antibiotics into him soon, they'd have to amputate. And amputation – especially of a kid's limb – was Christian's worst fear.

'You've got to come,' Olu shouted across the bodies. 'It's not safe.'

'Olu, no. You've got to give me time,' Christian said, sticking a plaster over the drip in the boy's arm. A woman on the floor beside him was shivering with fever. Dan had started wrapping a bandage round another woman's head. 'We can't leave now.'

'Christian, we gotta go,' Olu pleaded, glancing at the door.

Gunshots punctured the wailing.

'Shit,' Christian said, his eyes locking with Olu's. And in that instant he knew that he should have listened. Olu's eyes said the same.

'What's going on?' Dan asked, worried now, but Christian didn't dare tell him. Saliva flooded his mouth.

'Come on. Quickly,' he said. 'Leave what you're doing.'

The women and children had started panicking now, the whole atmosphere in the hut changing, everyone tense with fear.

By the time they made it to the door, an open-backed jeep was pulling up outside in the square next to Olu's truck, followed by another truck, guerrilla soldiers hanging from it at all angles, some with their heads entirely covered with checked scarves, apart from a slit for their eyes. They were all carrying Kalashnikov rifles. Belts of ammunition criss-crossed their torsos.

'Stay behind me,' Christian hissed to Dan.

A man – clearly the leader – jumped down from the first truck. He flicked back his scarf and rubbed the side of his nose, then looked at Christian. His yellowed eyes had the dullness of someone inured to death. Despite how long he'd worked in the region, this was the first time Christian had come face to face with a group of rebels. He had to consciously stop his legs from shaking.

'What are you doing here?' the rebel leader asked Christian in English. 'You should not be here.'

'We came to help the people. The women and children,' Christian said, trying to keep the fear from his voice. 'We're doctors, from the aid charity. We're here in peace.'

The rebel soldiers were jumping down from the second truck now, spilling like vermin into the square. A young boy fired his weapon into the air and laughed in a chilling display of machismo. He was still a child – twelve at most.

The leader flicked his head towards the hut. Three of the rebels pushed past Dan and Olu, and tore off the door.

'Please,' Christian begged the leader. 'Don't—'

But his words were cut off by the rattle of machine-gun fire and the screams of the women and children inside the hut.

'No!'

It was Dan who'd shouted.

Christian saw anger flash in the leader's eyes. He walked up to Dan and punched him in the face. Dan stared back in horrified disbelief, blood streaming from his broken nose. The leader watched him, waiting to see how the Westerner would react. Dan had already learned his lesson. He stared at the ground.

Christian couldn't believe how brave he was being, how he hadn't been cowed by pain, even though the punch must have hurt. Or maybe Dan was just numb with shock.

'You will come with us,' the leader told Christian.

Two other soldiers now rounded up Christian, Dan and Olu.

'You have been very foolish this time, Doctor Erickson,' the leader said, as Christian stumbled towards the first truck, his hands on his head.

How did they know his name?

Christian felt real fear – the worst he'd ever known – flooding through his veins. He watched in horror as the second jeep swung round, the soldiers clamouring on board.

'I told you, man,' Olu said, his voice choked with tears. His eyes locked with Christian's, fear and blame clearly etched in them.

'If they take us now, they'll torture us,' Dan said. His voice was an urgent whisper. His eyes suddenly seemed much older than his face. 'We have to run for it. Get to the trees over there. Buy ourselves time.'

Christian stared at him and then glanced over at the scrappy outcrop of trees at the edge of the village. Was he crazy? The plan would never work. But there was no time to think of an alternative.

Ahead of them, the guards had piled into one of the trucks and it was moving away fast in a cloud of dust. Now the guards immediately in front clambered up into the next truck. Only one guard, with a rifle, remained behind them, pushing them forward.

Suddenly, Dan broke away and turned, smashing the guard across the side of the head with his elbow. The guard fell.

'Now,' shouted Dan. 'Run.'

Christian set off sideways, his heart racing, as all three of them barrelled towards the trees.

Commotion behind them. Shouting.

'Don't look back,' Dan said, gaining on him. A few more metres and they'd be in the trees. They could get lost in the village huts. Escape back to Olu's truck . . .

Bang. Bang.

The shots rang out. Olu was down, staggering ahead of him, kneeling in the dirt, then collapsing.

Bang.

To his side, Christian saw Dan hit the ground.

'Stop. Stop now.' It was the rebel leader's voice.

Christian staggered to a halt. He put his hands up in surrender. His breath heaved in his chest. In a moment, the guards yanked him back towards the truck. He felt a rifle in the small of his back.

Christian's vision was blurring through his tears as he stumbled between them. He looked over his shoulder one last time. Dan and Olu were motionless in the dirt.

CHAPTER THREE

Scooter Black couldn't help her foot tapping with nervous energy as she glanced again at the door of the studio from where she was sitting in the reception area, flicking again through the pages of *Vanity Fair* and stopping on the article about 'Sahara chic'. She couldn't concentrate on the new trend for African-print dresses.

Her whole body felt as if it was sparking with nervous tension, like her aura was crackling with blue electricity. Although Megs, the healer – the one all the celebrities were using here in New York – had assured Scooter that there was absolutely nothing amiss with *her* aura these days. It was a steady yellow. Peaceful. That's what she'd said. Peaceful . . . yet enlightened.

But she would say that, Scooter now thought, because she'd been to see Megs after her past-life healing course, her self-hypnotherapy session and her second session of training to become a reiki master. It sure had been a long and expensive road of self-enlightenment to get to steady, optimistic yellow.

She didn't feel so friggin' peaceful or grounded right now.

Why were they taking so long?

As she tossed the magazine on the low table in front of her, Scooter stole another look at the receptionist. She was the usual for these types of film offices. Scooter had seen countless receptionists like her before. The kind who thought that since they were here answering phones, they were practically an exec producer. The kind who thought that they could make eyes at the bigwigs and be noticed for a movie role. The kind who didn't tip waitresses like Scooter. The kind who exuded *smug*.

This receptionist – young, blonde, wrinkle-free – had hungry, judgemental eyes. She glanced up and caught Scooter's gaze, her fingers pausing above her keyboard. She pulled a face and cocked her head to one side. *Still waiting?* her look said. *You know what that means, right?*

But Scooter refused to believe what her look implied. The producer and director were keeping her waiting because Lindy Laine, who'd cut in at the last moment, had flounced into Scooter's spot for a screen test, claiming she had to dash off to a commercial. She'd already been in there for half an hour, and as the minutes continued to tick by, Scooter started to get more worried. What was she doing? Giving them all head?

I mean, they couldn't possibly want Lindy, could they? Everyone knew who she was – ex Australian soap star turned singer turned actress – but she had so much brand baggage *and* she couldn't act her way out of a paper bag.

Breathe, Scooter told herself. Keep calm. This is your moment.

She tried to remember the Sanskrit mantra her yoga teacher had taught her, but her mind couldn't relax.

How *could* she when Miranda, her agent – uber-agent – from YMC had assured Scooter that this was a shoo-in. *A shoo-in.* That the director, none other than Magnus Miles – another YMC client – *love-love-loved* Scooter's cameo in the indie Sundance winner she'd been in last year and had assured

Miranda that Scooter was his number-one choice and would put a word in with Brody Myers, the producer. This was Magnus's project. Brody would do whatever he told him.

Better late than never, Miranda had joked, as if Scooter must have been despairing for all this time.

She hadn't. She'd never given up hope, never given up the belief that stardom would be hers. That was why she'd spent all this time on self-discovery. To put her wish out there in the universe. To connect with her future on a tangential level.

OK, it was a bit of that and a bit of distraction to get over what Dean, her boyfriend of eight years, had done and the dark days that had followed his brutal departure from her life and severance of the future together she'd thought would be theirs. But Scooter was prepared to enlist the help of any higher form to guide her on her journey to a new future and to make her dream come true. And for it to happen.

It.

That thing that Scooter had seen so many times but had yet to happen to her. That illusive, intangible moment when it was possible to go from being a nobody to being a shooting star. To go from unknown to A-list, almost overnight. And 'it' was about to happen to her.

Which was why Scooter had done everything to get this job. She'd maxed out her cards to buy this Rihanna copycat dress and these crazy heels. She'd had her hair extensions taken out, had a full head of highlights and a blow-dry. She'd had her teeth whitened (again) and her Botox redone. And hell, she looked hot. She knew she did. And she could easily pass for twenty-five. Easy.

It's a shoo-in, she told herself, remembering Miranda's words. This bit is just the before. The before 'it' happens. The before I'll remember when I'm sipping Manhattans on the sun terrace of my Beverly Hills pad.

Now she heard voices and saw the far door gliding open against the thick carpet. She stood up, unable to sit any longer, smoothing the green dress over her yoga-honed curves and flicking her swishy red hair from each shoulder.

But there, coming through the door, was Lindy. She was laughing, and Brody Myers' fat hand was on her shoulder as he laughed too. Brody Myers. Scooter gulped at the proximity between where she was standing and the famous producer, but he didn't so much as look in her direction. Instead, he kept his hand on Lindy's shoulder. What were they laughing about? What could they possibly have in common? Scooter kept her smile locked in place. Brody Myers shouldn't even be here at the screen test. This was Magnus's film. Magnus, who *love-love-loved* Scooter's work.

The receptionist stood up. She glared at Scooter, telling her to wait. She turned, carrying a pile of papers, and walked over to Brody, who kissed Lindy on the cheek. Lindy put her thumb and pinkie up in a show of 'Call me' before sashaying away from him and towards Scooter, her schoolgirl coquetry immediately replaced by dark triumph now her back was turned to Brody. She didn't meet Scooter's gaze until she was right by her, obviously concentrating on her rear view, which Brody was studying admiringly.

'Better luck next time, sweetie,' Lindy said in her light Australian accent, tucking her clutch bag under her arm. She paused, looking Scooter up and down. 'I told them that someone was waiting and that they should give you a chance, but they're looking for someone young. And . . . you know . . . *recognizable*.'

Scooter walked all the way back from the offices to her apartment block in the heels and dress trying to pretend that this was normal attire. That she was just some girl about town and that she had somewhere important to be, but with each passing block, her confidence waned and her disappointment rose, along with her fury.

Her toes were raw with blisters by the time she made it to the stoop of her building. She snarled as her heel got caught in a storm drain and snagged. She needed to get out of this fucking dress and into her jeans. Hell, she needed to shout at someone.

The tiny apartment still bore the traces of Scooter's rushed departure earlier that morning. Her robe was on the floor, make-up scattered over her dressing table and bedcover. The head on the painted Thai statue in the windowsill shrine wobbled in the waft of air as Scooter slammed the door. Where exactly had her good fucking karma been at the audition?

Tripping across the tiny space between the door and the bed, Scooter kicked off her unaffordable never-to-be-worn-again heels and yanked at the zipper at the back of her dress.

She opened the closet shower and turned on the faucet. She'd shower away the hurt and disappointment, but as soon as she turned on the shower, she knew that there was no hot water.

The shower ran in a cold trickle, then colder, the pipes, deep in the bowels of the building, coughing. Scooter fiddled with the temperature control, shivering now.

'Great,' she shouted, twisting off the shower. The hot water had been cut off. And soon Doreen would cut off the water altogether. Scooter knew the score.

She stood dripping in the centre of the room, forcing herself to keep calm. Forcing herself to think.

Her phone trilled, making her jump. It was Rebeka 'With-a-K' from YMC. Where was Miranda? Scooter wanted to speak to Miranda. Her goddamned agent. The one who'd assured her that the job was a shoo-in. Not her irritating assistant.

'Hi, Scooter,' Rebeka said. Her slow, condescending faux-English accent made Scooter bristle. Another jumped-up receptionist. Scooter wouldn't mind betting she wasn't from England at all. 'Hold one second.'

Rebeka disappeared and was replaced by music, but even before the first note, Scooter recognized the song. It was 'Find Me', the song she'd helped Dean compose when he'd been depressed and convinced that he'd never be heard. The song that had broken him into the big time. The song that was playing everywhere, without anyone ever knowing it had been part-written by Scooter. About her and Dean and how they'd love each other always. And now it was playing on her fucking agent's office phone system.

'Did you give Miranda my message? *Messages?*' Scooter barked, as the music cut abruptly and Rebeka was back.

'Miranda is very busy, what with the party tomorrow night and everything,' Rebeka said in that tone that so annoyed Scooter. 'Sorry.'

'But you told her what I said?' Scooter shot back. She wasn't going to rise to Rebeka's jibe about the party. Everyone knew how high profile the YMC party was. And also Rebeka knew damn well that Scooter hadn't been invited. Only the top YMC earners ever got to go to the agents' party.

'Hmm . . . she was in a meeting.'

Scooter jutted out her jaw, looking at the sky, imploring it to give her strength. 'Just tell her to call me.'

'She's got a very busy schedule . . .'

Scooter growled with frustration and rang off. *Bitch*.

If Miranda wouldn't take her calls ... that was the beginning of the end.

She closed her eyes, giving in to the tears. 'Will someone just give me a fucking break?' she yelled. Then she picked up the Buddha statue and shouted in its face, 'All I need is one fucking tiny piece of luck, you asshole. Just one.'

CHAPTER FOUR

Kamiko had missed her stop. In fact, she now realized that she'd reached the end of the Osaka Monorail line, as the doors hissed open and stayed open, jolting her from her game with a blast of cold air.

She stared up, disorientated for a minute, her mind still lost in *Death Con 3* on her sweaty tablet. She saw that she was the last person in the carriage.

'Shit,' she swore, not for her mistake but because she'd very nearly completed the level in record time.

In the distance, through the rain-spattered window, she could make out the towering skyline of the city – the smart headquarters of Panasonic and Matsushita. Places she'd applied for jobs, but had never been accepted.

Because of her name, she guessed. Because Kadoma, despite all its workers, was a relatively small city. And she suspected that everyone knew, from all the newspaper and TV reports at the time, that her father, Isamu Nozaki, had committed suicide, having squandered and gambled away his good fortune. Kamiko thought briefly of the man she remembered, his tie undone, his hair greasy and dishevelled, his eyes blood-shot as he'd swayed on the doorstep with a bottle of whisky in his hand, tears running down his face.

He'd been a coward, Kamiko thought. A lousy coward. There was nothing honourable about hanging yourself in a public car park and leaving your family to live with the consequences.

She got out of her seat and slipped into the toilet cubicle. She'd done this more than once and knew the drill. The inspector would poke his head round the doors, while the driver walked to the other end of the train to go back towards the city. If he found her, he'd demand to see her ticket. Kamiko hadn't bought a ticket for years. She was an expert in dodging fares.

She'd have to wait in here for ten minutes, she guessed. But who cared? She wasn't in any rush to get home to that bitch, her stepmother. She took out a marker pen from the pocket of her slashed leather jacket and, choosing an empty part of the cubicle wall, wrote 'DIE' in graffiti script.

Satisfied with her work, she stared at herself in the smeared mirror above the metal sink and raked her black fringe further over her eyes. She'd cut it too short last time. Then she smudged a thick line of black eyeliner under her eyes.

Usually she scowled, or pulled a face at her reflection, but today she gave herself a break. After all, she was in a good mood, now that Aiko, her arch-enemy at the factory, had been fired.

The long daily grind at the sushi factory where she worked shifts dumping endless squares of bleached rice into plastic boxes had been unbearable today. It had all started when Aiko had come with Renjiro this morning and had flirted so pointedly with him that it was obvious that they'd slept together.

Kamiko had seethed all day in private, annoyed that she'd missed the signals so badly. Annoyed that for weeks she'd interpreted Renjiro's surreptitious glances in her direction in the clocking-out room as something else. Annoyed that she'd fantasized about his warm, hard cock filling her up, and how he'd pull her hair, lost in passion, and, how afterwards, as they lay in bed, he'd promise to take her away. Away from her home. Anything to get away from home . . . and from the horrible factory and from Kadoma.

Because that's what Renjiro had promised in those looks and the quiet, kind attention he'd given her. She'd listened attentively, as he'd spoken out over the production line about his uncle in Tokyo who ran an export business and how he was going to give Renjiro a job. A proper, well-paid job where Renjiro would wear a suit and drive a car and be able to afford his own apartment. Kamiko had thought he'd been saying all that just for her benefit. Not that Renjiro had ever discussed it with her directly. After all, they'd hardly said two words to each other, but Kamiko had been convinced of his secret softness towards her. But seeing Aiko's triumphant look, she realized it had all been a stupid fantasy.

So she'd taken her revenge.

Mr Akatsuma, the strict foreman, had discovered his missing phone at 3 p.m., just before their ten-hour shift was due to end. He'd sounded the alarm on the floor, halting the production line. It was a rare occasion and all the workers had looked up in surprise as he'd stood at the top of the steps with his office phone in his hand. In the brief moment of silence that had followed, there'd been a clear ringing tone coming from Aiko's pocket. Kamiko had feigned surprise with the others, delighted that her quick thinking had worked. She'd stolen the boss's phone from his office at lunchtime and had deliberately planted it on Aiko.

Kamiko didn't know what Akatsuma had said to Aiko after

he'd hauled her into his office, but she'd left five minutes later, red-faced, and had gone straight to the clocking-out room.

Now, as Kamiko heard the guard chatting outside on the platform and the train filling up with passengers, ready for its return journey to the city, she reflected on her success, letting herself feel the frisson of satisfaction that, for once, something had happened in her dull existence. No, even better, that *she*'d made something happen. It only made her want more.

Kamiko was still savouring her success as she walked slowly back through the dwindling light from the station to her what she scornfully called 'home'.

All the dwellings in this purpose-built suburb blurred into the same utilitarian blandness, the space in the pre-fabricated buildings utilized to the maximum, the walls so paper-thin that everyone knew each other's business. Her father had been so proud to move his family here when the suburb had been built. Since his death, other suburbs had sprung up – better, more affluent neighbourhoods, with shops and restaurants and bars, while this one had been cut off and devalued when the ring road had been built. Through the metal fence at the end of the road, Kamiko could see the rush-hour traffic and hear its never-ending roar.

Down at heel, the neighbourhood felt like a featureless waiting room to Kamiko and not like home at all. Rain wept from the thin laurel trees outside her house, and the scrubby rhododendron bush, which had once singled their house out as classy, had a dirty milk carton stuffed in its foliage. Its white flowers lay crushed on the pavement. Kamiko stamped on one of them with the steel cap of her boot, watching the delicate cream petals smear across the dirty pavement.

She wondered what would have happened if her mother had still been alive and life had panned out as it had meant to. Nora, her mother, had died when she'd been six, of blood poisoning. Kamiko only had sketchy details of her mother, although she'd overheard Shikego, her stepmother, gossiping on the phone about her. She'd spoken of Nora running away, back to her family in Tokyo, and of how Kamiko's father had brought her back. And then later, after he'd killed himself, she'd heard Shikego tell Hiroshi, her half-brother, that his father had been haunted by the ghost of his first wife and that she was the reason he'd killed himself and left Shikego and him all alone.

As Kamiko stepped through the debris of the cluttered hall, she found her stepmother in her usual place, slumped in front of the television, stuffing a bun into her face. Shikego had given up any attempts to work or integrate into society since she'd been left a widow. She spent her days eating sugary cookies and twitching the curtains, paranoid that the neighbours were spying on her, her shame of her husband's public suicide too great for her to be able to function normally.

She was wearing a black dressing gown, which bulged at her considerable girth, and the skin beneath her eyes was grey and saggy. It seemed impossible to marry the image of this woman with the smiling beauty in her smart designer suit who clung happily to Kamiko's father's arm in the gold-framed painting on the wall.

Kamiko felt an all-too-familiar sensation as their eyes met, saliva flooding her mouth. She clenched her pelvic floor to stop the reaction that had once blighted her life, but since she'd taken control a few years ago, finally summoning up the courage to threaten Shikego with a knife – frightening her stepmother into promising never to touch her again – Kamiko hadn't wet herself once. And with time she'd almost managed to pretend that Shikego had never had the power she once had over her.

Instead, she'd forced the vile memories away. Locked them deep inside her. But sometimes, like now, seeing Shikego's horrible mouth open, she remembered what it had felt like to be beneath her. How she'd made Kamiko kiss her.

The bile rose. Kamiko controlled it.

She wished she'd followed through with her threat and stabbed that vile bitch in her bed.

'What time do you call this?' Shikego screeched.

Scowling and refusing to answer, Kamiko slipped past her into the next room. Her sullen half-brother, Hiroshi, was sitting at the polished wooden table, doing his homework. He had spots and greasy hair, and everything about him made Kamiko's skin crawl.

'What's the matter with her?' Kamiko asked him, flicking her head back towards the living room.

'You owe her money. Rent,' Hiroshi said.

Kamiko saw Hiroshi tense as she walked towards him. He was such a coward.

'I don't owe her anything,' Kamiko replied, thrusting her face up close to his. 'This is my house. My father had *me* first. It's not my fault she's too fat and lazy to work herself,' she added. 'I'm the one who pays the bills.'

'You have an attitude problem, just like your mother did,' Hiroshi said, but as soon as he'd said it, his eyes flicked down in fear.

Kamiko pounced, as he knew she would. Her fingernails bored into his hand, like a spider bite. Her eyes blazed into his, daring him to cry out. How dare he bad-mouth her mother?

On the table she tipped out his pencil case where he kept

his money. She took the coins and notes, and put it all in her pocket.

'That's mine,' Hiroshi said, his eyes pooling with tears. She almost wanted to laugh at him. Did he really think she didn't know all his hiding places?

'Not now it isn't,' Kamiko said. 'You owe *me* rent,' she said, raising her eyebrows at him. 'For being an annoying brat in my house.'

Shikego came in, looking between Kamiko and her son, but Kamiko ignored her, her eyes flicking to Hiroshi's, daring him to tell on her, daring him to test her and see how much worse she could be. He kept silent and she brushed past him, running up the short flight of stairs to her room, slamming the door against Shikego's shrill diatribe.

In her room, Kamiko stood in the tiny cupboard and slid the razor blade from the edge of the sink. Pulling up her sleeve, she looked at the other tiny scars laddered up her forearm.

Finding a fresh section of skin, she pulled the razor slowly across the surface until a line blossomed with droplets of blood. She sighed when she saw the blood; the familiar exquisite sting of pain felt like a release.

She watched the blood for a while, amazed, as she always was, at its colour. Its intimate beauty. She waited until the clean line was all filled in with blood, and then the oozing phase began, when the blood spilled out of the cut and formed a trickle. She liked to watch it. Each time the thick, determined flow of blood took a slightly different path across her scars.

And then, almost as soon as it had begun, the ritual was over. The scar was already healing, her blood already clotting.

She washed her arm, seeing the white scar like a fish gill open and close in the jet of water.

She dabbed her arm with the small black towel; then, when the bleeding had stopped, she lay on her back and lit a cigarette. Now these precious few hours were hers. She knew that whatever the fallout from her run-in with Hiroshi downstairs, Shikego wouldn't dare challenge her in her room. She would stay here for a while and maybe go out later to Tiko's cafe in town.

She liked Tiko's place. It was in a grungy basement bar, and although he never noticed her, Tiko was cool. Now that Renjiro was out of the picture, she'd just have to resume her old crush on the cafe owner.

She reached across to the cabinet beside her bed and pulled over her laptop. She sat up on the bed, plumping the black cushion behind her.

Then, plugging in her earphones, she booted up the music as loud as she could and prepared to log on to her game. Her reactions wouldn't be as sharp now as she'd like them to be, but it was worth a try. She was just outside the top-ten players on the leader board. If she got to be in the top three, she'd win a cash prize. And if she got to be number one, then all her problems would be solved.

But just as she was about to boot up the game, she saw a message in her in-box from another game, *Second Life*.

She listened to the familiar signature tune of the game and quickly went through her sign-in procedure, zipping through the main area to the private sector, where she saw an invitation to meet a stranger in a bar. Was this a set-up? she wondered. Was she going to get suckered into a sales pitch?

You are Kamiko, the text in the stranger's avatar's speech zone appeared.

Kamiko sat upright, more alert than ever. How the hell did they know that? Her details were encrypted into *Second Life*. Nobody knew who she was. She hadn't told anyone her identity. Had she?

Who are you? she typed.

I have been trying to get your attention.

Kamiko's hope flared for a second. Could this be Renjiro? Had he found a way to talk to her in secret? But no . . . it was impossible. How would he know about her *Second Life* identity?

What do you want? she typed.

You have been specially selected to receive something that will change your life.

This was some kind of hoax, surely. Some kind of sales pitch. But even so . . . how did the person know who she was? She stared at the screen.

What? Receive what? she typed.

The key.

Two words and then the avatar was gone.

What key? What did they mean?

For the next five minutes Kamiko frantically searched, but she couldn't find any trace of the person who'd contacted her. She moved her avatar into the bar on the screen where the flashing neon light shone down. At the bar, she found a message – a postcard addressed to her avatar. It had a picture of a key on it in silver. On the back was the address of a mailbox service downtown and a box number.

CHAPTER FIVE

Harry Cassidy looped his finger inside the neck of his Thomas Pink shirt, trying to alleviate the friction he felt there. It didn't help. He swivelled slightly in his chair, looking at the numbers cascading down one of his screens. The London markets had been buoyant today, the traders chatting animatedly on their phones, some sitting, some standing, but now that the US markets were about to close, the tension was seeping away and he heard laughter and joking as the guys started packing up.

It was nearly 9 p.m. already and Harry had been at his desk since 6.30 a.m. with hardly a break. He felt tiredness pinching his eyes. Somehow the slog to the weekend, when he would get a break, seemed impossibly long.

'Gentlemen, my work here is done,' he heard Nick Grundy announce. Which character from which 1980s sitcom was he trying to be now? Harry wondered, inwardly groaning.

He glanced up to see Nick throwing his pen down on the desk dramatically. He was a big bloke who had an East End boxer's pug nose and a crew cut. The kind of guy who was ugly but convinced himself that he was a man's man. His outlandish and often revoltingly sexist escapades with the various women he saw were the talk of the desk.

Now Nick was swivelling his hips. 'It's time to come to Daddy. Oh, yeah, come to Daddy-O. You know you want to. We have celebrating to do.'

The others laughed and Harry sensed a shift in the whole atmosphere of the trading desk. When Nick made an announcement and claimed the day done with, he'd usually made a fortune. And when he demanded that you celebrate with him, it was only the foolish – like Harry – who said no. Those in Nick Grundy's gang got ahead.

'Bonio, Devil Star, Maximillius, my friends, step this way,' Nick said.

He pointed to the three other guys on Harry's desk, ignoring Harry, who cast his eyes down and picked up his phone, facing the other way in his chair.

He pretended to talk and clattered some keys on his keyboard, while surreptitiously watching Nick and the others walking between the desks, Nick leading the way like the Pied Piper. He knew that David Starbey – aka Devil Star – really *had* made a pact with the Devil this time. Dave's wife was pregnant and wretched with morning sickness and earlier Harry had heard him promising to be home early, but there was no way he could extricate himself from Nick's clutches now.

Why couldn't the others see what a phoney Nick was? He was all mouth and yet . . . annoyingly, that was what was keeping him ahead. As well as the no-trousers bit. Harry knew what would happen tonight. That he'd take the boys to his private club in the City and then they'd head over to Shoreditch, where he'd pay for the boys to get lap dances in the sleazy joint Nick practically lived in. He'd heard the endless stories of the beautiful girls who ground their thongs tantalizingly close to the boys' faces. Harry couldn't understand it. What was the point in getting that turned on when you couldn't touch them?

But Nick Grundy's philandering and drinking only seemed to make him more popular. He had a whole network of 'his boys', as he referred to his inner circle, on other trading floors across the City. Everyone knew Nick. And everyone knew that Harry was the butt of his jokes.

'Oi! You still sitting on that PLG stock, Harry Tights?' Nick called over on his way out. *Harry Tights* – one of Nick's nicknames for him.

'No, of course not. Shifted that hours ago,' Harry said, as if incredulous that Nick could even ask, but he felt his pulse racing, hoping the bluff had paid off. He'd bought more and more PLG stock in the last few hours, convinced that, like its rivals, the steel group's shares would start trading up and not down now they'd been bought out by the Chinese.

'You're not so dumb after all, then,' Nick said, laughing and slapping Dave's back as he led 'his boys' away from the desk towards the lifts.

Harry watched them go, annoyed that Nick was not only keeping tabs on him, but also drawing attention to him. Because everyone listened to Nick Grundy.

Harry waited at his desk until the lights in the skyscrapers twinkled against the black sky, watching the stock trade down steadily. He knew he ought to close out before the markets shut in the next two minutes and take it on the chin, but something about Nick's arrogance made him want to hold on. And as he watched the figures, a thought took hold and wouldn't leave his head. He glanced around him.

What if he went home and traded through the night? He could keep his position open and wait for Singapore to start trading. And if he traded the shares from home, then by the morning he might be able to manoeuvre his way out of this scrape without anyone knowing.

He knew it was the kind of thing that would get him fired on the spot, but nobody would ever know, and by the time morning came round, he would be back on top. As he grabbed his jacket and stuffed his laptop in his bag, he told himself that it would all be OK. He had to get ahead. He had to find a way to beat Nick Grundy.

It was a matter of self-respect.

Down in the lobby, a janitor was polishing the vast marble floor with a noisy machine.

'Night, Mr Cassidy,' the night guard said from the front desk. Harry smiled at him and raised his hand. He couldn't shake the feeling he was being watched on the CCTV, that the mighty powers in the top office of the prestigious American bank knew exactly what he was doing. He knew that if his boss, Blake Saville, were here and not skiing in Verbier with clients, then Harry would never have got away with what he'd just done. Blake would have made his nightly patrol of the desk, making each trader account for their day, but in his absence, they'd been left to their own devices.

His boss would never find out, Harry assured himself, gripping his laptop case in his sweaty palms. Not, that is, until Harry had made a killing and tripled the profit on his desk. Then Blake would have to come good on his hint that Harry may be promoted and get his own desk and his own team. And then Nick wouldn't dare look down on him.

Harry stood in the thin drizzle of the night feeling confident. He knew he ought to go back across the river and let himself into the soulless apartment building. When he'd moved into the des-res high rise in the Docklands, the agent had assured him that it would be stuffed full of young City professionals like him. Or – as the agent had put it, leaning in close and overwhelming Harry with aftershave – 'top totty'. That had turned out to be a false promise. He had yet to meet any neighbours, and right now what he needed was some company. Someone to distract him for the next few hours until the Far East markets opened and he could trade.

It had started to rain lightly, but even so in the deserted plaza a group of kids skidded by on their small chopper bikes and BMXes, their hoods drawn close about their faces. They swerved to stop and look at Harry, their faces curious and malevolent. Then behind the kids, he saw the yellow light of a taxi cab.

He darted towards it, his hand in the air.

The kids, annoyed, spat on the pavement and turned away, to carry on balancing on their pedals and shouting abuse at each other.

'Where to, mate?' the cab driver asked, looking at Harry in the rear-view mirror.

'The Savoy,' Harry said.

It was the first place that came out of his mouth, but as Harry sank back into the safety of the black cab for the journey to the West End, looking at the lights reflected in the puddles on the pavements, he realized that it had come as no surprise.

As Harry walked into the Savoy bar fifteen minutes later, he was delighted to see Dulcie Davies was still on her shift. It was a promising omen. Tonight would be a good night.

He watched as she stretched her neck to one side and he wondered whether she'd been to one of the gruelling dance classes she'd told him all about. She liked to keep her hand in, she'd told him, having trained as a dancer for years in Sydney. She certainly had the physique for it. She was slim, with long limbs and the kind of pert bum he had to stop himself staring at. She was pretty, too, with dark hair, a cute button nose and enquiring eyes.

He'd met her a couple of months ago, when one of the guys on the desk had had his leaving drinks at the Savoy. Nick Grundy and the others had ordered copious bottles of champagne and had got progressively more loud and leery. Nick had pinched Dulcie's bum, after making several overt passes at her. She'd given him short shrift, whispering something in his ear that had made him shut up.

Harry had stayed behind to pay the bill and had apologized, which is how they'd got chatting. He'd been so desperate for her not to see him in the same light as the others. He'd walked her to the bus stop, pretending they were going the same way, just so that they could chat.

He doubted someone as bohemian and cool as she was, with her travelling stories and plans to make it to South America, would ever consider going out with someone as ordinary as he was, but Harry couldn't help but wish.

'Oh, it's you again,' she said, as he walked towards her, but her smile was friendly. 'Are you stalking me?'

'Just passing,' he lied. 'I thought I'd drop in for a nightcap.'

'So, what'll it be?' she asked, as he hitched himself onto the bar stool.

He put his laptop case on the empty stool next to him. 'I'll take a rum,' he said. 'Make it a dark and stormy. Has it been busy?' he asked, as she poured his drink.

'It'll get busy in a while, I guess.'

Dulcie poured in extra rum and handed the drink over with

a smile. As Harry took it, his finger brushed hers. The sudden connection gave him confidence.

'Can I buy you a drink?' he asked.

'No, thanks,' she said, moving away and making light of the moment. 'I don't drink.'

'What, like not at all? Not even water?'

Dulcie smiled at his weak attempt at humour. 'No, I mean not here. Not at work.'

'Oh, I see. Maybe another time, then? Out of work?'

She shot him an 'I don't think so' look, but even so, he wasn't disappointed.

'So, how's it been at the coal face of the financial markets?' she asked, changing the subject. 'You still working with that idiot?'

'I'm afraid so,' Harry said. 'And you're right: he is an idiot. He makes work hell.'

'Oh, the hard life of the rich banker,' she teased him. 'Hang on, I'm being deafened by violins.'

'All right, all right. God, you sound just like my family,' Harry said.

Dulcie smiled and raised an eyebrow. 'Touched a nerve, have I?'

Harry shrugged. 'All my family are up North. Dad is one of those guys who runs the youth football team and thinks our village is the be all and end all of everything.'

She folded a tea towel and put it on the wooden bar between them. She rested her slim hand on top of it. 'I take it he doesn't approve of you working in the City?'

'No. He thinks all I care about is money. According to him, the recession is all my fault. Personally.'

'And isn't it?'

But Harry didn't have a chance to answer, or defend himself, because her attention was drawn to the door.

'Fuck,' she whispered. She ducked down, then peeked behind him, over his shoulder. 'Don't turn round and don't say anything,' she said under her breath.

Harry swivelled on the leather bar stool to see a good-looking man in his late thirties with wavy hair swaggering in. He grinned at Dulcie, finishing his phone call and snapping his mobile shut. He was very tall with foppish light brown hair, the fringe of which he now smoothed. He had an expensive-looking signet ring on his little finger.

Dulcie rolled her eyes at Harry, a flash of annoyance on her face. 'I said not to look.'

'Who is he?' Harry whispered.

'Nobody,' Dulcie hissed. 'Just ignore him.'

'Babe,' the man said, stretching his arms out wide, 'you didn't pick up when I called you.'

So he wasn't a nobody, then, Harry thought, but someone Dulcie knew. Harry noticed his slurred words, but also the propriety in them. His accent was undeniably posh, although Harry suspected from the way he was dressed, in scruffy red jeans and boots, that he probably played down his aristocratic roots.

'Hello, Guy,' Dulcie said. Harry could see her bristling with irritation.

'Oh, don't be like that. Haven't you got a kiss for me?' Guy said, brushing past Harry and leaning across the bar.

'I told you. I don't want you to come in here,' Dulcie said, backing away from him. 'You'll get me fired.'

'If you'd just be with me, you wouldn't have to work at all,' Guy countered. He reached right over the bar and grabbed Dulcie's arm and pulled her roughly towards him.

'Didn't you hear what she just said?' The words were out of Harry's mouth before he'd had a chance to think. 'Let go of her. Now.'

'Who the fuck is this jumped-up twat?' The aggression was clear in Guy's voice as he turned to Harry.

'Don't call him names,' Dulcie said, rushing to Harry's defence.

Harry felt his cheeks flush, not just because Guy had insulted him, but because Dulcie had taken his side.

'What are you, some estate-agent prick? Who the fuck wears a suit like that these days?' Guy said, flipping the lapel of Harry's Reiss suit.

'He's a friend. And he works for a living,' Dulcie said pointedly.

'Oh, yeah. Where?' Guy demanded.

'America Bank,' Harry replied, disarmed by his aggression. 'Not that it's any of your business.'

'Just as I thought, then. A City twat. Well, you're not interested in guys like that, are you, princess? She's an artist,' Guy said with a sneer, turning his attention from Harry back to Dulcie. 'Now, come on, say hello to me nicely.'

He leaned across the bar and tried to grab Dulcie again. She pushed him away. 'Stop it, Guy. Please. Not in here. Now go away.'

'Just leave her alone,' Harry said, taking a grip on Guy's forearm, intent on steering him away.

He wasn't sure what happened next, only that it happened so fast and hard that by the time he realized Guy had hit him, he was on his back, looking at the blurry chandelier, and was only vaguely aware of Dulcie shouting as blood cascaded down his throat from his nose. He closed his eyes as Guy's fist descended on him again.

CHAPTER SIX

Christian sat inside the prison cell on the rough wooden bench watching the guard pacing on the other side of the barred door. It had been four hours or more since the awful events at the village, when Dan, Olu and Christian had tried to make a run for it, with disastrous consequences. Christian had been driven here to a highly fortified concrete bunker in the bush. The guards had shoved him roughly into this cell and he had no idea how long he was going to be kept here.

A thin shaft of moonlight broke through the high bars, illuminating the prison cell with its smears of blood on the wall. He felt the acrid stench of stale urine and sweat attack the back of his throat. He could see his hand shaking, his brain somehow refusing to process what had happened.

Dan had been shot. Olu too. They were both dead. And it was Christian's fault. Guilt and anger washed over him in waves. It had been his pride that had led them to the village. His desire for a rookie like Dan to see Christian as some kind of fearless saviour. His desire to show Dan the *truth*.

Christian hadn't even asked him any questions – about where he was from. His family. His girlfriend. Other people whose lives would be ruined now the charming young American had gone. And Olu's family too – his wife and kids. He'd told Christian once how much they meant to him.

Christian shook his head, tears pooling in his eyes.

Footsteps shook him out of his grief. The guard unlocked the door and opened it. He gestured with his rifle for Christian to get up. He used his rifle barrel to prod Christian and steer him down another corridor and past another metal door.

So this is where it starts, he thought. They're taking me off to be tortured. His guts writhed with fear.

The room beyond was lit by a bright bare bulb and a buzzing blue fluorescent tube caked in dead flies. Below it was a metal desk with another metal mesh-enforced door behind it. It opened and an older soldier with a terribly scarred face came through. He was wearing a dirty camouflage jacket.

He stood in silence gazing at Christian, who tried hard to stop himself shaking. He needed the toilet so badly he was terrified he'd piss his pants. From behind the door, he heard the sound of whistling coming nearer and nearer. An old Sinatra song, which seemed so incongruous in these surroundings that it only increased his fear.

The door opened and another man entered. The guard stiffened and averted his eyes.

The man in the doorway was tall and lithe, despite his long white robes. Christian saw the glint of expensive gold bracelets and a Rolex on his wrist and knew immediately that he was Colonel Adid. This was the megalomaniac who had galvanized an army from his appearances on YouTube. A man on the UN's and the FBI's 'Most Wanted' lists. A man who knew exactly what he wanted and how to get it. Through an unpredictable mixture of charm, cruelty and the kind of rebel-rousing spin that made disciples of his despots. It was his eyes that gave him away. They were brutal . . . crazed. He flicked his pink tongue against the back of his white teeth.

'And so you are here.' He spoke in perfect English, as if he'd been expecting Christian for tea. The rumours must be true, then, that Adid was English public-school educated. Yet Christian sincerely doubted he had gleaned any form of social conscience from it at all.

He walked up to Christian and stared hard at him.

'You were trespassing on my land,' the colonel said, tut-tutting as if he were admonishing a child.

'I didn't mean . . . I mean, I was doing my job. With the aid agency. That's all.'

'OK, Doctor, I am a reasonable man,' he said, rubbing his hands. 'But I do need to send a message to those who do not respect my authority. And I do not believe your aid agency has paid sufficient taxes.'

'Well, I can look into that, but I did what I thought was right. I did not mean to offend you. Sir,' Christian added. He cringed, hating himself for grovelling to this odious man. This man who had killed scores of people, razed whole communities and spread fear like an infection through an entire region.

Besides, he wanted to add, he'd already got his pound of flesh. His men had already killed Dan and Olu.

The colonel walked away, his hands behind his back, as if considering Christian's proposition. Then he nodded to the stiff-backed guard.

Christian knew at that moment that appeal was useless. That he would be tortured and killed and his body never found, his family never informed. They would show no mercy. He knew that in his bones.

He felt the guard tug at his jacket. What were they going to do? Strip-search him? Christian looked at the ceiling, trying not to cry.

Then something dropped on the floor. Christian stared at the guard, who picked up the white padded envelope that had fallen out of his jacket. He put it on the desk. Christian had to suppress a surge of grief. Kenneth, Malene and his little nephews. What would they make of his death? The home he'd avoided for so long seemed too precious now he'd never see it again.

The other guard – the older one – picked up the envelope and ripped it open. Christian was expecting it to contain letters from his brother, the family news that Christian knew for sure he'd never read now, but there was no paper in the padded envelope.

The guard peered inside, tipping a small black box onto the desk. It looked like a jewellery box. Classy and neat – all the more a reminder of the civilized outside world. He raised his eyebrows at Christian and opened the box. Inside, on a velvet pouch, was a silver key.

Christian saw the colonel freeze as he looked inside the box. He talked rapidly to the guard in a language Christian didn't understand. Then he looked at Christian.

His expression had entirely changed. Gone was the cruelty. In its place was something else Christian didn't recognize. Or, rather, he did, but he couldn't believe that he was right. Because what he saw in the colonel's dark, intelligent eyes was surprise, and – more than that – *respect*.

'This is yours?' he asked, holding up the silver key-shaped pendant. It glinted in the fading light.

'Yes,' Christian lied, trying to keep the surprise from his voice, never having seen the strange key-like object before. He knew he had to act now on pure instinct. It was his only chance.

The colonel stepped round the desk and came closer to Christian. He stared into his eyes for a long moment. Christian felt his pulse racing.

'In which case I sincerely apologize,' he said.

Apologize?

Christian tried to keep his look of dignity as the colonel barked at the guards and he was given back his jacket.

'Please, please,' he said, gesturing to Christian, 'come, come, come.'

The colonel led Christian through the door behind the desk into a short corridor and then out through another door into a quadrangle.

He marched across the scruffy yard, past a cage, where Christian saw thirty or so badly beaten men squashed in together, clearly dehydrated from the sun. They must be the men from the village, he thought. He felt their eyes boring into him as he followed the colonel to the far buildings, which were connected by a covered walkway. What must they think? he wondered. That he was a friend of the colonel's? That when he saw them in the cage, he didn't care?

But he had no time to stop. He cast his eyes down and away, ignoring their outstretched hands. The colonel appeared not even to see them. He opened a steel door with a key from his pocket and smiled warmly at Christian, inviting him inside.

Christian felt nauseous with adrenalin as he followed the colonel through to a crowded storeroom, which was stacked high on both sides with equipment – shovels and hoses, drills and sanitation kits, see-through bags of what looked like clean folded children's clothes and a whole shelf of medical kits too.

Anger swelled inside him. All those televised fundraising appeals that went on across Europe for his aid charity and the millions of ordinary people who'd given money to buy medical kits for the most needy, and here they all were. Pristine and new. Confiscated. Stolen. Taken from the drought-ravaged communities and shoved into a locked bunker – just for the colonel's satisfaction.

They walked through another door at the end into a make-shift garage. Several robust-looking trucks were parked inside, as well as two new gold Mercedes. How the colonel had got them here along those roads Christian had no idea. He couldn't believe the man's audacity. In this barren, scorched land, here he was hoarding all of this. The rumoured corruption of it was only too familiar to Christian. The people talked of little else. Seeing it up close like this made it seem fantastical, as if the rumours were just a pale whisper of the actual truth.

He followed on, trying not to react, fighting the urge to run, all too conscious of the guard behind him, and remembering poor Dan and Olu lying in the dirt. Anger and fear made his legs tremble.

He stopped behind the colonel, who opened another steel door with a key and dismissed the guard, who retreated. The colonel gestured for Christian to come inside.

It was cool in the room beyond, an air-conditioning unit humming quietly in the corner. The floor was covered in rugs, and studded leather sofas made a seating area at one end in front of a giant plasma screen. The scene before him wouldn't have looked out of place in a city apartment in Oslo, but to find it here in the middle of the African bush felt like a punch to the gut.

A jug of water was on the table on a bright yellow and brown tablecloth. Christian felt his salivary glands screaming for it. The colonel poured a long glass and handed it to him.

'Please, drink, my friend.'

Friend . . . ?

He went to a fridge as Christian greedily gulped the water. Christian eyed him warily. What was this? Some kind of psychological torture? Was Christian only being shown this to make the deprivation and torture that must surely follow all the more impossible to bear?

'You will want something stronger after that,' the colonel said, all smiles and charm now as he cracked open two cold beers. He handed one to Christian. So much for his Muslim principles, Christian thought, seeing the colonel take a swig of beer. The desk behind him had three laptops and four satellite phones on it. If there was only some way of using them . . .

'So, Doctor,' the colonel said, ushering Christian to sit in a comfortable armchair. He put the silver key pendant on the arm of the chair next to Christian and tapped it with his pale fingertip.

He smiled, then whipped off the long white robes he wore with one quick movement. The flap of white material through the air made him seem like a conjurer. And certainly it felt as if the colonel had magically transformed himself, as underneath his robes, he wore jeans and a Hawaiian shirt. He grinned, seeing Christian's surprise, then undid the poppers of his shirt to reveal a similar key hanging on a gold chain round his neck.

'I have the key too. Our membership makes us brothers now, you see.'

He said it proudly, as if Christian should be impressed. As if they really did share some sort of connection, some sort of brotherhood.

'I see,' Christian bluffed, not seeing at all. *What the hell was going on?* What the hell was this key? And why had Kenneth sent it to him?

Or maybe, right now, that doesn't matter, he thought. Maybe this wasn't some kind of psychological trick and this key, whatever the hell it was, might really somehow miraculously save his life.

He stared at it like a man who had just been dealt an ace in a game to which he did not know the rules.

Bluff, he told himself. Look like you know what you're doing. And pray that luck is on your side. Because wasn't that the way any true gambler ever really won?

Pretending to look nonplussed, he picked up this strange key-like object that had brought him to this bizarre situation and studied it, his mind desperately trying to catch up.

The key was thick and silver. A small embedded jewel – a diamond? Christian wondered – glinted. Clearly, on its own, the object was worth a considerable amount of money, but surely not enough in itself to bring about such a change in attitude in the colonel. No, it was what it signified – the 'membership' the colonel had referred to – entry into some elite club that was worth so much more.

Could he use it to bargain his way to freedom?

'I got mine in Dubai, from a sheikh,' the colonel said proudly. 'It was a possession he was unwilling to give up, but he lost it to me at cards and, as you will know yourself, Christian, honour and trustworthiness are everything where the key is concerned.' He laughed, clearly delighting in how clever he'd been to obtain the key. 'I would never give it up, my key,' he said, fingering his necklace like a talisman. 'I didn't believe him, of course, when he told me what it does.'

'It unlocks . . .' Christian bluffed, shaking his head as if the answer were unbelievable. He took a sip of beer to stop himself having to finish the sentence.

'Luxury,' the colonel cackled. 'The very gates of Heaven. Yes.' He laughed again, raising his bottle to Christian's. 'I went straight to the airport and showed them my key, to check if it really worked. I was upgraded to first class straight away. And now wherever I show my key, I am treated like a god. Not here in this hellish land, where the drought rages, of course. The key cannot fix that sadly. It will not bring me rain. But when I leave for some time away, it is invaluable. So tell me, where did you get yours?'

'It's a new one,' Christian said, stalling for time by coughing. 'My old one . . .' He shook his head, as if it were obvious that it had been lost. 'It's a hazard of being a doctor.'

Christian's mind was reeling. So this key signified unlimited luxury. He pictured a world of first-class lounges and luxury casinos, but he couldn't imagine himself in any of them.

Think. He had to think. He had to use this information to his advantage.

'Let me see, let me see.' The colonel put out his hand for Christian to hand over the key.

'I guess now that we know we're both key-holders, it changes everything,' Christian said. 'Now that we're both . . . brothers.' He stood up, putting his beer on the desk. He needed his mind to be clear, despite how good the cold liquid tasted. He needed to find the nerve to follow this through.

His eyes scanned the computers and phones. He'd be able to contact base from those phones. He'd be able to get them out of here. His mind was racing.

'Your key is different to mine,' the colonel said, studying the keys side by side.

Christian watched as the colonel pressed the diamond and the silver key came apart. The end he held in his hand had a USB connection. The colonel grinned at him, a flash of white teeth. He grabbed his laptop from the desk behind him – a state-of-the-art Apple Mac, Christian noted. Then he plugged the key into the side.

Christian stared at him, wondering what was going to happen. What the key would reveal when it was plugged into the computer. Whatever this key-club thing was, the colonel was certainly in awe of it. It was confusing, considering this guy was as corrupt as hell.

'Look at this. This is very interesting. See how it's personalized? It says, "Hello, Christian." Your key knows who you are. And there's more.' The colonel peered closer at the screen. '"Fill in your details and then you can request whatever you desire."'

The colonel's voice expressed as much disappointment as it appeared impressed. Did the fact that this key had been tailor-made for Christian mean that the colonel could not use it himself?

'Whatever you desire, huh? That's impressive,' he said. 'What do you desire?'

'Well, there is one thing I desire,' Christian replied, feeling put on the spot. But now was his moment. His chance.

'Go on . . .'

'As key-holders,' Christian said, thinking on his feet and stalling for time, in order to pluck up the courage for his request, 'honour and trustworthiness are all. And as brothers of course, we have a duty to look after each other. We wouldn't want a key-holder to fall into bad repute . . . ?'

He left the question hanging in the air. The colonel nodded.

'And I have contacts,' Christian lied, 'who would be most grateful to know that another key-holder helped me out.'

'Well, sure. As a gentleman, I give you my word.'

A *gentleman*. Christian almost scoffed at him. Colonel Adid was a maniac.

Christian attempted what he hoped was a friendly smile and not a terrified grimace.

'I know that my straying to that village annoyed your men. I understand that you want to maintain your power. But as a key-holder, I am asking you for a *gentlemanly*' – he stressed the word – 'favour.'

'What is it?'

'I want you to let those men – those prisoners back there – go.'

The colonel let out an expansive belly laugh, but it had a steel edge to it. Christian felt the hair on the back of his neck stand up. He'd pushed him too far.

'I'll take them back to the aid base so they can be relocated elsewhere,' Christian quickly continued, 'away from here. Away from your lands. You won't ever need to see them, their families or any of my staff again.'

'You ask me a big favour.'

'You are a key-holder. You understand that this would be a privilege I would appreciate greatly. And one that' – Christian prayed the lie he was about to tell would seal the deal – 'would naturally be paid back by other key-holders, such as myself, to you tenfold down the line.'

There. He'd said it. His lie was out. As he looked into the colonel's eyes, he wondered, Was it even really a lie at all? Because the colonel did not look in the least bit suspicious. And when a man like this, so accustomed to duplicity and death, showed not the slightest scepticism, Christian had to wonder if what he had himself just said was not really a lie at all.

The colonel paused for a long minute. 'I will do this. But only if you get me a diamond key like yours.'

'OK. Or you could have that one? I mean, it would be more useful to you than to me.'

As soon as he said it, he realized how pathetic he sounded.

The colonel laughed and slapped him on the back. 'I would not take your key, my friend. It is yours. It's very clear. No . . .' He paused. 'What I want is my own. One that is like this. Personalized for me.'

Christian nodded. 'Sure. Of course,' he lied. 'I can arrange that.'

'Good.'

The colonel's grin was wide. Christian felt relief flood through him. Had he really just guaranteed his freedom?

'But,' the colonel suddenly continued, making Christian flinch, 'if I find out that you have told anyone about this, or about my key, or if you do not fulfil your promise, I will kill . . .' – he paused, his evil eyes glinting – 'let's say one hundred children.'

He grinned, but Christian knew that he wasn't joking. He'd been a fool to get his hopes up. The colonel was insane. And this threat only proved it.

'You can tell no one,' he reiterated, 'because I will find out. I have spies everywhere. Even in your aid agency, there are people who answer to me.'

'Sure. I understand,' Christian said, but his voice cracked.

'In which case, my friend, we have ourselves a deal.'

CHAPTER SEVEN

'Hey, watch it, lady,' Scooter heard, as her shoulder bumped against one of the commuters coming out of the subway.

'Bite me,' she cursed, in no mood to apologize. She dodged through the crowds and across the gridlocked street through the blaring horns of the yellow cabs and headed for the flickering neon sign of Ronda's Diner on the pavement opposite.

Yet as soon as the familiar bell clanged above her head, and Ronda looked up from behind the wood-effect counter, Scooter knew that she couldn't ask her boss for money. Not when she saw the way Ron was wiping down the surfaces, the weight of the world on her shoulders. Her basset hound-like eyes locked with Scooter's.

'No joy?' she asked, in her heavy Brooklyn accent, as the door shut behind Scooter, sealing her in. The diner wasn't busy at this time of night and most of the bottle-green banquettes were empty, but the air was filled with the fuggy, sugary smell of doughnuts and frying burgers.

Feeling Ronda's gaze on her, Scooter felt almost winded by Ronda's lack of surprise. She almost turned round and walked back out through the door. Especially after her elaborate goodbye speech a few days ago.

'You're a good waitress, kid,' Ronda said, dumping a set of overalls on the counter, 'and you're in luck. I didn't fill the vacancy yet.'

'I haven't come back to work,' Scooter said, but already she knew she was defeated. Already she knew that she didn't have a choice.

'Listen, I know you've got fancy dreams of being an actress and all that, and I ain't saying that's wrong . . . it's just you gotta be realistic.'

Scooter knew Ronda meant well. She knew that she was trying to be helpful, but her lack of belief in Scooter's dreams was hard to cope with right now. Up until Lindy came out of that screen-test room earlier, Scooter had been living such a different life in her head and this . . . *all of this* . . . had seemed so far behind her. Now the reality of her actual life came crashing back.

'One, you get double the tips of all the others,' Ronda said, fixing Scooter with a 'listen to me' look, her enormous hips slumping to one side as she put her arm akimbo, 'and two, the customers like you.'

Scooter swallowed down a wave of humiliation and nodded as Ronda pressed the overalls into her hands. She lifted the familiar tabard over her head, looking at the old ketchup stain on the front of the pocket.

'Hey, Scooter,' Sanjay yelled from the kitchen, flipping a burger. 'Ronda won the bet. Five dollars said you'd be back for the evening shift.' He chuckled good-naturedly.

'Go check on the fellas in the back, would ya?' Ronda said, with a half-apologetic shrug. 'Oh, and a package came for you earlier. I said I'd give it to you. It's behind the bar.'

Scooter looked at the pile of junk mail and the small brown

package on top. She often had items delivered here rather than to her apartment block, where Doreen would intercept them.

She couldn't bear to think about what she'd ordered online that she'd forgotten about. Whatever it was, it would be going straight back. She saw the posh packaging and groaned. Was it earrings? That skinny snakeskin belt? What had she justified to herself this time?

She opened the package, pulling out a black box with a silver key embossed on the top. She opened the box and on a velvet pouch was a silver key. What the hell was this? She wouldn't have ordered a keyring, would she? She scanned her memory, guiltily remembering the online shopping spree she'd had a few weeks ago when she'd been high on ice cream.

'Hey, we're thirsty back here,' she heard Gabe call.

Groaning, she put the pretty silver key back in the box, shoved it into the front pocket of her dirty overalls and walked through to the back bar. She'd have to deal with it later.

Gabe and the Polish guy from the pawnshop were playing pool in the back room, where there were four tables under the low lights. The other tables were empty, but Gabe's had a few balls still left on the table.

'Not going to Hollywood?' Gabe asked, straightening up and scraping the chalk over his cue. His shirt was untucked and he heaved himself up to his full height, affording Scooter a flash of his flabby white belly. She could tell he was showing off. As if she and Gabe had some sort of connection. As if their familiarity gave him a chance.

'Not today, Gabe,' Scooter said, forcing a smile onto her face.

'Good. Bring us a beer, sweetheart. Make it a couple.'

She went to the pump behind the bar below the television

and started to pour two beers, but as she did, she absent-mindedly looked up and saw that the TV was showing an advert for *Space Titans*, the new HBO series.

The screen was filled with Mona, who was trussed up in some sci-fi leather corset, her toned thighs flashing above knee-high metallic boots. Her pout and dark tousled hair made her look like a pin-up from a comic book.

This was Mona? Who used to moan all the time about PMS and who went to bed with the same collection of teddies she'd had since she was nine? Mona, who Scooter had single-handedly nursed from a bulimic insecure wreck to an actress who believed in herself. Mona who'd stolen Scooter's future.

She felt an inner snarl starting somewhere deep inside her. A snarl of injustice and fury that ripped through all the nonsense of her crystal healing.

This was her own fault. Her own fault for being too god-damned nice. Just like she had been today with Lindy. Because it had been Scooter who had put Mona forward for the casting. She'd meant to have gone herself, but Ronda had had to take her dog to the vet to have it put down, which had meant Scooter had promised to look after things in her absence. So when the casting had come up, Scooter had called Mona and told her to go in her place. As a favour. As a little pick-me-up for her insecure, angst-ridden friend.

Never in a million years had Scooter expected Mona to ace the audition and to actually get cast. Not only had she managed to impress the client but the ad had been an unexpected hit, having gone viral on YouTube, and the image of Mona walking through a fountain in a cotton dress had hit home with teenage boys across America. Overnight mousy Mona had got the call for an HBO casting in LA. Scooter had had to feign delight.

'Hey,' Gabe shouted over. 'Watch it.'

Scooter realized the beer had overflowed over her hands and was cascading into the tray and spilling onto the floor.

'Sorry,' she mumbled, dumping the beers on the counter and leaving the mess.

She ducked into the washroom. She took her cell out of the back pocket of her jeans and stared at it.

What if she just called Mona one more time? What if she told her she'd seen the ad, that they should . . . you know . . . get together and hang. She could embellish a bit. Tell her that she'd met Brody today.

She dialled Mona's number, clutching the phone with both hands.

But nothing happened. Not like the other times, when she'd gone straight through to answer machine. The phone was dead. Mona had changed her number and Scooter knew in an instant that it was because she'd severed her old life. She'd severed *her*.

Scooter stared at herself in the mirror. She looked scared, she realized, the skin tight around her eyes.

Think, she willed herself. Think, think, think.

She had to get to see Miranda. She had to meet Magnus, the director who loved her work. Wouldn't he be at the YMC party? But how was she going to get into the exclusive agency party when Miranda wouldn't take her calls?

There had to be a way. Some way of unlocking her future. Some way that 'it' would happen to her.

Jay.

As soon as he sprang into her mind, she tore her eyes away from her reflection. Jay was from another life, an old life she'd healed. With crystals. Lots of crystals. Jay was from the days when she only thought about her next fix, when her life had been a mess.

But much as she wrestled with her conscience, she had to face facts. Jay was her only chance. Jay would get her into the YMC party. Of course he'd be going. He was at every party, privately dishing out overpriced cocaine to anyone who wanted it and could bear to listen to his A-list stories of debauchery.

Even the thought of him seemed to conjure him in her mind. Jay, with his husky laugh, his cockney accent, his skinny-hippy-David Bowie look, his delight at entering a party with his entourage – of which Scooter had always been his favourite. He'd told her often enough when they'd been high. Despite all the mess afterwards, those days with Dean when they'd partied with Jay, they sure had been fun.

But that was then and this was now. She'd moved on. Healed herself, hadn't she? Contacting Jay didn't mean she had to be the person she'd once been, she assured herself. She didn't automatically have to be the life and soul of the party. The one who cajoled everyone into having a good time with her. She was different now.

She dialled his number, surprised that it was still etched into the muscle memory of her fingers, as if her body was already betraying her.

She half expected him to have changed phone, just as Mona had, to have cut her off too. But Jay turned no one away. She remembered that now. Just as she remembered his long dirty-blond hair and pale wolf's eyes. Remembering, too, how often they'd been together, staggering away from parties in the dawn light – always the last to leave, arm in arm, laughing.

She tried to justify herself as his phone rang, but she felt her hands slippery with guilty perspiration. She wasn't going to give up her dream. Desperate times called for desperate measures. 'It' was going to happen. To *her*. Soon. Because if she back-pedalled any further from here, she'd fall off the cliff of obscurity and she might as well be dead.

'Hey, Scooter, baby,' Jay said, a smile in his voice. 'So you're back.'

CHAPTER EIGHT

Harry woke up and for a moment had no idea where he was. He was on a strange navy-blue sofa in his shirt and boxer shorts, but as he started to sit upright, the pain in his head kicked in.

'Fuck,' he whispered, his palm going to his nose, but it was so painful he could hardly touch it.

Through the crack in the bedroom door opposite, he could see Dulcie lying on the double bed in a skimpy pair of grey shorts and little vest top, a rose tattoo on the top of her hip. One of her long, lithe legs was hooked over a mound of cream cotton duvet and for a second Harry had the overwhelming urge to replace himself with the duvet and bury himself in her arms. Then he remembered what had happened last night and he groaned again.

He staggered the few steps towards what he assumed must be the bathroom door. The cupboard above the sink was open to reveal shelves full of girl apparatus – stuff that he found naturally intriguing. The kind of things he hadn't seen since he lived with his girlfriend Clare ten years ago: nail-varnish remover, cotton-wool buds, pots of moisturizer and eye cream. He closed the door of the cupboard and yelped when he saw his reflection in the mirror.

The bandage round his head was dried with blood, as were the plasters over his nose. Both of his eyes were black, livid bruising across his whole face.

Tentatively he touched his nose. He winced.

'Not pretty, huh?'

It was Dulcie, slouched against the doorway. She looked hot, her hair still messed up from sleep, and as she clawed at the back of it with one arm, her camisole top rode up to reveal her freckly belly. Despite the throbbing in his head, Harry felt an erection starting in his shorts.

'Are you going to work?' she asked, yawn-talking. 'You asked me to wake you up, but I overslept.'

Shit. Work. Harry hadn't even thought about work. And now he remembered the trade and the PLG stock position that was still open. He felt as if icy water were cascading through his guts.

Holy shit. The position was still open . . .

He was supposed to have traded through the night, but then Guy had hit him and . . .

'Fuck! I've got to go,' he said, panicking and rushing past Dulcie.

'Shouldn't you call in sick? You might be concussed,' she said, watching as he hopped into his trousers and then fiddled with the laces on his brogues. As he put his head forward, his nose was so painful it felt like he was being punched again.

'Thank you for looking after me,' he said, remembering their cab dash to St Thomas's Hospital's accident and emergency department. The long wait, the nausea and the pain. 'I'm sorry for . . .' He faced her. 'I'm sorry for everything.'

'Guy's an idiot when he's off his head. He got a blue from

Oxford for boxing apparently, so I guess it could have been worse.'

Could it? Harry wondered. He'd completely blown it. Dulcie winced at him, screwing up her face.

'It's really bad,' she said.

'Thanks,' he said. He wanted to kiss her cheek, but she backed away, giving him a pitying look.

'I'll see you around,' she said, closing the door after him.

The traffic was hideous, so Harry had to brave the Tube, then the DLR to the office. The nearer he got, the sweatier he became. He hardly noticed how people backed away from him, wincing at his face.

He didn't care, though. All he could focus on was getting to the trading floor and seeing what had happened. His damn laptop had run out of charge, so he had no way of knowing how bad the situation was. Even so, he was hoping, against all hope, that the PLG stock had risen overnight. If it had, then he could close out his position and nobody would be any the wiser, although his head kept churning round and round the logistics of how he could ever cover his tracks.

He ran into America Bank, bursting through the turnstiles with his pass, the only one in the lobby. He was late. Painfully late. The clock above the lifts showed it was gone half past eight.

The lift took forever to come, and as he rushed out into the reception area, he could see Blake Saville, his boss, in his glass-walled office above the busy trading floor. Even from where he was standing, Harry could see that his tanned face was stern. Any goodwill from his skiing trip had clearly evaporated. Did he already know what Harry had done?

'Hey, Harry,' Judith, the receptionist, said. She always sat on the front desk and she usually had a friendly smile for him, but this morning he could barely acknowledge her. 'Wow,' she gasped, as she took in the state of his face. 'Oh my God, what happened?'

'Never mind,' Harry growled roughly at her, storming past to the trading floor.

'Wait,' she called after him. He stopped and turned to see her standing and holding out a Jiffy bag towards him. 'There's a package for you.'

'For me?' he said, annoyed that she was delaying him.

'Yeah. It was delivered by courier. Hey, are you OK?' she asked, handing over the package.

Harry ignored her, ripping open the bag and pulling out the box inside. A small square envelope had his name embossed on the outside. Harry lifted out the thick cream card to read the message. *Sorry about last night. I hope this makes up for it.*

Harry felt himself swelling with anger, realizing the gift must be from Guy. He'd told him he worked at America Bank. So he must have had this delivered. Like some present could ever make up for what he'd done. The cheek of the guy. What on earth could make up for smashing in his face? He was a lunatic. The memory made Harry nauseous. He only hadn't pressed charges so that Dulcie could keep her job.

And now what was this? Had Guy sent him a watch or something? He ripped open the box. Inside was a silver key pendant.

'What the fuck . . . ?' Harry muttered. Confused and in turmoil, he ripped the key from the black velvet pouch and stared at it.

'Oh my God,' he heard Judith say, 'do you know what . . .'

But Harry was in too much of a panic to listen. He stuffed the key into his pocket. It might be valuable. Hell, he might have to pawn it just to get a meal very soon.

'Throw this lot, will you?' he said to Judith, dumping the box and Jiffy back on her desk.

'A thank-you would be nice,' she muttered, but Harry had already turned to leave.

As Harry approached his desk, his throat was dry. All of the traders were already hard at work. Dave stood up, staring at Harry.

'What happened to you?' he asked, failing to mask his surprised laugh as Harry logged on to his screen. 'Hey, look at Harry Tights,' Dave called out.

'Leave it, OK,' Harry said, annoyed that Dave was talking like Nick. He was a nice guy who should know better.

'What happened? You get beaten up?' Dave continued, enjoying his audience and the laughs of the others. 'Did you get mugged?'

'Yeah, by a girl probably.' Nick laughed, staring over Harry's partition and coaxing the others to come and stare too.

But Harry put his head down and tuned out their banter, barely able to bring himself to look at the screens. As he logged on, his heart nearly stopped. His position was even worse than he could have imagined in his worst nightmares. His shares had plummeted during the night.

What had he done? Even before he got the calculator out, he knew he was down millions. Tens of millions. He was torn between whether to puke or run, paralysed into doing neither.

Think.

He had to pull himself together and work out what to do.

Yet as more faces gathered above his partition to laugh and jeer at him, he felt as if he were drowning.

Three hours later Harry sat in the cubicle of the unisex toilets with his head in his hands. He'd been in here for ten minutes and knew he had to find the courage to get up and unlock the door, but he couldn't move his body.

Inside, his guts were twisting. He could feel the slick of sweat across his back, even though he'd changed last night's blood-spattered shirt for the clean shirt in his desk drawer. A crisp white shirt could not mask the feeling that he was walking around with a neon arrow pointing down at his head. It amazed him that nobody had yet noticed what he'd done.

But they would. Oh, yes, they would. And then . . .

'Oh Jesus,' he groaned aloud.

Maybe it would be better if he just ended it all. He'd never had a suicidal thought before, but now he imagined himself taking the tourist lift to the thirty-third floor and walking out-side onto the viewing platform and throwing himself over the edge like a sack of potatoes. That would be one way to solve the mess he was in.

Yet he knew, even as he imagined it, that he'd never go through with it. How he'd freeze near the edge, cowering away, as he always had done when his father had taken him for consti-tutional hikes in the Yorkshire hills around their village. He remembered his father's disappointment, not believing Harry that the vertigo made him feel too sick to breathe.

Besides, what if his suicide attempt didn't work? What if he made a bloody mess of the sparkling marble tiles way down on the plaza but didn't die and had to live with the shame of his botched attempt and spend the rest of his life in a wheelchair and a nappy, getting fed through a straw? Or what if he landed on someone? A woman, or a child?

He could hear the almost indiscernible tick of the second hand on his watch. His guts twisted again.

He knew the decent thing to do was to turn himself in. Go straight to Blake Saville's office and explain what he'd done. Although he knew there was no explanation, other than pride and greed. And stupidity. Surely better to do that than to be at his desk when they came for him. When Nick and the others realized what he'd done. When the authorities came and took him away.

Which they would.

Because he'd broken the law – not only of the trading floor, but the bank and the financial regulators.

Oh, and how Nick would love it, he thought bitterly. Of course he would. Harry getting publicly roasted. That would be something to dine out on tonight. But very soon it wouldn't be funny. Not when the repercussions of the magnitude of Harry's fuck-up were made clear. If the press heard about it, the whole team would be investigated. In fact, the whole trading desk might have to go. They might all lose their jobs. Even Dave, with a new baby on the way.

He lurched to his feet, thinking he might be sick. He had to leave. Go somewhere. Do anything. Just . . . just disappear. It would be easy, wouldn't it? Would anyone miss him? Would Dulcie miss him?

Dulcie. Lovely long-limbed Dulcie. For a second the image of her sleeping this morning flashed into his head. She'd never speak to him now. Not ever again. No woman would.

He leaned his hand on the tiles above the toilet bowl and put his other hand in his pocket, closing his eyes and waiting for the bile to rise and come out. But then he felt something in his pocket. The wave of nausea subsided.

'What the . . . ?' he said out loud, suddenly remembering the package Judith had given him earlier. So much had happened he'd forgotten about it entirely.

He pulled out the strange key-like object and stared at it, turning it over in his palm. And suddenly a chink of memory cut through his panic.

The key.

No, it couldn't be . . . could it?

He remembered now the conversation at the desk last year when Nick Grundy had talked about a key. How he was desperate to get hold of one. How his mate in Ibiza had had one and they'd been treated like VIPs wherever they went.

But this couldn't be the same key, could it?

Harry let himself out of the cubicle and rinsed his face at the sink. Then he swilled his mouth out and forced himself to calm down.

He had a key. Not necessarily *the* key, but right now he was out of options. This was all he had to work with.

He walked back out to reception, trying to appear breezy. Judith was standing behind the desk, packing her make-up bag into her handbag. She was probably off for her lunch break, Harry concluded.

'Hey,' he said.

She wasn't a bad-looking girl, he realized. Nick and the others teased her relentlessly with the kind of sexual banter that would have sent weaker girls running to the HR department, but Judith took it all in her stride.

'Oh, it's you,' she said. She was clearly put out about earlier.

'I just . . .' Harry began, 'I just wanted to apologize for earlier. I was a bit rude. I was late, you see, and—'

Judith shrugged, her eyes softening. 'Don't worry about it.'

Harry smiled back, grateful she was being so gracious.

'I just wondered,' Harry said, stepping closer, 'if you still have that packaging I gave you.'

'Sure,' Judith said, ducking below the desk. 'I kept it back. I mean, it's not every day you get sent the key, right?' she said, leaning over the desk conspiratorially. Her eyes were shining with excitement. Harry felt his heart race.

'You don't know who sent it, do you?'

'It came by courier, but, Harry, I mean, who cares?' Judith said in an excited whisper. 'You're just so lucky to be chosen. Half those guys out there would kill for a key like yours. Alice who works upstairs for Sir Menzies says he has one and he couldn't live without it.'

Harry nodded, feeling his knees trembling. Oh Jesus. This was for real.

'You know, do you mind keeping this just between us?' he asked her.

'Of course. Discretion is my middle name.' Judith grinned.

'In that case, perhaps you'll let me buy you a drink one of these days.'

CHAPTER NINE

In the grungy cafe in Kadoma, weak morning light spilled in through the barred basement windows, but Kamiko hadn't been to sleep and she still felt wide awake.

She watched Tiko yawn and rub the back of his head, where the green-dyed Mohican gave way to his shaved scalp. She imagined herself reaching out and touching it. He stretched in his swivel chair and Kamiko glanced down at the bare flesh above the top of his jeans and blushed when she saw that he'd caught her looking. He smiled at her and she felt a hot flush run through her.

Did he fancy her too? Could it be possible?

Yet everything was possible, after last night.

She'd been here for hours, she realized. She'd come straight from town when she'd got the key from the safety deposit box. She'd come straight here and had logged on to the *Second Life* game to find out who'd given it to her, to find out if there had been any more messages.

She hadn't even noticed Tiko shutting up shop, or that she was the last customer to leave. Then she'd realized he was staring over her shoulder. He'd casually asked if she wanted any help and had given her a beer on the house, and before she'd known it, she'd started talking.

She'd sworn him to secrecy at first, though, and he'd told her to chill out. In here, he only had to spend an hour with his computer in the back room and he'd have the online history of all his customers. There was nothing she could say that would surprise him, he'd told her.

At first he hadn't believed her when she'd shown him the small silver key she'd got from the safety deposit box near the station. They'd both been surprised when they'd studied it and it had come apart to reveal the USB port.

Kamiko had plugged it in, to find that Tiko's computer screen had been automatically replaced by a screen welcoming Kamiko.

It must have some kind of fancy programming to be able to come up with its own screen straight away, she'd realized. She'd studied the series of security questions about herself – ones that had seemed unduly thorough – such as her mother's date of birth and full name. Questions she'd had to wrack her brains to answer.

But then a page had appeared in fancy script.

Hello, Kamiko. What do you desire?

Kamiko had hesitated as to what to request first. With Tiko's help, they'd both decided that the first thing she should do to test the key was to ask for the thing she desired the most: a credit card with unlimited credit.

And cash. That was what she desired. Cold, hard cash.

She had typed in the request a minute ago, but nothing had happened. Now, though, the screen blinked into life and they both jumped together to look at it. She could feel Tiko's arm brushing against hers as they read the details for an appointment at the bank in town in a couple of hours. She bit her lip and stared at the screen.

So the key would give her cash. But how much? She looked at Tiko and then at the blinking cursor on the screen.

Is there a limit on the money I can get?

Yes.

How much?

You'll have to find out.

She'd have to find out? So this was a game, then? She felt her pulse racing. The key was talking to her. But who was behind it? Who was typing this?

Who is this? Why have I been chosen?

That is for you to find out.

How?

Just be yourself. That is all that is asked of you.

So there it was. That proved it. This was a test. Just as she'd thought – she'd been singled out because of her gaming skills. Someone, somewhere, was playing a new type of game. But out here in the real world and not in cyberspace.

'Bring it on,' she said, smiling at Tiko.

Are there other key-holders? Is this a competition?

Perhaps.

Yes or no?

Just be yourself. That is all that is asked of you.

'That phrase again,' she said to Tiko. 'What do you think it means?'

He shrugged. 'What it says, I guess.'

'How much money do you think I'll be able to get at the bank?'

'I don't know, but I wouldn't go and see the bank manager

looking like that,' he said, looking at her ripped jeans and dirty black shirt.

She looked down at her grungy attire.

'You've got to dress the part,' he said, 'if you're going to play the game.'

'Do I?'

'They might know who you are, but in my experience, to get into one of those places, you have to be smart,' he said. He sounded like he knew what he was talking about. But then, he would. He was a grown-up. With his own business.

'I guess,' she said, biting her lip. She felt self-conscious. Like the kid she was.

'Do you own a suit?' he asked.

'My stepmother does.'

'Then get that.'

'Won't I look stupid?'

Tiko shrugged. 'I reckon you could pull it off. Put some make-up on. Tart yourself up a bit.'

Kamiko smiled, seeing him lean back in his chair, his arms behind his head. Once again his black T-shirt rode up. She could see the top of a tattoo on his navel and felt a sharp rush of sexual desire. When she looked at him, he smiled slowly at her.

'Why are you looking at me like that?' she asked.

'You know why. Because I want to fuck you,' he said.

Kamiko was still buzzing as she arrived home at eight o'clock. She had a smile on her face as she entered the empty house. It was only as she turned her key in the lock that Kamiko realized that it hadn't even occurred to her to go to work. Without calling in sick and with no prior warning of her absence, Mr Akatsuma would be freaking out by now.

Fuck him, she thought. He could go to hell.

She knew the house would be empty. Hiroshi would already be at school, and Shikego would no doubt have taken him and be shambling around the supermarket aisles by now. She was glad to be alone.

She needed a moment to pinch herself. To celebrate what had happened. Because she could hardly believe it.

She probably shouldn't have told Tiko about the key, but somehow he'd made it so easy to confide in him. And it had felt good to share the monumental news with someone. Someone who got it. Who clearly wanted to share in her excitement.

And then . . . then he'd told her how much he wanted to fuck her.

Have sex . . . *with her*.

At first she'd been terrified. She'd never imagined anyone ever wanting her. But the way he'd said it, as if she were normal . . . it had felt more intoxicating than she'd ever dreamed.

As he'd taken her hand and helped her pull down her jeans, a million doubts had crowded into her head, her crippling in-securities making her want to scream out and run away. But he'd held her so tenderly, kissing her and whispering compliments into her hair, that she'd forced her fears away.

She'd squeezed her eyes shut as he'd entered her, feeling like she was watching herself from a corner of the room. It had been fast and she'd been fascinated by the noises Tiko made and how strange it felt to have him against her and in her.

Afterwards he'd smiled at her. 'Are you OK?' he'd asked.

She'd nodded, squeezing her lips together, wanting to punch the air. She'd had sex. And all because of the key. If it had unlocked that dream so quickly, what others would follow?

She felt dizzy with the prospect.

Tiko was right. It felt like a game. A more sophisticated one than any of the games she'd ever played online. If this was real, and it was a test, then she was going to win. Of that she was certain. She was going to push this thing as far as it could go. If someone wanted to give her luxury, then she was going to claim it. All of it. The only limit was her imagination.

Now, knowing time was tight, she pushed open the door to Shikego's room. The blinds were down, and the bed was unmade, a crumpled dent where Shikego's body had been. A purple robe was flung across the edge of the bed, discarded tights on the lino floor. God, her stepmother was a slob, she thought, wanting to be done with this. She shuddered with a kind of deep-seated revulsion that made her feel poisoned. She needed to find what she was looking for and get out of here fast.

But then she saw something poking out from under Shikego's pillow. She pulled out a luxury travel magazine. Is that what Shikego went to sleep dreaming of? Kamiko thought scornfully, as she flicked through the pages, each adorned with high-end spas and beautiful resorts in Australia and Dubai. Did that fat woman fantasize about herself by that pool or in that hotel suite? Would she find other young girls there to do unspeakable things to? Was that her plan?

She flung the magazine down and stepped towards the wardrobe, pulling it open. That fat bitch was thin once and she wouldn't have thrown out her wedding clothes – even though she'd sold everything else. She always looked at herself in the framed wedding photo in the living room and lamented about how beautiful she'd been and how wonderful she'd looked in her one designer suit.

Kamiko screwed up her nose at the smell coming from her stepmother's closet and the messy pile of slippers and shoes at the bottom. Quickly she ransacked the hangers of the stuffed wardrobe, her disdain increasing as she discarded the contents of each one. Unable to get to the far reaches of the cupboard, she pulled the clothes out, dumping them on the floor in big brown and black piles.

Eventually, at the back, her hand felt the crinkle of a cellophane cover. Throwing more clothes away, she eventually found Shikego's wedding suit. She reached up and took down the hanger, ripping off the cover.

The suit was of a plain fawn tweed with a pink and gold thread running through it and big gold buttons. It was very late 1980s, Kamiko thought, holding it up against her and looking in the mirror, but passable as retro. This would have to do. She had to charm the bank manager and get her hands on credit cards and cash.

Her mind raced at the thought. What if she typed in that she wanted a personal shopper? In Tokyo. She could go to Tokyo . . .

Was it only yesterday that she'd dreamed of going there with Renjiro and being his girlfriend? The idea seemed laughable now, when she had the key to as much luxury as she dared take. To think that she'd aspired to being a little housewife and how impressed she'd have been that he wore a suit and worked for his uncle.

Fuck that, she thought, smiling to herself.

She put the jacket on, posing in the mirror, already preparing for the meeting with the bank manager. But as she smiled, her fingers connected with something in the pocket of the jacket and Kamiko pulled out a small plain brown envelope. Inside was a black velvet pouch. Curious, Kamiko fiddled with the knot until it yielded. She tipped it up for the contents to fall into her hand, but nothing came out. She felt inside for anything, feeling a folded piece of paper. She took it out and unfolded it.

She looked at the Tokyo address and the date. Then she squinted, trying to read the writing:

This is for you and your new wife. It is a wedding present. In return, I ask that I can see Kamiko. If you wish, you can send her to me. I will bring her up and I can pay you in similar diamonds.

Diamonds? This package had once contained a diamond. She squinted at the name: Murushi.

A faint memory stirred. A woman's voice. 'Uncle Murushi. He will take care of you.'

Murushi. Yes. She was sure of it. He was her mother's brother. A man she couldn't remember ever meeting, but someone who had some connection to her.

Had he really paid her father and stepmother in diamonds? Because, if he had, then where had the money gone? And why had they never fulfilled their part of the bargain and let Kamiko see her mother's family?

Kamiko stared at the note, reeling at what it implied. That there had been a choice. That she could have lived with her uncle. Her rich uncle. And if she had . . . then she'd never have been subjected to Shikego's warped and disgusting whims.

Diamonds.

There had been diamonds.

Diamonds that had been given for her freedom.

The significance of this information seemed too hard to process. To think that it had been here all this time when Kamiko had slaved at that factory day after day and her real uncle – a member of her family – was rich enough to send diamonds. Worse, to think that her father had committed suicide having thought he'd bankrupted his family. And all the time that bitch had this in her possession. This promissory note. For more money.

Kamiko let out a low moan of disgust and fury. If Shikego had been there right at that moment, she had no doubt that she'd kill her.

But aware that time was running out, Kamiko tore the pink blouse off the hanger. It was disgusting, but the high collar would hide her tattoos, so Kamiko took that too, tossing the empty hanger on the pile of clothes.

Then she stopped, cursing herself for being so careless. She must not let Shikego get involved in this. Her stepmother – hysterical at the best of times – must not suspect that Kamiko had taken the suit, or had even been in her room, or that she had left for good.

Kamiko quickly and carefully replaced the clothes in the wardrobe. Soon, she'd returned the room to how she'd found it. Then she scribbled a note to Shikego telling her that she had gone away with a friend for a few weeks and left it by her bed.

She went to her room and got changed into the suit and carefully applied tasteful make-up to her face. Then she took out her savings from the locked box beneath her bed, along with her passport. A few moments later she slammed the door with a resounding thud and, with a smile on her face, walked quickly away from the horrible house in Kadoma forever.

CHAPTER TEN

Harry had never been to the thirtieth floor of the America Bank office block. He wasn't even sure how he'd made it into the executive lift and pressed the button, but somehow he'd been carried here, as if his actions were no longer his own, but he had nothing to lose. Not now.

As he stepped out of the lift, it was like stepping into a luxury Mayfair mansion, his feet sinking into the thick cream carpet. He strode towards a desk at the far end of the corridor where a beautiful girl was standing. She was wearing an immaculately tailored grey suit, which showed off her curves. Her lustrous dark hair was piled tastefully on top of her head, a dark fringe cut straight across her forehead accentuating her almond-shaped eyes. Harry looked instinctively and saw a grape-sized sapphire adorning her ring finger. A girl like her was bound to be taken.

'Can I help you?' she asked, her perfect eyebrows knotting together as she stared at Harry. He could tell she was trying not to flinch at his face.

'You must be Alice,' he said, trying to inject a note of confidence into his voice.

'Yes, I'm Alice Henry,' she said, but there was a question in her voice. She glanced nervously towards the rosewood door.

'Is Sir Menzies in?' Harry asked.

'Yes, but he has appointments, and I'm sorry, but . . . who are you?'

Harry smiled, his confidence flaring for real. Cole Menzies was in the building. He wasn't having lunch with the governor of the Bank of England, who was rumoured to be his best friend, or away on his mega-yacht.

Alice stepped smartly behind her desk, putting the expansive chunk of polished teak and glass between them. Behind her there was a spectacular view over the whole of London, a tiny sliver of Thames winking in the bright sun next to the Millennium Wheel. She rattled a few keys on a slim, state-of-the-art keyboard and a screen rose from the desk.

'I'm Harry Cassidy. I'm from the twelfth floor. I know I don't have an appointment, but I really need to see him about an urgent matter.'

'I'm afraid that's completely out of the question.'

Harry placed his key gently down on the desk in front of her.

She continued to rattle the keyboard for a second; then her attention was caught by the key. Her eyes darted to him, and her fingers froze in mid-air. She looked confused, then smiled at Harry, as if seeing him in a completely different light. She squeezed her lips together and clicked them out again, as if she'd made a decision.

'Would you excuse me for a moment?' she asked, standing up.

He could hardly believe it. It had worked. The key had worked. Just as he'd hoped it would.

She walked quickly to the rosewood door, knocked on it

lightly, then slipped into the office, her eyes meeting Harry's for an instant.

A moment later the door opened and Sir Cole Menzies came out.

Harry had seen him once before giving a speech, and once, briefly, at the tail end of a Christmas office drinks party for a handful of select clients. He was small with a rotund belly and red cheeks. With a fake white beard, he wouldn't look out of place as a Father Christmas in a department store.

'I hear you want to see me?' He had a twangy Texan accent that seemed incongruous given his opulent English surroundings. Behind him, Harry could see that the walls of his office were lined with antique books.

'Yes, sir. If you can spare five minutes?'

'Sure. Come in, son. It's fine, Alice.'

She gave him a look to enquire whether he really would be OK with a man who had a broken nose.

'You should see the other guy,' Harry whispered to her as she slipped out of Cole's office and he thought he saw a blush in her cheeks as she rolled her eyes at his lame joke.

'So, who are you, and what do you want?'

Harry was taken aback by Sir Menzies' abruptness, although his tone was not unfriendly.

'I'm Harry Cassidy. I work down on twelve on Blake Saville's team. There is a situation that you should be aware of,' Harry said. 'That I think – I *hope* – you can help with.' He tried to sound deprecating and charming at the same time.

'Oh?'

'A trader on my floor has been trading PLG stock.'

Cole Menzies pursed his lips. 'Has he now? That's not a wise decision.'

It came as no surprise to Harry that Sir Cole Menzies would have been aware of that particular stock. He was one of the shrewdest men in the City.

'I know, sir. Exactly. The thing is . . .' Harry faltered for a second, daring himself to blurt out the enormous lie he'd prepared. He hadn't consciously prepared it, but now that it was about to come out of his mouth, he realized that his Machiavellian subconscious had been working on this audacious save-ass plan since he'd entered the lift. He cleared his throat and looked straight at Sir Menzies. He had to appear as truthful as possible to pull this off. He gripped the key in his pocket to give himself confidence. 'Well, you see, the trader involved is called Nick Grundy and it's come to my attention that he's been using my screen to keep a position open. Overnight.'

Sir Cole Menzies' steel-grey eyes locked on Harry's. 'But that's impossible.'

'It's not. I know it's not supposed to happen, but it's easy to do if you have no regard for the rules.'

'But all that stock . . . it's gone—'

'Down. Yes, sir. Seriously down. I'm afraid the situation is critical.'

'Why haven't you dealt with this?'

'I tried to last night, but . . .' Harry gestured to his broken nose, amazed at both his acting and his quick thinking. It was all too plausible now that he'd challenged Nick and lost.

Cole Menzies looked at his face and winced. 'Yes, well, I know some of those boys on the floor are volatile. I take it you haven't told Blake?'

'He only came back in this morning.'

'Does he know you've come to see me?'

'He would never have allowed it,' Harry said. 'And Nick,

you see, Nick is very popular on the floor and Blake believes everything he says. He'll say it was me. I know he will. Even though it wasn't,' he added quickly. 'Although it really looks that way.'

Sir Cole Menzies shook his head. 'Goddamn it. I thought Blake had you lot under control.'

'It's not Blake's fault. Nick went against the rules. If you don't mind me saying, I think his ego is, well . . .' Harry left the implied description of Nick's monster ego hanging in the air.

'Despite what you think, I do like to know what's going on in my own bank.'

'That's what I thought. That's why I'm here.'

'And tell me . . . ?'

'Harry. It's Harry Cassidy, sir.'

'Tell me, Harry, why did you think I'd help you?' His eyes glinted. He already knew the answer. Alice must have already told him. This was just a test.

'Because of this,' Harry said, placing the key on the desk.

Cole Menzies studied it for a moment. 'I see. Well, yes, that does change things. How did you come by one of these, Harry?' He picked up Harry's key almost reverentially.

'I was told I had been specially selected,' he lied. 'I only acquired the key recently.'

'Well, you are a lucky young man indeed. As you've already seen, this key will open doors wherever you go.' He walked round the desk and gripped Harry's shoulder in an avuncular way. 'Do you like horse racing?'

'Of course.'

Harry was astonished that Sir Menzies had changed the subject so abruptly.

'The helicopter will be here shortly. I'm off to Ascot. Why

99

don't you come with me? There's some colleagues I'd like you to meet.' He pressed the key back into Harry's hand. 'I'd keep that safe if I were you.'

Harry smiled, still holding his breath, hardly daring to believe what he'd just done. 'Sure. I'd love to. Thank you.'

'You may want to clean up a bit. See Alice out in reception. She'll sort you out. Lance, my physician, should still be around from this morning. Actually, tell her to call Mr Fayed in Harley Street. He'll take a look at you and fix you up. He'll even give you a movie-star nose into the bargain if you like.' Cole Menzies laughed at his own joke.

Harry smiled, feeling giddy with the sheer magnitude of what he had just done. Cole Menzies had believed him. Would he get away with it? *Could* he? And what would be the consequences of Sir Cole Menzies taking him at his word? At the very least, Nick Grundy would be finished. As in totally.

He realized that the older man was staring at him. 'That's very kind of you. But, sir, the open position?'

'Yes. You're right. We'd better see to that.'

Sir Menzies picked up the phone on his glass desk and punched a few buttons. In a second he was through to Blake Saville.

'I have it on good authority your trader Nick Grundy has an open position on the PLG stock,' Cole Menzies barked into the phone. 'He's using another trader's identity. Sort it. Now. I don't care how. You can report back to me when the situation is half as bad as it is right now. And fire Grundy. Immediately.'

Jesus, Harry thought. Blake would be quaking in his boots. And Nick was getting fired. This was beyond his wildest dreams. Or nightmares. Because there was no way back from this. Not ever.

As he stared at Sir Menzies on the phone, he wondered whether this buzz he was feeling was triumph or fear. Was he relieved by the fact he'd just saved his own ass? Or thrilled by the new power he'd exerted? Or horrified at the enormity of the lie he'd just told?

Whatever it was, he'd never felt this feeling before. It seemed impossible that he'd been almost suicidal less than an hour ago. It was as if he'd stepped outside himself. Walked out of his skin, like a butterfly emerging from a cocoon.

Sir Cole Menzies replaced the receiver.

'That should do it,' he told Harry.

'Shouldn't I be there . . . you know . . . to help?' Harry faltered, although being down on the floor was the last place he wanted to be. He felt he should at least offer to be the stand-up guy Sir Cole Menzies had mistaken him for.

'No. Best not. If you've already had a run-in with this Grundy character, I'd stay up here. He'll be leaving the building within the next five minutes or so and then we won't see him again.'

'But the trade? The open trade.'

'That's Blake's headache now, not ours. Let's go and get some fresh air and get to know each other. I think you and I are going to get along very well.'

April 1995

Mack lay on the bunk in his cell reading, although he wasn't concentrating. If he looked out through the bars in the window, he could just make out the hills in the distance. He missed his binoculars. He'd had them until two years ago, but he'd lost them in the raid that had left him without a cellmate. It wasn't a pleasant memory. There hadn't been many pleasant memories here at the grim Yorkshire jail where he'd served just ten years of his sentence.

Now his eyesight wasn't good enough to make out any detail above the soft purple heather, but he knew the red kites were up there. He missed the fleeting sense, when he studied them, that he wasn't in this awful place and that he might be free to soar himself. He felt an affinity with the elegant birds and how they circled their prey, watching, waiting, then swooping in for the kill. It was exactly what Mack intended to do.

He indulged himself in a moment of fantasy. Of course, it wouldn't be easy to track down Voss, but if Mack was ever granted parole, then he'd spend every waking moment of his freedom doing just that.

And when he found him . . . he'd remind Voss that he owed Mack. Oh, he owed him big time.

After all, Mack had kept his word. He'd never breathed a word throughout the police investigation, or the highly publicized trial. The train robbery had gone down in history as the most lucrative heist of all time. And throughout the blame and the public outrage, the behind-the-scenes intimidation that had bordered on torture, Mack had stayed silent.

Nobody had ever found out that it had been Mack who'd perfected the plan for the robbery. Nor had he told anyone about where he'd hidden the bag of diamonds, next to the disused railway track. It had taken all his strength to crawl up the siding and dig a hole with his bare hands to bury the diamonds.

There wasn't a day that went past when he didn't picture that very spot in his mind. That tiny place on the earth that was just his. That held his future in it.

And as each year crept by, his certainty and hope built. Because no one knew about the diamonds, not even Voss. Mack had kept that part of the plan just for himself. Because he'd known all along the diamonds would be in that train. Voss had just known about the gold, but Mack had known that the recovered diamonds had gone to the bank in Nice and would be shipped to Paris at some point. Most likely when they'd ship the gold bullion in the safe. And his gamble had paid off. Best of all, he'd managed to get the bag of diamonds out of the safe without anyone seeing.

Hackett may think he'd had the last laugh, shooting Mack and leaving with the gold, but he hadn't known that right there inside his jacket Mack had a bag of diamonds worth ten times the value of the gold.

And as far as Mack knew, Voss still didn't know. The

location of the diamonds remained a mystery. Which meant that the diamonds were there. Mack's diamonds. His collateral. His future.

The police knew the diamonds were missing, of course. Mack reckoned that they would have happily tortured the information out of him, but Mack had feigned total ignorance of the diamonds all along. And now, ten years on, their attention had turned to other cases. Andy Harris, the chief inspector who had led the investigation from the UK, when the French investigation had turned out to have been such a shambles, had finally retired.

In some ways, Mack felt sorry for him. That he'd ended his professional career on such a bum note, never having cracked the great Mack Moncrief. He'd felt quite affectionate towards the affable inspector. In another life, they may even have been friends. Which is why there'd been so many times when Mack had wanted to shop the gang. He'd wanted to shop the bloody lot of them. The thought that Voss had got the cash had made Mack's blood boil. He'd got away with it and Mack was powerless to stop him being out there, gloating.

But he couldn't. He knew he couldn't. He just had to wait. And, over time, he'd managed to distil the fury to a pure, deadly venom. He didn't want his share of the money. He just wanted his life back.

The hideous bell jangled Mack back to reality. He calmly put the leather bookmark he'd tooled on an inmates' course long ago back into the library copy of *The Count of Monte Cristo*. He'd read it many times over, but he still took it out whenever it became free. It gave him hope.

Mack stepped out of his cell, taking in the steel structure of the internal hall of the prison. He moved calmly and slowly, using his stick for support. Miraculously, he hadn't lost his leg after Hackett had shot him, but he would limp badly now for the rest of his life.

The other prisoners were noisy and excitable, almost drowning out the sound of the guards running their truncheons along the steel balustrades. The inmates were always like this on days when visitors came. Yet the shoving sea of grey boiler suits in the walkway flowed around Mack, giving him space to move at his own pace.

Downstairs in the visitors' hall, Mack smiled when he saw that Barry had arrived and was at the corner table. He was busy laying out the chess set as it had been at the end of their session a fortnight ago. Mack wondered if today would be the day that they finally finished their game. He'd been dreaming of potential moves and he wouldn't mind betting, from the look of concentration on Barry's face, that he'd be taking it equally seriously. Over the years they'd both become good at the never-ending game of strategy, and even though it was usually Mack who won, Barry still gave him a run for his money.

It must have been five years now that Barry, a volunteer prison visitor, had been coming to see him and Mack appreciated it. He'd grown to respect the simple family man who gave him a glimpse of the outside world.

Barry must have known what Mack was inside for, but he never asked him about it, or let on that he had read his files, or seen the news reports. He must have been aware before he started his prison visits that Mack was one of the jail's most infamous inmates. One who had never resorted to violence, but had earned himself a reputation as someone not to mess with. But Barry had always been friendly and respectful, brushing aside any allusions to Mack's crime, and Mack had come to like and trust him.

Mack always felt a surge of respect for this modest man who gave up his time voluntarily. Would Mack have been so selfless, if his life hadn't spiralled out of control? If he'd lived the normal, cosy life he'd assumed was going to be his?

If he ever got the chance to walk free again, then he wondered if he'd ever do something to help others too. Something philanthropic. Something to change other people's lives. Not something small – something big. Life-changing. That would be satisfying, surely.

But the thought brought a wry smile of doubt. He couldn't think about the person he might become. His sentence was fifty years and he'd only served a fifth of it. The only way he'd get out of jail was when they carried him out in a coffin.

'So, how's your week been?' Mack asked, as they settled down to their game.

'Aye. My boy, he made me proud yesterday,' Barry said with a chuckle. He had such a dour Yorkshire accent and Mack wondered, as he often did, whether Barry opened up to other people the way he did on his visits to Mack at the jail. There was something about Barry, about his honesty, about his certainty about who he was and his place in the world, that appealed to Mack.

And now Mack smiled too, noticing the way Barry's eyes lit up, the same as they always did whenever he talked about his son. He was only a toddler, but the little boy meant everything to Barry. Mack listened intently, imagining every detail, as Barry talked about playing football in the backyard and how he'd ordered a proper goalpost for the lad's birthday, even though he could ill afford it. He knew that Barry's meagre wages as a care-taker were stretched to the limit with his young family and every treat was a sacrifice, and this latest one was the most extravagant yet. One that Barry had yet to tell his wife about.

'I know what she'll say,' he said, rolling his eyes at Mack, and Mack felt the warmth that he always did when Barry confided in him about his family. 'She'll say that we should buy a bike for Gina first, but I can see so much potential in the boy and I want him to have the best, you know.'

'We all want the best for our children,' Mack replied, trying to sound comforting. 'I'd feel the same way.'

'Have you got kids, Mack?' Barry asked.

Mack looked at him sharply. He realized now that, in all their years together, this was the first time Barry had asked him such a direct question about his family. He'd let Barry tell him all about his family and yet he'd never shared anything personal with him.

He regretted it, although Barry had never seemed to mind. Mack was so used to keeping secrets, much as he wanted to return the favour and confide in Barry, he didn't want to start being careless now, yet a small confession slipped out nonetheless.

'I haven't seen them since . . .' He trailed off. He couldn't bear to think of that awful time he'd last seen them. When Voss . . .

'Sorry, Mack. I didn't mean to stir up bad memories.'

They played on in silence for a few more minutes. Mack was glad Barry hadn't pressed him for details. He knew he mustn't give away anything personal, even to Barry. Not in here. Not ever. It was too dangerous. Not when Voss still had them. All of them. His family. Mark, just a sweet boy – the same age as Barry's son, and Tara too, his baby princess. And Kate. His Kate, who he missed so much it felt as if it would crush him.

Familiar fury pierced him in the chest. He mustn't think about it, he told himself. He must hold the faith. Hold the faith that they were alive. That Voss hadn't harmed them. That he'd kept his side of the bargain. But the faces of Kate, Mark and little Tara, the last time he'd seen them, cowering behind Voss, were imprinted on his brain.

'Do you really want to do that?' Mack asked, turning his attention back to the game, forcing his mind away from the pain. He watched as Barry hovered the queen above the board, the realization dawning on his face that if he put the piece down, then Mack would win.

'Ah, you get me every time,' Barry said with a good-natured laugh, putting the queen down anyway. He looked at the board and scratched his head. 'I'll miss these games of ours.'

Mack stared at him. 'Miss them. Why? Where are you going?'

'Nowhere.'

There was a pause; then Barry leaned forward. 'I'm not supposed to tell you, but I've let the cat out now.'

'Tell me,' Mack pressed.

Barry leaned in even closer and lowered his voice. 'They're thinking of moving you.'

'Moving me?'

'I put in a good word, you see. I was asked to recommend prisoners for relocation. You're going to Aberdeen. To a Class B prison. You know, with a little more freedom, a little more trust. On account of how you've kept your nose clean in here. And my report, of course.' He smiled, and shrugged self-deprecatingly.

It was all Mack could do not to jump across the table and hug him. He hadn't expected such a sudden surge of emotion. He only survived in here by concentrating on one day at a time.

Now he felt hope swelling inside him. He was getting out of this dump. And OK, he might be locked up somewhere else instead, but he was going home to Scotland. Somehow being on Scottish soil would make the remainder of his sentence seem more bearable.

'You recommended me?' Mack asked.

'Well, you're Scottish. I thought you'd like being there. And because you're a good man. I know that. Ten years inside is a long time for a man with your reputation to keep out of trouble. Maybe they've realized you're not such a great threat after all.'

Mack nodded, too emotional to speak.

Scotland.

Home.

It was a further two months before Mack was told officially of his relocation plans. And a further six before the day came when he was put in the back of an armoured van with three other prisoners. A total of eight months to think on the prospect of being transferred to another institution and all the changes it would mean.

The jail at Aberdeen was an imposing place with high granite walls and initially Mack wondered whether the transfer really was an improvement. After a strip search, he was introduced to various members of staff, including the prison chaplain.

'I don't do religion,' Mack told him bluntly.

'Is that so?' The chaplain laughed. He had fair hair and a foreign accent, Mack noticed. He looked at the priest, confused by his reaction. He was certainly a jolly fellow, considering the job he did.

'You might want to take solace in the Church once you get

to know your cellmate,' the chaplain called after Mack. 'The last one did. He couldn't stand the talking.'

'What does he mean?' Mack asked the guard. He felt a horrible sinking feeling starting inside him. He didn't want to share a cell. Not when he was used to being on his own, keeping himself to himself. What if he was in with some thug, or a nutter, like he had been at the beginning in the last place? But he still knew how to take care of himself. And he wouldn't be able to do anything until he'd got the lie of the land. Even so, his hackles were up as they approached the cell and the guard unlocked it.

'The Father is referring to Tobias Asquith, your new cell-mate. He's quite a character. You'll see.'

The cell was light and bright, Mack noticed, walking in. In fact, it was tidy and clean. A chess set was on a small table between the beds. No bunks in here. One wall had been chalked with a mural. An astonishingly detailed scene of a place that looked as if it might be the Riviera. Somehow it completely changed the atmosphere of the cell. A man was kneeling on the floor by the bed, adding the finishing touches. He stood up, wiping his hands on his prison boiler suit.

'Good luck,' the guard said to Mack with a wry grin. 'Don't play cards with him.'

'Why not?'

'The guy's the biggest fraudster in town,' the guard said. 'He'll get you every time.'

'Peter,' the man said, tipping his head to one side, 'I told you there were to be no hard feelings.'

The guard rolled his eyes and shut the door with a resounding thud.

Mack stared at his new cellmate. Despite his regulation prison clothes, he had the demeanour of someone who was in a yacht club in the South of France. A paisley scarf tied at the neck helped. As did the cigarette-holder he now picked up. With the mural behind him, he really could have been standing on the deck of a private yacht. He had an American twang to his clipped English, Mack noticed. His blue eyes shone with amused intelligence.

Mack felt his objections to this new cellmate bubbling up – the smoking, the affectations – and yet they all stalled on his tongue as the man grinned widely at Mack and extended his hand.

'Ah, Mack Moncrief, the great train robber,' he said. 'How very delightful to meet you at long last. Tobias Asquith at your service.'

Mack nodded, bemused. He shook Tobias's hand, not used to this level of civility from inmates. In fact, he'd quite forgotten it. His large hand felt rough in Tobias's smooth grip.

'You are Mack Moncrief?' Tobias checked.

'Aye. What's it to you?'

'What's it to me? What's it to me? My dear chap, it means everything. I've been on a campaign to get you into this cell ever since I heard you were heading our way.'

'Oh. And why's that?'

'Because a man who has the nerve and skill to plan something as audacious as that train robbery is just the man I need,' Tobias said, lowering his voice.

'Need for what?'

Tobias leaned in close. 'Our escape.'

Mack rubbed his temple. He couldn't help but smile. This guy . . . his confidence . . . was quite disarming. 'You're planning on escaping?'

'With your help.'

'And what makes you think I might be able to help you?'

'Well, you're the explosives expert, right?'

'Wrong. I worked for the army disposing bombs, not setting them off.'

'But you blasted open that safe on the train, didn't you?'

Mack shifted uncomfortably, then brushed past him to the empty bed.

'What if I could get you semtex and a detonator?'

Mack burst out laughing. He placed the copy of *The Count of Monte Cristo* on the empty bedside table. It had been a leaving present from Barry. The irony of this current conversation was not lost on him as he stroked the cover.

'Really? In here? Are you out of your mind?'

'They say I am, but it's all smoke and mirrors, my friend. I'm really quite sane. Although I do stray into the realms of genius occasionally.'

Mack stared at him, amused despite himself, then slapped the wall. 'Have you not noticed these walls? Even if we did have explosives, we couldn't make a blast in these – we'd kill ourselves. Then there's the small issue of the quad outside and the fence . . . oh, and the lookout towers.'

'Aha!' Tobias grinned. 'Oh, ye of little faith.'

CHAPTER ELEVEN

It was a hot, humid night in downtown Rio. The sun had set an hour ago, but the sky was still light through the palm trees and the lamps along the streets, the noises from outside infusing the night with excitement.

'We're nearly there,' Nat said. 'Feeling in the mood?' She wiggled her hips and clicked her fingers and Julia could tell she was itching to get dancing. She was wearing a short pink skirt and a cropped top that showed off her toned stomach. With her dark hair raked up in sparkling clips, Julia had no doubt that her friend would get lucky tonight.

Nat grinned at Julia beside her in the cab and Julia smiled back, pretending to share her mood, but the truth was that she felt too guilty to enjoy herself tonight. She shouldn't be out having fun when Vovo was so sick at home. Her grandmother had been worse than ever this evening before Julia had left to meet Nat. She'd been trying to tell Julia something when a coughing fit had seized her and left her exhausted. She'd left Marcello in charge with strict instructions to check on her regularly.

Julia looked out of the window to the lights of the Avenida Rio Branco, where the skyscraping banks and travel agencies behind the silhouetted palm trees reminded Julia of the wealth of the city and the vibrant, buzzing downtown scene she had glimpsed from the edges but had never been part of.

They were approaching the splendid buildings of the Theatro Municipal, near the National Library, where the cab would drop them at the plaza. Julia thought again of her class and how wonderful it would be to bring them here, or to the Museu Nacional de Belas Artes to show them all the classical and contemporary Brazilian art. Then she remembered Senhora Azevedo. There was no point in even thinking about it.

'We can walk,' Julia said, tapping the glass of the yellow cab, seeing the taxis lining up. The cab fare was so expensive already, but Nat had insisted on hiring one, even though Julia had wanted to come by tram. She was relieved when Nat handed over the money.

Outside, away from the air conditioning of the cab, the night was sticky, the sweet fragrance of the sugar-doughnut vendors filling the air. As they linked arms and walked towards the plaza, they were passed by a group of flamboyantly dressed transvestites and some roller-skating men in skimpy shorts. Julia laughed at their blatant exhibitionism as they turned and did a bow for the girls, extrovertly calling out compliments.

There were people everywhere and it was noisy. A samba band in the centre of the plaza was competing with the high-energy capoeira dancers, their rippling torsos delighting the crowd as they performed their weird mixture of martial-arts moves and tumbling dance to the throbbing beat of the *berimbau* and tambourine. Julia couldn't help but smile and dance a bit with Nat. The carnival atmosphere was infectious and now, out here, she forgot all her commitments at home, just as Nat had assured her she would. In fact, Julia realized, it felt great to be out.

They headed through the crowds to the Largo da Carioca, where the wide pedestrian mall was filled with street vendors hawking leather goods and cheap clothing. Taking in the surroundings, Nat and Julia chatted happily, as they always did, Nat recounting the trials of her office life and Julia sharing her fury at Senhora Azevedo telling her not to give the children ideas.

'Silly cow,' Nat said. 'Doesn't she realize how amazing you are? She's so lucky to have you at that school.'

Julia smiled, glad to have the fierce loyalty of her closest friend.

'A weird thing happened,' she said. 'I found a wallet.'

'Hooray for that. Was there money inside it?' Nat asked.

Julia nodded. 'Lots. But no ID. No way to return it to the owner. Just a strange card with a phone number written on it. I feel so guilty about it. Like it's this weight hanging over me. I should call the number and hand the wallet back, but I haven't. Every time I think of doing it, something stops me.'

'To hell with that,' Nat said. 'Listen, if there's anyone who needs a break, it's you. Spend the money, I say. Finders keepers.'

'You really think so?'

'You've got too much Catholic guilt. That's your problem.' Nat laughed. 'What are you planning on doing? Handing it in to the cops? You know they'd only steal it for themselves.'

Julia laughed too, but she wished she could share Nat's optimism and pragmatic approach to the wallet. She gripped her handbag tighter, feeling the wallet inside. She'd kept it with her since she'd found it and tonight was no exception. She'd thought about leaving it at home, but she'd felt it was probably safer to keep it with her. She couldn't risk Marcello or Fredo finding the money, yet at the same time she knew she couldn't spend it either.

'I mean, why don't we just blow the lot? You could get new

shoes . . . new dresses. Look. Look at that one,' Nat called, beckoning her over.

Julia looked longingly in the shop window. Would spending loads of money on some nice dresses really solve anything, though? It might cheer her up for a while, but it wouldn't alter the fact that Julia was nearly thirty and she was poor. All her life she'd been poor. All her life she'd had to put on a brave face and remind herself how lucky she was. But she wasn't lucky. Not in any real sense. And walking around in 2,000 reals' worth of designer dresses wasn't going to solve anything. She'd soon find herself poor again. And she'd also be a thief.

'Come on, it's down here,' Nat said, dragging her away from the brightly lit window.

They turned off the market, past the charcoal artists and down a side street. Here, beyond the buzz and skyscrapers, the buildings were from another, more stately era. Vovo used to clean a law office around here when Julia had been young, she remembered now as they turned into the Rua Goncalves Dias and passed the designer shops and then the Confeitaria Colombo, where Julia had always longed to take Vovo so she could soak up the atmosphere of the mirrored tea room where Rio's intelligentsia used to gather. For years Vovo had wanted to take tea in that tea room. And now she never would.

She should have done more, Julia chastised herself. She should have made the effort to make Vovo's dream happen when she was still healthy. After all, it had been Vovo who had done everything for Julia, bringing her up single-handedly after her parents had died in a fire when she was barely four. Julia couldn't remember her parents, although she'd stared at the framed photograph that Vovo kept by her bed often enough. They were just a fact, rather than anything more meaningful. People who meant nothing to her. But Vovo had never let Julia feel their loss. Her grandmother had given her enough love to more than make up for a mother and a father and had filled the rickety apartment with laughter, working day and night to make sure that Julia never went without. It was Vovo who'd made Julia follow her dream to become a teacher and now it was too late for Julia to show her how much she cared – how grateful she was. How had life slipped through her fingers like it had? How had 'one day' come and gone without her noticing?

'Come on. This should be fun,' Nat said, pulling her down the narrow alleyway to where a crowd was gathering.

Just as Julia had suspected, the crowd outside the swanky new bar were all young and beautiful, all the girls in high heels and short skirts posing in the queue, the thumping music spilling out onto the street. Nat walked to the front of the queue and waved her tickets at the good-looking bouncer in his hip jeans and blue shirt. He unclipped the red rope for them to pass, and grabbing Julia's hand, Nat pulled her into the corridor inside, where neon lights made everything blue and Nat's teeth look insanely white.

An achingly cool black girl in a skimpy silver dress stamped the back of their hands, and then an unsmiling suited bouncer opened the door to the club. Julia wondered whether he'd have been more charming if she and Nat were younger. She felt ancient in here and badly dressed too, in the little black dress and strappy sandals she'd borrowed from Nat. Didn't Nat feel, as she did, that this all felt a bit desperate? Like they were trying too hard?

But clearly not. Nat was grinning wildly at her and started dancing and laughing as soon as they entered the club. Music hit them full force, like a wave, as they stood at the top of the metal stairway. The club below was mobbed, lights criss-crossing the crowd by the neon-lit bar. Beyond the bar, a larger group was dancing. The DJ's box was high up on a dais and he pointed at the crowd, who roared back their approval.

Nat and Julia fought their way down the steps to the bar, where the good-looking bartenders twirled bottles in the air as they mixed cocktails. Music throbbed and the crowd even at the bar swayed to the music. Julia wondered how long it would be before she got a headache.

Nat bought them both a cocktail and Julia took the smallest sip. Unless she started spending the money from the wallet, she couldn't afford to buy any more than one drink in return, so they'd have to make it last.

Within moments Nat's face lit up in recognition, and pulling Julia away from the bar, she wriggled her way through the crowd to where a girl was standing near the dance floor. Nat greeted her, kissing the pretty brunette, and introduced Julia. The girl – whose name Julia missed – shouted over the music and beckoned them to follow.

They went towards the raised area at the side of the dance floor, where a group of people sat on a banquette and stood round a table. They clapped and cheered as Nat approached. And as Nat was swallowed into their greetings, Julia wished that she hadn't come out tonight. Nat didn't need her here, she realized, watching her friend kiss several people. She was just being kind, cutting her a break, because she knew how dismal Julia's life was. She watched Nat laughing and waved as she was led onto the dance floor by one of her colleagues' friends.

Julia watched Nat flirting with the guy, twirling in his arms, as she took another minute sip of her drink. She looked at the flashing lights, wishing she could get in the mood, but she only felt more isolated and out of place.

Why couldn't she be like Nat and join in the fun? After all, wasn't she always complaining to Nat about being single? It was over three years since she'd split up with Andreas. But whenever she'd been in a situation where she could have met a man – gone home with him even – she'd baulked at the idea.

Maybe Nat's earlier comment was spot on. Maybe she did have too much Catholic guilt to have fun. Ever since she'd been a child and Vovo had taken her to the ornate Portuguese church, she'd been scared of doing the wrong thing. She thought of the priest she'd confessed her teenage angst to and how she'd been a good girl, always doing the right thing, just to see a smile on Vovo's face.

She hadn't been to confession for years, though. Not since the abortion, which she knew she could never talk about with the priest – or anyone apart from Nat, who had held her hand throughout the whole ordeal. She'd given her the money to pay for it and now Julia realized that she shouldn't have told Nat about the money in the wallet. They hadn't discussed the abortion or the money since, but maybe Nat was expecting Julia to pay her back someday. Like today. Yes, she thought, maybe she should pay off her debt to Nat with the money she'd found. That would be the right thing to do.

It was strange, she thought, that while she felt guilty about all sorts of things, Julia hardly ever felt retrospective guilt about the abortion. Nothing, in fact, but relief that she'd made the right decision. There was no way she'd have been able to have a baby. Not without giving up all her dreams of making a better life for her and her family. But recently she'd been aware of a sense of future guilt on the horizon. Because she was twenty-nine. And what if that one time with Andreas had been her only chance to have a family of her own? It was a thought she rarely had the courage to face head on, because when she did, like now, she felt herself recoiling in fear.

She cautioned herself to stick to the facts. She couldn't have had a baby with Andreas. After the abortion, he'd called Julia a murderer and had tried to make her feel terrible, so she'd ended their relationship, thanking her lucky stars that she hadn't gone ahead with the pregnancy and been tied to a man like Andreas for the rest of her life.

But where were the alternative men? If she wanted the polar opposite of Andreas, it was hard to find. She'd had a few flings with a couple of men since. She'd even had a brief affair with her friend Tim at school, but in the end they'd both been too paranoid about being found out and losing their jobs. Senhora Azevedo would definitely have had something to say about them being a couple.

Now, she felt someone sidle up to her and heard a male voice shout, 'Hi,' above the music. She smiled, looking at his gelled hair and typical Brazilian dark good looks. She glanced at Nat on the dance floor and her partner, who both made encouraging faces. They'd clearly put the guy up to asking her to dance.

She turned to the man, who shouted his name. 'Tony,' she thought she heard. She smiled, but she could see automatically that he wasn't her type. He was wearing a shiny black satin shirt undone to reveal his waxed chest and well-defined pecs. As he led her onto the dance floor, his aftershave was overpoweringly musky.

Julia tried to smile again as Tony's eyes locked on hers. She could see the intent in them. She could see the single track of his mind and his assumption that she was on a similar track, hurtling towards him.

Without a smile, or any sense of irony, he put his arm up with a flourish, like a matador, and gripped her tightly, his hand exploring the curve of her waist. She wriggled in his grip, but he only took it as a sign that she wanted to be held tighter. She felt his face nuzzle into her neck; then his lips were on her ear.

She felt herself recoiling from his touch. She didn't want his hot breath in her ear. She didn't want to do this. She pushed him away and, turning, ran off the dance floor.

She walked quickly past the bar and through the door, surprising the bouncers, who were clearly not used to seeing people leave – especially so soon after arriving. She looked at the queue of expectant girls waiting to go in and take her place. They were welcome to it.

But still Julia felt a pang of guilt for leaving. She knew she should have stayed to check that Nat was OK, but Nat was a big girl who could look after herself, and she was among acquaintances who, from the look of it, would soon be friends.

She sent Nat a quick text, telling her she was fine and going home, then walked back towards the plaza, where she hoped to catch a tram. But as she wandered back through the crowds, she felt disconnected and unsettled. Why was she feeling like this when she should be out having fun? Was it really guilt, like Nat had said? Because of the wallet?

Well, if that was it, it was ridiculous, she concluded, delving inside her bag for her phone and the wallet. She had to sort this out right now. Fortified by the last of the cocktail she'd downed before leaving the club, she took the card from inside the wallet and dialled the number. She would leave a message. At the very least find out where to send the wallet. Get it out of her life once and for all.

But to her shock, a man answered.

'Hello?' he said in English.

'Hi, you don't know me, but I have a wallet of yours,' she said, remembering her English. Her palms had begun to sweat.

'Ah, you must be Miss Pires,' the voice said, slipping into Portuguese. He had a local accent. 'At last,' he said. Julia could tell he was smiling. 'I was beginning to think—'

'How do you know my name?' she asked, worried now. Because if the man knew her name, then that would mean that the wallet had been deliberately planted. The man – this man on the phone – had wanted her to find it. And he knew where she worked.

'We know many things about you,' he said.

Julia felt the skin on her neck erupt into goosebumps. *We?* Who was *we*? This was all sounding very sinister. She felt her throat go tight. Never in a million years had she expected *this*.

'Who are you? I want to give the wallet back. I don't want the money. I don't know why you have done this—'

'There is no need to be alarmed, Julia. Please, I can meet you and explain.'

Julia looked around her in the busy plaza. She was surrounded by people, but she felt terrified. The man on the phone wanted to meet her? Right now?

'No. I don't want . . . I don't know—' She panicked.

'Please. Please don't worry,' the man interrupted. 'What I have to tell you is very important. Where are you? I can meet you now if you wish. Are you in Rio?'

How could he expect her not to worry? He was a complete stranger who knew her name. She stared around her, her heart beating wildly.

'Julia?' the man said. His voice was friendly. Calm. 'You're in Rio? Are you downtown?'

He said it as if it were a question, but somehow the surety of his tone made the hairs on the back of her neck stand up. Did he know where she was right now? Was he tracking her somehow?

No. It was impossible, she told herself.

'Julia?' The man waited for her to speak again.

'Yes,' she whispered, closing her eyes at the enormous risk she was taking. 'I'm by the *theatro*.'

'Stay there. I'll be with you very soon. No more than twenty minutes.'

Julia was silent. She heard the man sigh gently.

'I understand that this must be strange, but please, I promise you, I mean you no harm. What I have to tell you is good.'

But as Julia sat on the steps of the *theatro* fifteen minutes later, her palms were sweating. Her instincts told her to run, but somehow she couldn't move. This was crazy. Why had she agreed to meet a stranger, after dark? Even in a place as public as this, it went against everything Vovo had ever taught her.

She watched the parrots flitting between the wide avenue of trees in front of her. Behind her, the lights of the *theatro* blazed. Was there really any safety here in this public place? Nobody in the world knew where she was or what she was doing.

What did this man want from her? Who was he? How did he know her name? The questions stacked up in her head one on top of another. What was this? What had she got herself into? Why, oh, why hadn't she handed in the wallet as soon as she'd found it?

She was just about to leave when she saw a dark-haired man running up the steps towards her. He was wearing jeans and a nicely cut designer shirt. He looked like he'd hurried to get here, but he grinned widely. He had very white teeth.

'Hello, Miss Pires,' he said, reaching her and smiling.

'Who are you?' she asked, standing up and facing the man. He stared intently at her, not answering. She felt the anger and frustration that had been building up during her wait make her voice shrill and shaky. 'What do you want with me? I have the money. Here . . .' She reached into her bag for the wallet and thrust it towards him. He could go to hell.

The man seemed to remember himself and held out his hands to her. 'No. No. The money is a gift,' the man said, smiling again.

He was staring at her so intently Julia blushed. This was just *weird*.

'Take it. I don't want it.'

The man held up his hands. 'I can't take it. It belongs to you.'

Julia bit her lip. She felt tears of impotence welling up inside her.

'You don't want it back?' she asked. 'Then what do you want with me?'

'Only to tell you . . . to tell you that you are lucky.'

Julia let out an exasperated yelp. The Pires family weren't *lucky*. Her parents had died in a fire. Ricardo, her older brother, had got into trouble with the police and then into drugs and had taken off years ago, leaving Vovo and Julia to bring up his son, Fredo. What was lucky for the poor kid about living in the favela? What was lucky about Vovo needing medical care none of them could afford? No, none of them were lucky. She'd certainly never been lucky in her life. The only things she'd ever got were through hard work and sheer bloody perseverance.

'You have been selected to receive a key,' the man told her, his tone soothing.

'A key? What key?' she interrupted.

'A key that will unlock your future. A key to solve all your problems.'

He smiled as if he'd just revealed a magic trick. Julia stared at him. Was this guy for real?

Quickly he took a box out of his pocket and opened it. Inside was a silver key-shaped pendant with a diamond on it.

'Here. This is it. It's yours. Take it.'

Julia looked at the little silver key and the diamond on it glinted. It was the same key that had been printed on the glossy card. It looked classy, not cheap. She felt herself looking at it, her curiosity piqued, despite herself.

'Why me? Why should I get this?'

'As I said, you have been chosen. Seriously. There's no catch. This is for you.'

'I don't understand,' Julia said, still staring at the key.

'I have been trying to find you to give it to you. I was supposed to get it to you before, but it's been . . .' He shook his head, deciding against explaining. 'It has been so hard to get your attention. It doesn't matter. All that matters is that you're here now and I can give it to you. Please take it,' the man continued, smiling. 'This key is very special. It will unlock all of your dreams.'

All of her dreams? What *were* her dreams? To get a better apartment. To give her schoolchildren better opportunities. To find a heart replacement for Vovo? To magic Fredo into a better life where he wouldn't succumb to the pressure of his peers like his father had? To find a kind, compassionate, funny, rich husband for herself? Was he really saying this key was going to get her those things? She almost laughed at the absurdity of it. They'd clearly mistaken her for someone else. Someone whose dreams were achievable. Someone whose dreams could be bought. And that was just it. The whole thing didn't seem right. Nothing about it seemed right. Nothing came for free. She knew that. It was a basic law of life.

'I don't want it. Thank you, but whatever this scheme is, I don't want it. I don't know how you know about me, but this is a mistake,' Julia said, taking off down the steps. 'You've got the wrong person.'

'Please, Julia, take it.'

'No.'

Julia ran faster. She had to get away. But just as she was going down the final step, her phone rang in her bag. It must be Nat, she thought, realizing Julia had gone. She should explain why she'd left – although now she wished she hadn't. Maybe she could go back to the club. The thought of the noise and the dancing suddenly seemed very appealing.

But it wasn't Nat; it was Marcello.

'Thank God, Julia, you're there,' he cried.

'What is it?'

'You've got to come now. Please, Julia. Quickly. It's Vovo. She's dying.'

She could hear the panic in his voice, but even though she knew she should be practical, she felt her eyes flood with tears. Not Vovo. Not now.

She told Marcello she'd be there as soon as she could, then set off to the square. She'd almost forgotten all about the man when he took her arm and stopped her.

'Go away,' Julia said, a sob in her voice. 'Leave me alone. I've got to go.'

He held the box out to her. 'Just take the key. You must take it. You have to. Use the key. I promise it will help with whatever you need,' he said, staring at her intently. 'Trust me.'

CHAPTER TWELVE

The prestigious annual YMC agents' party was in full swing on the enormous rooftop of their brownstone warehouse in Manhattan. In the early evening light, the skyscrapers around had fallen into soft relief and the sky above was a soft mauve. Fairy lights twinkled in the artificial trees as Scooter tottered in her Louboutin sandals from the bar to the far end of the party, beyond the sprung dance floor to where the big agents were holding court. Around the sides of the party, open tents were filled with low seating on silk rugs, the tables adorned with candles and flowers.

On the stage next to the dance floor she heard a few wolf whistles and applause as the sexy salsa band came on, replacing the acoustic guitarist. In a moment the night was filled with guitars and the husky voice of Carlos Bossa, the Brazilian singer, was everywhere.

A waiter blocked her path, holding out a tray of sumptuous-looking canapés, the miniature beef burgers crying out to be gobbled up. He was good-looking and clearly on show, desperate to be seen.

'Did you know . . . if you don't mind me saying . . . you look seriously hot in that dress,' he said in a practised drawl.

Scooter gave him a withering look. He was only hitting on her because he thought she might be a player. But she wasn't. Not yet.

'They're delicious,' he continued, but she put up her hand and shook her head. She knew the score. Those calorie-laden morsels were just a temptation. No actress would dare eat a carb in public after 6 p.m. Especially not here, where everyone was watching to see who had arrived and who was with whom.

Seeing he was not getting anywhere, the waiter brushed past her.

'Hey,' she called out, stopping another waiter in his tracks. She took one of the flutes of champagne from his tray and downed it in one. She hadn't had a drink for months, but one wouldn't hurt, and right now she needed some courage.

She felt jittery and on edge. She'd come with Jay, who'd schmoozed his way through security as usual, Scooter hanging on to his arm like she always used to. But now she'd left him by the bar. Without being so obviously in his entourage, and on her own, she was expecting to be found out at any second. Wherever she looked she saw security guys with their discreet earpieces. She knew she had to find Miranda and do what she came here to do, before her nerve deserted her.

'Scooter! Oh my God, Scooter Black.'

Scooter would have recognized that voice anywhere. It belonged to Lara Hill and she couldn't help but stare at the pregnant belly of the woman with swishy dark hair who was wearing a very bright orange dress as she raced towards her through the crowd, waving wildly. In a second Lara had engulfed her in an overbearing hug.

'I didn't know you were still in town,' Lara said, splaying her manicured nails on Scooter's arm. 'And I had no idea you'd be here. Wow,' she said, as if impressed. She opened her mouth and let out a wide-mouthed 'Ha' of sheer awe.

Scooter smiled unsteadily at her ex-friend Lara, remembering in a rush all the skiing holidays they'd been on: Scooter and Dean, Lara and Billy. Like a crackly rose-tinted movie of another life, she remembered the Colorado apartment Billy's producer had loaned them and how they'd all shared hot tubs together. She remembered how Lara had confided in her about her and Billy's terrible sex life and how Scooter had given her advice and tips.

And another time – in the summer – how she'd varnished Lara's nails and plaited her hair on the road trips they'd taken in the van, drinking and playing cards, then singing by the camp-fire to Dean's guitar. Lara had told Scooter that she was like a sister. The best friend she'd ever had. But in the almost two years since Dean had left a note on the kitchen table telling Scooter that it was over for good between them, Lara hadn't called once. Or, more specifically, she hadn't called Scooter *back* once. Because Lara, if anyone, must have had some inkling as to Dean's state of mind and the reason he'd so cruelly detonated his relationship with Scooter. But she'd gone radio silent, when she must have known how much Scooter had been hurting. *Some sister*.

'You know, you haven't changed a bit. And you don't even look like you've had much work,' Lara said, her eyes raking over Scooter's face. Scooter smiled uncertainly, not sure whether it had been an insult or a compliment. She remembered now that Lara rarely thought before opening her mouth. She decided to change the subject.

'So, you've been busy, I see,' Scooter said, raising her eyebrows at Lara's enormous bump. So much for the disastrous sex life, then. She must be doing something right at long last. She grabbed another glass of champagne from the next passing waiter. Her hand was shaking. She felt something bitter and snakelike – was it jealousy? – coiling round her insides.

'Would you like one?' the waiter asked Lara, but she patted her bump protectively and declined.

'I know. Me, refusing champagne!' She laughed at Scooter. 'But I haven't touched a drop for nearly two years. And now I have my own macrobiotic food company, it's just made the world of difference.'

'Oh my God. Wow,' Scooter said, still in shock. Lara had always been kind of grungy. A proper tomboy. And that had been her appeal – the way she drank beer and smoked roll-ups. But here she was . . . all groomed and healthy.

'It's been a perfect pregnancy. Billy wanted me to put my feet up tonight, as it's so close to my due date, but I said, "Hell, no." You know me. I don't want to miss a party. And now I've seen you, which has just made my evening.'

'So, do you know if it's a girl or a boy?' Scooter asked.

'It's a boy. Billy has all these plans about how they'll bond. And Dean too. He'll be godfather, you see,' Lara said, but stopped, realizing she'd said too much.

Scooter felt betrayed all over again. Dean and Billy and the little baby. Of course Dean would be godfather – not that he had a religious bone in his body.

If Scooter and Dean were still together, it would have been Scooter who organized the baby shower. Scooter who chose the godparent gift with Dean. Hell, she might even have a baby herself. The thought hit her like a bolt, tearing open the wound of Dean's betrayal all over again.

Maybe it wouldn't hurt as badly if she hadn't loved him so

much. But she had. She still did. But Lara, Dean, Billy, they'd all moved on. They were grown-ups. And what was she? A waitress. Just the same as she'd been fifteen years ago.

'So you see him?' Scooter asked, annoyed that her voice sounded so husky.

'Dean? All the time. You know he's living near us in West Canyon? We see Mona a lot too.'

'Oh?'

Why did they see Mona? Scooter's ex-best friend. And, more importantly, how the hell did Mona get to have a place in the Canyon?

'Mona. You must know about Mona and Dean,' Lara said with a guffaw. 'They've been together for a while now.' She squinted at Scooter.

Was Lara pretending to be confused, or had she enjoyed delivering this knife-wound? 'We haven't kept in touch,' Scooter managed.

Mona was dating Dean?

'He's doing so well. His songs are everywhere these days,' Lara gushed.

'I know,' Scooter managed, the bitterness of it all threatening to swamp her. She wondered if Lara knew that it was Scooter who'd co-written 'Find Me'.

'Isn't it just awesome!' Lara laughed. 'To think, when he was really struggling, and now look at him. You know he just did the soundtrack to Billy's film? In fact, we're all going to Cannes for the premiere. That's providing Junior here hurries up and gets born on time.' She laughed again, patting her bump affectionately.

Scooter forced a fake smile onto her face. 'That's so nice. Dean always wanted to go to Europe.' They'd planned to go together. Paris, Italy, London. It had all been worked out. Dean had told her it would be an 'unofficial honeymoon'.

'I know. We're doing it in such style this time. Billy has co-produced the movie, so we're staying on a yacht and having this mega-party.' She did jazz hands to accentuate the word 'mega'.

'Wow,' Scooter said lamely.

'The best bit is Dean's band will be performing. He says he can't wait. I mean, talk about the most A-list audience *ever*. Hilarious!'

Scooter felt suffocated. She had to get away from Lara. 'Sounds great. I hope you have a good time.'

Lara made a sympathetic face. Scooter had obviously failed to mask how much this got to her.

'So,' she said, grabbing Scooter's arm. 'Enough of all that. I want to hang out and hear about all your successes. I'm so glad you've made it as an actress. You've got to be super successful to have come here, right? I came with Courtney.'

'I'd love to, Lara, but there's my agent,' Scooter said, removing Lara's hand from her arm, 'so I'd better go and say hi. I'll catch you later.'

Scooter ducked away from Lara before she had time to protest. She marched straight over to Jay at the bar. 'I need a line,' she hissed in his ear.

Jay turned and looked at her over his shoulder. His slow smile made Scooter even more impatient. God, he hadn't changed. Not one bit. Still the same sly old Jay. He had his long hair tied back in a ponytail and was wearing an old-fashioned suede jacket with tassels on the back, but somehow he was managing to rock the cowboy look tonight.

'Sure thing, honeybun,' he said. 'But I thought you told me

not to give you anything, no matter what you said. Those were your words.'

'I don't care what I said. I just need one now.'

Coming out of the bathroom into the sparkling corridor five minutes later, Scooter hated to admit it, but she felt more herself than she had done in ages. She could feel the cocaine hitting her bloodstream, her skin tingling all over.

'Wow,' she muttered to herself. She'd forgotten how good this felt. How focused it made her feel. Mona and Dean – the searing pain of the information – had somehow been dulled.

Telling herself to be confident, she went out through the doors into the starlit night and saw straight away that Miranda was talking to a group of people. She was wearing a figure-hugging royal-blue dress and high heels, her immaculate blonde bob shining. It was now or never. Not giving herself time to think, Scooter strode over to the group.

'Hi. I'm one of Miranda's clients, Scooter Black,' she said, stepping confidently into the circle. 'Hi, Miranda. Great party.'

She saw Miranda flinch and look sharply around, as if searching for a security guard. Scooter kept her smile in place as she introduced herself to the guys Miranda had been talking to. Jesus, she thought, as she extended her hand, that was Mark Wahlberg. Then she realized the guy next to him was none other than Dallas Laney. *Dallas friggin' Laney.* Possibly one of the hottest actors on the planet right now.

'You're with Miranda?' Dallas Laney asked.

'Yeah. I'm an actress,' Scooter said, smoothing her hair behind her ear and feeling her knees go slightly weak. Dallas Laney was simply a thing of utter beauty. *And he was talking to her.*

'Oh? Theatre?' he asked, clearly not having seen her in anything.

'I've just auditioned for the new Brody Myers film.'

'Have you? He's had terrible trouble funding that. I'm glad it's going ahead.'

'Yeah. Great vehicle for the actress, though,' Mark said, looking at Miranda.

'Scooter, could we discuss this privately?' Miranda asked. Her tone made Scooter prickle all over. That supercilious put-you-down tone that agents like her had.

'I know. When Miranda put me up for it, she knew it was a shoo-in. Right, Miranda?' Scooter said, aware now that the others were looking at her, but somehow she couldn't stop herself. She saw Dallas Laney and Mark Wahlberg exchange amused looks.

'Scooter, you know, if you want to talk about this, then you could call my office on Monday.'

'But you won't take my calls. Rebeka "With-a-Fucking-K" stops them.' Scooter realized she'd said it out loud.

'The girl's got a point, Miranda,' said Dallas. He was clearly enjoying Miranda's barely concealed fury. 'I've heard Rebeka can be a bitch.' He smiled as he took a sip of his drink. His eyes twinkled at Scooter.

Miranda's rictus grin was frozen on her face.

'Well, she's here now,' Mark said, backing up Dallas and winking at Scooter. 'Talk to the girl. You two clearly have un-finished business.'

'OK. Don't go away, gentlemen,' Miranda said, relenting, as if it were all a joke. 'This'll only take a moment.'

She steered Scooter in an about-turn and led her up away

from the dance floor and band to a quiet corner of one of the side tents. Her fingernails dug into Scooter's arm.

'I don't know how you got in here, or what gives you the nerve to do what you just did, but don't you dare . . . ever . . . *ever*—' hissed Miranda.

'I'm sorry, but—'

'No, you listen up, Scooter,' she said, only just containing her anger. 'That was business, and whatever grievance you have, this is not the place to talk about it.'

Scooter knew that she had to play this right, but she felt her earlier confidence evaporating.

'You've been ignoring me and I just want an explanation. That's all,' she blurted.

'Jesus!' Miranda exclaimed. 'An explanation for what?'

'About why they didn't see me. You said . . . you said the part was practically mine.'

'You think I control these people? I can sense their moods, take their hints, but at the end of the day I can only do so much. I put you up for the part, and as I heard it, you let Lindy go straight in. *In front of you.*'

How had she heard that? 'She . . . I—' Scooter started, but Miranda held up her hand.

'You never let another actress get ahead of you. There is no room for "nice" in this business, Scooter. You've got to really want it.'

'I do really want it.'

'Well, if that's the case, why haven't you landed any roles? I mean, now we're having this honest chat, you might as well hear what I think,' Miranda said, furiously flicking her hair. Her eyes gleamed with menace. 'Because, you know, maybe you have to consider that you've missed the boat.' She raised one eyebrow at Scooter. Her words were aimed carefully and Scooter caught the glint in her eyes as she saw she'd hit her target. Right in the heart.

Scooter swallowed, feeling her conviction dissolving like a vitamin tablet, its effervescence dying, leaving her flat. But at the same time she knew she deserved this. That she'd brought all this on herself. Cocaine had always made her too bold. And now look where it had got her.

'Look, I know it's hard to hear, but it's just tough out there. To get parts for anyone. Even the A-listers don't get what they want. And you know, for you and the kind of parts I can put you up for . . .'

Scooter shook her head. 'I know what you're trying to say, Miranda, but I'll show you. I will, I'll prove it to you,' Scooter said, hating the begging tone that had crept into her voice. 'Just put me up for something. I'll ace it. I will. I won't let you down.'

Miranda held up her hand, clearly not wanting to hear any more. 'If you'll excuse me, I have a party to run. And, Scooter, can you please try not to embarrass me any more. Or yourself.'

The party was soon in full swing, but as the night filled with laughter and dancing, Scooter sat alone at the bar, her mind blazing with fury.

'Fill her up,' she told the barman, slamming her shot glass down on the counter for the fifth time.

The barman raised his eyebrows and poured some oily tequila into the glass. Scooter drained it in one.

'Again,' she slurred. She didn't care. She just wanted to drink until this all went away.

'Scooter. Hey, Scoots.'

She swivelled on the bar stool and squinted through the

crowd. Jay was waving from where he sat on a low Moroccan leather couch. He was surrounded by pretty girls on the seating round the candlelit table in the tent.

Scooter slid off the stool and staggered through the crowd towards him.

'Steady there.' Jay laughed, as she approached.

An actress Scooter recognized was sitting on the floor and had her arm draped across Jay's knee. She was from that show . . . Scooter searched for the name of it, but she was too drunk.

'Scooch up,' Scooter told Jay, bumping into the table and squeezing onto the seat next to him. The actress looked put out, but readjusted herself to be closer to Jay.

'You know Scooter?' Jay told the assembled crowd. Scooter put her hand up to the mumbled hellos. 'She's been sober for – what, like two years?' he checked with Scooter.

'I've fallen off the wagon tonight,' she slurred.

'I missed you, babe.' He laughed, patting Scooter's knee. 'My God, her and Dean . . . they were like the craziest, you know.' She pulled a face, annoyed he'd told these strangers about her and Dean, but even so, she was glad she was sitting down. Jay would look after her. He always had.

'So what happened then?' the actress asked. Scooter realized Jay had been in the middle of a story. She sat back as he leaned forward. The lights above her on the tent were blurring and spinning. Who the hell was that chick? Why couldn't she remember anything?

'Oh, yeah. So this guy who called told me he knew this businessman who wanted a stag party to end all stag parties. The works. Money no object. I didn't believe it, but then a first-class ticket turned up to Las Vegas.'

Scooter listened to him, remembering now how Jay liked nothing more than this. Telling a story, spinning a yarn. Tales of debauchery. That was his thing.

She hiccupped loudly, then giggled.

Jay turned to her. 'You OK, babe?' he asked.

But Scooter couldn't speak. She had serious head spins. She shook her head and waved her hand for him to carry on.

'So I get there and there's this Larry Ash guy,' Jay continued. 'He's like . . . seriously loaded. Worked his way up from nothing, apparently. But he had this crazily exclusive key thing.'

'What key thing?' the actress asked.

'It's like a little silver key. A handful of people get them and then they can do anything. I mean, let me tell you about this guy . . .'

'Euuw.' The actress made a revolted noise and Scooter realized she'd slumped down behind Jay. 'What's wrong with her?'

Scooter felt Jay propping her up.

'Scoots? Scooter, don't pass out on me, babes,' he said.

Scooter tried to concentrate, but everything was spinning.

'So this key thing is amazing,' Jay continued. 'We went to Vegas, but it's hard to book those big suites. Especially on Fight Night. But this guy arrives at, like, the MGM Grand, shows this key thing he's got to the manager and we were given the top sky loft. Like free for a whole week.'

'I got one of those,' Scooter slurred, her brain picking up on what Jay was saying. And at exactly the same time she remembered the actress's name. She'd been in that series about the desert island. Alicia Knowles. That was it.

'Scooter, mate, don't you think you should, you know, chill out for a bit?' Jay said, holding up her shoulder.

'No, seriously, Jay,' Scooter slurred, desperate for him to hear her. 'Someone delivered it to me. I don't know who, but I've got one of those keys. You've got to believe me. I'm serious. I'll show . . .' But what had she done with the key? She faded out as she retched and, knowing she was going to puke, pushed Jay out of the way and threw up in Alicia Knowles's lap.

CHAPTER THIRTEEN

In the stuffy sitting room of the apartment in the favela, Julia's grandmother Consuela Pires was on the floor, slipping in and out of consciousness. The old woman looked deathly pale and her breathing was shallow and laboured as Julia held her hand, desperately willing her to hold on. Through the open door to the bedroom, Julia watched Fredo, her nephew, gingerly picking up the pieces of broken glass that lay next to the treasured photo of Julia's parents on the floor.

'Where is the ambulance?' she hissed, staring at Marcello, who was on the phone. He was looking at the television, which was on mute but was still showing the football. Her uncle, his side profile to her, revolted her. Now in his late sixties, he took no responsibility for himself or the apartment whatsoever. Tonight he was wearing his usual attire of a stained vest and shorts, his hairy belly bulging out.

'Fredo, turn off the TV,' she called. He scooted through and flicked the switch.

'They said we'll have to wait,' Marcello said, blushing. 'There's been a coach crash on the freeway. All the ambulances are out. The operator didn't know how long it would be.'

'Why don't we get her in a taxi?' Fredo asked, turning away from the blank TV.

'We can't move her,' Marcello said, crouching down next to Julia.

What was she trying to say? Julia clutched her grandmother's hand, tears blurring her eyes. She should have trusted her instinct. She should never have gone out with Nat. She should have stayed by her side.

'When did you find her?' she asked Marcello again.

'I heard a crash coming from her room. The pictures by her bed were smashed on the floor.'

She stared at Marcello, hating him for not paying attention, knowing that he'd been watching the football with the sound turned up. She caught the tang of beer on his breath. Had poor Vovo had to smash the photos she'd always loved just to get his attention? He'd promised he'd look in on her and now, as his gaze fell away from Julia's, she knew she'd guessed the truth.

'She's trying to speak,' Fredo said.

'Don't crowd her,' Julia said, pushing him out of the way.

'Vo, Vo, I'm here now. Everything is going to be OK,' Julia said, trying to sound reassuring. But it wasn't going to be OK. Nothing was going to be OK if Vovo died on the floor in front of them.

Vovo let out an incoherent gurgle, her eyes straining to open. Julia felt the pressure on her hand as Vovo tried to squeeze it.

'Your mother . . .' she managed, then was wracked with a spasm of pain.

Fredo let out a yelp of alarm. 'Do something, Julia. Do something.'

Julia felt her heart racing with panic. At that moment she

remembered the man from earlier. *Use the key. I promise it will help with whatever you need.*

It couldn't be true, could it? Could that key he'd given her help her now? But how? What did it do? Did she have to ring that guy? Ask him for help?

Julia ran to her room and pulled out the silver key from the box. She turned it over in her hand, wondering what the hell to do with it, but then, as she pressed down on it, it came apart. She saw that one side could be fitted into a computer.

So that's what he'd meant.

She grabbed her laptop and booted it up. Then she slid the key into the USB port on her computer.

Her home screen disappeared and in its place a page appeared.

In fancy script, there was a prompt.

Hello, Julia. Please answer some security questions and then you can request anything you desire.

Julia. They knew her name. But it wasn't only that; this all seemed like something from a fairy tale. Desire didn't come into it. Not here in the favela. Not when it was a matter of life and death. This wasn't about desiring a new handbag or a pair of shoes.

She shouldn't be doing this, she thought, as she hit the return key and filled in the questions, her name and birthday, the name of her first school, the date of her first communion. Why could that be relevant? How could anyone possibly know if these answers she was giving were correct?

This felt all wrong. And sinister too. Why would someone who wanted to know all this about her help her? How did they know who she was? Couldn't it just be a scam? Some kind of identity theft? She read about that all the time in the papers.

'Julia. Julia, hurry up. What are you doing?' Marcello called.

She stared at her bedroom door and then back at the screen as a new page came up, with a new prompt.

What do you desire?

Wasn't it worth a try? She had nothing to lose. Not now. She found her hands flying over the keyboard.

Medical care for my grandmother. Fast. Heart failure. Hurry.

She pressed the enter button. Nothing happened.

She stared at the screen. Of course it wouldn't work. She'd been a fool to think it would. She threw the laptop aside and hurried up from her bed, feeling foolish. She'd wasted precious minutes when Vovo was dying. Just then her computer beeped. She went back to look at it.

Ambulance on way. Specialist cardiac team at St Saviour's Private Clinic on standby.

All of the neighbours came out on the street as the medics carefully carried Vovo down the rickety steps of the favela's alleyway to the pristine green and white private ambulance waiting on the street at the bottom. Julia hurried next to her, as the green-suited, proficient medical staff clamped the oxygen mask over Vovo's face.

'Miss Pires, you can come with your grandmother if you wish,' the nurse said, smiling at her.

Julia stared at Marcello and Fredo, seeing the concern and disbelief in their faces. But there was no time to explain. And no way of explaining how she'd conjured a private ambulance out of thin air.

'Stay here. I'll be fine. I'll call you and let you know what happens,' she told them.

'Will they save her?' Fredo asked.

Julia cupped his cheek tenderly and kissed his forehead. 'I hope so, baby.'

Julia got into the back of the ambulance beside Vovo. It was jammed with the latest technology, and as she met the gaze of the smart nurse, she felt embarrassed that they were here, aware of how shabby her street was. The nurse smiled, injecting the contents of a syringe into Vovo's arm as the ambulance driver gently shut the doors.

'This will ease the pain,' she said.

The ambulance started on the long descent down the hill, negotiating the potholes in the road. Julia watched the favela disappearing behind her through the back of the ambulance window, and as she gripped Vovo's hand, she felt as if she were entering into a different world. One where she'd left her family and everything she knew behind.

Soon they were travelling on the freeway and then into the smart suburb. The houses on either side of the wide tree-lined street got smarter, the cars in the driveways more expensive. Julia had never been to this part of the city. She held Vovo's hand and soon she felt the pressure of her fingers.

'She's trying to speak,' Julia told the nurse, who was sitting in the back on the other side of the stretcher.

The nurse gently removed the oxygen mask from Vovo's face.

Her grandmother's eyes were wide with fright.

'Julia, Julia, where are we? Where are we going?' she whispered.

'We're going to St Saviour's,' the nurse told her gently, leaning down close.

'But how? We can't afford . . .' she said, her eyes going from the nurse to Julia.

'It's OK, Vovo,' Julia said. 'Your lottery numbers came up,' she lied, squeezing the old lady's hand. 'Just like you said.'

Julia stared up and caught the nurse's eye. How much does she know? she wondered. Did this seem as outlandish to the nurse as it did to Julia? Did the ambulance regularly go to the favela to collect patients? She sincerely doubted it.

'Is it your first time at St Saviour's?' the nurse asked Julia.

'Yes,' she said, feeling a wave of embarrassment. She felt she should explain, but she couldn't. How could she tell the nurse about the key, or the man she'd met only earlier this evening, and how she'd typed in her 'desire' on the strange webpage.

'It's a wonderful hospital,' the nurse said. 'Your grandmother will be in good hands.'

But who would pay for it?

Julia stared at Vovo, gripping her hand tighter.

If she had to pay, then she'd just have to worry about that later. For now all that mattered was making sure Vovo wasn't in any more pain.

There was a small bump and the ambulance entered a wide driveway of a modern building. A set of glass front doors opened and a team of theatre nurses rushed through with a gurney and drip.

Vovo was lifted onto the trolley; a new oxygen mask was strapped to her face. A tall man with soft green eyes and a white doctor's coat chatted briefly to the nurse from the ambulance, then felt Vovo's pulse. Julia noticed his designer shoes beneath his trousers.

'Miss Pires, I'm Doctor Sanchez,' the man said, coming over to her and shaking her hand. He was disarmingly good-looking. That she'd even noticed at a time like this left her feeling ashamed and all too aware that she was still dressed for a nightclub. 'I'll do an assessment, but it's probable we'll put your grandmother into heart surgery right away,' he told her.

'Oh, thank God. Thank you,' Julia said, her eyes filling with tears. 'She's not going to die?'

'Not if I can help it.' He smiled, touching her arm. 'But she's not in great shape.'

Julia heard the warning in his voice and leaned over Vovo. 'They're going to make you better,' she said, tears dripping onto Vovo's face. She wiped them from her soft skin. Vovo didn't open her eyes, and in a moment the trolley had slid away, the doctor following it.

A nurse in a smart uniform came over and smiled. She had a pretty crucifix necklace against her tanned skin and perfect make-up. Julia wondered if that was for Doctor Sanchez's benefit. She'd never been to a hospital or clinic like this where everyone was so well groomed. Julia brushed away her tears.

'Miss Pires?' the nurse said.

'Yes?' Julia asked, confused. How did she know her name? Why was she being treated like royalty?

'Please come this way. There's a private suite upstairs where you can be comfortable. We will give your grandmother the best care possible, I promise,' she said.

She led her through another set of doors into a pristine corridor to a plush elevator with mirrored panels, then down another corridor where the nurse unlocked a door with a swipe card. Inside, the rooms looked like a hotel suite.

'We will keep you fully informed about your grandmother's

progress. If you want, you can go home. Or you can stay here. I think you'll find the facilities very comfortable. Do help yourself to the refreshments.' She smiled, giving Julia the key card.

Julia walked slowly across the clean beige carpet and sank onto the soft sofa, marvelling at her surroundings. She ran her hand over the smooth leather of the sofa and the cashmere cushions. Through the door, she could see a very comfortable-looking bed. Across the room, a modern plasma-screen TV was cased in a tasteful cabinet. Glossy magazines were stacked on a low table.

She took the silver key the man had given her out of her pocket and stared at it.

What was happening to her? What did this all mean?

She thought about the man with the dark hair she'd met, who'd given her the key. She'd been so suspicious of him – rude even – but all he'd been was friendly. He'd only wanted to help her. Like he was some sort of guardian angel.

And what if he was?

What if this wasn't all wrong and suspicious, as she'd automatically assumed? What if this key was a force for good? It had already saved Vovo's life. What else would Julia be able to do with it? Who else would it be possible to save?

She stared at the key and knew without a shadow of a doubt that it had already changed her life forever.

CHAPTER FOURTEEN

Harry relaxed back against the soft cream leather of the Daimler, looking at the lights of Trafalgar Square, as the driver guided the sleek black car through the heavy traffic towards the Strand. His head was buzzing from the day he'd just had. The helicopter ride from the city to Ascot had been exciting enough, but his day at the races had been off the scale.

Harry had been the beneficiary of several City corporate hospitality gigs in his time at the bank, but nothing had come close to Cole Menzies' extravaganza at Ascot. Not only had they had the best seats in the house, but Harry had also met legendary trainer Russell More and had topped it all off with a five-g win on Dark Secret – a bet that had impressed the hell out of Cole and his friends.

He'd been having such a great time that he'd hardly had time to consider the magnitude of how he'd fixed his open-trade problem and had had Nick Grundy fired in the process. It had barely been mentioned all day. If there had been any fallout at the bank, Cole seemed entirely unruffled by it.

Now, having dropped Cole off at his club in Pall Mall, Cole had insisted on his driver taking Harry on. He was alone for the first time all day. Glancing at the discreet chauffeur in the front,

Harry took his phone from inside his jacket. There were seven messages and twenty-eight missed calls.

'I'll get you for this. I'll get you. You'll see,' Nick's voice hissed down the line. 'You're a fucking liar, Cassidy.'

The venom in Nick's voice felt like a stab in the guts. Quickly Harry turned off the phone. Then, for good measure, he opened the back and pulled out the battery and SIM card. He would get a new phone tomorrow. He didn't want anyone from his team to have his number. Not now. Not now he could start afresh.

He looked at his reflection in the glass of the car window. Everything would be OK, he assured himself. No matter what happened with the key, or how and why he'd got it, he had Cole Menzies' protection now.

Besides, people like Nick Grundy deserved to go down. OK, so he hadn't actually done anything wrong in this instance. But that didn't mean he wasn't wrong. He was wrong in every way. The way he'd always mocked Harry. The way he'd treated women. His bragging. His arrogance. His greed.

Nick Grundy had chosen to live by the sword; well, damn it, he'd now died by it too. He'd have done exactly the same thing if their positions had been reversed. Of that Harry had no doubt.

Which is why Harry wouldn't – couldn't – afford to feel guilty. He'd beaten Nick. That was all. He'd beaten him and this was his prize: to be greater than Nick could ever have been.

And, by God, he was going to make every second count.

But even so, he wondered what Nick and the boys were doing now. And how bad the fallout had really been. He wondered whether the bank had managed to hush up what had happened or whether it would be the talk of the City. If it was, he knew Nick's network would rally round him. Did that mean there'd be a witch hunt? Would they try and track down Harry? Maybe Nick was waiting for Harry outside his apartment right now.

Or, no, on second thoughts, Nick's gang might not have rallied round, Harry thought. It was the City after all. They'd probably done as others of their kind had done for decades: turned their back on a failing friend in order to save their own skins.

To be on the safe side, Harry wouldn't go home, he decided. In fact, he could move in to the Savoy for a bit, he thought, until he was sure the whole PLG stock disaster had blown over. That way, nobody would ever guess where he was. And he'd be safe there, particularly now that Guy had been banned from coming anywhere near the building.

But there was a thought . . . He owed Guy now, didn't he? For sending him the key. For all it had brought. Should he try to make contact with him? Harry wondered. Not now, of course. Not yet. In the next week or so perhaps he'd try to find out all he could about the mysterious silver key. For now he was just going to enjoy it.

'The Savoy, please,' Harry told the driver, pressing the intercom button.

That was the place for him. And of course he'd be able to see Dulcie all the time. Plus, there was no way she'd be able to resist him, once she'd discovered his change in fortune and he'd confided in her about the key.

Yes, he thought, pleased with his decision. He didn't need to go back to his apartment at all. He could leave his old life behind altogether. The thought felt thrilling.

In the morning he'd have a lie-in; then at midday he was

going to Cole's private surgeon, Mr Fayed, who had shifted his appointments at his Harley Street clinic in order to fix Harry's nose. Then, after a few weeks off to recover, during which time Cole had offered Harry the use of his yacht in the Med, Cole had suggested that Harry come and see him to brainstorm a few options about his future at the bank.

In Sir Menzies' opinion, Harry's talents could be put to much better use than on the trading floor. He'd told Harry that now that he was a key-holder, he was a very important asset to the bank indeed. He could fulfil a more ambassadorial role. Doors would open for him. That's what Cole had said. His exact words. And he hadn't been wrong. So far Harry had felt as if he'd stepped through a door into a parallel universe, where life was easy and fun and where a click of his finger, or of his keypad, at least, could make all of his troubles disappear. And there was only one person he wanted to share it with, and if his lucky streak continued, then this would be the icing on the cake.

Dulcie was finishing her shift and putting on her coat when Harry strode into the bar.

'Good news?' she asked.

'I've had the most incredible day,' he told her, leaning over the bar. God, she was pretty, Harry thought. To think that this morning at the bank, he was worried that she might never speak to him again. But now he was here with a very real chance. A very real chance to kiss those peachy lips of hers.

'Good for you,' she said, looking at him suspiciously. 'I've had a shitty one and I'm very tired,' she said pointedly. 'So forgive me if I don't stop and chat.'

But Harry wasn't going to give up that easily. He walked with her through the bar, talking as he did about the strange package and the scandal at work. How Nick Grundy had left his trading position open overnight and had tried to make Harry take the fall for it. As he recounted the lie he'd told Cole, it felt more and more like the truth.

And he told her, too, about the key. How he'd used it to gain access to Sir Cole Menzies to help him prove his innocence. And how Sir Menzies had taken a shine to him and had asked his private physician to sort out Harry's face, before whisking him off in a private helicopter to the races.

'Wow,' Dulcie said, clearly surprised. 'That is a bit of a full-on day.' She looked more closely at him. 'Your face is so much better.'

'Do you think Guy sent me the package? Do you think he gave me the key?' Harry asked, glad she was impressed. 'I mean, it must have been him, right? It must have been an apology for beating me up. That's what the message implied, anyway.'

Dulcie shrugged into her coat and pulled a sceptical face. 'It all sounds a bit cloak and dagger, especially with that message. It doesn't make sense. Guy wouldn't give anyone anything. Certainly not you. Not even if he felt very guilty.'

She had a point. Harry realized his assumption about Guy might be very wrong.

'Well, someone has,' Harry insisted. 'Someone has decided to change my life.'

'Are you sure this isn't a wind-up?' she asked, stopping. They'd nearly reached the lobby and stopped to let some guests past. The doorman smiled at Dulcie.

'No. I swear it's the truth,' Harry said. 'This thing is life-changing,' he insisted. 'I can get anything I want.'

Dulcie smiled mischievously. 'Go on, then,' she said. 'Impress me.'

'Well, OK, how about I book the best room here? The best room they've got.'

'What, here? In the Savoy? Yeah, right. Have you any idea how much that would cost?' She fixed him with a doubtful look. 'It's concussion. I said you'd have it. You can walk me to the bus stop.'

But it was Harry's turn to smile mischievously now.

'Watch,' he said, turning to reception.

'Don't,' she said, reaching out to stop him. 'You'll just embarrass yourself. And me.'

He stopped. 'Trust me, OK?' he said, surprised at how sure of himself he felt as he walked towards reception and talked to the smart woman behind the wooden desk.

He'd prove himself to Dulcie. He'd get a suite here – just as he'd decided he would in the car earlier. He'd take Dulcie up to the top floor. To the top of the world. And very soon she'd be on top of him.

'Excuse me, what suites do you have available?' he asked the woman.

'Let me see, sir,' she said. 'I'm not sure if we have any . . .' Her fingers rattled over the keyboard.

Harry grinned at Dulcie, who rolled her eyes. Reluctantly, with the hands in the pockets of her coat, she walked towards him. She was clearly embarrassed. The receptionist glanced at Dulcie, recognizing her.

Harry put the key on the reception desk. The receptionist looked at the key, then up at Harry.

'Certainly, sir. Let me just check. I think the Ambassador Suite is available.'

'Jesus.' Dulcie shook her head.

'I told you,' Harry whispered. 'It's like magic.'

'Here we are, sir,' the receptionist said, handing over the plastic access card. 'Please help yourself to the bar, and there's a freshly stocked kitchen, although we can send up any meal from the restaurant. Will you both be staying?'

'Er . . . no,' Dulcie said, glancing sideways at Harry. 'We are *not* together.'

'Come on, Dulcie. Don't you want to know what it's like up there? Just come and see it with me,' Harry said, grabbing her hand.

Harry was still smiling as they arrived at the suite. Harry put the key card in the door and turned on the lights. Before them was a vast room with an oak four-poster bed. A sea of thick blue carpet led to a wall of windows framed with sumptuous blue drapes. Beyond them, lights twinkled over the River Thames.

'Isn't it great?' Harry said. 'Come on. Come in. Stay and have a drink.'

But Dulcie remained in the doorway, her hands in her pockets. 'No.'

'Why not?'

'Because you shouldn't be here,' Dulcie said. 'Because even if that key thing did get you in, you're still going to have to pay. Nothing's for free. You must know that. There's no such thing as a free lunch. Isn't that what you City boys always say?'

'No, it's not. Relax. Sir Menzies says the key is like a private members' club where the elite get a sort of free upgrade.'

'So, if that's the case, then why would anyone – let alone Guy – give up such privileges to you?'

Harry felt his bubble bursting, but he kept the smile on his face. Why was Dulcie trying to ruin this? Why wasn't she excited, like he'd hoped she'd be? And, worse, what if she was right? What if there really was some kind of debt accruing for all this luxury? And not just financial, but something more insidious? Something worse?

Screw it, he thought. Now wasn't the time to start worrying. Now was the time to have fun.

'Who cares why this is happening? Why don't we just enjoy it?'

'There's no "we", Harry. I'm not having any part of this,' she said. 'I meant what I said. There's no such thing as a free ride. I mean, what have you done to deserve all this? Tell me that.'

Harry felt his cheeks burning. She was right, of course. He hadn't done anything. Apart from defend her. And then lie. And cheat. To save himself.

Harry stepped towards her. 'Why *shouldn't* it be me? Dulcie, I promise you, I'm not trying to do anything evil,' he said. 'This is just a bit of luck. Anyway, you let me stay last night with you. Let me treat you. Stay and have some drinks and dinner with me.'

He was close to her now and he put his arms round her waist. But as soon as he did, he felt her flinch and knew he'd overstepped the mark.

Dulcie moved back and pressed her hand to his chest, gently but firmly keeping him at bay. 'Look, I like you, Harry. I do,' she said. 'But this feels all wrong. I'm sorry I'm . . .' She turned and walked to the door.

He couldn't believe it. She was turning him down. She was turning this down.

'Dulcie, please,' Harry said.

But it was too late. She'd already gone.

Annoyed with himself, Harry flopped down on the bed. He wished more than anything that Dulcie hadn't gone. He didn't want to be alone. He hadn't been trying to buy her, only to share his good fortune with her. Idiot that he was, he hadn't explained properly, and now it was too late.

He went to the fridge and took out a beer, then flicked on the television. All these trappings of success were making him horny. Especially when he'd thought things would have gone so differently with Dulcie.

He put on the adult channel, watching the girls on screen, draining five more beers. His head was light, but he knew there was no way he could sleep. On a whim, he called the reception.

'You wouldn't happen to have . . . I mean, you don't have a number for . . . ?' Harry rubbed his forehead. What was he doing? What was he thinking? 'It doesn't matter,' he said, putting down the phone. Of course he couldn't ask the Savoy to get him an escort. What had he been thinking?

Then he remembered his key. He got it out of his coat pocket and turned it over in his hand, remembering that earlier he'd accidentally pulled it apart. He pressed the diamond and the key came apart in his hand once again.

Booting up his laptop, he plugged in the end. He was surprised at the security procedures, answering questions about himself – his place of birth, his first school, the name of his first pet and his height. Whoever had designed the key had meant it to be only for him. But soon he was through the security and another page appeared, asking what he desired. Steeling himself, he typed two words: **A woman.**

The cursor kept on blinking.

Maybe he should be more specific, he thought.

He paused, his fingers poised over the keys. 'Fuck it,' he said aloud, typing his description. He might as well see where this would lead. And who knew, maybe the key could deliver his dream woman? Yeah, like that babe on the front of that issue of *FHM* he had at home. She was seriously hot. That half-Asian model: LaMay. She'd been in at least two of his recent fantasies, so he had no trouble describing her.

An hour later Harry was starting to feel sleepy and was just thinking about calling it a night and going to sleep when there was a knock at the door.

It couldn't be . . .

It must be the concierge, he thought, as he quickly padded over the thick carpet in his underpants, catching his reflection in the dressing-table mirror. He sucked in his abs.

He opened the heavy door a crack. Leaning against the doorpost was one of the most beautiful women he'd ever seen. She had dusky skin and piercing greenish-grey eyes, her black hair cropped short against her head. She was wearing a long green dress that accentuated her womanly curves.

It was only when her eyes met his that it hit him. It *was* LaMay. It was the model from *FHM*.

Jesus. That meant . . . that meant that his key could make even his most outlandish dreams come true. He felt faint with shock.

'Hi. You're Harry, right?' she said in her sultry voice. 'Can I come in?'

She knew his name? Well, she must do if she'd been summoned by his key. Even so, Harry was so shocked he almost fell back as she eased herself through the doorway. With long catwalk strides, she glided past him as if she was entirely familiar with the room. Her shawl fell from her shoulders and she dropped it on the chaise lounge at the foot of the bed, claiming her territory. Then she headed towards the bureau against the wall between the sumptuous long blue drapes. Harry stared at her, breathing in her heady perfume.

She turned and smiled and flicked her eyes towards the door, which he closed.

'So tell me, Harry, would you like a little something to get you in the mood? Shall we have champagne?'

Harry was finding it difficult to swallow. He felt an erection springing rock hard in his pants, making his shorts flare out. He subtly tried to adjust himself as he reached for a towel from the bed.

'I was about to take a shower,' he said.

'Maybe we can do that later.'

Later?

We?

He had a fucking supermodel in his room suggesting they shower together . . . ?

Harry saw that she'd opened the bureau to reveal another drinks cabinet and a sound system, and she took an iPod from a small slot and studied it for a few seconds, then fitted it in the dock. In a moment the room was filled with soft, ambient music – the kind Harry assumed was played in only the most chic beach resorts in Miami and Ibiza.

'You're . . . you're . . .' Harry began, his mouth dry, as she swayed her hips and opened the fridge, taking out a bottle of chilled champagne. 'You're LaMay? *The* LaMay?'

'*The* LaMay. I like that.' She laughed, shrugging her shoulder. 'Are you going to be the gentleman?'

'Sure,' Harry said, stumbling towards her to take the champagne from her hands.

She smiled wryly at him. 'You know, I feel a little over-dressed like this,' she said.

'I should . . . um . . . There's a dressing gown somewhere,' Harry said, fumbling now with the wire twine round the cork. But as soon as he said it, he felt ridiculous, especially when LaMay laughed.

'You're cute.'

Harry popped the champagne cork, froth spilling down the neck of the bottle. He grabbed the champagne glasses and clumsily filled them.

'I don't. I mean, I didn't think they'd actually send someone. You, I mean . . .' He stumbled over his words, feeling at once slightly panicked and intensely horny.

'They?' she said.

'The, um, the organization . . . the people . . . whoever. I mean, you must know who they are, right?'

'I just got a call from my agent. And the address and room number and details about you, of course. I've stayed here before. I like this room. And when he told me the amount for one night . . .' She shrugged again and smiled at him. 'I thought, Hell, why not? I was in the mood for a little company myself.' Harry couldn't believe what she was telling him. He stared at her, but she simply stared back. She was clearly unashamedly up for it. And she clearly thought he was loaded. 'So now that I'm here, why don't we just relax and have some fun together?' It wasn't so much of a question as an invitation. One Harry knew he was powerless to refuse.

She arched her eyebrows as they both took a sip of champagne. She made a few comments about the room and the bar downstairs, but Harry could barely concentrate on the small talk. He couldn't stop staring at her. He'd never had a woman as classy as LaMay telling him he was cute before. When she realized he was not responding, she put her champagne glass down and slowly smiled.

'Instead of you putting more clothes on, why don't I just take mine off?' she suggested.

Harry gulped. She turned so her back was to him and unzipped her dress. It fell in a pool by her feet and she stood naked before him except for the slightest silk thong.

Harry physically had to stop his mouth from falling open as she turned to face him. He'd thought she'd had the most incredible breasts he'd ever seen when he'd studied her photo on the front of the magazine, but up close and in the flesh, they were magnificent. And her skin . . . her skin was perfect.

'Would you like to touch me?' she asked, seeing him staring at her. 'I'd like that. You know, I really like my breasts. I call them "my girls",' she said, cupping them gently and offering them to him.

He stepped towards her and raised his hand to touch her breast. She smiled, her eyes narrowing with pleasure.

'Wow,' he mumbled.

'You like that?' she whispered. He felt her hand reach down and flick away the towel round his waist, then grab him through his boxer shorts, squeezing his length.

Could this really be happening? To him? She was here in his room, and she wanted to have sex with him?

'Hmmm. Nice,' she said appreciatively.

'Oh God,' Harry sighed, pulling away to look at her. 'Do you have any idea how amazing I think you are?'

She kissed him fully on the mouth then, groaning with pleasure. It felt incredible to be pressed up against her. Her lips parted and her tongue flicked against his and he felt his insides erupt in butterflies.

And then he was lost. In a frenzy of kissing, he felt his confidence grow as it became clear that it wasn't an act. She really wanted him.

But just as she'd sunk to the bed and had wriggled down his shorts, there was a knock at the door. His hard cock was centimetres away from her perfect, glistening lips.

She stared up at him. 'Shouldn't you get that?'

Harry couldn't bear it.

The knock came again. Growling with frustration, he rearranged himself back into his shorts and ran for the door, opening it a tiny crack.

Dulcie stood in the hallway, her hair wet from the rain.

'Dulcie!' he said, his voice too high. He could feel himself blushing. What the hell was she doing here?

'Maybe we should talk. You know . . . about this key business. About what it all means, and whether you should—'

'Who is it?' It was LaMay calling from inside the room, but from the closeness of her voice, Harry could tell that she was out of bed and on her way to the door.

'Who's that?' Dulcie asked, her face tense with shock.

'Nothing, really.' Harry panicked. How was he going to explain LaMay in his room? 'It's . . .'

Dulcie pressed her lips together. He thought he saw her eyes welling with tears. 'You have company. Oh . . .' she said, backing away. 'Well, you didn't waste any time.'

'Dulcie, I can explain. I didn't . . . I mean, it was the key. She just turned up.'

'Who turned up?' she said, her tone disgusted. 'You have a call girl in there?'

'No, not at all,' Harry said, leaning out into the corridor, round the door, but it was difficult, as he was half naked. 'It's LaMay,' he mouthed to her.

He was still so astounded by what had happened he wanted Dulcie to be impressed.

She spluttered with a sarcastic laugh, 'LaMay? The super-model LaMay?'

'Yes.' Harry's eyes were wide. 'She's here.'

'Fucking hell, Harry,' Dulcie said, her look withering as she turned on her heel. She clearly didn't believe him. 'I really think you need your head examining.'

'Seriously. Dulcie, wait—'

'Oh, Harry?' LaMay was calling him from inside. Harry glanced desperately over his houlder.

'Screw you,' Dulcie called, her voice choking, as she ran for the lift. 'Go on. Have your fucking call girl. I thought you were different, but you know you're just the same as all those others.'

CHAPTER FIFTEEN

It was late afternoon when Kamiko finished her shopping spree and went back to Tiko's cafe. Her appointment at the bank couldn't have gone better. Mr Narimoko had been so sweet and accommodating. Kamiko had asked for several credit cards and, her confidence buoyed, for a cash advance of ten million yen. Even saying the words had given her a thrill. She'd been sure that the bank manager would laugh, but he'd simply nodded and smiled and asked her to wait.

Kamiko had never imagined seeing that much money in her life, but five minutes later he'd brought out a large envelope containing bundles of 10,000-yen notes. He'd handed it over asking no questions, but wishing her a pleasant day. Then, on her way out, a cashier had passed her a wallet with three silver credit cards in it. There had been no mention of how she'd pay off the cards, or pay back the cash.

Terrified and thrilled in equal measure by her success, Kamiko had gone straight to the train station and bought two small holdalls. Then she'd paid for two long-term luggage lockers, dividing the cash between each locker. She had no idea when, but she was pretty sure that having a stash of cash would come in useful.

Then she'd taken her credit cards and hit the shops. She'd never imagined anyone paying her any attention in designer boutiques, but the assistants seemed to fall over themselves to help her. Shikego's suit had helped, of course. That and pretending that she knew exactly what she was doing.

She'd been positively fawned over in Hanshin, the exclusive department store, where she'd bought the sexiest black under-wear she'd ever imagined owning. Then, her confidence growing, she'd gone to the Lolita shop in Umeda – a shop where she'd never even dreamed that she'd be able to afford anything – and kitted herself out with a completely new outfit. It was a kind of red tartan punk dress with ripped tights and the coolest boots. She'd also bought Tiko a pair of purple snakeskin jeans.

Best of all, she'd bought herself a camera. A state-of-the-art professional Nikon. The kind of sleek black beast she'd always longed for. She couldn't wait to take pictures of her new life with it.

But now, as she approached Tiko's cafe, she knew that the biggest challenge of her day lay ahead. She had no idea how Tiko would feel about what had happened earlier – although it had consumed most of her thoughts. Would he ignore her? Pretend it hadn't happened? What if he thought she was really uncool?

As soon as she pushed open the door, though, all her doubt vanished as Tiko grinned at her.

'Hey, gorgeous,' he said, kissing her across the counter of the cafe and making her blush. *Gorgeous*. Nobody had ever called her that before.

She told him quickly about her day – omitting the part about the note she'd found about the diamonds and playing down her meeting at the bank. She didn't tell him about the cash – only that she'd got a credit card and had been shopping. She searched his face for signs of surprise, but he didn't seem to be giving her his full attention, his eyes straying to her lips.

'Have I got something . . . ?' she began hesitantly, self-consciously putting her fingertips to her lips.

'No.' He smiled. 'You're just . . . very kissable,' he said, leaning over to kiss her lingeringly again. She giggled, both embarrassed and delighted at his attention.

She reached down into her pile of bags and gave him the trousers she'd bought and felt a warm wave of pleasure pass through her as he laughed with delight.

'I love them. Thank you,' he said, kissing her again.

It made her feel good. She'd never bought anyone a gift before.

'I really want to change out of this hideous thing,' she said, lifting the stiff jacket of Shikego's suit.

She'd had plenty of opportunity to change in the shops, but somehow wearing this suit of Shikego's had felt like a sublime act of revenge. For every second she'd worn it and every yen she'd spent, she'd known just how infuriated her stepmother would have been if she could see her. How horrified she'd have been that Kamiko had defiled her most precious memory.

Kamiko had never felt this empowered. Or this free.

Tiko stepped behind her, putting his hands under her jacket. 'I rather like it. It makes you look like a sexy older woman.'

Kamiko laughed, turning round in his arms, and he kissed again, his tongue probing her mouth. She flicked her eyes towards the customers, but Tiko shrugged. He led her to the back room and quietly shut the door, pulling down the blind over the glass window. He steered her towards the bunk, hitching up her skirt as they kissed more passionately.

She liked the way he tasted – of Diet Coke and cigarettes

– and the way he smelt too. As he enveloped her in his arms, she smelt the sharp, sexy tang of his body odour and saw the black tattoo inscription in the soft flesh under his arm.

She'd never had this effect on men, ever, and she couldn't help but delight in the sensation. Was it really just the clothes? Or the intimacy they'd shared discussing the key? Or was it the key itself and the knowledge of what it could get that was now making him press his hard cock against her so passionately?

'I want you,' he breathed. And that's when she realized that this was what she'd wanted to hear most of all. That it wasn't just the clothes, or the key, but herself – Kamiko – who was turning him on.

And it was right then at that moment that she made the decision. She was done with being a victim. She would not let her stepmother into her head. Not ever again. What she did – Shikego – that was gone. Locked away. Over. The frightened little girl that Kamiko had been? She'd gone too.

From now on Kamiko was going to be her own person. Her own sexual person. Starting right now. With no flashbacks. No memories. She would wipe her hard drive clean and replace it with only happy memories.

Still kissing her, Tiko moved, then broke away momentarily. He pressed a button on his speaker and the loud rock music ratcheted up. She laughed, deafened, her senses overwhelmed as she ripped off his T-shirt.

Despite her vow of caution, Kamiko couldn't help giving in to the feeling of being wanted, and the heady sensation that she knew what she was doing.

She grabbed his jeans, fumbling with the button, setting him free. He pressed her hand round him. Feeling a wantonness she'd never felt, she slid back on the bunk, fully hitching up her skirt.

He pulled aside her thong and lifted up her legs so that they were wrapped round his waist. She thought she ought to stop and think about birth control, but it was already too late. Tiko gasped as he entered her and she stared at his face as he thrust inside her, amazed that her body could be giving his so much pleasure.

He moved quickly inside her and she felt herself gasping and sweating. For a moment she thought he might come, but he seemed to remember himself and slow down, kissing her again.

'Let me taste you,' he whispered. Then he knelt before her, burying his face up her skirt, his tongue finding her and lapping at her. He pressed her to him, sucking her hard, his tongue probing her. She felt his fingers enter her and her breath became ragged as the sensation became more intense. Her thighs quivered as they pressed round his head. And then it happened. Like a cascade, she felt herself come.

She felt dizzy and weak, her whole body flooding with endorphins. She'd never experienced anything like it.

'Take off your shirt,' he said, pulling open the buttons of Shikego's silk blouse. He ran his hand over her tiny breasts, gasping and leaning forward to suck her nipples hard. Then he stood above her and, massaging himself, came over her chest, his eyes fluttering with his orgasm.

'Fuck, you turn me on,' he gasped. Then he smiled and kissed her and she gasped with shock.

Afterwards she couldn't stop smiling at Tiko as she unwrapped the tissue packages she'd bought, showing him her new clothes.

'I was busy while you were gone,' he told her, as she got changed. 'Researching your key.'

'Did you find out anything?' she asked him.

'There,' he said, pointing to a neat pile of printed A4 sheets. 'That's what there is. There's nothing else online about a key. I can't see any kind of new reality game involving a key. It's a bit of a mystery to me.'

A customer tried the door, but Tiko shouted out for him to wait. He slipped out of the door, and alone in the back room, Kamiko read the information he'd gathered.

The information was about BGZ, a marketing organization based in Zurich who administered the key scheme. The picture of their keys looked exactly like the one Kamiko had been given. She read on. The key scheme had been set up as an elite corporate gifting scheme for top businessmen. An upgrade gimmick for the very rich and very powerful. Ironic, really, Kamiko thought. Perks for just the kind of people who didn't need an upgrade. But free credit cards like the ones she'd been given today? Free money? There was no mention of that kind of perk at all. Plus, the design of her key, the one she had in her possession, seemed to be different to the one described on these pages. None of them incorporated a USB, or a diamond.

So what did that mean? Did her key come from a different corporation? Or just another department of this key organization? A secret department that was more exclusive and elitist and not to be shared on the corporate website?

So many questions. All without answers. And the biggest question of all was this: why on earth had one been sent to *her*?

As Kamiko scanned the papers, she was even more determined to find out the truth. The head offices were in Switzerland, and the organization was run by a woman called Martha Faust. Kamiko folded up the papers and put them in her bag, deciding that Martha Faust was most definitely on her to-do list.

'So what do you want to do now?' Tiko asked when he

returned. 'I've closed the shop, which is a first on a weekend. You are having a wicked effect on me.'

'I thought we could go to Tokyo,' she said, hardly daring to hope that he'd come with her. If he didn't agree to come, she'd go alone, but Tiko grinned.

'Sure,' he said.

'I've always wanted to go to Tokyo Dome City.'

'Then what are we waiting for?' he said, already punching numbers into his till to cash up. 'Oh, did you know Black Pearl are playing at the Dome tonight?'

'Wow. Black Pearl. I love their stuff,' Kamiko said, lacing up her new boots.

'Why don't we see if we can get tickets with your key thing?'

Kamiko smiled to herself and logged in to her key page.

'Ask for three tickets,' Tiko told her.

'Three?'

'Susi will kill me if I go to see Black Pearl without her. They're her favourite band.'

Kamiko's smile dropped. Didn't he want to go with just her?

'Who is Susi?' she asked, trying not to sound as jealous as she felt.

'She's just a friend. Like you are.'

'You sleep with her?'

'Sometimes, when we're both lonely. She likes girls too.' He smiled, putting his forehead on hers. 'Oh, don't look like that, my sweet Kamiko,' he said. 'You're my girl now. But you'll like Susi. Believe me, it'll be loads of fun. Be cool, baby.'

But as soon as Kamiko met Susi in the sleek black lobby of the five-star Tokyo hotel that evening, she didn't feel cool. She felt instantly intimidated. Susi was the kind of girl who'd always bullied or ignored people like Kamiko. She had peroxide-white hair and big brown eyes and perfect skin and was at least twenty-five. She was wearing a mesh top that showed her black bra, and Kamiko could tell immediately that she and Tiko had some kind of bond between them. It had been so much fun hanging out with Tiko all day, but now, seeing him with Susi, she felt childish and silly. She felt jealous and upset too. She'd had sex with Tiko earlier, but she wasn't sure how much it meant to him. He and Susi were lovers too. He'd told her as much. Had he told Susi about *her*?

Could she really bear to share him with someone like Susi? Because she couldn't work out exactly what their relationship was, or where she stood in it all. On the way into the limousine that had arrived to transport them to the concert, Kamiko had grabbed Tiko's hand, wondering whether Susi would be jealous, but she didn't so much as glance their way.

Inside the Dome, it was loud, the support band having already started their set. The bouncer led the way up to their VIP seats and Kamiko watched Susi confidently climbing the metal stairs two by two in her stilettos, her bum peachy in her soft grey leather trousers. She was acting like she owned the place, like she'd seen and done all this before, so Kamiko didn't say anything as they were led to their private box, even though she wanted to jump up and down with excitement.

Be cool, baby. She reminded herself of what Tiko had said. Well, if that's what it took to win him from Susi, then that's what she'd be.

Kamiko could see the security guys eyeing up Susi and Kamiko wondered how it was possible to get the kind of aura that Susi had. But even without an aura, it was nice to be treated for once like she was somebody, Kamiko thought. She really liked this feeling of people being deferential to her. Hell, the feeling of stuff – *real* stuff – happening. For the first time in her life she was actually living. First the shopping trip, then the hotel in Tokyo, the limo and now this.

It was way beyond her wildest fantasies. It felt unreal – like she was in a virtual-reality scenario and this was all a game.

Be cool, she told herself again. She had to keep her wits about her.

'You want it to be really mind-blowing?' Susi asked, as the music started. 'Why don't you take one of these?' she said, her eyes flicking down to a pill in the palm of her hand.

Kamiko felt crazily out of her depth and so inexperienced, but she was determined not to show it. Was this another test?

'What are they?' she yelled above the music.

'You'll like it,' Susi shouted back, smiling.

Tiko winked at her and nodded.

Trying not to show how nervous she felt, Kamiko swigged back the pill with some beer. This was all a confidence trick. She was sure of that. She had to pretend she knew what she was doing and show no weakness. No matter what happened, she was still in control.

She felt Susi next to her. Then she leaned across and kissed her cheek. Kamiko smelt her warm, musky perfume.

'You are a good girl. I like you,' she said.

When she felt a hand caressing the small of her back, Kamiko didn't know whether it was Susi's or Tiko's, but she didn't care.

Half an hour later Kamiko felt like she was flying – soaring high above the stadium – and yet at the same time the music throbbed through her. Kamiko screamed harder than she'd ever screamed as Black Pearl came on stage.

Kamiko grinned across at Tiko, who mouthed, 'Awesome,' at her. Then he leaned over and kissed her fully on the mouth and Kamiko knew that everything was cool, just as he'd promised. She felt Susi watching them and felt a pull deep in her crotch. This had to be the most exciting night of her life.

Later, much later, Kamiko was still high and excited as they all stumbled through the door to her hotel room.

'Do you want to see my tattoos now?' Susi asked. They'd been discussing them in the limo. She smiled, her heavily made-up eyelids drooping. 'They're not as good as yours, but you might like them.'

She slid the thin mesh top over her head. She lay down on the bed as Kamiko took pictures of her back with her new camera, zooming in on Susi's perfect skin and the leopard on her shoulder.

Then she patted the bed and Kamiko lay down next to her. Susi smiled, stroking her arm.

'I like you taking pictures,' she whispered. 'It's sexy. You're sexy. Did you know that?'

Kamiko giggled shyly.

'Don't dismiss it,' Susi said. 'Tiko told me you were hot, but I didn't believe him, but, baby, you are . . .'

Kamiko felt terrified and exhilarated all at once. What was going to happen? She'd never been this close to a girl before like this. Especially one as hot as Susi. She looked at her nipples through the gauze of her bra. She fancied Tiko, of course she did, but she found Susi intoxicating in a way she'd never thought possible.

'You ever tried MDMA powder?' she asked.

Kamiko hardly knew what it was, but didn't want to admit

it. She shook her head. Susi's finger continued to stroke her arm.

They both giggled as Tiko came and stood at the end of the bed.

'What are you two up to?' he asked.

'You know, I'd like to watch Tiko fucking you,' Susi whispered to Kamiko. 'I think that would be really horny. Would you like me to watch you together?'

She thought about how exhilarated she'd felt when Susi had watched Tiko kissing her at the concert. How much more exciting would it feel to have her watching them having sex in this private hotel room?

Kamiko noticed a look passing between Susi and Tiko. Had they planned this? she wondered.

'I'm up for anything,' she said.

'So.' Susi grinned. 'You know what I gave you earlier?'

Kamiko nodded.

'Did you like it? Shall I give you some more?'

She put her finger on Kamiko's lips, pressing down on her bottom lip. As Kamiko stared at her lips, it was all she could do to stop herself grabbing Susi and kissing her. She couldn't imagine how it would actually be to make out properly with a girl. In front of Tiko. She longed to hold Susi and press against her, to know what it would feel like to take one of her soft pink nipples in her mouth.

Susi laughed, looking at Kamiko and obviously seeing the hunger in her eyes. 'Only a day and look how we've corrupted you. You're not so innocent now, are you?' Again she looked at Tiko and he nodded.

'So this stuff will blow your mind, but it tastes horrible,' Tiko said. 'I'll put some in your drink. Here.'

Tiko handed her the glass.

'Drink up,' Susi whispered.

They chatted for a while and Tiko put some slow, sexy music on; then Susi lay back on the bed and leaned in close to Kamiko. 'I want to kiss you so much,' she said.

Kamiko bit her lip. She wasn't sure what was going on. She closed her eyes and leaned forward to kiss Susi, but their lips didn't meet. After a moment she opened her eyes. Susi's eyes were narrowed, watching her intently. Then, seemingly satisfied, she moved away, grabbing her top.

'Where are you going?' Kamiko asked. Her brain was fuzzy. She didn't want this to stop, but they were moving away from her now. She couldn't concentrate, couldn't formulate her words to make them stay.

'Will she be OK?' she heard Susi say.

'Of course she will,' Tiko said. He was standing at the foot of the bed, watching her, as Susi pulled on her top and boots.

Kamiko made an incoherent noise, trying desperately to grasp her words, but it felt as if she was in quicksand.

'Oh, little Kamiko,' Susi said. Gone were her soft smiles. 'That wasn't ecstasy we gave you,' she said. 'It was Rohypnol.'

Kamiko felt fear rip through her. She tried to get up, but her limbs felt like glue.

'Shh, shh,' Susi said, pushing her back on the bed. 'The best thing about all of this is that in the morning you won't remember a thing,' she told Kamiko. Then she turned to Tiko. 'You got the key?'

'Of course I have,' Tiko said. 'The key to everything,' he joked, throwing Kamiko's silver key up in the air and catching it in his hand. He gripped it tightly. 'Come on, let's go.'

A moment later the hotel door slammed.

CHAPTER SIXTEEN

Sylvie Lachard, Christian's boss at Afri-Aid, stared at Christian over her desk in the headquarters in the NGO compound in Gigiri, Nairobi, and rubbed her forehead. He noticed that she hadn't aged well in the last five years. The stress of her job had clearly taken its toll. She was tall with fine black skin, but there were deep creases in her forehead and grey hair at her temples.

Christian shifted in his seat, recrossing his legs. He felt uncomfortable in his smart trousers and leather deck shoes. He suspected that she knew that he was lying about what had happened at the colonel's compound and how Christian had managed to get the prisoners to safety. He felt as if his guilt was written all over his face. He hadn't dared tell Sylvie about the key. He couldn't forget Colonel Adid's threat, or what he'd promised in return for the liberation of the prisoners. Or the fact that he'd told Christian he had people in Afri-Aid who were beholden to him. No, Christian had to keep quiet, keep his promise and pray that Sylvie bought his story.

But it wasn't looking good. Christian had assumed his coup would have been grounds for celebration, but the team leader back at the base camp hadn't been pleased with the sudden influx of refugees and had started asking lots of questions.

The prisoners hadn't been happy either. They'd wanted revenge for the slaughter of their fellow villagers. Christian had tried to explain to them the terms of their release and had tried to make them appreciate that he'd got them and the surviving members of their families to safety, but after their initial euphoria at being reunited with their loved ones, the men had keenly felt their loss of pride at having been ousted from their village.

His conscience had taken a further battering when he'd filled in the report in the camp office, knowing it would be shown to Dan's family. In smudged pen, he'd written a letter spelling out the young doctor's bravery, concluding that he knew the risks before he'd died. That it had been Dan's plan to run from the compound, rather than to get captured.

But it was a lie: Dan hadn't known the risks, couldn't have known them. He'd only been guessing and acting on gut instinct. The truth was that they should never have been anywhere near the colonel's region at all. It was Christian who'd gone in there, regardless of the risks. Which made him responsible for Dan and Olu's deaths, and no one else.

This version of the truth formed part of the same report that Sylvie had in front of her on her desk and was reading, a disbelieving look on her face. She made occasional exclamatory noises and Christian felt guilt churning inside him. He mustn't panic, he told himself, but it was hard not to. For the first time in his life he wanted nothing more than to run away.

Last night he'd stayed up in his hotel room and had booted up the new laptop he'd bought in Nairobi. He knew he had to try and get another key. No matter what. After what the colonel had told him, he'd been feeling constantly paranoid. This had been the first chance he'd had to log on.

He'd been surprised at all the personal security questions

the key had asked him. Not only the name of his first school, but the colour of his first boat.

How could the key know he'd even owned a boat? Let alone what colour? How would they know it was orange?

Eventually a page had come up.

Hello, Christian. What do you desire?

He'd stared for a moment at the fancy font. He had no choice: he had to go for it. He started typing.

I need another key.

Not possible.

The two words had appeared within a second.

You don't understand. I need another key for someone else. Someone who is threatening me. Someone who will kill innocent children if I do not get him one.

There was a pause.

This is not possible. The key cannot do this.

Christian had growled with frustration. Of course the key could do it. Shouldn't it do anything Christian desired? Wasn't that the point? Well, he desired this, for Christ's sake.

He'd tried again.

I am in danger. You must help me. You must get me another key.

There was a shorter pause before the next reply.

This is not possible. The key cannot do this.

Did this mean that he was talking to a computer? Why the same answer?

But whatever he did – and he'd tried several more times – the key simply refused his request.

Who are you? Christian had typed.

The key cannot tell you this.

Christian had puzzled over it all night. Who the hell was

behind the key? Why wouldn't they help? And more importantly, what the hell was he going to do if he couldn't get another key for the colonel?

He should have insisted on giving the colonel his own key, insisted that he take it, but the colonel had been almost deferential towards Christian's key. He'd wanted his own. And now Christian was trapped, with no way out of this mess.

He shifted again in his seat now, as Sylvie sighed, finishing the report.

Above the pristine water cooler was a picture of a starving African child with flies crawling around his nose – the emotive international image of the aid charity. Next to it were framed certificates from various organizations around the world, commending Afri-Aid. He thought back to the colonel's supply rooms. He hadn't told Sylvie about that. He doubted she'd be able to bear it.

Sylvie's tired eyes bored into Christian's. 'And that's your story, is it?' she asked, flipping her pink nails against the report.

'It's the truth,' Christian lied.

'You got Colonel Adid to agree to release the prisoners? That's what you expect me to believe?'

'He was a reasonable man,' Christian said. 'In this case.'

He knew she knew he was lying. He could see it in her eyes.

'Is there something wrong, Sylvie?' Christian asked, trying to bluff it out, but Sylvie's tired eyes met his and he knew it hadn't worked.

'Well, you and I know the answer to that one. Yes. There is something very wrong. The bottom line is, you went against every directive, every rule of Afri-Aid. You should not have been anywhere near that zone and now you have compromised our whole charter here. No matter how much good you've done, I cannot afford to have a loose cannon in the ranks.'

'What are you saying, Sylvie?' Christian asked, scared by her tone.

'I think we have no choice but to let you go,' she said quietly.

'So I'm losing my job because I helped?' Christian was appalled.

'No, you're losing your job because you ignored the rules and you negotiated with that megalomaniac,' Sylvie said, not hiding the bitterness in her voice. 'I'm sorry, but that's the way it has to be, Christian. Our whole organization cannot work effectively if we have mavericks like you in the field.'

'Sylvie,' Christian appealed, 'do something. You need doctors like me. This is crazy.'

'I'm sorry, Doctor Erickson,' she enunciated, using Christian's surname for the first time in years, 'but I can't help you. I think it's time that you took a break anyway. You've been on the front line for too long.'

Christian left the office feeling dazed. He could hardly believe what had just happened. But as he went back to the Intercontinental Hotel to check out, the reality of his encounter in Sylvie's office sank in. He was no longer an Afri-Aid doctor. He was out of the job that had defined him for every minute of every day for the last six years.

Perhaps Christian deserved to get fired. The guilt in him told him that after what had happened to Dan, he'd had it coming. And yet his pride smarted. To think of the risks he'd taken for Afri-Aid and he'd been chucked out on his ear. Time after time he'd gone into the rebels' territory and helped the people who needed it most and now they threw the book at him. He was still muttering to himself as the woman behind the counter handed him his credit card.

'I hope you had a pleasant stay, sir,' she said.

'Yes, I did, thank you,' he said with a smile, amazed at his sudden ability to lie so easily. He hated hotels like this at the best of times and was glad to see the back of it.

Last night there'd been a conference and the delegates had got drunk in the bar and he hadn't been able to stand watching their posturing when their fellow countrymen were being beaten and tortured. There seemed to be nobody who cared about justice in this place. Not any more.

Downstairs, he loaded his rucksack into the boot of the waiting cab.

'Where are you going to?' the cab driver asked. He had a colourful jacket on and a big smile. His jolly manner only made Christian feel more weary.

'I don't know. I guess I want to go home,' he said.

'Where's home?'

'Norway.'

'The airport, then?'

Christian sat in the back, looking out of the window at the busy city streets, feeling rattled. He didn't want to go to Norway, but then, he had to find out how Kenneth had got hold of that key and why he'd sent it to Christian. He thought about his brother and his father and how he would explain his sudden unemployment. They had both warned him about how emotionally damaging his career in aid work could be. He hated to go back there now and prove them right. Not when he was burnt out, just as his father said he would be.

'You look tired,' the cabbie told him, and Christian smiled to himself.

'I have been working for a long time.'

'Then you should have a holiday. Are you going on holiday to Norway? Won't it be cold?'

'Yeah, I guess so.'

'If I was going on holiday, I would go to a beach instead. Somewhere hot and exotic.'

Christian smiled at the friendly face in the rear-view mirror. The football boots dangling from the mirror danced jauntily.

He felt hemmed in, closed in by the city. He couldn't shake the sense of claustrophobia. But it was more than that. It was an inbuilt disgust. He'd been to the far stretches of civilization, to where the tribes that lived there existed on next to nothing. And yet, despite all their hardship and lack of material possessions, they laughed and loved harder than anyone he'd ever met in a city. He'd found their rich spirituality humbling. And now that he had been banished from Africa, he knew that it was this, more than anything that he'd miss. He couldn't shake the feeling that he'd been cast out when he didn't deserve it. When he had so much more to do.

'Where would you go if you could go anywhere?' he asked the driver.

'Me?' The driver grinned in the mirror, clearly delighted with the question. Christian saw from his ID on the dashboard that his name was Jomo. 'South America, for sure. I would go and see my team play at the Olympics in Rio. Wouldn't that be something?'

'I was on my way to South America when I came to Africa,' Christian said.

He stared out of the window as Jomo started talking animatedly about his team, thinking of the young man he'd been six years ago. How he'd carried the guide to South America in his backpack. How he'd fantasized about climbing mountains in Chile. How he'd wanted to dip his toes in the sea on Copacabana Beach and go and see the view from the Cristo Redentor, the Christ statue overlooking Rio. He remembered now how it was the only one of the Seven Wonders of the Modern World his mother had never made it to. He remembered telling her before she died that he'd go there for her. One day.

All those dreams he'd had back then, he thought sadly. That certainty that he would walk all over the globe. That he would travel and learn and expand his horizons, with no fear of what the future might hold, just like his mother had when she'd been young. She'd been a pioneering aid worker who had never lost her love for travel. It had always been something Christian had taken for granted about her, but now he thought about how brave she'd been to travel alone all round Europe and Asia, as well as parts of South America. He always assumed that he'd inherited her inbuilt assumption that people would be kind and honest and treat him – and each other – decently, but he no longer felt like that. He'd seen too much brutality to ever feel truly safe again.

Where had that confident young man he'd once been gone? he wondered. Because the idea of getting on a plane, with no plan and no direction, seemed terrifying. He saw now that Jomo's indicator was blinking. As the signs for the freeway leading to the airport came into view, the car sped up.

Once Jomo took him to the airport, should he really go to Norway? A new thought occurred to him. If the colonel had eyes and ears everywhere, then maybe it would be better to disappear for a while. Lie low until the colonel forgot Christian and his threat to kill a hundred children if Christian didn't procure him a key.

Because that wasn't going to happen. Not anytime soon. That wretched key had made that clear last night.

So where would he go? If the world was his? If he could go anywhere? He wondered now, as he looked out of the window, if it was possible to reclaim the enthusiastic young man he'd once been and go and explore Chile and Brazil. Perhaps, if he stood looking over the city of Rio, looking at the view his mother had always wanted to see, then he might start to feel brave again.

Jomo slowed down as they approached departures and stopped in the only vacant space. There was commotion everywhere, with large families travelling with stacks of suitcases and taped-up cardboard boxes, but rather than feeling daunted, Christian felt excited to be leaving.

He paid Jomo and got out of the cab to collect his rucksack.

'Hey, man, where are you going to go?' Jomo asked, handing over the rucksack.

'To do what I should have done a long time ago,' Christian said.

October 1998

In the cell, the night reading lights were on for a minute more. Across the hallway, Mack could hear the banter of inmates in other cells – the usual catcalls before lights-out. But in here, there was a tense silence. Mack's hands were sweating. He pulled at the sleeve of his orange boiler suit, trying to relax his neck muscles. He hadn't been this nervous since the night of the robbery all those years ago, but he knew he must hold it together. Tobias was relying on him.

He glanced over at his cellmate and friend, who was sitting on the bed opposite, reading a book. Behind him, the mocked-up dummy of Tobias's body was immobile under the sheets.

Tobias looked calm and Mack could see his eyes scanning the sentences, but he knew his friend well enough to know that his casual stance was a mere illusion. His mind was whirring too. Mack could almost hear it.

It had taken ages for him to trust Tobias, but spending twenty-four hours a day with someone was a good way to get to know them. Tobias was easy-going and easy to like, and despite wanting to keep himself to himself, Mack couldn't help being drawn to him from the first time they'd met.

His life fascinated Mack. In fact, Mack often joked that he no longer needed novels, now he had Tobias to listen to. As far as he could make out, Tobias Asquith had been a kind of global playboy, flitting around the world and fraternizing with a whole host of wealthy eccentrics in the art world, who never suspected once that the art forger they all most feared was right among them. His stories were full of descriptions of fancy yachts and gorgeous women, sumptuous food and always a reference to a splendid wine.

Mack didn't judge Tobias for his criminal actions – partly because he was paying for them by this stint in jail, but also because Tobias had a staunch morality to selecting the people he ripped off. He'd only ever targeted those who'd hoarded precious art for money's sake. Those were the kind of people he despised. The kind of people who cared only for wealth.

In return, bit by bit, Mack had told Tobias his own story. Tobias had listened intently, asking intelligent questions, until he knew all the details about Voss. His sense of moral outrage about how Mack had been wronged had been such a relief. It had been like a balm to an open wound. Every doubt Mack had ever had, everything that had troubled him, had been absolved by Tobias's faith in him as a wronged man. It had made Tobias more determined than ever that they should escape jail and right those wrongs.

The only thing Mack held back was the secret of the diamonds. That was until a year ago, when Tobias had shared the details of his biggest job – the theft of a Titian from a Japanese electronics tycoon – and Mack had suddenly changed his mind about telling Tobias everything. Because behind the small painting, Tobias had found a 'criminally easy' safe fully loaded with a stash of diamonds. He'd 'liquidated' them in Tokyo, through a backstreet diamond dealer who had owed Tobias a favour.

And that's when Mack had told Tobias about the diamonds that he'd buried in France. It had felt so good to share his last secret. He told him he'd puzzled for years about whether anyone from forensics had managed to retrace his movements the night of the robbery, but nobody had ever known the full story. Nobody had known that Hackett had shot him before making off with all the gold.

Again and again he told Tobias the story of how he'd dragged himself, bleeding, up to the top of the bank to bury the bag of diamonds. And then how he'd crawled further before falling down the steep bank the other side into a storm drain. As the weather had broken and the clouds had disgorged furious rainfall, he'd waited, lying in the concrete trough, delirious with pain and despair.

When he'd finally been discovered by a farmer, the rainwater had carried him five miles away from where he'd hidden the diamonds. The farmer had called the police, who had been all too keen to take him into custody. The train robbery had hit the headlines by then. Mack had claimed his innocence, but the train guard had recovered enough from his gunshot wounds to identify Mack straight away.

With each retelling Tobias had become more convinced that the diamonds must still be there. Where Mack had buried them.

And that's when the plan for their escape had really taken shape. They would escape prison and go to the Scottish Borders to Lady Hillary Markham's stately home. Tobias claimed that she had a soft spot for him, and that he'd promised to find the

Constable that had gone missing from her estate. He was absolutely certain that the dotty old lady would provide the perfect refuge for them.

Then, after lying low, they would go to France and find Mack's diamonds.

And then Mack could get his family back. The way Tobias had said it made it all sound so simple.

A whistle blew. The lights went out, plunging the cell into momentary darkness, before the thin gloom of the corridor lights cast shadows in the cell. Mack and Tobias didn't move.

Any moment now the faulty fire alarm Mack had rigged up over the past week when he'd been on kitchen duty would go off in the catering block. Officers would be diverted there to check it out, but would find nothing. But those precious moments were all they needed.

Mack sensed Tobias looking towards him.

Three, two, one . . .

Another agonizing second, then . . .

A fire alarm went off in the distance. Noise erupted into the night. Every cellmate was up, shouting, clanging their bars. Security lights flickered along the dark corridors. A guard shouted for everyone to pipe down.

Tobias gave a quick nod. Mack was up in a second.

Together, they moved his bed, heavy with his own dummy body, to expose the hole below it. It had taken Tobias months to get the architectural plans for the jail, but this vital knowledge had given Mack the belief that their plan might work. It had taken the last six months to assemble all the elements, but now the moment had come.

Two minutes later the two of them had moved the bed back over the hole and had shimmied under the floor and into the vertical ventilation shaft that ran down the outside of the building. It was hot and cramped, and despite the practice run, Mack felt his heart pounding. They'd removed the security grilles and rigged up ropes, so their descent was fast.

They kept moving and soon they were level with the ground, the shaft twisting back into the building. They burst through the ventilation hatch and into the empty corridor, the guards having gone to investigate the alarm, as they'd hoped they would.

They ran quickly, dodging through the corridor and then up through the next shaft. This one was thinner and more difficult, but it was only a few metres long.

A minute later they broke up through the hatch into the aisle of the chapel. It was eerily quiet, the pews empty. Moonlight shone in coloured shafts through the stained-glass window. Mack was first through, pulling up Tobias. They replaced the grille quickly, running up the aisle and behind the altar to the wooden door. It was locked, as they knew it would be. Mack knelt in front of it, unwrapping the toolkit from his pocket.

'Hurry,' Tobias whispered. 'They'll be checking the cells soon.'

The whole prison would be in lockdown mode until the all-clear was given. Mack just hoped that when the guards checked their beds from the door of their cell, they'd see what they thought were Tobias and Mack sleeping soundly. It wouldn't be until 7.30 a.m. that they discovered the dummies. By which time Mack and Tobias would be well on the road.

The room beyond the door was dark, but they moved quickly through it and Mack felt a stab of guilt at the huge deception he was about to pull off. He'd been in here often lately, having struck up a friendship with Teis, the prison chaplain. He hoped that when Teis discovered what they'd done, he wouldn't think that Mack had used him. Even though it would seem that he had.

Because over the course of their intellectual debates and heated chess games, Mack had subtly prised information from the unsuspecting chaplain. Until Teis had felt so comfortable in his company that Mack had found out exactly when the two junkie prisoners in D Block had died and, more importantly, the protocol for their bodies leaving the prison.

The brief prison funeral had been today at 9 a.m and now, late at night and after hours, the undertakers would load the bodies into the van and drive them away to the crematorium.

Sure enough, in the cool room beyond the chaplain's private room, Tobias and Mack found the two black body bags in exactly the same place as they'd been earlier today. They looked at each other and smiled. The last, most crucial part of the plan had fallen into place.

They unzipped the body bags, revealing the emaciated corpses of the two tragedy-bound inmates. It took two minutes to remove the bodies, putting them back in the coffins where they were stacked by the door. Every prisoner who died used the same coffins and Mack could see up close how scuffed they were. After another frantic minute of heaving, the corpses were hidden in the closed coffins, which were restacked against the wall.

'I'm not sure I can do it,' Tobias said, curling his nose up at the smell of the body bag, despite the fact that this had been his plan. That he'd thought this bit would be the easiest.

Mack shook his head in amused exasperation. Tobias was such a snob.

'Get in,' Mack commanded, watching Tobias crawl onto the slab and into the body bag. He did up the zip, patting his friend.

'Lie still,' he whispered. 'I'll see you on the other side.'

Then he crawled into his own body bag, but the zip was difficult to close from the inside and at the top it got jammed, which left the last inch open.

He waited in the darkness and the cold, his heart pounding. Mack felt his nose itching and prayed he didn't sneeze. He was so close. So very close to freedom. The plan had worked so far, but he knew from bitter experience that things could still go wrong, even when you thought you'd got away with it. But the thought . . . the thought he might be out of prison and free to go and find his family . . . it felt like he could almost hear an orchestra of angels playing in the distance.

He forced himself to focus and not count his chickens. He wasn't free yet. Footsteps approached and Mack tensed.

It was Teis. Mack pictured the chaplain he knew so well. His blond hair and easy laugh. Sure enough, he smelt a whiff of pipe-smoke and heard more footsteps. Then a buzz from the phone on the wall. Mack heard Teis pick it up.

'No. Everything is fine here,' he said. 'It was a faulty alarm, was it?' He laughed. 'You've been reading too many thrillers, Jack,' Teis said. There was more banter; then Teis rang off. 'Sure. Let them through. I'm ready. I'll open the back doors now.'

He hung up the phone; then there was the sound of doors opening and a van pulling up. There were more voices as Teis greeted the undertakers.

Mack lay still. Every muscle in his body ached. His nose itched like crazy, but most of all, he could only think how obvious it was that he and Tobias were in the body bags. They were both so much bigger and heavier than the emaciated junkies.

Tobias's body bag was the first to go. He heard the

undertakers grunting as they heaved him off the slab and carried him out through the doors and into the van.

Then Mack heard lone footsteps. Someone leaning over him. He tensed, keeping still. Then fingers on the zip of the body bag, just above his nose.

And then . . . the zip opened.

CHAPTER SEVENTEEN

In the French chateau, Scooter sat on the pink velvet window seat of her spectacular designer bedroom admiring the view from the turret window. She inhaled the wisteria-scented air, her eye drawn to the fields of sunflowers in the Provençal valley and the spires of the pretty town in the distance. She had never stayed somewhere as beautiful in her entire life. In the far distance, a tiny shimmer of blue revealed the coast.

My God, she thought. I'm actually here. In France.

It hardly seemed possible that so much had happened in such a short space of time. When was the YMC party? she wondered, counting back the weeks. Not even two months ago, but it felt like a lifetime.

She could barely remember anything about the party after her showdown with Miranda, although she'd heard more than enough from other people about her behaviour that night.

When she'd woken up in Jay's apartment the following morning, he'd given her his rescue remedy: a toxic-looking green smoothie and several strong painkillers, as well as the lowdown on the events of the night before. As she took small sips of the disgusting drink, he told her how she'd committed career suicide and ruined his chances of pulling when she threw up all over the actress he'd been chatting up.

'It was fucking disgusting,' Jay said. 'Poor Alicia. She won't be forgetting you in a hurry.'

'Oh God,' Scooter groaned.

'You did say something interesting, though. About a key?' Jay said, clattering around in the kitchen of his loft apartment, a cigarette dangling from his lips.

'Did I?' Scooter sniffed, her head in her hands.

'Yeah. You said you'd been sent a silver key.'

'Did I?' she mumbled, the words 'career suicide' rolling round her head.

'I don't think for one second it might be the same thing – I mean, why the hell would you have a key? – but ever since you said it, it's been bugging me. Because I have to know. Because if you have the same key thing that this dude in Vegas had, then, man . . .' He trailed off as he looked at Scooter, who had been weeping profusely again. 'Forget it. Sorry. Forget it,' Jay said, shaking his head as if to obliterate such a ridiculous thought.

But as it had turned out, it hadn't been a ridiculous thought, although it had taken Scooter a while to realize it. After the party, she'd lain low, brooding over the screw-up she'd made of everything. It hadn't helped that a courier had delivered a letter to her apartment informing her that YMC no longer wished to represent her and that she should cease all contact with the agency with immediate effect.

Then Doreen had told her that she'd doubled the rent and Scooter could either pay up or push off by the following week. Things had got so bad that even Ronda at the cafe – a depressive herself – had been irritated, hinting to Scooter there was no shortage of waitresses queuing up to take her place if she didn't buck up her ideas.

'You're usually so cheerful,' she'd lamented. 'You're bringing everyone down with your long face. Is it really that bad? Whatever's bugging you?'

But hell, yeah, it had been that bad. Scooter hadn't had the heart to tell Ronda just how bad things really had been, that in a week she'd be homeless, that she'd wrecked her career and her future, and had bankrupted herself on credit cards.

Then, just when her life hit rock bottom, Scooter found the key again in the pocket of her tunic at work and remembered what Jay had said about it at the party. She took the key home and studied it, wondering what on earth she was supposed to do with it. She'd almost thrown it away, but as she pressed the diamond the key came apart in her hand, revealing a USB port.

She plugged it into her laptop and was astonished to discover that she'd been selected for some sort of special offer.

They even knew her name.

At first she had no idea what to do with the key. She ought to have been excited, but instead she'd felt angry, assuming it was just some sort of scam, designed only to get her more into debt. So when the screen asked her what she desired, she'd typed: **Who are you? Why have you chosen me?**

Because you deserve it.

That had been the answer. She didn't deserve it, did she? **Is this a scam?**

This key can make your dreams come true. What do you desire, Scooter?

She'd laughed mockingly at the screen. Someone was out there claiming they could make her dreams come true. Well, that was a load of horseshit for a start. And what did she desire? For

Dean to be sorry that he'd left her? To tell her what a big mistake he'd made and that she was the love of his life after all? Yeah, like that was ever going to happen.

Or for Miranda to take her back on the books and finally get her a decent part in a movie? Or for Mona to return her calls? No, for Mona to return her calls and to admit what a bitch she'd been? Or for some computer program to magic her up a new apartment and new clothes? Hell, a whole new life.

Like any sort of upgrade service could ever manage *that*.

And that's exactly what she'd carried on thinking, right up until a few days later, when Jay arrived as she was packing up her room.

'You have no idea how long it took me to find out where you actually live these days,' he said, walking into her small apartment and turning up his nose. 'You look like shit.'

'Nice to see you too. Why are you here?'

'To see how you're doing. I was worried when I hadn't heard from you.'

Scooter scowled at him. 'A drug dealer with a heart. How very touching.'

'Don't be like that, babe,' Jay said, looking hurt. 'I mean it. I've been worried.'

Perhaps it was his concern for her, or perhaps it was just that she felt so sorry for herself, but Scooter broke down then and sobbed. When she'd finished, she'd told him that she'd found the key after the last time they'd spoken. That it was just some kind of sales gimmick, right?

Jay demanded that she show him the key and she'd dug it out of her bedside drawer and chucked it at him. When Jay held it in his hands, he'd started jumping around her apartment.

'Oh my God!' he yelled. 'Oh my God. Scooter, baby, you have no idea what this means.'

'What does it mean?' she asked, dumping clothes into the plastic sack she'd been holding.

'This is it. *The* key. This is your get-out-of-jail-free card.'

'Yeah, sure it is,' she said, shaking her head, tears threatening to fall again.

'I'm serious. This will get you into places – loads of places.' Jay grinned like a Cheshire cat and Scooter saw a plan whirring in his mind.

'What places? I have nowhere to go. No money to go anywhere. I'm homeless in less than twelve hours.'

But his grin didn't waver for a second. In fact, it just got more intense.

'Let's say you did have someplace to go,' Jay said. 'Say, just for a minute, you could go anywhere. Where would you go?'

Scooter had shrugged. 'To Cannes, maybe,' she told him, spiralling off into a rapid fantasy about driving down the Croisette in a fancy limo. How she'd step out onto the red carpet and see Dean in the crowd. How he'd be amazed by how incredible she looked and realize what a fool he'd been . . .

'Then that's what will happen,' Jay said, booting up her laptop. 'Watch this space.'

Jay helped to move her stuff into storage and out of Doreen's clutches and, through the key, hired a swanky furnished loft apartment in SoHo for a few weeks. Sprung into sudden luxury, Scooter felt wrong-footed, worrying all the time that she was about to be presented with a bill, but Jay assured her that it wouldn't happen. And he seemed to be right, as each day went by and no debt collectors came. When she'd questioned the key about what was required of her, when they would demand payment, it had replied: *Be yourself. That is all that is asked of you.*

Before she knew it, the Cannes trip had started to take shape. Through her key, and with Jay egging her on, Scooter had organized a private plane to bring her and Jay and his entourage of party people all the way to Nice.

Scooter didn't mind the others. She didn't really feel like she had a choice to say no to all the hangers-on when Jay had been so kind to her. Besides, it was fun to be with the fashionable crowd from Manhattan, including Declan, a wry-witted Irishman who was obviously completely in love with Jay, and whom Jay was blatantly stringing along; Trudi, a club DJ, and her girlfriend, Siobhan; BoBo, a daytime-TV hairdresser who had already worked magic on Scooter's hair; as well as Ulrika, Heidi and Rolf, three achingly hip young models, and their photographer, Barney, who Scooter thought was really sweet.

They'd partied non-stop all the way to France from JFK on the private plane last night; then, just as Jay had promised, with the most cursory of passport checks they'd all piled into the minivan waiting on the tarmac and had been driven on the twisty road down the coast and up here into the hills to the villa Scooter had procured through the key. She'd asked for **A villa or house. Like, the most exclusive accommodation near Cannes,** but nothing had prepared Scooter for this place. The gravel drive with its avenue of plane trees and rolling lawns only hinted at the grandeur of the house beyond, but Scooter had gasped when she'd seen the old stone building on the top of the hill. It wasn't so much a villa as a chateau. A proper chateau that looked as if it had been built for a medieval lord, complete with ancient-looking turrets and crenulations, and formal gardens stretching around it. It was like something from a dream.

'There you are!'

Scooter turned from the window to see Jay bursting into her room.

'Man, this place is awesome. Have you seen the art downstairs? That is some serious kit.'

'It's beautiful. I just can't get over it. Look at that view. I could die looking at it. It makes me want to start sketching and wafting around in floaty dresses,' Scooter sighed.

'Yeah, right,' Jay said. 'No offence, but you're not floaty-dress-girl material. You know what we need to do?' he said, bouncing on the four-poster bed on his bottom and propping himself up with the pile of embroidered cushions. 'The others all agree on this one.'

Outside, Scooter could hear whoops of delight and splashing from the pool.

'What?'

'Throw a party. A proper kick-ass party. This place is made for it.'

Scooter pulled a face, thinking of Lillian, the formal French housekeeper who'd greeted them earlier. She didn't look like the kind of person who'd approve of the chateau being trashed.

'We won't be allowed.'

'Allowed?' Jay laughed. 'Who's in charge? You are, honeybun,' he pointed out.

'But I don't even know why this is happening, or who is paying for it all.'

She knew Jay hated her questioning her good fortune, but she couldn't help it. Why was this happening to her? What had she ever done to deserve all of this? It didn't make any sense. This wasn't an upgrade. It was a whole life transplant.

Jay and all his friends kept telling her how lucky she was

and how lucky they were to know her, how grateful they were that Scooter had included them in her adventure, but she felt more out of control and detached than ever. And the key wouldn't answer any of her questions.

'I told you, babes – chill. If there's one thing I know, it's that some people have shitloads of spare cash. And if you, for whatever reason, happen to be on the receiving end of that, then cushtie, right? Roll with it.'

'Really?'

'Think about it. We can get the word out and throw a party on the night of' – he winked at her mischievously – 'Dean's premiere, perhaps?'

She knew Jay was gently trying to cajole her into taking revenge. After she'd told him what Dean had done and how he'd left so suddenly, breaking her heart, Jay was firmly on her side. She regretted now that she'd let slip back in New York that Dean was here in Cannes.

'Oh, I don't know. I don't want to ruin his party.'

'No? But I bet you wouldn't mind showing him just how cool your own life turned out to be too, huh?'

'I guess,' Scooter said, but she felt torn. The anguish that had burned within her had dimmed now that her fortunes had changed so dramatically. She wasn't sure she even wanted to confront Dean any more. Then she remembered that he was with Mona now. And that Mona would be here in France with him.

'How would we organize a party at such short notice?'

'The key. Ask your magic key, princess, and see if it has an answer,' Jay said, jumping off the bed and doing an elf-like dance across the thick carpet.

Scooter laughed, shaking her head, but Jay was right.

'I do feel like this is a fairy tale.'

'Too right. You're even in a friggin' turret!'

The fairy godmother who materialized later that afternoon came in the form of a small Frenchman with a sculpted goatee and sideburns, and round blue-lensed glasses. Scooter's first glimpse of him had been from underwater, at the bottom of the pool.

She'd been looking up, feeling triumphant at having clearly won the game. Fuelled by several bottles of wine over lunch, Scooter was delighting in being the life and soul of the party. And when Declan had asked her what her party trick was and she'd told them she was an expert at holding her breath underwater, he'd insisted that she show them all. So now, on this her third attempt, her lungs were burning, but she knew she'd broken her record of three minutes underwater.

But, distorted through the swimming pool, she heard BoBo and Declan shouting at her to surface and saw an unfamiliar figure standing by the poolside looking down at her.

Reluctantly she pushed her feet against the blue tiles at the bottom of the pool and surfaced into the sun, expecting applause, but instead a stern-looking man stared down at her.

'Zat is very impressive,' he said.

Declan made eyes at Scooter. This guy was clearly someone important.

Despite the heat, he was wearing a navy suit with wide white pinstripes and lace-up patent boots.

'*Je suis* Pierre,' he said, looking Scooter up and down as she climbed out of the pool, her breath-holding victory forgotten. She grabbed a towel, conscious of her skimpy bikini. 'I have come about ze party.'

He had sculpted eyebrows and a thick mop of black hair,

which was swept up into an exaggerated quiff. She offered him some of the delicious white Chablis they'd all been drinking, but he refused and introduced his equally serious-looking assistants.

'We have no time,' Pierre declared. 'Come. Show me,' he said to Scooter, gesturing for her to follow.

Urging the others to come with her, Scooter followed as Pierre swept up the path through the gardens and into the house, making little grunting sounds as he looked over the space, sometimes framing the air with his hands, sometimes shaking his head, so that his hair wobbled.

When Pierre made it to the hall, Scooter, Jay, Declan and BoBo watched as he came to a stop in a comically theatrical way. Had there ever been anyone more camp? Scooter wondered. She eyeballed Jay, who swigged from the beer bottle in his hand. She could tell he was about to start giggling. Barney, the photographer, came out of the kitchen to see what was going on. He winked at Scooter. Trudi and Siobhan came out of the cinema room to see what was going on too.

'I am moving my schedule to organize ze party for you,' Pierre announced. 'I was going to do ze Miramax Ball, but I've delegated zat to someone else.'

'Really?' said Scooter, astounded.

'You do want ze biggest and best and most talked-about party in this most star-studded enclave of ze world?' he checked. 'In less than a week?'

'Yeah, I guess . . .'

'Well, zat is why you have me. I will create you a – how you say? – a one-off event. A night that every guest who is here, no matter how famous they are, will tell their grandchildren about and whisper, "I was there."'

Scooter nudged Jay, who was already silently impersonating him saying 'one-off' in his French accent.

Pierre started talking in rapid French to his two assistants, one of whom started scribbling notes in a black book, while another stared intently at an iPad, nodding as Pierre spoke.

'Do you realize who that is?' Barney said, sidling up to Scooter.

'No,' Scooter said, leaning in close.

'That is Pierre Fitzroy. He's like . . . *a god*. He practically invented Fashion Week.'

'Oh my God. Pierre Fitzroy,' Ulrika said, startled, coming out of the kitchen. She immediately pouted and struck her model's pose, then, as Heidi and Rolf joined her, started talking in excited whispers.

'So, what is ze reason for this party?' Pierre demanded. 'Are you launching a movie, a company, a product . . . what?'

'Reason?' Scooter mumbled. She didn't have a reason.

'People won't come unless there is a reason,' Pierre said. 'How are you able to do this – host a party?'

'It's, well—' she began.

'It's a secret,' Jay interrupted. 'It's, um . . .' He looked at Scooter.

'Yeah. There is a reason for the party, but we're keeping it under wraps. And maybe it'll be good to keep everyone guessing, you know?'

Pierre considered her answer for a moment, his finger on his lips. 'A secret. OK. Well, zat could work. Ze Secret Party. We could work zat. What theme did you have in mind?' Pierre said.

'Theme? Well, I hadn't thought about it that much,' Scooter said, looking to Jay and Barney for some help. 'We just want a kick-ass party.'

'Yeah. Lots of music. Good bands,' Jay added. 'But it's got to be exclusive, right?'

'Yeah. Totally exclusive. Only the best people can come. We need a vibe. A buzz about it,' Scooter said, liking the fact that everyone was on board.

'Reiss,' Pierre barked out, nodding at Scooter's request. One of his assistants typed furiously on the iPad. 'Get Reiss.'

'What about black as a theme?' Barney said. 'Scooter Black's black party. It sort of works.'

'*Bon*,' Pierre said, clapping his hands. 'Black is perfect. Chic. Mysterious. We are agreed. Believe me, ze Secret Party will be ze party zat everyone will still be talking about in ten years' time.'

Scooter felt a shiver of excitement running down her spine. Jay was right. This was her fairy tale and she was damn well going to enjoy every second of it. She turned and grinned at Declan and Jay.

'Man, is he for real?' Jay gasped, as Pierre and his assistants stalked off towards the front door, already talking quickly into their phones.

CHAPTER EIGHTEEN

Julia sat in Senhora Azevedo's office, watching her diminutive boss, who was sitting on the other side of her desk. Julia had been called out of her class a few minutes ago, but hadn't been given a reason. Now she watched her boss, who looked between a piece of paper in her hand and up at Julia, over the top of her glasses.

'Thank you for being so understanding about my leave from school,' Julia said nervously. 'My grandmother is recovering well, so I won't be taking any more days off.'

It was true. Vovo's operation had been a success and she was in recovery, although it wasn't as quick as they'd hoped. Maybe that was because Consuela was loving every second of being waited on hand and foot in the private hospital. She had nothing but praise for the food and the nurses, who had all taken a shine to her.

'That's not why I've called you in here.'

'Oh,' Julia said, glancing towards the door as she heard a blast of noisy children. She wondered how nineteen-year-old Maria, her new teaching student, was getting on with the class and whether they were playing up. Maria had been recruited as part of a new scheme to rehabilitate past drug offenders and

Julia had been finding it hard to break down her brittle exterior and nurture a more giving attitude. She needed to get back and supervise.

'I have been contacted by the school authority,' Senhora Azevedo said, standing up and staring at Julia over her glasses. 'Apparently they have a fund available for a class trip. A substantial trip.'

'Oh?' Julia said again, but her voice had gone hoarse.

When Julia had told Nat about what had happened with the stranger after she'd left the nightclub and how an ambulance had turned up and taken Vovo to a private hospital, Nat had been amazed.

Julia had sworn her to secrecy, but it had felt good to offload her anxiety on Nat and to admit how torn she felt all the time. Torn between feeling terrified that it was all a trick and she was about to be ruined by enormous medical bills for Vovo and elated that something magical had happened and that Vovo had been saved. Not to mention the stress of all the lies she'd told Fredo and Marcello about Vovo's lottery win – the only excuse she'd been able to think of to explain what had happened. It simply hadn't felt right to tell them about the key. Not when she couldn't explain it herself. Not until she'd found out why she'd been given it.

Nat had given her a big hug and told her to calm down and think positively.

'But what if it's a trick?' Julia had said.

'There's only one way to test it. Think of something complicated that you really want. That you couldn't possibly get by yourself. And ask the key to make it happen. And then you'll know whether it's good or evil.'

Which is when Julia had had the idea about her class trip.

Nat had been horrified that Julia wanted to use it for something so mundane.

'What about travelling? You could get plane tickets to anywhere. We could go to Europe – London, Paris, Amsterdam. You've always wanted to go to Amsterdam.'

'But Vovo is still in hospital. I can't just leave. Besides, I don't want to go anywhere. There's enough places on my doorstep I've never been to,' Julia had replied, unsettled by Nat's disappointment in her. 'It's the same for the kids. If there's one thing I really want, it's to get them out of that school and to open their eyes.'

And so Nat had helped Julia type in her desire into the key's webpage. She'd asked for her class to get to go on a trip round Rio.

'Do you know anything about this, Julia?' Senhora Azevedo asked, interrupting Julia's thoughts. 'Did you apply for this grant behind my back?'

'No, of course not.'

Julia felt her cheeks burning. She hadn't dared to expect a response. Let alone one so fast and so clever. This was totally legitimate and above board. Signed off by the authorities. How had it been possible? The people behind this key organization . . . that guy she'd met, how much power did they have?

'Because the grant has been given on the proviso that it is your class that benefits.'

'My class?' Julia bluffed.

'Some kind of lottery between schools, apparently,' the headmistress said, scanning the letter and holding her glasses. 'All the classes were entered, but yours won. The grant available will be more than enough for you to take the whole class somewhere educational. Abroad even.' She flapped a cheque in the air. 'Although that is a ridiculous idea. And this money – from the local authority – it could fix so much at the school. I'm not sure why your class should be the only ones to benefit from such a fortuitous piece of luck.'

'We don't have to spend it all,' Julia said. 'We would only need enough for them to explore the city.'

Julia wanted to remind her boss of how damning she'd been about Julia's class project when she'd asked them to imagine an ultimate school trip in Rio. How she'd told Julia off for giving the children ideas. Now it was going to happen. All thanks to her. And her key, of course. She wanted to punch the air.

Senhora Azevedo rubbed her head and pursed her lips, still clearly suspicious. 'OK, well, if you insist that you can do it, then it's up to you. Personally, I can't think of a worse headache than taking those kids anywhere.'

A week later Julia was starting to understand why Senhora Azevedo had become so cynical about school trips. They were to be out of school for a day, yet planning it was taking up all of Julia's time. Sorting out the itinerary was one thing (although having a big budget certainly helped when it came to transport and gaining access to the museums), but the bigger problem was dealing with the children, who were all so over-excited Julia doubted they'd ever be able to behave in a public place.

Her pleas to some of the parents to come and assist had fallen on deaf ears and the staff were stretched to capacity. Which only left Julia and Maria, who was difficult to motivate at the best of times. That was until Julia offered her an upfront cash bonus for the day. She still had the money from the wallet and she felt better about spending it on Maria, who was working in the school for next to nothing. When Julia gave her 1,000 reals, she was overjoyed.

The money had the desired effect. On the day of the trip, Maria turned up early. She'd clearly spent half the money on a new wardrobe, and her hair had been dyed blonde and braided. Plastered with the kind of make-up the headmistress would never have allowed, Maria winked at Julia, then bossed the kids onto the bus, doling out more attitude than any of them dared to give back.

Within minutes Maria had all the kids singing, then organized a game to get them to pair up, making it so much easier to chaperone the kids around the first two museums. By the time they'd all got to the samba workshop in Lapa, everyone was into the swing of it and having a great time.

After enjoying lunch in the Parque Nacional da Tijuca, they moved on to the Cosme Velho and waited for the Trem do Corcovado to take them up the mountain to the statue of the Cristo Redentor, Rio's glorious landmark. The seventy-metre-high statue of Christ with his arms outstretched was known the world over and Julia couldn't wait to see the view from up there.

'Have you been before, miss?' Margarite asked excitedly, trying to frame the top of the mountain with the camera on her mobile phone.

'No. My grandmother always said she'd bring me, but we never made it.'

Another regret, Julia thought. Why hadn't she made the trip happen? How had life and work got in the way until it was too late? Well, if Vovo ever made it out of hospital, which Julia very much hoped she would, this place would be the first on the list. It felt as if the key had given Julia a second chance. A chance to do the right thing. And she would.

Julia couldn't help feel a childlike excitement as she and the class bustled inside the red carriage of the cog railway that would take them up the steep mountainside. It was an old-fashioned train, modelled when the statue had been first built, and Julia liked its sedate old-world charm and its leather seats and open wooden windows. The kids were soon all seated, while a few stood with Julia, who clung on to an overhead handrail.

'Room for one more,' the guard said.

Julia smiled and turned to see the final passenger – a man – jump into the carriage and cling to the metal bar. He had his side profile towards her, as he hitched his small rucksack over his shoulder, so she could see his slim build in his light combat trousers. He was tall, and his long arms were tanned, his muscles strong as he grabbed the handrail. He took his baseball cap off and she saw that he had fair skin and hair.

The train began moving with a jolt, making all the kids scream with excitement. Julia beamed at them, loving the way their expressions had become so open. But she soon found herself drawn back to the man, who was ducking down, to look out of the window at the view through the trees. As the bumpy train made its ascent, she saw the line of light brown stubble on his jaw and the pendant hanging on a leather string round his neck. She knew she should tear her eyes away from him, but somehow she couldn't. He was so different, so unusual compared to the dark-skinned men she was used to. It wasn't so much that the man was good-looking, although he was, in a dependable sort of way; it was just that there was something familiar about him, although she was certain he was a complete stranger. And then, as if sensing that Julia was looking at him, he turned and his eyes met hers and he smiled.

And that's when she felt it. Like a bolt of electricity mixed with a sense of certain recognition that, for one brief second, made the kids, the rest of the carriage, the whole of Rio melt away, and she was suspended in his stare, as if twirling slowly round, airborne in the glittery shafts of sunlight.

Julia felt a blush start in her cheeks and she looked quickly away. She was embarrassed by the noisy children. She turned her attention to a couple behind her who were fighting and began calming them down by pointing out the view to them. All the while she felt the stranger's gaze on her.

The train travelled at a stately pace, clanking up the track and through the trees. As the track grew steeper, the view became ever more breathtaking. Julia fanned her face, aware that she was perspiring. It was hot in the carriage, but it was better to come in the afternoon, rather than risk the view being ruined by the morning clouds.

After a few minutes she stole another glance at the man, but he was staring right at her. She turned quickly away, pressing her lips together to mask her shocked smile. What was happening to her? She could almost hear her own heartbeat.

'Have you seen that guy?' Maria whispered unsubtly.

'Shh,' Julia implored her, widening her eyes.

Maria stole another glance at the man, behind Julia's back. 'He's definitely checking you out. And he's hot, right?'

Julia shook her head, widening her eyes even further at Maria to tell her to stop. This was not the time or place to even think about meeting anyone. Besides, the guy looked foreign. He was a complete stranger. A tourist. He probably didn't even speak Portuguese.

So what if she found him attractive? That just looking at him made an unfamiliar tug start in her abdomen? She mustn't stare. She was a teacher, here in a position of responsibility. This wasn't meant to be about her.

But even without looking, she'd already memorized every detail of him. Maria was right. He *was* hot. She liked the open buttons of his crumpled blue linen shirt, but most of all she liked his eyes. Those soft, enquiring grey eyes. The eyes that were making the carriage feel overwhelmingly hot.

She busied herself with the children as they leaned out of the open train windows and marvelled at the view through the trees, which was getting clearer and clearer. Some of them were used to views over Rio, living at the top of the slum, but those views were ordinary, like wallpaper. Just part of their daily life. But this, it now became apparent, as the children stopped their chattering and descended into hushed awe, was something different. This was magical. Like they had found themselves looking through the eyes of an eagle, or an angel of God.

But even as she thought it, drinking in the magnificent view herself, her body – her whole body – could feel that the man was not gazing at the view at all. He was gazing at her.

When the train came to a stop at the top, she bustled the children off, trying to prevent them from running off to the souvenir stand. She did another headcount and, finding that she still had all the kids, turned away to see if she could see the man, but the stranger had gone. He had to be here somewhere, she told herself. She strained on her tiptoes to look around the crowd. He couldn't have just disappeared.

She felt a sudden stab of panic, like she'd lost one of the children. But it was him she was missing. No one else. She knew that somehow she had to talk to him. No matter what.

But Maria reminded her of more pressing things, like trying to get the children to line up on the steps to the statue so that she could take a photograph for the school newsletter. They were a ragtag bunch, Julia realized, seeing the other tourists keeping away, as she bustled them into place. Julia was so fiercely proud of them all the same.

She took the photo, making them all smile. She smiled herself when she saw the picture on her camera. Senhora Azevedo wouldn't stop her putting this on the school's website, surely.

Soon the kids had dispersed, some to the chapel underneath the giant statue and others to scamper up the steps to look at the concrete statue itself, which was vast up close – even bigger than it looked from below. It was beautiful. The smooth, strong lines of the stonework so familiar and yet so extraordinary now she was right next to it.

It was only when she'd herded most of the children up the steps that she saw the traveller from the train standing on the top viewing platform taking in the view.

'Say something to him,' Maria urged, seeing that Julia had spotted him.

'I can't,' Julia said.

Maria deliberately pushed her and she edged closer to the man.

As she stepped up to the viewing platform, Julia could see the man's face from side on, his eyes shining as he looked down at the skyscrapers far below, the yellow crescent of beach, the smile of white surf and expanse of blue fading into the distant haze.

Up here there was a fresh breeze and it was strangely peaceful. Birds flew far down below them, and a helicopter buzzed below too, across the city. In the distance, hang-gliders soared around Sugarloaf Mountain.

Julia didn't want to interrupt the stranger, although she

knew a comment about the view would not make her seem too stupid. It was incredible. She took a step closer, her palms sweating, but right at that moment she heard a scream.

She turned to see that Eduardo was up on the wall near the steps. He looked as if he was walking along the ledge for a dare, as he kept glancing backwards to the other children, who jeered and catcalled to him.

'No! Eduardo, no!' Julia shouted, racing down the steps, panicking. 'Come down.'

Maybe it was her calling out that threw him off balance, or maybe it was Maria, who lunged for his leg at the same time, but Eduardo toppled backwards off the wall.

The children screamed as he disappeared from view.

Julia raced through the crowd, desperately looking over the wall, but all she could see was the tops of some trees and a sheer drop.

'Where's he gone?' Maria panicked.

'Eduardo!' Julia shouted, her voice shrill.

'Oh my God,' Maria gasped. 'What are we going to do?'

'Move.'

Julia heard the accented English and turned to see the man from the train, the man she'd been about to speak to when she should have been keeping an eye on the kids. He thrust his backpack into her arms, then sprang up onto the wall.

'What's his name?' he shouted.

'Eduardo.'

The man went to the far side of the wall and, grimacing with effort, lowered himself over the edge, calling out Eduardo's name.

'I can see him,' he called out in a strained voice.

'Oh, thank God,' Julia said.

'He's caught on a tree.'

Julia held her breath as the man climbed down, out of view. She hoisted herself as far over the wall as it was safe to go without falling. She could see the man cajoling Eduardo into giving him his hand, but she could tell the poor boy was terrified he was going to slip. His feet dangled in thin air, his T-shirt snagged on a branch. Below him was a sheer drop of thousands of feet.

Julia gasped as the man extended his hand. For a second it looked like he was going to overbalance. She covered her mouth in shock, saying a silent prayer.

Then, just as Eduardo slipped and screamed, the man swung forward and grabbed him under his arm. Momentarily, it looked like they would both topple, but the man was strong. With a grunt of exertion, he yanked the boy up and round onto his back.

Five minutes later he'd hauled him up to safety. Eduardo still clung tightly to his back as he climbed up the wall. Julia held out her hand, helping the man hoist himself over.

'I've got you,' she told Eduardo, pulling the terrified boy into her arms. He was shaking like a leaf.

His classmates clapped and cheered, but Julia knew it was not a cause for celebration. She could feel her knees shaking too as she knelt next to the man and Eduardo. If he hadn't caught on that tree . . . If the man from the carriage hadn't saved him . . .

'He's OK. He's had a shock, that's all,' the man said, wiping the sweat from his brow with his sleeve. He was out of breath.

He smiled at Julia and again, despite the child between them, she felt a tug somewhere deep inside her.

Without warning Eduardo shot up out of Julia's arms and shouted at Paulo, pushing him backwards.

'Hey,' Julia said, going to pull him away. 'Enough.'

It took a few minutes, but eventually she managed to calm down the fight. When she looked around for the man, though, to talk to him and thank him properly, he'd gone.

She searched everywhere, but she didn't see him again until she was on her way back to the train, herding the kids in front of her. He was at the kiosk, buying a postcard. Relief washing over her, Julia broke away from the kids and touched his arm. He looked at her hand and then into her eyes and he smiled. He looked so calm and unruffled. You'd never be able to tell that he'd just saved a boy's life. Not to mention Julia's career.

'I didn't have a chance to thank you,' Julia said, speaking carefully so that she got her English correct. She'd studied at night school for years to learn the language properly, but since she'd been teaching she'd had to give up night school and she was rusty. It felt good to be speaking English again though. She realized now how much she'd missed the conversation classes.

'You don't have to. I was glad to be able to help. You look like you have your hands full.'

'It's my first school trip with the class. They are a bit over-excited. I hope we didn't ruin your visit.'

'Not at all.' He smiled at her and she felt that strange breathless feeling again. She could feel herself blushing in the awkward pause.

'I had to bring them here,' she said, as if they'd been talking all the while. The blush got worse. She should stop talking now and let the man go. 'I always wanted to come up here.'

'Me too,' the man said with a gentle smile. He followed her gaze to the view. 'My mum always wanted to come here. She was a fan of Hitchcock films and I think she fancied herself as Ingrid Bergman in *Notorious*.'

Julia nodded, but she felt deflated. She couldn't claim to have understood his film reference and now felt inadequate. He was obviously a cultured, well-travelled man. What could she possibly have to offer someone like him, when she'd already proved how incompetent she was at her job?

'Thank you again. I'm afraid I can't ever repay you.'

'You can if you agree to meet me again,' he said, his eyes boring into hers. 'Let me buy you dinner. Or at least a drink?'

At first she didn't think she'd heard him correctly, but then Julia saw that he was serious and was waiting for an answer.

'But I don't even know your name,' she stumbled, laughing.

'Christian. My name is Christian Erickson,' he said.

CHAPTER NINETEEN

Kamiko sat on the high wooden seat in the far corner of Starbucks, in the warm, cinnamon-scented fug, and bit her nails, nervously looking through the steamed-up window at the posh Zurich street, with its smart trams and clean cars. She'd drunk two large black coffees and her foot jiggled with nervous tension. She'd been in here since seven this morning, and now, at nearly half past eight, the workers were starting to arrive.

She saw two people in business suits come into the cafe, laughing and talking in German. As the door closed, Kamiko felt a blast of cold air.

She watched the man and woman, and wondered if they were having an office affair, as they seemed very friendly for work colleagues and kept touching each other.

It was a cold day but sunny and they took off their gloves and laughed about keeping their sunglasses on as they sat at the window bar just along from her. She saw them both say something and glance her way. She knew she looked out of place in her black jumper, boots and ripped leggings, but she didn't care what they thought.

She picked up her camera, pretending to be busy, shielding the screen from the glare of the sun and scrolling back to the photos she studied endlessly, hoping that another viewing might give her some vital clues.

She stopped at the all-too-familiar images. There they were, Tiko and Susi, laughing and pulling faces at her camera. Then there was a run of pictures of the concert at Tokyo Dome. The lights and lasers. Susi's pupils black and dilated from the drugs they'd taken.

Then there were the shots from the hotel. She slowed down through them, stopping at the one of Susi with her top off. The way she was looking at the camera – at Kamiko – still made a strange longing fill her abdomen. Until she remembered how she'd woken up alone in the hotel bed with a terrible headache, and Tiko and Susi gone. With her key and her phone.

She'd gone straight back to Kadoma, but Tiko hadn't been there, just a grubby card on the door of the cafe saying that it would be closed until further notice. It was when she'd seen that that Kamiko had realized just how stupid she'd been. How badly Tiko and Susi had used her. What a gullible fool she'd been to trust them. She had realized Tiko had seen her registering her details on the key and knew her security passwords. He had said himself that he only had to check his machines and he knew everything.

Which meant that Tiko and Susi could use her key. They could get anything they wanted now. Anything at all. When the key was *hers*.

And she'd decided there and then that she would find them, no matter what.

Ever since that moment a hard, black flame had burned within her. Nobody was going to give her all this and then rip it away. She was not going to go back to Kadoma to her shitty life. Not when she'd been singled out for an upgrade. Which is why she'd decided to track down Martha Faust and find out the truth about the key organization and get another key for herself.

Kamiko scrolled now through the photos from yesterday, when she'd arrived at the airport, stopping at the shots of this very Zurich street and the smart headquarters of the marketing organization that administered the key scheme.

She scrolled forward, coming to the set of pictures of Martha Faust going through the revolving door of the office block opposite, in her smart grey suit and black-framed glasses, carrying a takeout coffee from this very Starbucks cafe in her gloved hand, a smart leather dossier tucked under her arm. She looked every inch the powerful fifty-something businesswoman Kamiko had suspected she would be.

Plucking up the courage, Kamiko had quickly gone into the building and taken one of the glossy brochures from the smart reception area, and had spent yesterday doing her homework in the cheap hotel she'd found.

She'd read all about Martha Faust: her glowing academic credentials, her rise through blue-chip organizations in Europe and the States, her work as a brand ambassador, her famed marketing prowess. The key scheme had been Martha Faust's baby. It had been her idea to bring luxury brands on board as a gifting opportunity for top businesspeople. Kamiko was no closer to finding out any answers, which is why she was here today, waiting for Martha Faust, determined to confront her.

She didn't have to wait long before Martha came into the coffee shop, greeting a few people she knew. The barista behind the counter seemed to know her order, as she handed over a coffee with a smile.

Kamiko slipped off her seat, turning her back to the door as she packed away her camera. Then she quickly slipped out of the door, following Martha Faust across the bustling street and through the revolving door into the building opposite.

The reception area was busy, but she spotted Martha passing into the lift. Quickly she read the floor guide and saw that the BGZ offices were on the tenth floor. Shielding herself with the crowd, she managed to slip through the double doors, finding herself in an empty stairwell. She quickly climbed up the twisting flights of stairs and was out of breath by the time she made it to the tenth floor.

The BGZ offices' reception was smart, with lots of low tables displaying magazines and books. A fluffy fawn carpet made everything seem muted. As Kamiko entered through the glass doors, past the exotic fish tank, she saw a young guy in a grey suit behind a reception desk. He had a chiselled jaw, but acne scars on his skin. Kamiko could tell straight away that he thought he was important.

He looked Kamiko up and down, his eyes registering shock and distaste, and spoke to her in German, but Kamiko shrugged.

'I here to see Ms Faust,' she said in English. She'd been learning English on language tapes for years, but this was the first time she'd got to speak it properly and her voice shook. It sounded right in her head. She stared at the receptionist hard.

The young guy looked confused. He went back to his desk, picked up a phone and talked quietly into it.

Kamiko stared at him, enjoying the fact that the receptionist was so clearly intimidated.

'Follow me,' he said, quickly walking round the desk and marching briskly down a corridor. At the end, he opened the door and waited for her to pass. She chewed her gum and slunk past sullenly, delighting in his discomfort.

Martha Faust was sat behind a fancy oak desk and was on

the phone. She held up a manicured finger, asking Kamiko to wait.

Kamiko strolled across the posh office, looking at the vintage adverts framed on the walls as she waited until Martha Faust put down the receiver on her desk.

'Can I help you?' she asked. She smiled at Kamiko. Her face was unwrinkled and she clearly cared for her skin. She was wearing a green woollen dress, and her figure was trim. She looked well put together and entirely in command of her domain.

'You know who I am,' Kamiko said, turning to face her. It was a gamble, but she could see that it had paid off. She saw Martha Faust's face register shock.

'Do I?' she asked, her eyes flicking away nervously. 'We haven't met.'

'I am key-holder,' Kamiko said.

'Well, I'm afraid I don't know all the key-holders. There are lots of them.'

'But none like me,' Kamiko insisted. 'I'm not top businessperson.'

She walked towards the desk and sat down in the comfortable chair opposite Martha, acting as if she had all the time in the world. She could tell the older woman was uncomfortable.

'Why are you here?'

'Because I have a problem,' Kamiko told her, careful to get the English right.

'Oh?'

'Someone stole my key. And I want another one.'

Martha Faust clasped her hands on top of the desk and pressed her lips together. She stared at Kamiko for a long moment; then obviously seeing that Kamiko had no intention of leaving, she sighed. She glanced at the door and leaned forward, lowering her voice.

'Kamiko. Yes, well, in truth I am familiar with your case, but I still can't tell you anything, I'm afraid. And I certainly can't issue another key.'

What did her 'case' mean? Kamiko watched her pushing the papers around on her desk.

'Why not?'

'It's complicated, I'm afraid.' Martha Faust stretched her fingers on the desk. 'It's impossible to issue another key. Absolutely out of the question. You only get one chance.'

One chance? At what? Kamiko wondered. At winning? How was she meant to win, or succeed, or take her chance as best she could, if she didn't even know the rules by which she was meant to be playing?

At that moment the phone on her desk rang and Martha Faust jumped.

'Excuse me,' she said to Kamiko, picking up the receiver and listening.

She turned away in her chair and Kamiko picked up the stapler on her desk.

'Yes, yes,' Martha said, in a lowered tone in English. 'Of course I'll be at the reception. I'll have to go home first. I'll be at the chalet.' She glanced back at Kamiko, her face clouding. 'No, not that one. Didn't you know I've got a new place in Gletch? It'll only be a half-hour drive from there. I've got to go . . . OK.'

She rang off, then stood up. 'Miss Nozaki, I'm sorry, but I have a very busy day ahead of me. I'm afraid I can't help you more.'

'I'm not leaving until I find out what is going on,' Kamiko

said, leaning back in her seat and putting one of her boots on the edge of the desk.

'There is nothing "going on". The key-holder scheme has been around for years. The part you're involved in is a recent add-on, if you like. Separate to the main scheme but operating on the same principles. Quite frankly, I'm very much regretting agreeing to it at all.'

'Agreeing to who? Who is behind it all?'

'I can't tell you that. I'm sorry. That is none of your business. You have to leave now.'

'No.'

'I insist that you leave,' she said firmly, then marched to her office door and opened it, waiting for Kamiko to go.

A few moments later Kamiko stood on the street, feeling annoyed. Why had Martha Faust dismissed her so quickly? What was she hiding? She was more convinced than ever that the key was some sort of game. A game Martha Faust was clearly keen to distance her organization from, but one to which she alone knew the rules.

Seeing a yellow taxi, Kamiko put up her hand. She got in the back and asked the driver if it was possible to get a train to Gletch.

'It is way too small for a train station. It's halfway up the mountain. People usually ski there.'

'Oh. Well, can you take me there?'

'By road? I guess. But it will cost you.'

Kamiko sat back in the seat. She would go to Gletch and find Martha Faust's chalet. Even if it meant waiting for her until she came back later. Martha Faust would have a computer at home. She must do. Something that would give Kamiko a clue as to what was going on. It was just a question of finding it.

CHAPTER TWENTY

The midnight-blue mega-yacht gleamed in the bright afternoon light, towering above the neighbouring boats on the harbourside in Cannes. Owned by Russian billionaire Serge Lebekovski – the oil magnet turned film producer – it was the venue of the Brightside Pictures reception and Scooter could sense the buzz about the party even as she stepped out of the white limo. Music from the jazz band wafted on the breeze, and bunting fluttered on the ramp.

Looking up, Scooter could see the party on the deck, the select guests seemingly unaware of the bank of paparazzi and their telephoto lenses on the quayside, but all posing nevertheless. Nobody on board could possibly be having as much fun as she had been having, though. This had to be the week of her life, Scooter thought.

She felt invincible as she walked out in front of the cameras with Declan, Jay, Barney and the girls. Her hair had been coiffured into a trendy side-bun by BoBo, who had made a few calls and had had a movie stylist come to the chateau to sort out Scooter's wardrobe. For today, she'd picked out a pale orange Roberto Cavalli sundress with heels to match and she felt sensational.

It was good to be out of the chateau for a while, though staying there this past week had been magical. The party had been organized like a military operation and Scooter couldn't wait. People had been transforming the chateau for days and now the buzz was building to a fever pitch. It was going to be the party of the year. And she was throwing it. The sense of power it made her feel was intoxicating.

She'd quizzed Pierre's assistant Max about who was paying for it. All he'd said was that Pierre seemed happy with the arrangement, which was a first. Apparently, a 'substantial' banker's draft had been sent to his company. When Scooter had asked how much, Max had laughed and told her that Pierre only ever worked for the top budget and would not have bumped the other party unless the fee had been 'significant'. As the client, Scooter was not to worry, he reassured her. She hadn't had the nerve to ask who had sent the draft. She didn't dare shatter the illusion. Because everyone was treating her for the first time in her life as if she really was somebody.

So much so that Pierre and his assistants had checked every decision with her, and she'd surprised herself by how practical she was and how creative she'd found the decision-making process. Pierre, who famously despised working for clients but seemed to adore Scooter, had pulled out all the stops, hiring in Reiss, a 'celebrity fixer', who had been busy spreading rumours about the party to get the hype started.

Now Reiss himself appeared in person by car. He was in his early thirties and was wearing leather jeans and a cropped leather jacket – a look any straight man would find difficult to pull off, but Reiss exuded a cool confidence and charisma. He lifted his glasses and smiled at Scooter.

'We meet at last. I'm Reiss. Pierre sent me,' he said, slipping his phone into his pocket. He had an American accent with a French twang, but had the sort of in-the-know aura that Scooter had started to recognize from being around Pierre. He was handsome, with dark hair and a deep tan. He looked . . . well . . . rich. 'Sorry I'm late. I've had a few busy days.'

'That's OK,' Scooter said, smiling back.

'Your party is going to be sensational,' Reiss said, holding out his hand for Scooter to step onto the kerb. 'But we have to ramp up the mystery factor. Now, here's what I want you and your friends to do,' he instructed, as they were all waved straight into the exclusive party by the black-suited bouncers.

As Scooter stood on deck half an hour later, taking in the spectacular panoramic view of the shoreline, she felt as if she'd been transported into the pages of a celebrity magazine. But rather than feeling awed and insecure, for the first time she felt as if she belonged.

'Hi,' a man said. She turned to see a good-looking guy in blue linen trousers and a crisp white T-shirt standing next to her. 'You look familiar. Have we met?' he asked, pushing his aviator shades up into his mop of dark hair. His blue eyes were as twinkly as the sea. Scooter felt her heart thump once, very hard.

'You're Dallas Laney, right?' she said, although it was ridiculous to ask. *Everyone* knew who Dallas Laney was. 'We met briefly at the YMC party.'

'Ah, yes,' he said, remembering. He started smiling – that multi-million-dollar smile that made him one of the most sought-after actors in Hollywood. To be on the receiving end of it was quite something. He pointed his finger at her. 'You were the one who stood up to Miranda.'

Scooter shrugged. 'She'd been stringing me along for ages. I had to get to her somehow, but it was probably a bad judgement call. She wasn't very happy about it.'

Did he know the rest? she wondered. How she'd got spectacularly drunk and thrown up on Alicia Knowles? She wondered how long it would be before she could laugh about that particular episode, like Jay was so fond of doing.

'So I gathered,' Dallas said with a smile, and she realized straight away that he knew. That everyone probably knew what a fool she'd been. She felt a blush rise in her cheeks. 'Hey, we've all done crazy stuff, though, right?'

Scooter remembered now that Dallas had been caught up in some sort of teen scandal. It was only recently, since he'd famously hit forty and got sober and clean, that the work had come his way again and he'd been enjoying a spectacular revival. And, God, if she'd fancied him in all those teen flicks, it was nothing compared to now. The guy was to die for.

'Actually, I admire someone who has the balls to stand up to the agents occasionally,' he continued. 'Have you found new representation?'

'I'm considering my options. Put it that way. In the meantime I'm just enjoying being here and catching up with people.' She liked the way that sounded. As if she was important. As if all of these people were people she could see at any time.

'Where are you staying?' he asked.

Did he know? she wondered. It had been like this for days. People fishing for invitations to her party. It was all so exciting.

'In the hills. Chateau Marmond.'

'I know that place. Tom and Katie had it a couple of years back. How did you get that?'

'A little bit of luck,' Scooter said with a shrug. She could tell that Dallas was reappraising her more favourably by the second.

'You're not the one throwing that party tonight everyone's talking about?' His eyes were bright as he leaned in close. He smelt gorgeous. 'The Secret Party?'

Scooter smiled, raising her eyebrows. 'My, how rumours fly,' she said. 'It's quite a small bash – or so Pierre says – but that's by his standards. Would you like to come?'

'Me? I'd love to, but I've, er, I've sort of committed to stuff.'

Like the party at the Martinez tonight, no doubt, Scooter thought. The premiere party for the film Dean had scored the soundtrack to. The party where Dean and Mona, along with Billy and Lara, would be centre stage.

'Oh, come on,' she said. 'I know you like a party, and this one is very exclusive. I've got limos coming to pick up a few select friends. There's a couple leaving from the Martinez later.'

But she couldn't say any more, because a familiar face filled her vision.

Mona had acquired herself a new nose, and her narrow frame was squeezed into a sculpted red dress that made her look like a Barbie doll. She was every bit the kind of woman Dean had once claimed to despise.

'Hi, Scooter,' Mona said, easing into the conversation. She looked between Dallas Laney and Scooter, her eyes flashing venom, as if she couldn't believe what she was seeing. 'Dallas,' she added in a simpering low coo, 'how nice to meet you.'

'Oh. It's you,' Scooter said, keeping her voice flat and uninterested, as if she'd seen her yesterday. She leaned in, whispering into Laney's ear, 'I've got to deal with this one.'

'OK,' he whispered back. 'I'll catch you later.'

And he kissed her, right there and then, on the cheek. Then, lingeringly, on the other. His skin was soft and warm. She wanted to drink him in. She could happily drown in his scent. 'I take it this is making her pissed, right?' he whispered, and Scooter laughed. She liked him for being intuitive enough to pick up the tension between her and Mona. But not half as much as she liked the way his chest was pressed up against hers.

He glanced at Mona behind them, then winked at Scooter.

'I'll catch you at the Secret Party,' he said, this time in a whisper loud enough for Mona to hear. 'Limo outside the Martinez.' He pointed his finger at Scooter and she smiled again as his gorgeous eyes bored into hers. 'I'll be there.'

Then he turned and left. Scooter stared at his strong shoulders and pert butt. Fuck . . . he was just gorgeous. And he'd promised to come to her party. She wished Mona would disappear so that she could revel in the sensation of having been kissed by Dallas Laney, but Mona stepped in closer.

'*You* know about the Secret Party?' Mona said incredulously, as soon as he'd left. 'The one everyone is freaking out about?'

Scooter turned slowly towards Mona. How dare she talk to her like this? Like nothing had happened. Like she had the right to butt in on a conversation. Like she still had the right to talk to Scooter, after everything she'd done. After using her, dumping her and stealing her boyfriend.

Then she remembered what the key had told her: *Just be yourself*. Well, she would, damn it. Mona didn't intimidate her now. Not one little bit.

'Yeah,' Scooter said, 'actually, I do.'

'But the film is opening tonight. Whoever is organizing that party is *deliberately stealing the guests*. And this is Dean's big moment. He's playing at the after-party, but no one will be there.'

Scooter bit down on her triumphant smile. Those very

words, coming out of Mona's mouth, felt like all the victory she needed.

She cocked her head at Mona, noticing properly now how very odd she looked. Her eyebrows were so high up her head she had this startled look about her.

'Ah, yes,' she said, her tone as steely as she could make it. 'Dean. I hear you're together now,' Scooter said, daring her to look away.

Mona shifted uncomfortably. 'Yeah, well, we are. Who told you, anyway?'

The way she said it made Scooter realize how much she'd wanted to keep it a secret. Out of guilt? she wondered. No, it was more to do with Mona's little power trip. Of believing that she was better than Scooter.

'Lara.'

Scooter let the revelation hang as a waiter came over with drinks. Mona must think that Lara was one of her best friends now. Now that she and Dean and Lara and Billy hung out together. Lara was a snake in the grass who had loved nothing more than ratting out Mona.

But if Mona was upset, she tried not to show it. Instead, she took the opportunity to flirt with the waiter and ask him about the drinks. Scooter waited patiently, refusing a drink herself. She wanted to be sober for this. She noticed Mona's hand shaking as she took the glass from the tray.

'So you're still working, then?' Mona said, taking a sip of her drink and spilling it down her mouth. 'I mean, you must be if you're here, but I thought—' Mona began.

'You thought what?' Scooter interrupted. 'You thought I wasn't worth bothering with? Is that it? Even though it was *me* who got you your first break, you thought you'd just drop me and run off with the man you knew I still had feelings for. Is *that* what you thought?'

A flush rose on Mona's neck. 'No. Of course not. It wasn't like that.'

'Oh really? Wasn't it? Because the way I see it is that I helped you out and you stabbed me in the back,' Scooter said, spelling it out for her. It felt so good to say it. To have called her on her behaviour. She felt power surging through her. Man, this felt good. Mona gawped at her, astounded that Scooter had had the nerve to be so honest.

'Which, as far as I'm concerned,' Scooter continued, 'really doesn't give you the right to even speak to me. Or interrupt my conversations.'

She sensed someone by her side and turned to see Jay. He squeezed her elbow. Thank God. He was here, just when she needed him.

'Oh, look who it is. The viper,' Jay said, his eyes narrowing at Mona as if she were some kind of a joke. Scooter could have kissed him then. She could tell the effect his scorn was having on Mona.

'Come on, babe,' he said to Scooter, amusement dancing in his eyes. 'We'd better get ready for the party.'

'You mean you're going?' Mona asked. 'To the Secret Party?'

Jay laughed. 'Going? Of course she's going. It's *her* party.'

'Hey, Scooter' – she heard voices behind her and turned to see Ulrika and Heidi – 'save a place for Jack and Delores in the Carlton limo at seven. They're all coming up. It's going to be awesome.'

Scooter saw Mona register what Jay had said and that it had just been confirmed by the hip young group of people.

'It's *your* party?' Mona said, the penny finally dropping.

'Tonight. Your party is the party tonight?' She gulped, as if this fact were unbelievable. 'The Secret Party?'

'And guess what, Mona? You're *not invited*,' Jay said. 'Oh, and by the way, your nose job is a disaster. If you'd kept your best friend, maybe she'd have told you that.' Jay grabbed hold of Scooter's arm and walked towards the exit as Mona squealed behind them. 'Was that as satisfying as you'd hoped?' he asked in a low voice.

Scooter could feel Mona's eyes on her as she walked away. 'Oh, yes.' She giggled. 'Oh, yes, it really was.'

CHAPTER TWENTY-ONE

Ten miles down the coast from Cannes, Harry breathed in the sunshine as he steered the wooden tender towards the small port. His favourite Paul Smith shirt flapped in the warm breeze, and he noticed, as he slowed right down and grabbed his straw trilby, that he had a satisfying tan mark below his new Tag Heuer watch.

Leaning over the side of the boat as he approached the quayside, he caught sight of his reflection in the clear deep-blue water. He hardly recognized himself. He had a new designer haircut, thanks to a top stylist in Ibiza, and his skin glowed with a healthy tan.

He'd always wanted to party in the South of France, but had never had the friends or cause to come. After his nose surgery, Cole had insisted that Harry take the yacht for a few months 'to hang around the Med'. He'd jumped at the chance.

He'd been toying with the idea of asking the key for a yacht anyway, after his incredible night with LaMay. He reasoned that if the key could magic her up, then the sky was the limit. A spell on Cole's yacht would give him the chance to find out whether a yachting life was the life for him.

He'd discovered that it most definitely was. In fact, he'd been having the time of his life. He'd had a blast over in Ibiza and had stayed for a few weeks in Palma in Majorca. No matter where he went, thanks to his key, there was automatic entry into every exclusive party. He thought about how he used to envy Nick Grundy for gathering people around him, but now Harry *was* that guy, but on such a far-out scale. If only Nick Grundy could see him now. He'd shit his pants with envy.

Approaching the quayside now, Harry slowed the engine to guide the small vessel in. He liked these morning trips he made by himself. It was fun being on the yacht, but sometimes he needed a break from the staff constantly being there to attend to his every need. It was quite overbearing. It seemed that if you had a mega-yacht, you had to have the people to run it too. It was a very small niggle in an otherwise perfect arrangement. Besides, half an hour to himself was really all he needed. Just a tiny bit of space to pinch himself. To remember that this truly was happening to him. And this morning more than ever before, he wanted time away – to reflect on his impromptu birthday party last night.

He smiled to himself, thinking of the two girls still asleep in the master birth on the yacht. He'd buy them both flowers, he decided, before he went back to wake them up. Or would that be too cheesy? Maybe he should buy them jewellery, or something from one of the designer boutiques. It would be nice to show his appreciation for the special birthday present they'd given him last night. He felt heat rising in his cheeks even thinking about it. Man . . . they'd blown his mind.

He'd met Yinska through his new friend Reiss, whom he'd met in Ibiza. Reiss was a crazy guy – half Parisian, half American – who had the best coke Harry had ever tried. And he'd tried his fair share recently – enough to consider himself quite the aficionado.

Reiss had turned up when Harry had first arrived in Ibiza and had put in a request to the key for a 'discreet party organizer with supplies', hoping that he'd be able to get into a party at Pacha, where he'd overheard that several of the models he'd seen around the exclusive harbour would be. Reiss had come to the yacht and they'd clicked instantly. When Harry had shown him his key, Reiss had assured him that he could get into Pacha with it anyway. He knew others with keys like it who were waved straight through to the VIP area and enjoyed free champagne all night.

The drugs were a different matter, though, and Reiss was more than happy to oblige. When Harry had invited him to stay and hang out, Reiss had seemed glad to accept. And he was so much fun to party with. Being with Reiss made Harry feel like the coolest guy on the planet. Harry loved the feeling of being 'in'. He was 'in' with the most 'in' crowd.

It was because of Reiss that Harry had ordered Rupert, the captain, to hot-foot it from the Balearics here to the South of France, where Reiss was 'finessing' a few of the bigger parties at the film festival. What a life that guy had.

As a little thank-you for his lift over to France, Reiss had organized an impromptu birthday party for Harry on board *Menzies' Millions*. It had been a gathering of the most beautiful people Harry had ever seen. The most beautiful of all had been Yinska. Harry had immediately liked her accented English and her sense of fun. Last night she'd introduced him to her friend Anya, another blonde bombshell, who hardly spoke any English, but it didn't matter. He'd picked up 'birthday present' and the look between her and Yinska, and realized conversation was the last thing the pair of them were interested in. It had been every porn fantasy he'd ever had rolled into one – or three.

He shook his head, still reeling from the experience. He wished he had someone to tell how amazing it had been, but Reiss had left the party just before Harry got up, to disappear off to Cannes.

He thought of Dulcie and guffawed out loud at himself. He couldn't tell *her* about his threesome with the Russian models! She hadn't even believed him about LaMay. Even so, he felt a dart of shame.

The truth was, he missed her. Or at least the thought of what she could have been to him. But Dulcie was a fool, he reminded himself. She'd had her chance to come on this crazy ride with him and she hadn't wanted it. There'd been plenty more gorgeous girls since then gagging to take her place.

He threw the rope onto the quayside and tied the sleek wooden tender to the iron buoy. He remembered tying up a boat on holiday in Scotland once. On a small loch. Why had they been there on holiday? He couldn't remember. Except that his father had hired a static caravan on a wind-blown hillside. He remembered his legs being sore with nettle rash and the rain pounding on the roof as his mum and dad played gin rummy by candlelight. He remembered, too, the sunny days fishing on the loch with his dad for hours. What had they even talked about?

He shook the thought away. He didn't want to think about his family. He realized now that maybe they'd tried to get in touch with him on his birthday yesterday, but he hadn't given them a second thought as he'd been having so much fun.

He should have called his mum to tell her that he was OK. She was probably starting to worry about him, he thought, realizing that there was no way she could track him down. He hadn't been back to his flat for weeks and weeks, and he'd destroyed his old mobile phone and hadn't given his parents his new number.

He knew he ought to feel guilty about worrying her, but the more hedonistic and pleasurable his life became, the more he felt as if he could never go back to the person he'd once been. He certainly couldn't even attempt to explain to his mum and dad what had happened to him.

In a parallel universe, how stifling his life could have become, he mused. If he'd never left home or worked in the City, if he'd stayed in Yorkshire like his father had wanted. If he'd hung out with those dull, narrow-minded friends from home. If he'd had a birthday bash in the village hall, like his parents had done for his sister Gina's thirtieth – an event he'd promised to show up to, but had deliberately snubbed, spending the day watching the Grand Prix instead. He couldn't think of any worse fate.

Instead, in this his amazing new life, he'd danced through the night on a mega-yacht with sensationally beautiful models who had then fucked his brains out. Compare and contrast, he thought, smiling to himself.

He pocketed the keys, although this was such an exclusive quayside Harry doubted anyone would nick his tender. In every direction, luxury yachts were moored up. Over the road, behind the avenue of blossoming trees, he could see the row of exclusive cafes and restaurants with their pretty striped awnings. The air was filled with birdsong and the clinking of masts.

'Hey there.' Harry looked up to see a blond man calling out to him from along the quayside as he stepped off a luxury white powerboat onto the concrete. He was athletic-looking and had an American accent. He looked vaguely familiar.

'Harry, right? Francis Lordain,' the guy reminded him, as Harry approached. 'Futures desk.'

'Of course,' Harry said, inwardly swearing. This was the last place he'd expected to run into colleagues. Besides, he only remembered Francis vaguely. He'd been much more senior in America Bank than Harry.

'How you doing?' Harry said, shaking his hand.

A blonde girl now appeared at the top of the walkway to the yacht. She was wearing a large floppy hat and big designer shades. She had a kaftan top over skimpy shorts. As she walked towards them, Francis holding her hand to steady her on the quayside, Harry could see her athletic build and imagined that she was a keen tennis player. No surprise that a guy like Francis would have a hot chick like this.

'This is my wife, Annabelle,' Francis said, and Harry shook hands with her.

'You can call me Bella,' she said.

'Hi, Bella,' Harry said, but he could tell that she was obviously furious that Francis had run into a colleague, and as Francis started talking about America Bank, Harry saw her fidget with her rattan handbag, irritated. Before long the conversation had turned to Nick Grundy.

'Nick sure was a rotten apple,' Francis said. 'I mean, he was quite a character, but the whole desk went because of him. Quite a scandal, huh? Although, they hushed it up, of course.'

This was news to Harry. He'd deliberately avoided any contact with the bank – apart from the odd conversation with Cole, who was waiting for the 'right opportunity' for him, until which time Harry was on extended paid leave. He hadn't dared ask what had happened to Blake Saville or his old team. And now he knew. Dave and all the others were out of a job and Nick Grundy was totally in the shit.

'What can I tell you? He was corrupt as hell,' Harry said with a shrug.

'You don't seem to be doing so badly out of it, though?' Francis said, slapping Harry on the top of the arm.

'You know what, I have to admit life is pretty sweet,' Harry said, smiling at Bella, who raised an eyebrow in a dismissive way. It felt good to show off. Like he was a big player.

'Why don't you come over to the yacht later and have some supper?' Francis asked. 'We'd be happy to have you. Wouldn't we, Bella?' He put his hands on his hips and nodded up at the chunky powerboat next to them, as if Harry should be impressed.

Bella looked distrustful and then worried that a banker was going to cramp her style.

'I'd love to, but I'm supposed to be heading into Cannes.'

'Right. The film festival. Annabelle and I came down for a film premiere.'

'I do locations,' Bella interjected, her tone making it perfectly clear that she considered herself vastly superior to both Francis and Harry.

'Oh. So you might know Chateau Marmond, then,' Harry said.

'Yeah.' Bella laughed, like Harry was an idiot. 'Of course I do. It's, like, the holy grail of Cannes property. Why do you ask?'

'Because that's where I'm going tonight. There's some kind of private party . . .'

This news seemed like an electric shock to Bella. She took off her sunglasses and stared open-mouthed at Harry.

'The Secret Party,' she gasped. She had very pretty blue eyes and Harry felt a shimmer of desire. 'You can't mean you're going to the Secret Party? You're absolutely sure? The one with a black theme?'

'Yeah, that's the one.' Harry nodded, remembering that Reiss had given him a black shirt for his birthday and had told him to wear it tonight. He'd had no intention of going to the party, hoping that he'd be able to recover from last night on the yacht with the two Russian girls. He'd been thinking of a quiet candlelit supper in one of the chic waterside restaurants. But seeing Bella's reaction, he changed his mind.

She turned excitedly to Francis. 'My God! I heard about that party from BoBo's friend Alex. Everyone is going apparently. All the A-list. Pierre has styled it.' She turned back to reappraise Harry, putting the arm of her sunglasses in her mouth and looking him right in the eye. He held her gaze, knowing exactly what she was thinking. After all, he'd had enough women in the last few months to know what that look meant. She was considering fucking him. He stared right back, raising his eyebrow a little in a sardonic look he'd practised a few times lately.

What was happening to him? Harry wondered. The more action he got, the more he seemed to want. And women were just throwing themselves at him.

Make hay while the sun shines. Wasn't that what Reiss had said? He felt a twitch in his shorts and imagined what Bella must look like naked.

'Well, why don't you come along?' Harry said, as if it was no big deal.

'Seriously?' Bella asked, smiling now. 'But that's impossible. That party is private invite only. There's no way we could—'

'Sure there is,' Harry said, laughing. He wanted to blurt it out. That nothing was impossible for him. Not now. Not now that he had the key. Not now he knew all the people in the know. He could get just about anything he wanted.

Even her.

'Don't worry about it. I'll get you in. I'm going in the helicopter anyway, so there's plenty of room. Why don't you come for supper on my yacht instead and we'll go after that?'

It was Francis's turn to look startled, as it dawned on him that Harry had access to a helicopter.

Harry's mind fast-forwarded with logistics. He'd have to get rid of the Russian girls, he realized. But that wouldn't be a problem. He could meet them at the party, perhaps. Or maybe he'd let them go altogether. He'd already got the best he was going to get out of them. And Bella had caught his attention now.

Bella stared quizzically at Harry, not quite believing it. 'OK, then. Sure.'

'Which yacht are you on?' Francis asked.

Harry pointed to the enormous yacht moored a hundred metres away and finally understanding shone in Francis's eyes.

'That's Cole's yacht, right?' Francis said, clearly trying not to sound shocked.

'Yeah. He gave it to me for a few weeks,' Harry replied, gratified to see how impressed Francis was that he was on *Menzies' Millions*. 'I'm in the process of getting my own.'

'Lucky you.'

'Well, come and hang out and enjoy it with me,' Harry said with a smile.

'Sure. OK. We'll come at seven or so.'

'I've got to get something to wear!' Bella squealed, jumping up and down with excitement.

'You're in the right place,' Harry said, nodding over at the parade of shops.

When Bella turned to leave, she winked at him and he felt his cock twitch again.

Man, he was on a roll.

CHAPTER TWENTY-TWO

Kamiko stared through the view-finder on her camera at the front door of Martha Faust's chalet. She'd been in Gletch for the best part of the day, walking around and spying on each of the houses in the small hamlet, although most of them seemed to be empty. She'd almost given up believing that she was in the right place, but then fifteen minutes ago she'd seen Martha Faust arrive in a sleek BMW. She'd entered the chalet and the lights had gone on. Kamiko had tried to track her through the windows, using the zoom lens on her camera, but she guessed she must have gone to the back of the property. Now one of the main lights dimmed and she tensed as Martha Faust opened the front door.

Just as she'd hoped, the older woman was going out. She watched as she got quickly into her car and drove away. Kamiko snapped her on her camera.

As soon as the car had disappeared round a bend in the road, Kamiko ran across the street and up the drive. She pressed herself against the wooden boards of the tall building and edged round the garden to the back of the property.

It faced the ski slopes, though now, off-season, there were patches of grass through the thin dusting of snow. This place was clearly pretty posh. She saw a sleek cable car snaking up the hill to the station at the top.

When she was quite convinced that nobody was coming, she found a large stone and broke the side window next to the back door, smashing the glass out with her boot. Then she quickly pulled on the latex gloves she'd brought with her, reached inside and opened the back door.

Inside, the chalet was warm. She walked up the stairs, adjusting one of her gloves, though after years in the sushi factory, they felt like a second skin. She had no intention of being discovered, but it was best to be on the safe side and leave no fingerprints. She turned the handle of the door at the top and walked into the main hallway.

The hall floor had dark brown boards, polished to a high shine, with Indian silk rugs on them. The dark green walls were covered with tastefully framed artworks. A flowering orchid sat in a Chinese bowl on an ornamental table. Martha Faust's work bag – the one Kamiko had photographed her with – was next to it.

Kamiko went to it and opened it, but found only a make-up bag, which she rummaged through, unwinding a lipstick and sniffing it. She found a folder with papers she couldn't under-stand, and a glossy diary too, which she flicked through, but nothing seemed to spring out at her as useful.

The hallway opened up into an open-plan kitchen and sitting room, and walking through, Kamiko idly ran her glove over the polished white counters, wondering what it must be like to own this designer haven, with the view of the slopes outside. There was an empty bowl with a spoon and a discarded napkin on the kitchen counter, and one of the high comfortable-looking stools was out of place next to it.

Kamiko walked over to the state-of-the-art cooker, seeing some soup in a saucepan on the hob. She picked up the spoon and ate a mouthful straight from it. It was still warm, and liking the taste of the lentil and ham broth, she gobbled up several more spoonfuls until it was finished.

She left the empty pan and went to explore the living area beyond the kitchen. It had a swanky revolving wood-burning stove suspended from the ceiling, and fur throws decorated the squashy sofas. A huge picture window looked out onto a teak deck with a large wooden hot tub. Looking through another door, she saw that downstairs there was a room for skis and boots, and a sauna. This place really was some pad.

Kamiko thought back to the horrible cluttered house in Kadoma and the contrast with this understated designer elegance couldn't have been greater. She felt a surge of bitter jealousy. So Martha Faust had a job and had to work, but how did she get to have this perfect life? It wasn't fair. Kamiko wanted this for herself, and unless Martha Faust gave her another key, it would never be hers.

Again she felt a familiar sense of panic rising. The same panic she'd had since Tiko and Susi had stolen her key. The feeling that she was losing time. If this was a game, as Martha had hinted, then she had to get herself back in it. And fast. *You had to be in it to win it*. An old lottery jingle spun in her head.

Others were in it. Others were winning maybe. She didn't know how many, or who. All she knew was that they weren't her.

Going upstairs again, Kamiko found two spacious double bedrooms – rugs, throws and fireplaces in each. A single silk robe hung on the back of the en-suite bathroom door. At the end of the corridor was a closed door and Kamiko opened it to discover a study built under the eaves of the chalet, with a floor-to-ceiling glass window behind the desk. A hunting gun hung over the mantelpiece.

She walked over to the desk, looking at the sleek black computer and phone. She picked up a silver-framed photograph of Martha Faust with two men. They were all laughing. Was one of the men her husband? Kamiko wondered. Maybe the blond one, with the red scarf tied foppishly round his neck, who was looking at her in the photograph. There seemed to be no sign that Martha Faust was married or had children.

Kamiko sat at the desk chair and opened the drawers of the desk. In the bottom drawers, there were some neat folders filled with bills and correspondence, but the top three were locked. Curious, Kamiko took out the Swiss army knife she'd bought at the small shop round the corner from her hotel in Zurich last night and picked the locks, prizing open the drawers.

She went through each drawer, starting with the bottom one. It was full of papers and a packet of photographs, but they were all of a building site. Perhaps they were of this house being built.

In the second drawer, Kamiko found a folder containing legal-looking documents, written in German. She suspected that it was a copy of Martha Faust's life insurance and will.

In the top drawer, there was nothing, apart from a few pens and odd trinkets. Kamiko reached right inside, noticing that the back of the drawer dipped down slightly. Which meant that the front of it had to have a false bottom. Prising the base of the drawer away from the side, she lifted the green felt-covered panel and slid her hand into the dark gap. There was nothing there. Then, just as she was about to withdraw her hand, the tip of her latex glove connected with something that felt like metal.

She scrabbled around, stretching her fingers, until she'd got the object. She pulled it out. It was a heavy, old-fashioned key.

She turned the key over in her palm, wondering why it had been hidden in the false bottom of a locked drawer.

It must be a key to a safe.

Kamiko's eyes scanned the room, thinking as logically as she could; then she got out of her seat to explore. Think. If I was programming this room, where would I put the safe?

The safe was under an oil painting of glens and mountains in the corner alcove next to the fireplace. The old-fashioned contraption that was buried in the wall clunked open as she turned the key. Inside was a black velvet box containing a very sparkly diamond necklace and bracelet. Kamiko took them both out, holding them up to the light, seeing the pattern they threw on the wall. They must be worth a fortune.

She remembered the note that she'd found in Shikego's wedding suit. The one she still had in her backpack. Her uncle Murushi had been something to do with diamonds. Perhaps if she found Murushi and gave him this necklace, he would be able to tell her how much it was worth.

The thought of stealing something so valuable filled her with a strange and thrilling fear. She'd stolen things before, of course. All the time. Money from Shikego, sweets from her half-brother, Hiroshi. Stealing an expensive diamond necklace and bracelet, though, was in a different league.

Then she remembered her meeting with Martha Faust. The woman who'd refused to give her another key, or tell her the truth. Yes, Kamiko deserved something if she wasn't going to get another key. Something to secure her future.

She stuffed the necklace and bracelet in the pocket of her jacket, putting the black box back in the safe, which is when she noticed that there was something else at the back. It felt like a folder, but she couldn't reach it.

Kamiko looked around her, trying to find something to stand on, finally hoisting herself up using the mantelpiece and throwing herself forward towards the safe. Using the momentum she had, she shoved her hand into the safe and pulled out the folder.

She'd got it, but no sooner than she had, it fell out of her grip, papers cascading to the floor.

Cursing, she bent down to pick them up. Which is when she saw the photograph and her breath caught in her throat.

The photo was of her.

It was stuck to a piece of paper with Kamiko's name and address on it and details of her job at the factory. She stared at the photograph of herself. It had been taken recently. But where? She was staring out into the middle distance and Kamiko realized she'd been photographed on the monorail that she'd taken every morning to the sushi factory. But who had taken this picture? And why?

Her hands were shaking as she stared at the picture. Here was evidence. Evidence that Martha Faust not only knew who she was, but was concerned enough to lock her details in the safe.

She grabbed the folder. Nothing was written on the plain brown card. Quickly she scrabbled around on the floor and picked up the other pieces of paper. Four others. Four other profiles just like hers.

She laid them out over the carpet, staring at the other people who had shared the safe with her. Were they key-holders too? They must be. Four others. That was it.

Her mind raced over the implications of this find. Four others. That meant almost certainly one or more had got ahead.

What had they claimed from the key? Were they all living a life of luxury already? Had they got way ahead of her?

She picked up the sheet nearest her and studied the picture of a woman from New York. Scooter Black. She looked like an actress, Kamiko thought. Stuck-up. A show-off.

She grabbed the next page. Then there was a girl with dark, exotic features and long wavy dark hair. *Julia Pires*, she read. In Rio.

Rio? As far away as Rio?

What on earth connected her and this girl from Rio and the girl from New York? It didn't make sense.

Then there was a man who looked like a boring commuter in a suit with a frown on his face, Harry Cassidy. And another man who had the shadow of a beard and was very suntanned. *Christian Erickson*, she read, *last stationed in Africa*. She flicked over the papers again, memorizing their faces.

So these people were her rivals. And the game was global. Her heart raced with the magnitude of this information. But it was a game, she remembered. And now she knew what she was up against, she felt a plan starting to form. Because if she was going to be denied her key, then what if her rivals were denied theirs too? Wouldn't that level the playing field? Wouldn't that make the people behind all this come forward and reveal themselves? And she could get to them all now she knew who they were and where they lived. They wouldn't be hard to find at all.

To find . . . and to take out. One by one . . .

Kamiko was so absorbed in the strategy forming in her head that she jumped when she saw car lights flash over the paper and realized that the light had faded. She'd thought Martha Faust had gone for the evening, but now she heard the car stop outside the chalet and its door slam. Kamiko shrank back against the wall, willing the shadows to swallow her up, as she heard the front door open downstairs.

Outside, it had started to rain. Kamiko looked at the spatters on the window, her mind whirring. Martha Faust couldn't be home already, could she? Kamiko cursed herself for getting carried away and looking around the house. She'd assumed she had plenty of time, thinking that Martha would be gone for hours, but now she realized what a stupid assumption she'd made. Maybe Martha had only been going on an errand. Or maybe she'd cancelled her plans altogether for this evening. And now Kamiko was trapped. How long would it be before Martha discovered the broken back window, or the empty soup pan? How long before she raised the alarm?

Kamiko quickly shut the safe and put the oil painting back on the wall in front of it.

She could hear the front door unlocking and then Martha Faust talking on the phone in German. Her voice was light, and she laughed occasionally. She could hear her in the kitchen, the fridge door opening and closing. Then she heard her end the call and the squeak and pop of a cork coming out of a bottle, then the glug of liquid in a glass.

Kamiko strained her ears, wondering whether she'd seen the empty pan, but Martha came quickly upstairs, humming to herself. She crossed the open doorway and walked along the corridor into the bedroom. Kamiko saw light spill out into the hallway as she turned on the bedroom light.

Kamiko crouched beneath the desk, listening to the hiss of the shower, then wardrobe doors opening and closing. She felt her legs cramping in the small space, but she didn't dare move. There was no way she could get into the corridor and downstairs without risking Martha catching her.

She forced herself to stay silent, although her heart was thumping so hard she could almost hear it.

Stay still. Be invisible. She'll go out in a minute and then I can slink away and figure out what this all means.

A slice of light crept across the Indian silk rug in the study. Kamiko made the toes of her black boots shrink back from it. She saw in the reflection of the glass Martha Faust hovering in the doorway, fastening an earring, before shrugging her shoulders into a thick fur-collared brown suede coat.

Kamiko willed her to close the door again, but then, clearly remembering something, Martha stepped inside the study and turned on the overhead light. Kamiko held her breath. If Martha Faust came behind the desk, she'd see her . . .

She watched the reflection in the window, seeing the older woman walking across the carpet, nearer and nearer to the desk. She was still humming to herself and fastening an earring. She leaned over and picked up a piece of paper with some writing on it from the pad by the phone. Then she stopped and Kamiko realized that the side drawer wasn't closed properly. The one that had contained the safe key.

Martha Faust rushed round the desk and pulled open the drawer.

And then it happened. Their eyes met.

She jumped back and screamed when she saw Kamiko crouching beneath her desk.

'You! It's you!' she cried, her hand splaying on her chest as she backed away. 'What are you doing? What are you doing in my home?'

Kamiko lurched forward from underneath the desk, holding out her hands, as if to tame a wild animal, but she couldn't explain, and as Martha's eyes stared into hers, she could see how angry and threatened the otherwise-composed woman felt. Her eyes were wide with terror.

She backed towards the fireplace and reached above it for the hunting gun. In a second she'd grabbed it and held out the cumbersome weapon, pointing it towards Kamiko as she stood up.

'Get out,' she commanded. 'Before I call the police. How dare you break into my home?'

'Tell me,' Kamiko said, scooting down and picking up the brown folder from the carpet by the desk. 'Why have you got this? Who are other people?'

Martha's face was ashen with fear. 'Get off that!' she shouted desperately, reaching for the folder, but Kamiko was quicker. She snatched up the file above her head. 'Give it to me!' Martha Faust was furious now. Her arm came up to grab the folder, but Kamiko stopped her, her hand catching Martha Faust's chin. She fell backwards, dropping the gun.

Kamiko saw it skid away towards the window and, leaving the folder, lunged for it and snatched it. She reached it at the same time as the older woman, but Kamiko had a stronger grip. She wrestled it away from her.

'Let it go,' Martha Faust shouted. 'Let go.'

She grabbed hold of the barrel of the gun, trying to wrench it free of Kamiko's grasp.

Bang.

The noise of the gun was so loud Kamiko's ears rang. A split second later Martha Faust fell away, gasping in shock and pain. Kamiko recoiled, horrified that the gun had gone off.

Martha Faust continued to back away, clutching her stomach. Blood seeped between her fingers. She looked at the gunshot wound and then at Kamiko, who was still holding the gun, her hands shaking. She looked startled, then disbelieving.

Kamiko stared, unblinking. She hadn't meant to shoot her. This shouldn't be happening. Why did she even have a loaded gun in her study?

She dropped the gun, which went off again, making both women jump. This time the bullet went through the plate-glass window. An unpleasant creak started as a crack ran up the glass, like a fissure through an ice sheet.

'Call an ambulance,' Martha managed, through clenched teeth. 'Use the phone on the desk.'

Kamiko stared at the woman on the floor, scrabbling backwards now to prop herself up against the wall. She was shivering, her teeth chattering, despite the thick suede coat she was wearing.

Kamiko stared at the blood, transfixed by the deep red liquid seeping out. An unstoppable life force flowing away, free. It was beautiful.

She could see her own reflection in the cracked glass and Martha Faust on the floor. What had passed in the last few moments was so dramatic she felt as if she was watching herself on a stage and this was some kind of play into which she'd unwittingly stumbled centre stage.

Martha Faust coughed and then groaned. The blood was blooming into a dark stain on the rug. There was so much of it.

'Please. I could die of a gunshot wound like this. I will bleed to death without an ambulance,' she said, her voice a rasp. 'Quickly. You must be quick.'

Kamiko's hand hovered above the phone.

'First, you tell me. Why I given key? Tell me and I call you ambulance.'

Martha Faust's disbelieving eyes stared into hers as she realized that Kamiko was serious.

'I know that you have been chosen. Along with the others.'

'Chosen for what?'

'It's a test.'

'What kind of test?'

'One where there can only be one winner.'

She was right. Just as she'd suspected. This was all a game. Kamiko smiled. She couldn't help herself. In spite of the blood. In spite of the insanity of the situation she found herself in. She knew she'd been right all along. This whole silver key thing. It was a game. And now she knew the other players.

But she was the best game player she knew.

Martha Faust gasped. 'Help me,' she mouthed, but she fell backwards onto the rug, writhing for a moment, her breath rasping in agony.

Then she clutched at her chest, still gasping. A moment later she was still. Her eyes stayed open, her cheeks smeared with her own blood from the rug.

Kamiko stared at her. She stepped cautiously towards her and prodded her gently with the toe of her boot, but Martha didn't move. Her eyes were open. Dead-fish eyes already. Like the tuna in the cold room in the sushi factory.

Behind Kamiko, the glass continued creaking, then broke into a million pieces.

Shaking, Kamiko grabbed the folder from the desk and ran out of the room. As she slammed the study door behind her, she heard the wall of glass shatter to the floor.

CHAPTER TWENTY-THREE

On the famous Rio boulevard running the length of Ipanema Beach, Christian watched Julia as she took the coconuts with straws poking out of the top from the stallholder. The stallholder, dressed in a yellow vest, was deeply tanned and was talking in rapid Portuguese, pointing at the machete he'd chopped the coconuts with between Julia and Christian.

Although Christian didn't understand a word, from Julia's reaction he suspected that the man was asking if he and Julia were a couple. Or more likely, judging from the flirtatious twinkle in the man's eye, he was suggesting that Christian was lucky to be with someone as undeniably beautiful as Julia.

Julia didn't explain, but she rolled her eyes and smiled as she turned to Christian. She handed him a coconut.

'Cheers,' she said, flicking her dark hair away from her face so that she could put her lips round the straw. Christian had to rip his eyes away from the sheen of perspiration on her unblemished chest and concentrate on drinking the delicious fresh milk himself. It was hard not to stare at her. Just the way she was standing, the warm, gentle breeze blowing her skirt, filled him with an unfamiliar sensation – both of longing and awe.

Ever since he'd first set eyes on her on the train up to the

Cristo Redentor statue yesterday, Christian hadn't been able to get Julia out of his head. Last night he'd plucked up the courage to call the number she'd given him. They'd ended up talking for an hour. When she'd rung off, having agreed to meet him today, he'd hugged the phone and punched the air. And afterwards, for the first time since he'd left Africa, he'd fallen into a deep, happy sleep.

What was happening to him? He'd had his fair share of passing flings in Africa, of course, with a couple of the female doctors and aid workers he'd met, but they'd always fizzled out and gone nowhere. Misery, poverty, drought and a complete lack of privacy were fairly big passion-killers. But here, everything was different. Here, the atmosphere buzzed with life and passion. It was difficult not to be intoxicated by it.

He followed Julia now, as she walked towards the railings where they'd propped their hired bikes.

'There's so many people,' Christian said, looking across Ipanema.

'We Cariocas sure love the beach,' Julia replied, following his gaze to the esplanade, where the joggers and skaters whizzed past, then on to the expanse of sand beyond, where the shouts from the volleyball crowd mixed with samba music from a big beatbox and the laughter of children.

Julia pointed out the 'beautiful people', as she described them, crowded around the *calçadão* – the long wooden footway along the beach – totally unaware of personal space, just happy to be on the beach and having a party. Young women with smooth brown skin in tiny bikinis flirted with boys in the briefest of briefs, everyone posing and happily flaunting their bodies. In the distance, way out to sea, surfers caught the long breaking waves.

'The beach is all to do with status,' Julia explained to Christian. 'Up there you have the beautiful people. Then the revolutionaries. Then the gays. Then the artists,' she continued.

'Where do you go if you're a gay artist?' he asked.

'In between, I guess,' Julia said, smiling at him.

He loved the little overlap of her front two teeth, her lustrous full lips and the freckles on her nose.

'We have a phrase in Rio,' she continued. 'It means "Where do you hang out on the beach?" It says a lot about a person.'

'I see. And where do you hang out on the beach?' Christian asked.

'I don't.'

'But you must do, with this on your doorstep.'

'You think all we do is hang out in bikinis playing beach volleyball all day long?' Julia asked, laughing. 'I am *far* too busy.'

From what she'd told him already, Christian suspected that Julia was a workaholic, but he understood more than most how a job could be all consuming. It was yet another thing they had in common. He could tell what a great teacher she was just from the way she'd interacted with those kids. They all clearly adored her. And why wouldn't they? She was young and beautiful and passionate.

The fact that she was so busy made him even more grateful that she'd agreed to come to the beach with him today. He wondered whether it felt strange for her to be doing this – being a tourist on his account, explaining this place, showing him the ropes. It had been his idea to come here. On a date. He hadn't actually put it that way when he'd suggested it. 'A trip' were the words he'd chosen, not wanting to scare her off. He was still unsure of how she felt about him.

Did she *like* him or just like him? He hoped it was the

former. He hoped this was the start of something, not the end.

God, he thought, smiling to himself, he really was out of practice where women and romance were concerned. Just take it easy. Be yourself. Accept that what will be will be, he cautioned himself.

'Are you OK?' she asked, smiling at him curiously, making him suddenly fear he had just spoken his thoughts out loud.

He felt himself blushing and took another sip of his drink.

'Sure, sure, just feeling the heat, that's all,' he said.

She finished her coconut, put it in the bin and went to get back on her bike, ready to cycle away.

'Good,' she said. 'Just as long as you're enjoying our' – and there, did he detect a mischievous glint in her eyes? – 'trip so far.'

Trip. The way she said it, the emphasis and irony she'd put on it. He felt himself blush again, realizing that she'd understood that this was a date right from the start. Even better, then, that she'd said yes. She'd decided to come.

'Come on,' she told him. 'There's so much more I want to show you.'

They cycled further along the boulevard until they spotted some space on the sand near the water's edge. Weaving through the crowd, they spread out the beach towels they'd brought. Julia unpacked a picnic from her bag.

As they chatted, he told her about his time in South America so far. How he'd rubbed along with a group of European climbers for a while in Chile before coming to Brazil. How he'd immediately warmed to the chilled-out vibe.

'That said, when I first got here, I took a tour up to the favelas,' Christian told her, remembering his ride on the cable car.

'You did?'

'Some of those places up there scared me. I've been so used to poverty in Africa, but urban poverty is somehow so much worse. I can't imagine how grim it must be living there.'

'You'd be surprised how many people do,' Julia said in a small voice.

She seemed so caring towards other people, Christian thought.

Was he boring her? he wondered. He should be the fun guy, after all, not come across all heavy and judgemental about the city she lived in. He quickly changed the subject.

'That salad looks good,' he said, examining the bowl of tomatoes and peppers.

'It's my grandmother's recipe. We always used to bring it to the beach at the weekend when we were kids,' Julia replied, taking off her dress to reveal the light blue bikini beneath.

Christian had to stop himself from staring at her. She was so curvy and exotic and yet she seemed to be completely unaware of it.

'It feels good to be here,' she said with a happy sigh, offering her face up to the sun. 'I haven't done this for so long,' she said.

As she started rubbing sun lotion on her long legs, he wished he could grab the bottle and do it himself. He ached to touch her. God, the heat really was getting to him. He never normally fell for people this quickly. Or maybe it wasn't the heat at all. Or this crazily beautiful country. Maybe it was just her.

'Are you not hot?' she said, catching him staring.

He was wearing shorts, a T-shirt and a baseball cap. Was her question merely pragmatic, he wondered, or something else? Had she asked it because she felt disadvantaged, dressed as she was, or because she was curious to see what he looked like?

Well, nothing ventured, nothing gained. He stood, a little

self-conscious among all the perfectly tanned and toned bodies around him, and pulled off his T-shirt, sucking in his belly. He was in reasonable shape, thanks to a daily routine of crunches and press-ups, and he wasn't as pasty and white as some of the other European tourists he'd seen dotted around, but even so, he hoped she liked what she saw and wasn't disappointed.

Everyone else here – the locals – were so *professional* about this beach scene.

But as he stepped out of his shorts, revealing his bathing trunks beneath, he saw she wasn't even looking, but busy with the picnic bag instead. And as he sat down, she asked him about what food he liked and he forgot all thought of how she might be judging him. Instead, he relaxed.

He forced himself to look only at her face as they talked. And the more he did, the more he found himself looking into her dark green eyes, and the easier the conversation flowed. In fact, he found himself opening up to Julia in a way that he hadn't done to anyone in years. The way she looked at him when he talked made him feel for the first time as if he was being really listened to. He told her about his life as a doctor and his adventures in Africa, not trying to make it sound as impressive as he might have done, but compelled instead to be honest.

The only subjects that did cross his mind but he kept to himself were his encounter with Colonel Adid and how he'd subsequently been fired from Afri-Aid. And he certainly didn't tell her about the key.

The colonel's threat had faded since he'd been in South America, but it was always there in the back of Christian's mind. He still hoped that if he could just lie low for a while, then the whole thing would blow over.

Forget the key, he told himself. And all it stood for. Because who needed luxury, or an upgrade, when the promise of real happiness was right here in front of him? No, he concluded, even the richest billionaire in the world could not buy this feeling of happiness, this hope.

'Shall we swim?' he asked her, nodding at the sea.

They swam out chatting easily, the warm waves rippling around them. Then the water suddenly got deeper. Christian caught Julia when a wave broke over her. For a moment he held her in his arms, her legs against his. He could see the sun sparkling in the droplets on her nose as she laughed. He imagined her legs wrapped round his waist. He pictured her leaning in towards him and pressing her lips against his.

But then the swell of a fresh wave lifted Julia up and away from him. And the moment had gone.

They stayed on the beach for hours afterwards, the time melting away as they chatted and ate ice cream. Then Christian suggested that they head to a bar. He was worried that Julia might make a fuss and insist on going home to change and wash her hair, after everything she'd told him about the high-maintenance women of Rio, but she simply took a shower on the beach and dried off before putting her red dress back on.

Without make-up, her hair damp and curly from the sea, she took his breath away. How could it be, he wondered, that someone stripped of all their feminine artifice could be even more astonishing to behold? And that's when he realized what it was that had first drawn him to her: the openness in her eyes. A confidence that she liked who she was – and that this was enough.

They took the bikes back to the hire shack; then Julia suggested that they take a tram to the Santa Teresa district, where she knew a bar that did the best caipirinhas in Rio.

He'd been expecting her to take him to a sophisticated bar, but she led him into a tiny backstreet neighbourhood that he'd never have found without her. He felt as if he'd broken through into the real Rio. She pointed out the bar in the pretty cobbled square, but told him first she wanted to show him the Portuguese church.

As the evening sun shone through the stained-glass windows, illuminating the gold statues with shards of sparkling dusk, they slipped into a pew and sat side by side, their legs touching, as Julia told him about coming to the church as a child.

'Vovo, my grandmother, has always been very superstitious. She believes in good and evil forces,' Julia told him.

'And do you?'

'Not really. I'm not particularly religious any more. I used to be. The Catholic guilt has stayed, but little else. What about you?'

'Being a doctor makes you question religion. It makes you pragmatic. No matter what God people believe in, faith sometimes seems misguided and foolish when you see so much suffering. I've never been sure that faith brings the comfort people say it does,' he admitted, thinking of the villagers he'd seen that fatal day, shuddering when he remembered the women and the children in the gruesome makeshift hospital. 'I'm just not sure about doctrine for doctrine's sake,' he continued. 'But I guess that's because my father is a minister. He and my mother fell out about it.'

Why was he telling her this? He hadn't told anyone about that before. Because he couldn't stop himself? Because he felt it a duty to respond to her openness with his own? Because he felt he could tell her anything? Almost.

'So what do you believe in, then, Doctor?' she asked, her eyes shining. 'If you don't believe in gods or spirits or Fate,'

'I never said I didn't believe in Fate,' Christian said, surprised by the words even as they came out, but nonetheless knowing they were true. Because today, yes, he could believe in Fate. He'd believe in anything if it could make a day like today come true.

Back out in the square, they sat at a small table outside the old-fashioned bar and ordered another drink while Christian looked around, soaking up the atmosphere. Inside, a crowd of old men were gathered at the bar watching the TV high on the wall where a football match was showing, the volume turned up loud. A couple of little girls in pretty white dresses came out of a pastel-coloured house along the street and placed a small puppy down.

The boom of a microphone and the strum of some chords on a guitar signalled a small band setting up across the square. Old ladies appeared in doorways, bringing chairs out with them and gathering in groups. Darkness was closing in. Lights like strings of pearls glimmered in the black trees.

'I love it here,' Christian told Julia, smiling. 'I love all this architecture. I would never have known it was here unless you'd brought me. I could live here.'

He knew it sounded stupid, but he meant it. Why not? Why not set up a new life here? He could find work, couldn't he? And those people he'd seen in the favelas? They could do with his help, couldn't they? There must be a charity who could take him on.

Julia laughed. 'It's a bit haphazard, isn't it?' she asked, finishing her drink and eating the leaf of mint from the top. 'Don't you like all that minimalist architecture in Scandinavia?'

'It's not for me,' Christian said. 'It's been so long since I've had a proper home I wonder what it would feel like now.'

'Home is an attitude, isn't it? More than a place,' Julia said. 'That's what my grandmother always said.'

'Will you take me to your home?' he asked.

'Mine?'

'Yes.' Christian smiled, reaching out for her hand across the table and holding it. He was shocked that he'd so spontaneously taken her hand in his. It had seemed so natural. But now he looked down at their hands touching and wondered how she felt about it. He didn't pull away. And neither did she.

'I'd love to see where you live. Meet Marcello and Fredo. They sound wonderful.'

Julia bit her lip. 'But . . . it's not what you'll be expecting,' she began, withdrawing her hand.

Christian couldn't understand her reaction. Maybe he'd pushed it too far. Maybe it was too soon for him to have taken her hand. No, he sensed it. There was something else. A darkening of her eyes, as if, for the first time, he'd stumbled on something she wanted to conceal.

What was it? Something about her family? Her grandmother? He felt a tremor of doubt.

'If this is the moment when you're going to mention that you're mother to six wonderful kids, then please just do it as quickly as you can.'

'No.' She smiled, but it was a sad smile. 'No, it's not that.'

'Then what? I don't have any expectations, believe me. I just want to know about your life. See your home. I mean, it can't be that bad, can it? It's not as if you live in a slum or anything.'

Julia took a sip of her drink. She didn't look at him and she didn't smile.

'Why don't we dance? Come on,' she said, standing up.

'I can't,' Christian said, stalling, astonished and confused that she'd changed the subject so abruptly. 'I mean, not properly.'

'Yes, you can. I'll show you.'

Julia ran ahead under the coloured lights looping from the trees. Then she stopped and danced, her hips swaying in her red dress, her feet moving in time to the gravel-smooth voice of the old guy who was singing with the guitarists. He smiled when he saw Julia had taken centre stage on the cobbles and was beckoning Christian towards her.

She was so ethereal, he thought. Just when he'd got more intimate with her, she slipped away, but it only made him long for her more. Was this what it felt like, he wondered, to really fall for someone?

Because yes, he'd had relationships before, and yes, he'd convinced himself before that he might have been in love. But none of that compared to how he felt right now, as he walked across the square to join her. The music, the rum, the look in her eyes left him feeling heady, as if each of his senses was insanely heightened. He felt completely present. Completely alive.

She placed herself in his arms, putting his hand on her waist. He felt her hips press against his and he stepped back. 'That's it,' she cajoled. 'You got it,' she said, guiding him round. 'That's it – forward back, one, two, three.'

His hips moulded against hers, her slim thigh between his legs, her hand on the small of his back. The voices of the singers seemed to resonate inside him, until he felt himself becoming one with the music, with Julia.

'Shall we do it? Shall we try a spin?' he asked, noticing the other couples who had joined in.

She twirled away from him and then back into his arms. He

crossed his arms in front of her, feeling how she felt pressed up against him. When the song finished and they applauded, neither of them made a move to sit down. The old guys nodded to the crowd and upped the tempo.

Soon the street party was in full swing and Christian was laughing and twirling Julia away from him and spinning her back into his arms.

Whatever he'd felt before . . . that sense of belonging to this place . . . and to her, it had now morphed into something else, something less profound but equally wonderful. He was having fun. Real fun. Forgetting about everything else. The kind of fun he hadn't had in years. The kind of fun he'd thought he'd never have again.

'You're good,' she said approvingly, after a few more dances. 'A fast learner.'

He held her in his arms, her face close to his.

'Do you know something?' he whispered in her ear.

'What?' she asked, pulling away slightly and staring up at him smiling.

'I've been wanting to do something all day, but I don't think I can wait any longer.'

'What?' she asked, but her eyes told him that she knew. She moved her chin forward slightly towards his. And then their lips were touching.

CHAPTER TWENTY-FOUR

In the bordello-themed 'glamour booth' just inside the entrance to Chateau Marmond, Scooter smiled as Barney walked round her, clicking the shutter of his camera. He'd rigged up lights and a backdrop in order to photograph the guests as they arrived in an area immediately inside the grand front entrance. It was just one tiny aspect of the party Pierre and his team had planned.

In a moment Scooter herself would make her grand entrance to the party. She could already hear voices and music. Trudi must have started her first set on the decks in the ornamental flower garden, which was now a funky dance area, the flowerbeds encased below a Perspex dance floor.

'You're sure it's not too over the top?' she asked Barney, fanning out the skirt of her strapless dress.

'You can't be too over the top. It's your party. You can wear what you want. And, honey, if you're ever going to wear vintage Armani, then tonight is the night. Especially when you look as sensational as this.' He paused, inspecting the back of his camera. 'See?'

Scooter squinted over his shoulder at the screen on his camera. She hardly recognized herself. BoBo had done her usual magic with her hair, piling it into a big up-do, the few highlights she'd put in earlier accentuating her flame-red locks. Her eyes were perfectly made up with dark kohl, and the jet necklace showed off her freckly shoulders.

'Ahhh . . . there you are,' Pierre said, appearing with two glasses of champagne. 'The belle of the ball.'

He strode across the black carpet into the lights and kissed Scooter on both cheeks before handing her a glass. Barney snapped the moment.

'Sensational,' Pierre said, admiring her strapless ball gown, and she could tell he meant it. She flushed at the compliment. According to Heidi, Pierre was nothing if not frugal with his praise.

She touched her glass with his and smiled, thinking that the famous party planner looked pretty sensational himself. He was wearing black leather trousers and a sequinned black shirt and had a fascinator in his hair. He looked just as theatrical as the rest of the party he'd created.

'To a night of magic, darling,' he said.

'A night of magic,' she replied. 'Shit, I'm nervous.'

'Don't be. Tonight will be *fantastique*,' he assured her. 'It already is.'

'But what if everyone—' she began, but stopped herself. What if everyone found out what a fraud she was? she wanted to say. What if anyone found out that none of this was real? That she had no idea who was paying for it?

She couldn't think about that. It was too scary. And she was in way too deep to do anything but bluff her way through.

'Be yourself,' Pierre reassured her. 'Do what you do best: be completely up front with everyone. It's what makes you so special, darling. And for goodness' sake, Scooter, *enjoy yourself.*'

Yes. Pierre was right, Scooter thought, as she stopped in the grand hallway with him. Everyone else was enjoying her spectacular party and she damn well would too.

Through the back doors, the gardens were lit up in theatrical blue, for now, but she couldn't wait for her guests to see the laser show over the entire building later on. Around the pool, there were already fifty or so guests enjoying the sumptuous canapés that were being served by the masked waiters and waitresses.

Flares lit the path from the pool to where the black circus marquee had been erected for the spectacular acrobatic show, the troupe having been flown in from Vegas just for tonight. The trapeze artistes with their feather headdresses walked past the open flap inside the tents.

Out through the front door, another helicopter was landing in the garden. She saw two men and a very pretty blonde girl protecting their heads and ducking from the rotors, laughing and running towards the house. It was as if Chateau Marmond was a magnet and all the beautiful people were drawn to it.

As nine o'clock approached, more and more limos arrived and she saw Kirsten, Robert and Keira step out onto the gravel. Inside, Barney stopped them, luring them into his glamour booth for a shot. Scooter could tell he was having a ball. Not only that, she thought, those exclusive shots of the celebrities would be worth a fortune.

Scooter wondered what havoc the Secret Party was causing down in Cannes. Looking around, it seemed that already everyone who should be at Dean's film premiere was here, including Daniel Torene, the lead actor, who was at the roulette table in the drawing-room casino with Jay.

What would Dean say if he could see her now? Scooter wondered. She thought about how often she'd rehearsed her showdown with him in her head. How she'd tell him exactly what she thought of him and spell it out how much he'd hurt her. When they'd first started planning the party, she'd secretly hoped that Dean would come along. Now she prayed that he stayed away, and that Mona heeded Jay's warning. She didn't want Dean to ruin her night.

Besides, she couldn't help looking out for Dallas Laney. He would come, wouldn't he? She felt a bubble of childish excitement at the thought of seeing him again. Then she told herself to stop being ridiculous. He was Dallas Laney. He was so far out of her league it wasn't true.

'Hey, how you doing?' a guy in a black tuxedo asked her, walking over to her as she stood by the pool talking to Declan, who squeezed her arm and moved away.

The man was short and balding and was sucking on a cigar. Scooter would have recognized him anywhere. It was the famous producer Brody Myers.

'We haven't met before, have we?' he asked, as she introduced herself and they shook hands. They both took an espresso martini from the tray being proffered by one of the handsome waiters. It sure had been a whole heap of fun deciding on the black-themed cocktails, and they were certainly going down well with the guests.

'We nearly did. I was waiting to audition for you in New York a few months back, but Lindy somehow got in front of me and—'

'Oh,' Brody Myers said, his bushy eyebrows crinkling together. 'Well, I'm not sure how that happened.'

'It was annoying because Miranda, my *ex*-agent, said that Magnus loved my work and—'

'Magnus Miles? That buffoon? He doesn't have a clue. I fired him off the project ages ago.'

This was news to Scooter. Why hadn't Miranda just come clean and told her that Magnus had gone? All that energy . . . all those hopes. She realized now she'd been utterly out of the loop. She had been forever. Until now.

'I'm sorry I didn't see you,' Brody said. He sounded genuine. 'That was bad timing. We cast Lindy.'

'I know.' Scooter shrugged.

Brody Myers gave her a quizzical look. 'Oh? You don't think that's a good idea?'

'Not particularly,' Scooter said, remembering what Pierre had told her. It felt so empowering just telling the truth. And she could. Because this was her party. And that made her in charge. She felt confidence surging through her. She was going to grab this opportunity with both hands. The key had got her so far, but the free ride might not last forever, which meant she needed to get a job. And here it was, her chance. Right in front of her.

'When I read the script, I thought it would work so much better in another setting. Take the characters out of the city and put them somewhere small-town and make them – I don't know – older. More real. Then the dynamic with Ed works much better. Especially if you cast a heavyweight in that role, like a Clooney.'

Brody chuckled in surprise at her suggestions, but they were interrupted by several guests who came up to congratulate Scooter on her party. She could feel Brody Myers watching her.

'Scooter, let me cut to the chase,' he said, when they were on their own again. 'Have you ever considered producing?'

'Anything other than a kick-ass party?' she said with a smile.

'Seriously. I'm thinking about movies. You think in just the right way. You're smart too. I can see that.'

Scooter smiled. The great Brody Myers was flattering *her*.

'Listen – why don't you co-produce with me? Alter the script like you just said.'

'What? Just like that?'

He leaned in close. 'You've got the key, right?'

How had he found that out?

'You have no idea how lucky you are or how far you could go. They say Spielberg has one . . .' he said. He widened his eyes and let his comment hang in the air. His look said that the sky was the limit if she played it right.

'Scooter, come on, the burlesque show's going to be on in a second,' Declan called.

'I'm coming,' she called back.

And then she saw him: Dallas Laney was standing on the terrace overlooking the pool.

Scooter smoothed down her dress as she approached Dallas, biting back her smile. He was wearing a pair of designer black trousers and a black shirt with a loose white silk tie. He was scanning the crowd below. Was he looking for her?

'Hey, you,' she said, surprising him. 'Having fun?'

'Wow,' he exclaimed, his face lighting up. He paused, choosing his words carefully. 'If I may say so, you look . . . just beautiful.'

She was glad then that she'd chosen this dress. She did a mock curtsey. 'Why, thank you, kind sir,' she laughed. Wow. Dallas Laney had just told her she looked beautiful. And he meant it.

'It sure is a good turnout for a secret party,' he said. 'You having fun?'

She was *now*.

'Of course,' she replied. 'The trapeze show is on in a minute and then the bands start. We'll have to go down and dance.' She smiled at him, but she made no move to go. She could stand here all night staring at him.

There was a beat between them as their eyes met and then he looked down at his drink.

'Listen, I was thinking . . .' he said, rubbing the side of his face. 'Do you want me to talk to my agent about taking you on? He owes me, and I think he'd work well for you.'

Scooter knew that he was repped by John Cross, the most uber-powerful Hollywood agent there was. Who also happened to be the head of YMC. The agency that had ceremoniously dumped her after their party.

First Brody's offer and now this. Scooter's head was reeling.

'That's sweet of you, but after my little outburst at their party, YMC don't want anything more to do with me.'

'They don't mean that,' Dallas said. 'Agents change their minds the whole time.'

'Maybe, but I've an interesting offer from Brody Myers.'

'What?' she asked, picking up on the flash of disapproval on his face. Did he know something she didn't?

'Nothing.'

'What? You don't think I can handle Brody Myers?'

'I didn't say that.'

'You didn't need to.' She laughed.

There was another moment as their eyes connected. She raised her eyebrow quizzically.

He took a sip of his cocktail. He was clearly not going to tell her what he thought about Brody. Instead, he changed the subject.

'You know, I haven't met anyone like you before.'

'Oh really?' She couldn't keep the twinge of sarcasm from

her voice, but she immediately regretted it. He wasn't teasing her. He was being serious.

'You know – someone who is so confident and secure in who they are.'

Scooter shook her head. If only he knew.

'You just seem honest, and honesty, believe me, it's a rare thing. Especially in this game. And . . .' He paused and she thought he looked bashful. He covered it by taking a sip of his champagne. 'It's nice to find someone to chat to, you know.'

'How so?' she asked, stepping in closer, enjoying this intimate moment beneath the stars.

'Well, once upon a time I was just a regular guy from Detroit. With bad hair and bad breath, no doubt. But since all this fame thing, it's like . . . I don't know, it sounds ungrateful, but people don't really want to talk to me. They just want to stare. It makes me feel like a freak.'

Scooter cast her eyes down and smiled. That was exactly what *she* was doing.

'You can't complain,' she told him. 'You're Dallas Laney. International heartthrob.'

He rolled his eyes, embarrassed. 'Really, it's not that easy . . .'

'Are you seriously trying to tell me that your life isn't completely peachy perfect? You're rich and handsome and could date anyone you pleased in the whole world.'

'That's not necessarily true,' he interjected.

'OK, so I get it might be stressful. All the media pressure, yada, yada,' she said. 'But you're a man. It's a piece of cake for you.'

'I see. I stand corrected,' he said. 'And slightly told off.'

'It would be a travesty if someone like you didn't realize how lucky they really are,' Scooter told him.

He nodded, then took a little intake of breath.

'Would you go out to dinner with me? After all this Cannes madness is over?' he asked. 'That would make me feel lucky.'

He was asking her out. Dallas Laney was *asking her out*. Scooter's heart was thumping so hard she wondered if he could hear it. And he was being genuine. He wanted to take her out to dinner. Like a grown-up. Like he wanted it to be the start of something real.

She let out a gasp of a laugh. She couldn't believe this was happening. If only her high-school self could see her now! She wanted to pinch herself. And right at that moment she realized that this was 'it'.

It.

The moment she'd been waiting for all her life. The moment she took off and became a shooting star.

'What? What's so funny?' he asked, grinning too.

'Nothing. Just . . .' She laughed again, grabbing his hand. 'I'd love to, but first let's go have some fun.'

Dallas wrapped his fingers round hers. Through the open flap in the tent below, the trapeze artiste flew high into the air.

CHAPTER TWENTY-FIVE

Harry stared up at the trapeze artiste against the red silk interior of the tent and gasped as she connected with her partner, mid-swing, her body bending and somersaulting in time to the sexy soundtrack. He clapped and smiled with the crowd around him.

'Wow,' Bella mouthed to him.

So far this party had been rocking, and he was thrilled that he'd brought Bella and Francis and that they were having such a good time. It was difficult not to. Everything was of the most exceptional quality – from the canapés to the cocktails, not to mention this level of entertainment. Whoever this chick was throwing this party, she sure had some style. And some serious cash. This must all be costing a *fortune*.

He felt a little bit guilty that he'd dumped Yinska and Anya, not waiting for them before he'd left for the party, but it would have been too awkward to explain his relationship to them in front of Bella, who had been subtly flirting with him behind Francis's back all night. Harry was loving it. And the longer he kept stringing her along, the keener she got.

'You got any more . . . you know?' Bella said now, leaning up to talk quietly in his ear. She looped her arm through Harry's and her pert breasts pressed against him. They'd already had a cheeky line together before they'd left the yacht, when Bella had 'accidentally' found Harry in his cabin. She'd implored him not to tell Francis, who disapproved of all drugs.

'No, but I can get some easily enough. I'll need to talk to my mate Reiss. I think he's by the pool.'

'Wait,' she said, seeing him look through the doorway of the tent. 'I'll come with you.'

Harry watched as Bella went to speak to her husband, taking the opportunity to survey her extremely pert bum in the little black dress she was wearing. There were no discernible traces of underwear beneath it. Bella, all dressed up, was quite the little hotty.

Beyond her, on the stage, he watched the troupe of dancers with their black basques and feathered headdresses, who were now can-canning in time to the lewd trombone in the jazz orchestra. They were all seriously hot, and the sleazy jazz made him feel even more horny.

Bella turned and winked at him, and Francis turned too and waved to Harry as they chatted. He had no idea what excuse she'd made, but as Francis nodded to Harry, he realized that Francis seemed happy enough to watch the trapeze show by himself and let his wife go. He trusted Bella, no doubt smug in his status as her rich banker husband. But Harry was richer and, judging from the wink Bella now gave him, much more desirable – or least *appeared* to be, thanks to the key.

Bella linked arms again and they walked out of the tent, moving aside for another couple in the doorway, who smiled at them. The guy in the black shirt and white tie was chatting to a glamorous redhead, and as they passed, Harry thought they seemed vaguely familiar.

'That's Dallas Laney,' Bella squealed, barely containing her excitement. 'Oh my God, this party is epic. I really can't thank you enough, Harry, for inviting me.'

Me. He knew she'd said it deliberately. Not *we*. Not her and Francis. Just her. She snuggled in closer to him as they walked up the flare-lit path. Ahead of them, the chateau was illuminated with lasers, casting shadows of the guests onto the wall. He had to admit that he'd never seen so many beautiful or famous people gathered in one place. It felt so good to be one of them, to be a player.

'It's fun to have someone to share it with,' he admitted.

'You really mean that?'

'Of course. I like having you as my partner in crime,' he said. And he meant it. He liked hanging out with Bella. It's how he imagined it might have been if Dulcie had come along for the ride. Too bad Bella was someone else's wife.

She stopped and stared at him for a moment and there was a beat between them. He could tell she was longing for something to happen between them, but for once he was happy to wait. This money thing, the power that came with it, it was giving him confidence. She'd come to him. He was sure of it. As soon as he said the word.

The longer he put off giving her what she wanted, the more she wanted it. This new kind of sexual magnetism felt quite intoxicating.

Just as they got to the pool area, Harry saw a familiar figure break away from a group of people and come over.

'Reiss . . . hey, man,' Harry said, striking a slow high-five and hug with his new friend.

'Nice shirt, dude,' Reiss said.

Harry introduced Bella, who seemed suitably impressed by Reiss's evident coolness. Reiss gave Harry an amused look, clearly assuming that he and Bella were together. He liked the fact that Reiss thought that Harry was some kind of playboy. But hell, he could see why. He *felt* like one. Maybe he might even stay one. Maybe this was who he was now.

'I'm just going down to town to bring up some people,' he said. 'Word's got round quick about this party. Everyone wants to be here.'

'Hey, you got any more of that coke?' Harry asked, stepping forward to discreetly talk in his ear. 'I'm running low after last night.'

'Man, it's one big party with you, Harry,' Reiss teased him. 'I'll get some for you when I'm down in town. In the meantime go and see Jay,' he continued. 'He's staying here at the chateau, but the last I saw him, he was in the casino room. He's got long hair and is wearing a black trilby.'

Harry laughed, not sure that he'd ever find someone of that description in a party as big as this. 'OK, we'll try and find him.'

'He'll be the centre of attention. You can't miss him. Tell him you're with me. Watch him, though. The guy's a party animal.'

'Sounds interesting,' Bella said, making excited eyes at Harry.

Fifteen minutes later Bella had obviously completely forgotten about returning to Francis, and Harry was in no hurry to remind her. They'd found the crowd in the casino room, where a guy who fitted perfectly the description Reiss had given was hanging out with his friends. Harry introduced himself and explained that he was a friend of Reiss's, at which point Jay let out a whoop of delight.

'Welcome, my friend,' he said, kissing Bella's hand. 'Come join in the fun.'

This was the inner circle, Harry realized. Even cooler than the party outside.

There was such a sexy vibe in here. The room had been decorated to look like an exclusive club in Vegas, and smart waitresses walked around with trays of cocktails. The music was louche and low.

Jay, realizing Harry was a fellow Englishman, soon urged him to join him at the roulette wheel, and Harry stacked up the chips the croupier pushed towards him. They played together, laughing and bantering, until a crowd had gathered round. Jay ordered more champagne, and Bella laughed and clapped as Harry's stack of chips grew higher and higher. He had to admit that he loved being the centre of attention.

'You up for it?' Jay asked, pointing to the chips on the table. 'All or nothing?'

'Sure.'

'Oh, I like you, partner.' Jay grinned. 'You're my kind of man.'

Basking in the compliment, Harry made his bet.

'OK, I'm in. All on black. It seems appropriate,' he said, rubbing his hands together.

'Harry, are you sure? This is for real,' Bella whispered, her face clouding with concern. 'That's, like, fifty thousand euros.'

'Relax. I'm feeling lucky tonight,' Harry said, pushing his chips towards the croupier. 'All on black,' he repeated.

The roulette wheel turned. Jay clapped his hands. The music throbbed. Bella squeezed Harry's hand, and all around him everyone held their breath, making Harry feel, for one moment, like he was the centre of the universe and everything revolved round him.

Then the ball fell.

The crowd made a collective groan as it landed on red.

'Better luck next time, sir,' the croupier said. His smile was friendly enough, but his eyes were serious. Those chips meant real cash.

'Yeah, yeah, sure. I'll . . .' Harry didn't finish the sentence. He shrugged, putting a brave face on it, but even so, he felt the sting of losing. His key better stretch to paying off his gambling debts or he'd be fucked.

Jay put something in his top pocket. 'Don't worry. This will soften the blow, mate,' he said, leaning in close.

Bella slipped her hand into Harry's as they left the room and went out into the hallway.

'We'd better go back,' Harry teased her, but she eyeballed him and laughed.

'Come on, let's go and do some,' she said, knowing what he had in his pocket. 'Besides, I want to explore the house. I can't *not* look upstairs. This is location heaven.'

They ran quickly up the grand central staircase, past all the couples chatting. The throbbing beat of the band outside filled the air, the crystal chandelier sending sparkles all around the great painted dome on the ceiling.

'What's in here, d'you reckon?' Bella's eyes were shining as she opened a bedroom door to reveal a sumptuous room with gold walls and peach silk covers on the four-poster bed. They slipped inside the room.

With the door closed, the sound of the party was muted. The only light in the room came from the moonlight cascading through the arched wrought-iron windows. Harry walked silently across the carpet of the soft, shadowy room and turned on a bedside lamp.

'Don't turn it on,' Bella said, running her hand along the silk quilt. 'I like the moonlight. It's romantic, don't you think?'

She blushed as she said it, realizing how forward it sounded, but Harry smiled and obliged, turning off the light. Then he chopped up some lines on the bedside table with his credit card. He felt a momentary twinge of alarm. He'd been taking coke now for weeks and felt his body yearning for the thick line of powder. It took all his strength to offer the silver tube to Bella first.

'I don't normally do this,' Bella said, snorting a line and rubbing her nostril. He wasn't sure if she meant doing cocaine or finding herself taking it alone in a romantic moonlit bedroom with a man who wasn't her husband.

Harry snorted his line and came up for air, sniffing loudly. She laughed at him, biting her lip and balancing on one foot. She reached out and touched the front of his shirt.

Now that he was alone with her in a bedroom, he felt the desire he'd been holding back rearing up. The bed was right behind Bella. It would only take one move to topple her over and he'd be on top of her.

Bella stared at him, her big blue eyes narrowing.

'I'm never usually unfaithful,' she whispered, her voice shaking as she put her hand on Harry's chest.

Usually? What did that mean?

Harry put his hand out and brushed the strap of her dress from her shoulder. 'Uh-huh.'

'Don't,' Bella said, closing her eyes as he stepped towards her and kissed her neck. 'Seriously,' she said, but her voice was a whisper.

'I find doing something you shouldn't do is always the biggest turn-on,' Harry said, carrying on kissing the soft skin of her neck and breathing in her expensive perfume.

'Me too. I mean, there's been a few times. Francis is away such a lot. And it's only been with my tennis coach , , ,' She faded out as he kissed lower.

'I see,' he said, leaning down to kiss the top of her breast. She was quivering with desire.

He wondered whether her tennis coach had had a hard-on as eager as his, but he wanted to take his time. He wanted to kiss her all over. He brushed the other strap from her shoulder and gently pulled her dress down to her waist. She had pale nipples and she put her hands over her breasts as if suddenly ashamed, but he lifted them gently away.

'You're beautiful,' he told her, meaning it. He kissed each of her nipples, cupping one breast in his hand.

'Don't you think they should be, you know, bigger?' she asked him. 'I was going to have them done.'

'Don't you dare,' he said. 'Haven't you realized yet that you're the hottest girl at this party?'

She grabbed his shirt and pulled him on top of her then, falling onto the bed. He kissed her, smoothing the hair from his face. He liked kissing her, he realized, groaning as their tongues met.

'I so want you to fuck me,' she breathed. 'Oh God, I want you so much, Harry. I have done since the moment we met.'

She fumbled with the fly on his trousers and he undid his belt. She pushed down his Armani pants until his cock was free. He put her small fist round him, her sparkly wedding and engagement bands winking at him in the moonlight as she massaged him. It only made him want her more.

He hitched up her dress and, just as he'd suspected, she wasn't wearing any underwear. He surveyed her neat waxed pussy. Leaning down, he buried his face in her, licking her. She bucked, groaning, her hands clawing his hair.

Then he was on top of her, entering her, her legs wrapping round his back as he felt himself consumed by her.

Man, it felt good to fuck her. Even better than he'd imagined.

'Harry? Bella?'

They both turned their faces at the same time. Francis was framed in the doorway, his hand on the light switch.

'Fuck,' Harry swore, as Francis let out a primeval yell of fury and dashed across the room. Harry was up, hopping as he tried desperately to pull up his pants and trousers. His heart was pounding. Bella scrabbled away up the bed, trying to cover herself up.

'I should have done this on the yacht,' Francis thundered, reaching the bed and preparing to punch Harry.

'No. Leave him alone,' Bella screamed, lunging at Francis and knocking him off balance. 'It's not his fault.'

'Get off,' Francis yelled at her, 'you little slut.'

'Francis, no,' Bella cried.

'You told me you felt sorry for him. You told me he was *gay*.'

Harry glanced at Bella, astounded by her subterfuge, then seizing his moment, he dodged past Francis, still doing up his trousers as he ran straight through the door. He got to the top of the staircase and slid down the banister on his bum, just as he had as a child, making the people at the bottom of the stairs scoot out of the way laughing. Francis bounded down the stairs after him.

'You all right, mate?' Jay asked, as Harry sprinted into the casino room and stopped breathlessly, looking around for an exit route.

'No, spot of bother, mate,' Harry replied, glancing over his shoulder.

'Oh?' Jay called, dealing cards as if it was nothing out of the ordinary. 'Go over there, behind that panel, and take the door on the right. It goes through to the orangery and then you'll be in the garden.'

'Cheers,' Harry called, dodging through the crowd, apologizing to people for spilling their drinks.

He squeezed behind the fake wall panel, seeing an ornate room beyond with oil paintings on the posh wallpaper. He went through the heavy wooden door on the right and found himself in a long, conservatory-like room, lined with marble busts. Dodging past them, he dashed for the door at the end, turning the key in the old-fashioned metal lock.

Out in the garden, he ran round a line of tall hedges and realized he was in the garden next to the pool area. He ran towards the dance stage to try and get lost in the crowd. The music was thumping out, people were everywhere, but there was no way through the dancers. He was trapped on the edge of the crowd.

A woman reared in front of him. A tall, familiar brunette, her pretty features crumpled in fury. Yinska.

'Where were you?' she snarled at him in her heavily accented English. 'You promised you would bring me to the party. Anya and I came to the yacht to come with you, but you'd gone. You are so rude. After everything—'

'Honestly, I can explain,' Harry said, trying to placate her, but he couldn't explain and now he was aware that people around him had stopped dancing and were staring. Yinska started to advance on him, still swearing loudly.

Harry turned and glanced behind him. That's when his eyes

met with Francis's, who had come through the house and was now near the pool.

Harry made a break for it, leaping over the lavender beds to the far side of the pool, but Francis was fast. As Harry got to the end of the pool, Francis was there, striding towards him.

'Listen – I'm really sorry, but she came on to me,' Harry said, holding up his arms defensively as Francis rolled up his sleeves, ready for a fight, his face grim with fury. Harry backed away up onto the diving board, but Francis stepped up with him.

'Not my nose,' Harry pleaded as Francis advanced. 'Not my nose.'

But it was too late.

'You fucking prick,' Francis growled, throwing a punch that spun Harry's head sideways as he toppled backwards into the pool.

Harry swam into consciousness through a Valium haze, aware of his phone buzzing against the inlaid wood of the bedside cabinet. It took a moment to realize that he was in the master cabin of *Menzies' Millions*.

He wished more than anything that the boat would stop rocking. He could barely move his head.

He couldn't even remember how he'd got home from the party last night – or rather, this morning, he realized, noticing he was still fully dressed and daylight was clawing around the edges of his porthole blinds.

He remembered now. The helicopter taking off . . . Jay and his friends waving him off. He'd gambled all night with Jay, the story of him getting caught with Bella becoming more exaggerated with each telling, until he felt more of a playboy than a cad who'd fucked his colleague's wife. And that girl – the one whose party it was – who'd been there when the sun came up – Scooter, that was it, who'd told him not to worry about the croupier, that she'd handle it. Thank God. Man, she'd been cool. No wonder Dallas Laney had been following her around like a puppy dog. It sure had been one hell of a night.

With one hand he stretched out and grabbed his phone. Maybe it was Bella, calling to apologize. Or maybe it was Reiss with some good news. He was clean out of coke and pills, and he had the feeling that today he might really be needing some.

'Hi, Harry.'

The familiar Texan twang made Harry lurch awake.

'Cole?' Harry said, sitting up slightly.

His head was throbbing from all the whisky he'd drunk and from his bruised nose.

'So, you're in the South of France, I hear,' Cole said. Harry pictured him in the office. 'Pretty girls there, so I gather. You should watch yourself.'

What did *that* mean? Could Cole have found out about Bella? Or maybe one of the crew had said something about the Russian girls?

He cursed himself for not getting out of his obligation to Cole sooner. Or leaving his yacht. He should have just asked the key for a yacht of his own as he'd planned to and – when and if it had materialized – taken off, but he'd been too busy having a good time.

'I'm doing fine,' Harry said, gingerly placing his palm over his eye.

'Well, enough of a good time. I want you to fly back to London. I have a job for you.'

'A job? What sort of job?' Harry said.

He hadn't even thought of work, but now he remembered

that he owed Cole big time. That his free ride was bound to have come to an end at some point.

Because there had to be a catch, right? To all of this. To the key. At some point he'd be called to account and told what it was all about. Maybe that was why he'd been grabbing all he could, because deep down he knew it would have to come to an end.

But not today. Jesus, not today, he silently begged.

'I need you to offer some investment advice to a private client,' Cole said. 'And show her a good time while you're at it.'

'But—' Harry started to protest, but Cole had already hung up.

CHAPTER TWENTY-SIX

Kamiko watched Sir Cole Menzies replace the phone on the antique desk in his swanky London office. Behind him, through the floor-to-ceiling window between the shelves of antique books, the skyline of London shimmered in the midday sun.

She'd been in London for a week, trying to hunt down Harry Cassidy, and at last she had him in her sights. She felt a glow of triumph run through her and shifted in the stiff chair in her new Max Azria trouser suit and matching navy Prada shoes.

Thanks to Lisa Dern, the private investigator Kamiko had hired, she'd learned a lot about her fellow key-holder in the short time she'd been here. She'd found out Harry Cassidy's address, his bank details and his employment record. Lisa had also found out that he was in the pocket of his boss – this guy, Sir Cole Menzies – staying on his yacht and God knows what else, so it was on the Texan City man that Kamiko and Lisa had concentrated their efforts.

'All sorted. Harry is just the guy for you, Miss Lee,' Sir Menzies said. He looked pleased with himself. The silver pin at his neck sparkled in the sunlight, refracted through the diamond Damien Hirst skull on his desk.

'Please, call me Kim,' Kamiko said, trying to sound demure.

'Well, Kim, Harry is a gem and this is a perfect match.'

Kamiko smiled, the glow of satisfaction spreading. This fat, power-hungry American had no idea what he'd just done.

Now Kamiko turned to Lisa, who was sitting beside her. It was Lisa who had arranged the meeting and had talked her way in here. Posing as a sophisticated City agent, she'd made Cole believe that Kamiko, one of her high-end Japanese clients, had a considerable amount to invest. The more Kamiko and Lisa had worked on the pitch for today's meeting, the more they'd ramped up how much Kamiko was worth.

It had been Lisa who had suggested to Cole Menzies that a trader or financial expert from his bank was exactly the kind of person this young Japanese heiress was looking for in order to get a general feel of the UK financial markets. Their cover story, coupled with the false financial documentation Lisa had created, had worked like a charm.

Now Lisa stood up. In her black business suit, she looked every inch the slick City businesswoman, not the ruthless private investigator Kamiko knew her to be. She was blonde and slim, and Kamiko could tell that Cole Menzies was impressed by her. She saw the lascivious glint in his eye as he stared at Lisa's long legs.

Oh, yes, she thought, she'd certainly lucked out finding Lisa.

She saw Lisa return his look with a sardonic raised eyebrow. She was the perfect bait. It was no surprise to Kamiko that Lisa had lost her sexual discrimination case in the City and had then been fired from the police force for 'unacceptable behaviour'. But as a private detective, her natural sex appeal was certainly an asset. All the men they'd encountered on the way to this office had fallen over themselves to help her.

'I'm sure he is,' Lisa said, 'and as I said before, there is nothing better than local knowledge. We'll be in touch, Sir Menzies. Thank you so much for your time.'

Half an hour later Kamiko sat opposite Lisa in a crowded nearby Docklands wine bar.

'I fucking hate these places,' Lisa said, sipping her Diet Coke. Her posh English accent had gone, Kamiko noticed, still impressed by the act she'd put on. 'Full of City scumbags.'

'Like Harry Cassidy,' Kamiko pointed out.

'Yeah, like your Harry bloke,' Lisa agreed.

Kamiko hadn't told Lisa either her real name or anything about the key, and only a very sketchy story about her connection to Harry, claiming that he'd screwed her on a property deal that had cost her everything. And now she wanted revenge. A motive Lisa seemed to find perfectly natural and one the advertisement on her website broadly hinted was her area of expertise. Which is what had drawn Kamiko to her in the first place and, via a series of complex web addresses, had eventually secured her services. The first thing she'd said when Kamiko had telephoned her and she'd outlined her problem was that she'd relish the chance to take down a City guy.

'You find out more about him?' Kamiko asked, finishing her beer.

Lisa pulled across her YSL briefcase and delved inside, past her make-up bag, for her reporter's notebook.

'A lot. It seems Harry Cassidy has quite a gambling addiction and various unpaid debts to Internet betting sites. Let me see,' she said, flipping over the page. 'He's defaulted on his mortgage three times and had taken equity out of his flat to pay off debts.'

Kamiko was impressed that she'd found out so much.

'Oh, yeah, and there's more,' Lisa said, flicking over a few pages. 'I found out from one of the secretaries at America Bank that Cassidy used to work with a trader called Nick Grundy who got fired around the same time that Cassidy stopped going to the office. They hated each other, apparently.'

'That's good,' Kamiko said, leaning forward.

'I have an address for him over in West London.' She ripped out the sheet and handed it over. 'It's in Hammersmith, by the river.'

'You are very good,' Kamiko said.

Lisa looked at her. 'If you want to go the whole way, then you'll need someone in the press to act fast. I have a friend over at the *Mail* who would pounce on this. They love a bit of City-boy bashing.' She wrote a number on the pad, ripped it out and handed it to Kamiko, who thanked her again.

'You want extra work?' Kamiko asked.

Lisa shrugged and nodded, finishing her Diet Coke. 'Cash for information always works for me.'

She gave Kamiko a smile. She was obviously pleased that Kamiko had transferred the large fee in cash to Lisa's account yesterday without questions. Kamiko still had some of the cash that she'd got from the bank manager when she'd first got the key, and as far as she was concerned, Lisa was money well spent. She didn't care if that meant that she had to stay in a dive of a hostel and eat cheap food. All she cared about was finding out who was behind the key and how to win the game.

'This guy. He called Tiko,' Kamiko said, pulling out a photograph from her jacket. 'And this is Susi. They boyfriend and girlfriend. They bad people. Do bad things. I need to find them. You try?'

'OK,' Lisa said. 'Are they connected to Harry?'

Kamiko didn't answer. She finished her drink.

'Are you actually going to tell me what any of this is really about?' Lisa asked.

'Better you don't know,' Kamiko replied. 'I give you extra money,' she said, 'for expenses.'

She pushed a thick envelope of cash across the marble tabletop to Lisa, who looked around and took it. She looked inside the envelope.

'Nice doing business with you, Kim,' she said. 'I'll see what I can do.'

Kamiko took the Tube from the Docklands back to her grubby hostel in Tottenham Court Road. As she stared at her reflection in the glass of the train, watching the people coming and going, looking at the adverts and reading their newspapers, she reflected on how well today had gone. Better than she could have expected. She felt sure that she was already one step closer to winning.

It's a test . . . There can only be one winner. Martha Faust's words came back to her, along with an image of the dying woman on the floor of her study.

But Kamiko didn't feel any remorse. Not then and not now. In fact, she hardly felt responsible at all. It was Martha who'd attacked her first. Martha who'd kept a loaded firearm in her study. And Martha who'd been deliberately obstructive about the information she held about Kamiko. All she'd needed to do was tell Kamiko the truth and nothing bad need ever have happened.

Kamiko had scanned the Internet, but so far the police had no leads into Martha Faust's death. She'd read moving tributes from colleagues and friends outlining their sadness at her tragic death, but Kamiko had remained impassive. The news reports said that the police were trying to piece together the business-woman's last movements.

When Kamiko had read this, she wondered whether that smug guy she'd met at Martha Faust's office would remember that she'd been in Zurich, or whether they'd look as far as the CCTV in the Starbucks cafe. But even if they'd been able to identify her, the police would never guess Kamiko's connection to the businesswoman.

But thanks to Martha, and the papers she'd found in her safe, Kamiko now had a plan. And taking Harry – her fellow key-holder, her *competitor* – out of the equation was the next step. But she didn't want to kill him. Not if it could possibly be helped. Not now that Lisa was involved. There were other ways to get him, though, she was sure of it. A guy like that must have annoyed enough people.

Later that evening Kamiko took a trip to Hammersmith to track down Harry's old colleague Nick Grundy. She found his flat easily and was in luck. Just as she was about to ring the bell, the door opened and a scruffy guy came out with a newspaper under his arm. She followed him round the corner.

The pub he entered on the bank of the River Thames, next to a big green road bridge, was warm and inviting. A long wooden bar ran the length of the narrow room and various locals slouched at it, standing on the rough floorboards. At the far end, a barmaid polished glasses and chewed gum, occasion-ally filling pints for the customers. Framed pictures of rowing teams filled the walls, along with various seafaring artefacts including fake brass portholes and a row of rope knots.

Kamiko watched Grundy talking to the barmaid, who clearly tolerated but didn't like him. He bought a pint of beer and took it to a corner table, where he sat and drank half of it in one go. Then he put the paper on the table.

'So you are Nick Grundy?' Kamiko asked, waiting until he was settled, then walking to the table and standing above him.

He instantly repelled her. Not just because of his scornful sneer. It was more to do with the aura of depression that he carried around with him. Of a man beaten.

'Who wants to know?' he grunted.

'My name is Kim Lee.' She concentrated hard, keen to get the words out right. 'We talk about Harry Cassidy?'

'How do you know that wanker?' he asked, before nodding to the stool opposite him. Kamiko sat down.

It only took a few questions before Nick Grundy made it clear that he had quite a lot to say about his ex-colleague. He was obviously furious about being fired.

'I was better than him and he set me up,' Nick said, swigging his beer. He was already half drunk. He didn't mask the bitterness in his voice. Kamiko offered to buy him another drink to keep him talking. 'And now my reputation is fucked because of him.'

She bought more beers and his tongue became even looser and she struggled to keep up as he told her about the open trade he'd been blamed for, when he hadn't even been in the building. How Harry had somehow managed to bribe and corrupt the senior management, who had dismissed Nick without any right to reply. How even the employment lawyers he'd tried hiring had one by one dropped him. As if someone much bigger had been pulling the strings.

Kamiko listened quietly and sympathetically nodded. If the bank had performed such a sly cover-up, then that was the perfect way to expose Harry.

'He has girlfriend?' Kamiko asked.

'Nah. Too much of a wimp. He never used to come out with me and the lads, although he could have done if he'd only had the balls to ask.'

'So there was no one special?'

'He used to fancy the barmaid at the Savoy. The dancer. That's all I know. So what's all this about? Why do you want to know about this?'

Kamiko nodded. 'I think he is . . . how you say it? A liar,' she told Nick Grundy.

He laughed and raised his pint to her. 'I'll drink to that. Look, if you want to fuck him over, darlin', by all means be my guest. And count me in too.' His face had lit up, Kamiko noticed.

'You talk to newspaper? You tell them this? What you tell me?' she asked him.

''Course I bloody would.' He rubbed his hands together. Then he laughed. 'And the rest. Just make sure you've caught Cassidy first.'

New Year's Eve 1999

'Can you get them? Are they there?' Mack whispered in the darkness. He pulled at his aching leg in order to shift position, his trousers soaked through, the cold seeping into his bones.

'I don't know. I think there's something,' Tobias replied, his strained voice coming through the mist of freezing drizzle.

Mack crawled closer to him across the slippery wet mud to where Tobias was sprawled on the steep bank. Wearing all black, the only thing visible was his pale face.

They heard a train coming, and as it rushed towards them along the track, the force of it left them squashed and immobile against the bank, the deafening roar making Mack cry out against the thundering noise. The air felt as if it was being sucked out of his lungs.

As he lay pinned against the dirt, he looked at the strobing carriages and memories flashed before him.

Most of all he remembered Teis above him, staring into the body bag on the night they'd broken out of prison.

'Please, Teis,' Mack had whispered desperately in the dark. 'Please.'

Teis had looked terrified.

There had been more footsteps. The undertakers had been behind him, ready to take the bag to join Tobias in the back of the van.

Mack's eyes had bored into Teis's, hoping his friend the chaplain would not let him down. All it would have taken was one word and Mack would have been ruined forever. But it had been Teis more than anyone who'd known the truth about Mack. And all the reasons why he should escape: because he was innocent; because he had to get his family back; because that monster Voss still had them. It had been this that Mack had been relying on as he stared into Teis's eyes.

For a moment time had been suspended; then, with a tortured blink, Teis had zipped up the body bag without a word. Mack had heard him stand back; then he'd felt himself being shunted off the slab.

'He's a heavy one, this one,' one of the undertakers had said.

'He was a tricky soul,' he'd heard Teis say. 'Perhaps he'll be good in the next life.'

Mack had felt himself being carried between the men and out to the van. He'd landed with a thud on the cold, hard floor of the van. The doors had slammed. A moment later the engine started and the van had started moving, away from the prison and through the gates to the world beyond.

He remembered, too, that first gulp of freedom. How he and Tobias had broken out of the undertakers' van and made a run for it through the night, stealing a car and driving to the stately home in the Scottish Borders. He remembered those cosy winter nights plotting this trip to France in Lady Markham's game-keeper's cottage.

And as the carriages continued to thunder past, he

remembered the trip to France three weeks ago. How he and Tobias had sailed on a two-man yacht through treacherous seas and how exhausted and sick Mack had been.

He remembered, too, the shock he'd felt when they'd finally made it here and he'd seen that a new railway had been built along this once-disused track. He'd been convinced that the diamonds had been dislodged during the new building work and either buried for good or found by someone who had kept their discovery very quiet.

But Tobias had refused to let him give up, urging Mack to try and piece together where exactly he must have crawled to. Last night they'd methodically scoured every inch of this section of the bank, but the bad weather had forced them to give up.

Tonight was New Year's Eve. The night before the new millennium. It had a sort of prophesy about it, Tobias had said earlier, an optimism, like a gateway opening up to the future, but all night Mack had felt weary, tired and doomed.

Until now.

Lying side by side on the dark bank in the rain, their hearing slowly returned to normal after the train disappeared up the track, their eyes connected and Mack grinned, hardly daring to breathe. Because if this was real . . . if the diamonds really were here, then he would do whatever it took to find Voss and reclaim his family. Then he'd put this whole hideous millennium behind him and start again.

He thrust his fingers into the small hole in the soft ground Tobias had made with the trowel and there . . . the feel of sodden velvet. The sensation he'd been dreaming of for fifteen long years.

Mack shone his torch into the hole. A bright diamond sparkled in the dirt.

'You found them.' He laughed. 'Oh my God. You found them.'

Tobias laughed too. Then they were hugging, whooping with delight, sliding down the bank.

'Oh my God, it's just as you said,' Tobias gasped, once they shone the torch in the hole again. The diamonds sparkled like stars in the dark. He picked one out and held it in the light of the torch.

'I told you,' Mack said, as Tobias examined it. 'There's a whole bag of those in there.'

'But look at it, Mack,' Tobias said. He'd never heard such awe in his voice. 'It's the size of a marble and so beautifully cut.'

Mack grinned, hope flaring in his chest. These diamonds had been worth it after all. Worth every risk, every long second in jail. As they pulled out the diamonds one by one, dropping them carefully in the bag, Mack felt his soul lighten and lift. And plans – real plans – start to take shape in his mind. What he hadn't dared to hope for suddenly seemed possible.

As long as they could get them to Tobias's contact in Tokyo, then he would be rich beyond his wildest dreams. Forever.

And he would get back what was his. All he had to do now was find Voss and take back Kate, Tara and Mark. And then life would be normal. Back to how it should have been, before Voss's evil hold had ripped his life apart.

The thought made tears of relief and joy spring to his eyes.

'Oh my God, Mack,' Tobias breathed, as the diamonds kept on coming from the ground. 'How many more of these are there?'

Mack was clearly not the only one feeling emotional. Because his friend would be affected just as much. Mack had agreed to split the diamond haul with him. And now they were both rich, his friend would be able to undo the wrongs in his past too. He'd be able to find the daughter he'd never met and explain himself to the one woman he'd ever loved. The woman he'd left behind in America.

But wherever their lives took them, Mack thought, smiling at his friend, they would be partners forever.

Above them, they heard New Year's Eve fireworks erupting over the small town in the distance.

'Happy new millennium, my friend,' Mack said, and his heart filled with happiness at the thought of what the future would bring.

CHAPTER TWENTY-SEVEN

Julia woke up with a start. She looked at the chink of light coming in through the unfamiliar blinds, then smiled and bit her lip. She had her cheek resting against Christian's chest and she listened to the steady thump of his heartbeat as he slept, feeling her naked limbs against his. Contentment swept through her like a wave. Outside, she could hear the distant sound of church bells, the morning call of parrots in the palm trees and the hushed whisper of the sea.

She couldn't believe that she was here in bed with her new lover. She'd never imagined that she'd find anyone like Christian, who was funny, kind, intelligent, well travelled *and* amazing in bed. Not only had she found someone who could well be her perfect man, she was here with him in this apartment. Everything from the soft mattress beneath her to the fresh crisp white linen and cream silk quilt – it was the most luxury she'd ever experienced. And it was all hers. She sighed again, letting her mind luxuriate in every detail.

After her date with Christian on the beach and all the fun they'd had dancing, she'd been so tempted to go back to his hotel with him. When he'd kissed her, it had felt so right. But she'd resisted, knowing that however tempted she was, she shouldn't have sex with him on their first date. She knew that however frustrating, taking things slowly would only make them better.

She'd gone straight home and had called Nat, even though it had been the middle of the night.

'Hey, how did it go?' Nat had asked through a yawn.

'Oh God, Nat, it was just incredible. But . . .' Julia had been torn between joy and panic.

'What's the problem?'

'He wants to meet my family. He wants to see where I *live*.'

'So?'

'So, I can't bring him here,' Julia had exclaimed, staring around the pokey apartment, with its awful stained furniture and hideous kitchen piled high with washing-up, the leaking tap dripping on a pan. 'He thinks . . .' She'd trailed off. She hadn't been able to bear the thought of disappointing him. He'd already told her how alarming he'd found the favela. 'He'd run a mile if he saw this.'

'So? Make up an excuse.'

'I can't. He has nothing to do but see me. What am I going to do?'

'Why don't you try asking your key for an apartment?' Nat had said, as if it had been no big deal. 'They have serviced apartments, fully furnished and finished, down to the bed linen and cutlery, on that seafront development. I took a client to one the other day. They're amazing.'

'You think the key would be able to get me that?' Julia had asked.

'I don't know. It's worth a try, isn't it?'

And so that's what had happened. Spurred on by Nat, in the dead of night – without giving herself time to back out of the idea – Julia had asked her key for a fully furnished apartment with a sea view. By the morning she'd had a call from an agent saying the keys were ready to pick up.

She hadn't been able to believe how gorgeous the penthouse apartment had been. Two en-suite bedrooms with a balcony overlooking the beach. The open-plan living area had a white carpet and white built-in shelves full of books and squashy funky-coloured sofas and beanbags, and opened out onto a white kitchen with a central island, its drawers full of gadgets and utensils. It had felt like she'd stepped into the pages of a designer magazine. The kind of magazine she'd never been able to afford to buy.

Telling Christian she couldn't see him until later because she was visiting Vovo, Julia had spent a frenzied day shopping and stocking the apartment to make it look lived in. Then last night they'd gone out for supper. She'd suggested Luigi's place, knowing that the seafood was good and the atmosphere buzzing.

It had been a fun night. After they'd eaten a seafood platter together, she'd taken him over the road to a bar to see some of the dancers she knew who always performed in the carnival. Christian had been amazed by their flamboyant feather head-dresses and sequinned bikinis, and they'd both partied until late.

Then Julia had invited him back to her apartment. She'd explained that it was a new place and that some of her stuff was in storage, but she still wished she'd brought some photographs from home. Seeing it through Christian's eyes made the whole place seem so devoid of personality.

But Christian had been nothing but charming, and as Julia had led him onto the balcony to see the moonlit view, she'd felt a mixture of pride and relief that he'd believed that she might be the kind of person to have an apartment like this.

When they had finally gone to bed, she'd expected to feel

nervous, but with Christian, it has been just the opposite. He'd undressed her slowly, looking into her eyes. It had been so sensual and romantic.

In the candlelit bedroom, they'd explored each other's naked bodies. It had felt so intimate but so exhilarating. As they finally lay down and he entered her, he looked at her the whole time and they held hands, both delighted and entranced by the other person. She'd felt completely uninhibited, revelling in the way her body felt against his, loving the feel of his back, his buttocks, as she pulled him to her, wanting him to fill her body and mind completely.

They'd kissed endlessly, moving seamlessly from one position to another, each time delighting in a fresh sensation. Soon it had been too much. As she'd sat astride him, Julia had experienced one of the most powerful orgasms of her life.

Now, lying here in his arms remembering it all, she felt her desire stirring again.

Christian jerked and groaned in his sleep, his eyes flickering.

'Hey,' she said, worried now. She shook him awake.

Christian exhaled and looked at her, his eyes wide with shock.

'Are you OK?' she asked.

'It's nothing,' he mumbled, rubbing his eyes. 'Just . . . just nightmares.'

'What about?'

'Just . . .' he said.

'What?' She stroked his brow. 'You can tell me.'

'It's nothing. Just stuff that happened . . . in Africa. It doesn't matter.'

Christian kissed her back, brushing a lock of hair behind her ear.

'How did you get to be even more gorgeous in the morning than you were last night?' he asked.

She knew he was changing the subject, but she sensed this was not the time to press him for details.

Julia smiled and rolled on top of him. She could feel Christian's body responding to hers.

'Speak for yourself,' she told him. She kissed his neck, then the blond hair on his chest and down towards his stomach. 'God, you are so sexy.'

Afterwards they got up and went into the kitchen to get breakfast. The view out of the window over the sun-drenched beach made them both gasp and smile when Julia pulled back the curtain. She went to the kitchen to make coffee, thinking that this had to be one of *the* best mornings of her entire life.

'Nice coffee cups,' Christian said, pulling the brand-new crockery out of the cupboard.

'They are, aren't they?' Julia said, admiring the funky porcelain.

Christian laughed. 'You act like you've never seen them before.'

She turned away, trying to cover her embarrassment and shock. She'd almost slipped up.

'So, what are the plans today?' Christian asked, putting his arms round her waist and kissing her hair. 'Please tell me you don't have any.'

'Not many,' Julia said, already wondering how much of her day she could cancel. She just wanted to hang out with Christian and make everything else go away.

'Nat's coming over, and then I'm supposed to be preparing for this stupid assertiveness course Senhora Azevedo has me going on this week. Although it's a complete waste of time. I'm plenty assertive enough with the kids, in my opinion. Oh, yeah,' she said, remembering, 'and I'm supposed to be going to see Vovo at the hospital.'

'Again?' he said.

Julia nodded mutely, remembering the lie she'd told yesterday that she'd been with Vovo when she'd actually been moving in here.

'You make me feel ashamed,' he said.

'Ashamed? Why?'

'Because you're such a good granddaughter. You're always going to the hospital to see her and it has got me thinking . . . I must go home and see my family. My dad and brother.'

'You're leaving?'

Christian smiled gently. 'Come with me.' His eyes were bright as he held her hands. 'Come away with me. We'll go to Europe. I'll show you Paris, just like you wanted, and then we'll go and see my dad and brother in Norway.'

'Christian, I can't jump on a plane. And anyway, I'd have to book the time off from school.' There was also the small issue of the fact she didn't have a passport. Why would she, when travelling out of Brazil had never been an option before? But maybe the key would be able to magic one up. Suddenly, anything seemed possible today.

'I'll buy the tickets,' he told her. 'I can make it work.'

Julia said nothing. She could think of nothing better than jetting off to Europe with Christian, but at the same time it was true what she'd said. She did have responsibilities here. She couldn't just walk out on her job. Or Vovo.

And yet . . . yet did she really need to teach, when the key was helping her so much? But no, she banished such a reprehensible thought. Her job meant everything to her. She couldn't possibly let down the kids, not without someone to replace her – someone who knew them and would take care of them. Maria, her assistant, was doing a good job, but she wasn't qualified.

But still a nagging thought persisted. What if the key could magic her up a teacher to step into her shoes?

She couldn't believe she was even *thinking* like this, but all the things that had seemed so important – like her job, or even holding her family together in the favela – were suddenly slipping away. In this apartment, with Christian, she felt like a different person. One who wanted to be free. Who had options and choices.

Whoever, whatever was behind all this . . . then they'd meant her to have this luxury. She felt sure of it. Perhaps she deserved this new life she was living. And she deserved someone to share it with . . . didn't she?

She was still mulling over her future and Christian's offer later that morning, as she cleared up the coffee cups and he took a shower. These feelings were all so confusing. She felt guilty one minute and elated the next. She wondered what Vovo would make of all this if she could see Julia now.

Christian appeared in the doorway in a towel, making her jump. His hair was wet from the shower.

'Have you got a plaster?' he asked. She saw now that he'd nicked himself shaving and held a tissue to his neck. He walked towards her, stopping on the designer rug in front of the plasma TV. Behind him, the shelves were loaded with tasteful vases and books that she'd never read. Books that made her look like she had an intellect and view on the world that she'd never dreamed of having.

'A plaster?' she said.

'Yeah, just till it stops bleeding,' Christian said. 'You must have a medical kit?'

'Sure,' she said, but right at that moment she felt an altogether more real emotion slam into her chest. She turned away, feeling caught out. Of course she had a medical kit. But that was at home, in the tiny, hideous bathroom she shared with Fredo, Marcello and Vovo, with its dark green paintwork to hide the patches of fungus, and the buzzing electric light that was hanging off the wall.

'What's the matter?' Christian asked.

'Just . . .'

The justification she'd felt only moments ago about being here in the apartment vanished. In its place she just felt like the big liar she was. And here in front of her was this wonderful man who would leave her as soon as he'd found out what she'd done.

Because, as much as she tried to justify it to herself, she knew that Christian would be horrified that she'd used the key. He would be disgusted that she was happily spending someone else's money to improve her life.

He thought she was like him – decent and caring and hard-working – but she wasn't. She was just a freeloader who was only concerned about what he thought of her. She remembered the dark-haired man who'd given her the key outside the *theatro*. What would Christian say if he knew that a stranger was controlling her life? She felt yet more shame washing over her.

'Are you upset about me going back to my family?' he asked, his face clouding as he walked towards her. His arms were wet from the shower as he put them around her. 'You can come with me.'

'It's not that . . .' she began, putting her hand on his chest. She felt tears threatening to choke her.

'I was thinking, you know, just now in the shower. Why don't you take a few days off work? Get out of this training course. We can go on an adventure together.'

She stared at him. How could she possibly plan a future with him? How could she go on adventures with him when he'd got her all wrong?

'Julia? What is it?' he asked, his face etched with concern as fat tears of grief fell from her eyes. Because she saw now that she had to end this right here. She had to let him go. He deserved someone so much better than her.

'You don't know me,' Julia said.

'But I do,' Christian said, holding her face, kissing away her tears. 'I know all I need to know about you.'

'You don't. You don't.'

'Then tell me. What could be so terrible that you haven't told me, huh?'

She took a deep, shuddering breath, preparing herself. 'The truth.'

'And what's that?' He smiled gently at her. She loved his accent. She loved the way his soft eyes looked at her and his finger trailed across her skin. She felt a quivering in her chest.

'The truth is that I'm poor.'

There. She'd said it. She stared into his face, feeling frightened, as she waited for his reaction, but Christian laughed.

'It wouldn't matter if you were,' he said.

'It would to me.'

'You think money matters?'

'Of course it matters.'

Julia felt wrong-footed. She knew he hadn't understood. She'd told yet another half-truth. Of course he wasn't going to believe that she was poor when they were standing in an apartment like this. She wished that she had never asked the key for it. She wished she'd had the confidence to take him to her real home all along.

And now a strange buzzing interrupted their conversation. Julia quickly dried her eyes, realizing that it must be the door. Nat must be here already. But this was the worst possible timing. She had to tell Christian. She had to tell him the truth about the key. Even if it meant losing him, she had to come clean.

But at the same time relief flooded through her. Nat had bought her more time. For now.

She vowed to herself that whatever happened, that was it. She wouldn't use the key for anything else. In fact, at the first opportunity, she'd get rid of it. It was the only way to stop herself feeling so conflicted.

CHAPTER TWENTY-EIGHT

Harry pushed the key into the front door of his Docklands apartment dreading what he would find. Even though he'd got a cab from the airport, the rain on the short run into the building had already soaked his Italian linen jacket and he shivered in the gloomy hallway.

Why was the weather in this country so *shit*?

He pushed open the door with difficulty, noticing the mail stacked up on the mat. One letter on the top had 'IMPORTANT' stamped on it in red, from the mortgage company by the looks of things. He didn't bother picking it up. He dumped his bag on the floor and walked through the kitchen and living room, wondering how he could ever have thought this place was glamorous. It was a shithole.

And it stank. Man, it stank.

He walked over to the fridge and opened it up, screwing up his nose at the carton of rancid milk. He gingerly removed a pizza box with half a decomposing pizza inside and put it in the bin. Christ, were those mouse droppings on the floor? Gross.

He already knew what he would do. He would ask the key. Get someone to come round and clean up. Then he'd put the apartment on the market and tell the key to get him a proper place. Yeah, like a big pad out in Surrey or somewhere, with a fuck-off big pool and Jacuzzi. Tennis courts. Indoor cinema. The kind of place he could invite Reiss and his rich friends to party.

He kicked himself now that he hadn't sorted out such an essential before, but he'd been too busy having fun and getting high. And now it was too late.

He opened the last remaining beer in the fridge and walked to the black leather sofa. The cold apartment only served to remind him of how empty his life had been before he'd left America Bank. It was as if life back then had been in black and white and he'd just been a nobody, a drone, going back and forth to the bank. Whereas now he lived in colour. He could do whatever the hell he liked.

Then he forced himself to remember. He hadn't left yet. They were still paying him and he couldn't just do what the hell he wanted. He'd come back because Cole had asked him to. Because he hadn't been able to say no. Because, deep down, he knew he had a debt to pay. To Cole. Or to the key. To whatever the fuck this strange organization or brotherhood really was.

But still . . . *work*. He groaned at the thought. He didn't want to work. He wasn't cut out for it. All the way back to London from the South of France on the private plane, he'd been mulling over the possibilities in his head and how he should have told Cole he wasn't up to this strange investment meeting. Partly, Harry admitted, as a result of his own lies, Cole had clearly misplaced his faith in Harry's financial abilities. He wasn't in any position to advise anyone about anything. What the hell did he know?

But the way he'd framed Nick Grundy still haunted him. Not the fact that he'd done it. No, Grundy was a bastard who'd had it coming. No, what haunted him was that his deceit might still get found out. All it would take was for Cole to launch a proper investigation, to interview Harry's colleagues, to get some computer forensics guy in, or even just to review the CCTV of when Harry had been at his screen and had left the building that day . . . and he'd be screwed.

No, he had to be patient and play the Cole situation wisely. The old guy had been kind and clearly had a soft spot for Harry, so what he needed to do was keep him sweet. Then he'd gently extricate himself from the whole America Bank thing and quietly drop his connection with Cole. And quit for good.

With his key, he could go anywhere. Take off round the world. Australia, maybe. He'd always wanted to go there. Perhaps he could bag himself a waterside apartment in Sydney and see which rich women fell into his lap. He felt himself spiralling into one of his familiar fantasies. Him in an open-topped sports car, a blonde babe in running kit getting in beside him. Only this time he knew such a fantasy could really happen.

All in good time, he thought, forcing himself to be patient. He just had to sort his business out in London; then he'd be on his way.

It was only a matter of hours ago, but already his partying in France seemed like another lifetime. He thought of the models on the yacht and of Bella and felt his cock twitch with a yearning. Man, he needed to get laid. And badly. It was like having an itch he couldn't scratch.

He rubbed his face. He'd have a cheeky line or two just to settle himself and give him some energy for this dinner meeting Cole had set him up with. Yes, that would sort things. And thanks to the key finding him Reiss, he'd come home with a handy little stash.

He went to his bag and retrieved the leather wash bag and

the thick plastic wallets of cocaine he'd put in the side pockets. Asking the key for private planes sure had its advantages. No one had even so much as checked his passport, let alone his bags. Then he squirted some of the expensive Hermès aftershave from the bottle in his wash bag onto his wrist and inhaled the scent. It reminded him of sunshine and sex.

Back in the living room, he sat heavily on the sofa and tipped out the white powder onto the coffee table, clearing the take-away menus and old beer cans to one side. It was only then that he noticed the flashing light on his answering machine.

He leaned over and pressed the play button, chopping up the powder with his credit card. He listened to the machine telling him that he had over fifty new messages as he rolled a fifty-pound note in his fingers.

The most recent message was from yesterday at 11 p.m. As he tipped his head forward to snort the fat line of cocaine he'd chopped out on the glass table, he heard a familiar voice.

'Harry, it's Dulcie.' He paused, one finger over his nostril. 'I know we haven't spoken for a while, but I wondered if you wouldn't mind meeting me. I'm going to be at . . .' – she paused, her voice slightly shaky – 'a bar in Shoreditch tomorrow night. Forty-five Albermarle Lane. Say around ten thirty? I hope to see you there.'

Dulcie. There was a turn-up for the books. So, she'd seen sense at last. He might get a decent fuck in after all. Because if she'd left that message yesterday, that meant that she was hoping to see him tonight. Harry smiled to himself and snorted the fat line.

'Bingo,' he said to himself.

But that still left the problem of the dinner with Cole's

mystery client. He'd just have to charm her and tell her to fuck off, then head to Shoreditch alone.

Shit, it was going to be a long night. He looked down at the other line of cocaine. Maybe he should have that too, just to be sure. Keep him on his toes, so to speak. And take an extra couple of grammes for later. God knew, with what he had planned for lovely Dulcie later, he was going to need all the energy he could get.

'Harry, it's Mum.' The second message clicked in as he leaned down to snort the line. 'I know you aren't answering my calls, and they say you're away at work. It's just . . .' He could hear the emotion rising in her voice and her attempt to control it. 'Dad and I are worried about you, darling. Are you OK? We missed you on your birthday.' There was another long pause. 'I love you. That's all.'

Harry closed his eyes for a moment, finding it difficult to get the coke past the swelling in his nose where Francis had punched him. Frustrated, he rubbed the white powder round his gums, feeling his tongue numbing.

He knew he should call his mum and stop her worrying. As soon as she'd heard his voice and he'd fobbed her off with an excuse for his radio silence, she'd forgive him. She always did. She was his mother. That's what mothers were supposed to do.

But now, as he collapsed back on the sofa, the coke making his ears ring, he resented her unconditional love. He didn't want her weeping in the kitchen trying to cling on to him. He'd moved away. Moved on with his life. Why couldn't she just accept that?

He also resented the fact that his parents thought that the money Harry had made in the City was somehow different to theirs. They had no idea about how the world actually worked. They were so lower class and ordinary. How could he include them in his new life when he went to parties with the likes of Dallas Laney?

He gave an ironic snort of laughter as he imagined himself at home in the little Yorkshire terraced house and how he might describe the party in France to them. But even just the act of telling them about his life in that environment would feel demeaning. Because they either wouldn't believe him or would bring it down to their level. And he couldn't have that.

He deleted his mother's message and the following fifty messages one by one without even listening to them. It was only when he got to the fifty-third message that he heard a snippet of it.

'You're dead meat, mate. You won't get away with it.'

Harry pressed the delete button very quickly, erasing the vicious tones of Nick Grundy. He must have left that message, and scores of others, on Harry's machine when he got fired. Nick Grundy had his number. He must know where Harry lived.

Quickly he unplugged the answering machine from its lead as if it were on fire.

'Shit,' he swore.

He shouldn't have erased the messages, he panicked. If something happened to him . . . if Nick Grundy did something to him . . . then the tapes would be evidence . . .

He jumped, hearing the bleep of a text message on his mobile phone. He pulled it out of his jacket.

It was from Alice, Cole's secretary, confirming his reservation for dinner with Kim Lee.

CHAPTER TWENTY-NINE

Deep in the heart of the Brazilian rainforest, the sun shone in a clear blue sky above Iguazu Falls. On the metal viewing platform, Julia and Christian stood side by side and looked out on the spectacle of the 275 waterfalls spreading out on either side of them, the mighty rivers cascading over the edge of the cliff and plunging hundreds of metres down to the basin below.

They held hands, gulping in the mist of water, laughing at shimmering rainbows ahead of them, shouting to be heard over the rush of the most famous waterfall, Devil's Throat, which was swallowing water at a rate of millions of tonnes a second. Swallows swooped in and out of the clouds of mist, catching insects. A multitude of yellow butterflies danced in the air around them.

'It's incredible,' Julia shouted, her face shining with water. She was wearing the red waterproof jacket that the guide had offered. She even looked beautiful in that, Christian noticed, unable to stop grinning at her.

In the distance, far below, beyond the foam, the river gathered and meandered away through the rocks, sparkling in the sunshine, the deep green trees on either side resplendent with life. But Christian was scarcely taking in the view. He could hardly bear to tear his eyes away from Julia.

Everything about her fascinated him, from the way she spoke to the tiny freckles on her skin. It was as if he was utterly intoxicated by her. He really had gone nuts over this girl, he thought to himself, but he didn't care. So what if he felt like a love-sick teenager? What was wrong with wanting to hold her hand and feel his fingers entwining with hers? Especially when he knew that she felt the same way. Because that was the very best part of it all: the simply incredible fact that someone as wonderful as Julia had fallen for him. It made him feel ten feet tall.

Christian had planned the trip here to Iguazu Falls as a surprise, although it had taken some persuading to make Julia bail out of the course she was supposed to be going on at school and to call in sick. He knew she felt guilty. That boss of hers terrified her, but Christian had insisted it would be worth it.

They'd got up at dawn in order to get the helicopter from Rio. Christian had refused to tell Julia their destination, but now he was thrilled with her reaction. The smile on Julia's face was all the justification Christian needed.

After Julia's strange outburst in her apartment, he'd been convinced that he must take her somewhere to impress her. He knew how much she wanted to travel, how hungry she was to explore the world, and maybe that was why money mattered to her so much, he'd reasoned. Maybe when she'd admitted to him that she was poor, he hadn't understood what she'd meant. Maybe what she was really trying to tell him was that she wanted to be with someone rich. Someone who could show her the world.

The more he thought about it afterwards, the more convinced

he became that some sort of grand gesture, to prove himself to her, was the right thing to do. When she'd been at work, he'd trawled the travel agents, trying to book a day away, but at such short notice, every flight was fully booked.

He'd gone back to his hotel to change, but as he'd been dressing, his rucksack had slipped onto the floor and the key had fallen out of the side pocket. The light from the window had made it shine and before he'd given himself time to think, Christian had plugged the key into his laptop and had logged in his details. Then a page had come up.

Hello, Christian. What do you desire?

Sod it, he'd thought. Why not? Why not use the key this once? If someone wants me to have an upgrade, then this is the time to use it.

So he'd detailed the trip. How he wanted two tickets to come to Iguazu and somewhere exclusive and luxurious to stay for the night.

He wondered whether the key would be more forthcoming on this request. He was still smarting that he'd been refused another key for the colonel. An hour later there'd been a call from the front desk of the hotel to tell him that there was an envelope waiting for him at reception.

It had been like magic. Inside the envelope had been details of the helicopter that had been booked, as well as a reservation for the top suite at the stunning five-star Falls Lodge. As to who had delivered the tickets, he was completely in the dark. The receptionist said the envelope had been delivered by courier.

But someone somewhere wanted him to have a good time.

Christian had felt a momentary pang of guilt as he'd looked at the envelope with the tickets in it. It felt wrong to be having a good time when Dan and Olu were dead. But the nightmares he'd suffered about them were less and less frequent since he'd met Julia. And the nightmare, too, about how he'd promised the colonel that he'd get him a key like his own in return for all those prisoners' lives – that felt less real now so much time had passed.

Surely it had been a case of being in the wrong place at the wrong time, he reasoned. The colonel wouldn't even remember Christian by now. He was sure of it. He'd have moved on to bigger things. No, that dark day in the colonel's headquarters was in the past. Surely he made threats like the one he'd made to Christian all the time and never carried them out.

Besides, the moral fury he'd felt towards the key in Africa had changed now that he was free to use it on his own terms, just for himself. Because what harm could he possibly be doing to use the key to finesse a date or two with Julia? How long had it been since he'd considered his own pleasure? And when he thought of all those kids he'd helped, he started to realize that perhaps he did deserve spoiling.

Somehow, someone – probably someone Kenneth knew in Norway – had wanted him to have this upgrade service in his life to make that happen. In fact, the more he thought about it and that envelope that had come from Norway, the more that explanation made sense. It would have been typical of his brother to distrust something like the key, so he'd probably forwarded it on to Christian.

Christian remembered the kind of luxury upgrade the colonel had talked about that he and others used their keys for. Those sort of perks wouldn't have appealed to Kenneth at all. He was perfectly happy living his quiet but contented family life. What need did he have for first-class flights or exclusive accommodation? He didn't even have a phone.

If he could persuade Julia to come with him, Christian was determined to fly home to Norway with her and thank his brother. The more time he spent with her, the more important it became that he introduced her to his family.

But all in good time. Next week he planned to take Julia to Manaus, up the coast, where – with the help of the key – he had booked an exclusive jungle lodge up in the canopy. They were going trekking with a guide deep into the Amazon rainforest and would travel back on the mighty river itself. And then he had the most wonderful place in Colombo lined up. Maybe he'd ask the key for a yacht and make the journey in style. Could its generosity really stretch that far?

'Oh my God, Christian, this is so amazing,' Julia shouted over the noise of the water. 'But how did you . . . ? I mean, how can you afford it?' Julia said, staring into his eyes. 'I know doctors make good money, but still . . .'

'I used some savings,' Christian lied. He couldn't tell her about the key. Not just yet. Not when things were so wonderful.

He'd tell her about it in time, he assured himself. For now, he liked spoiling her. He liked being the guy who had conjured this magical trip out of nowhere. He liked making such a grand romantic gesture and seeing her eyes light up like they had.

She kissed him, clearly thrilled. Then her expression clouded, a questioning look replacing her previous joy, then just as quickly shifting into gritty determination. She broke away from him and walked right up to the edge of the railings. He watched as she reached inside her jacket and threw something silver over the edge. Christian saw it flash in the sunlight for a split second and then disappear into the raging falls.

'What was that?' he asked.

'Nothing. Something from the past, that's all.'

He wondered whether it had been a ring, although it had looked rather too big for that. Had she been engaged before? he thought. After all, he only had a very sketchy outline of her previous relationships.

Had that man who'd come to her apartment yesterday been an ex? he wondered, remembering how the stranger had banged on Julia's door. Christian had been so excited to tell Julia about his surprise trip that he'd flung open the door, expecting her to be home from work, but instead a rough-looking man had been standing there.

He'd been good-looking in a typical macho Brazilian sort of way. His jeans were dirty, but he had a pair of new trainers on. He'd been wearing a red and green football vest, but his overpowering aftershave hadn't been able to mask the stale sweat beneath it.

'Can I help you?' Christian had asked in English, making the man look confused.

'Do you know where she is?' he'd asked in heavy, stilted English. 'Julia?'

'At the school where she teaches. Shall I tell her you called?'

'No, no,' the man had said, frowning at Christian. 'Who are you?'

'I'm Christian, Julia's boyfriend,' he'd said.

He'd said it without thinking. Describing himself as her boyfriend had felt good.

The guy nodded, shuffling back towards the lift.

When Julia had finally come home from school, Christian had forgotten all about telling her about the man.

But no, Christian concluded now. Julia was too classy to be associated with the likes of a rough guy like that. And anyway, even if he was from her past, the past was just that. The past.

'Don't look so confused. It really doesn't matter,' she told him, laughing. 'It's just something I had to get rid of.' She leaned up and kissed him tenderly. 'I want to be totally honest with you,' she said.

'Me too,' he said.

'Which is why . . .' She sighed. 'Why . . .'

But Christian's gaze was torn from her smiling face. A man behind Julia, on the far side of the platform, was staring their way.

A man who looked exactly like . . . Dan.

Dan who was dead. Dan whom Christian had finally stopped dreaming about. Dan whom he'd put in the past . . .

Jesus. Was it his mind playing tricks on him?

He stared again, but there was a crowd of people in front of the Dan lookalike. When they'd moved on, he'd gone.

'What is it?' Julia asked him, frowning and cupping his face to draw his attention back to her.

'I thought I saw someone. I thought I saw someone I knew,' he said, but he was finding it difficult to speak. 'Sorry, what were you saying?'

'That I'll take you to meet Vovo,' she said. 'I want you to meet my family.'

'You mean it?' Christian said, forcing his attention back to Julia. She twined her fingers into his.

'Of course,' Julia said, her face lit up with a smile. 'Oh, Christian, I want to do everything I can to make you happy.'

Christian sat at the bamboo bar in the comfortable lounge looking at the lush gardens outside, the noisy birdsong clear over the ambient music. They hadn't been joking on the room brochure when they claimed this was the perfect place to unwind.

He smiled to himself, remembering his conversation with Julia and how good it had felt to admit their feelings for one another, and how magical the sex had been when they'd got back to their room upstairs. Now he had an hour alone while she had her massage at the spa. He sipped his beer, feeling so contented and relaxed that he didn't register that someone was next to him at the bar.

'Hello, Christian.'

Christian stared up at the man next to him. The man who had spoken. And his breath caught in his chest. He hadn't been imagining it after all . . .

Dan was wearing fawn trousers and a pink polo shirt. He no longer looked like the fresh-faced rookie doctor Christian had picked up that fateful day in Somalia. He looked older. His eyes were flinty, his face unsmiling.

'Dan' – Christian could barely speak – 'it *was* you at the falls . . .'

'I didn't want to interrupt. Looked like it was quite an emotional moment.'

Christian felt his cheeks pounding with blood. 'But you're . . .'

'Alive? Is that what you mean? Yes. No thanks to the colonel. Or you for that matter.'

Christian's mind went into overdrive as Dan ordered a beer for himself and slid onto the stool next to Christian like they were just two old friends sharing a drink. Like this was the most normal thing in the world. When it was anything but.

How had Dan survived? He and Olu, they were on the ground . . .

And Christian had left them. Left them at the compound when he'd driven off with the freed prisoners.

'I thought you'd been killed,' Christian said.

'Yes. I can see why you must have supposed that. In truth, right from the moment I realized that we were heading for the colonel's compound, I thought none of us would make it out alive.'

'You knew where we were going?' he asked, confused.

'Of course. I'd had intel on it for months.'

'Intel?'

Dan stared at Christian. 'I'm not really a doctor, Christian.'

'You're not?' Christian was confused. He'd seen him in action, in that makeshift hospital. He'd known what to do.

'That's not my first job, anyway. When I met you, I was working undercover.'

'Undercover? What do you mean?'

But even before Dan said it, Christian felt a sinking sense of dread. 'I work for the CIA.'

The CIA? Jesus.

And now Christian remembered how Dan had reacted to the rebels. How determined he'd been for them to run, but most of all, how he looked now. Like a man in control. A man with 'intel'.

But why was he telling Christian this now?

Christian picked up his beer and took a shaky sip, playing for time, wondering what this all meant. What Dan wanted from him. Because it couldn't be a coincidence him turning up like this out of the blue. No, he wasn't buying that. Not at all.

'I'll cut to the chase before your girlfriend comes back,' Dan said. 'It's Julia, isn't it?'

Christian felt his palms sweating. He knew Julia's name. What else did he know? He nodded dumbly. As he snuck a look up at Dan, he felt like the tables had turned on him. Like he was a little boy in trouble.

'I'm sorry, Dan. I don't know what to say,' he mumbled.

'I had to bury Olu's body myself.'

Christian closed his eyes. Poor Olu. His face swam into Christian's mind. A sharp stab of guilt hit him with almost physical force. He'd grieved for his friend – and for Dan – these past few months, but the fact remained that he hadn't even gone to see Olu's widow or children. He'd just wanted to get away. He'd been a coward. He should have at least told Olu's wife what a good man her husband had been, right up until the end. He owed Olu that and he regretted it bitterly now.

'Then I got picked up by the rebels as I was leaving the village. They took me way out into a compound in the bush where they held me captive for weeks. But eventually I got to speak to your *brother* Colonel Adid,' Dan said.

Christian felt a new wave of cold fear wash over him as he registered Dan's tone. *Brother.* So Dan thought he and the colonel were friends. Which could only mean that Christian had been kidding himself all along. The colonel hadn't forgotten him at all.

'He sends his regards, by the way,' Dan said conversationally, as if it were no big deal.

But it was.

Because he *knew*.

'How did you escape?' Christian asked, already dreading the answer. His voice was husky.

'Oh, I didn't escape. You don't *escape* a man like Colonel Adid. No, I made a deal with him.'

'A deal?'

'Come, come, Christian. You'd know all about making deals

with the colonel. He let me go on the proviso that I found you and got you to fulfil your promise to him.'

Christian felt panic swell in his chest as Dan took a sip of beer.

His promise. The promise he'd tried so hard to forget. The one that Dan – and the CIA – now knew about.

The colonel's manic grin was etched on his memory.

'But you've been a difficult man to find, Christian,' Dan said, his hawklike gaze connecting with Christian's terror-struck eyes. 'I knew you'd come to Brazil, from the flight records of course. But it wasn't until we saw a picture of you on Facebook on Julia's page that we traced you.'

Christian felt as if he were being tipped into concrete. *We*. He meant the CIA. They'd tracked him down through one picture on Facebook on Julia's page? He hadn't even realized she had a page, or that she'd uploaded a photo of him. How long had they been monitoring him? And why did they want to find him so badly?

'I don't know what you want with me. I thought . . . I thought this would all go away.'

'Did you? Then you were very wrong. Because the colonel says he's tripled his wager,' Dan went on. 'Three hundred children's lives. Unless you get him a magic key like yours.'

'I don't know where it came from,' Christian stuttered. 'I really don't. But the colonel can have mine,' he rushed on. 'Seriously. I can just give it to you.'

'He doesn't want yours. He wants his own. Like you promised,' Dan said reasonably. 'Your key is tailored, right? It'll only work for you. Because you've been approved by the organization, or whoever it is that's behind it.'

'But I don't know where it came from . . . who gave it to me. Why don't I just give it to you? You can find out.'

'Oh, believe me, we've tried that already. But neither the colonel's key nor yours comes from the marketing organization in Europe that administers them. In fact, they were quite horrified to find out that a man such as Adid had got hold of one.'

'That's because he got it from a sheikh in Dubai. That's what he told me.'

'Well, that explains it. But what's not explained is that you don't appear on their database at all. Anywhere. The key organization has never heard of you. And they haven't heard of these USB keys either. Like the one you have – and the colonel wants. And the one person who might have known, their CEO, was found dead recently, so we can't ask her either.'

Christian buried his head in his hands. This was terrifying. He felt completely trapped.

'But if you, if the CIA can't find out who's behind that, then what chance have I got?'

'Do you want those kids to die?' Dan's voice was harsh. Christian was not being let off the hook.

'No, I want to help them as much as you do. I want to—'

But then he noticed something in the other man's eyes. A darkening.

'That's not the only reason you want me to get him this key, is it?'

'No. It's vital you get a key for the colonel because it's the best chance we have of being able to track Adid and find out where he's going and where he's getting his funding from. We know he has links to al-Qaeda, but our intel suggests he has links to the very top. And that is information the US Government would very much like to know.'

'But you're still not telling me how the hell I'm meant to find another key. Whoever's behind all this is just as big a mystery to me as it is to you.' Christian panicked. 'I asked for another key straight away, but the key shut me out and said it wasn't possible. It's clearly a computer program. I can't get any answers out of it.'

'Then why don't you let us try?' Dan said.

'You want me to give you my key?'

Dan smiled a reassuring smile. 'Someone's chosen you, Christian. This isn't simply random. People don't just give money for nothing. You need to find out who is behind the key. And if you could meet someone from that organization in person, then you could explain everything about the colonel.'

'Do you think it would work, your guys hacking the system?' Christian felt his palms sweating.

'It looks like your best option right now.' Dan put his beer down on the bar. His look was deadly serious. 'Because you have two weeks to get another key or those children die.'

CHAPTER THIRTY

Harry surreptitiously stole yet another look at his watch as he sat on the plush maroon leather banquette of the Chinese Michelin-starred restaurant. His system was still swimming with coke and he wasn't hungry, although he'd ordered the chef's banquet.

He glanced at Kim Lee, the woman opposite, who was wolfing down noodles with her chopsticks, and tried to keep the disdain from his face as she spun the china bowls of food on the lazy Susan towards her and peered into their depths. It wasn't exactly ladylike. He'd never been out with girls who could eat like that, let alone any who would dream of eating so much at a meeting.

She was dressed in a black shirt and skirt that somehow didn't match and made her look like a schoolgirl. Her heavy eye make-up had the same effect of making her look younger. That sullen expression she had, staring out from behind a curtain of straight black hair, it was like she was still a teenager and Harry wondered what the other diners thought.

But it wasn't just the way she looked. She was just plain odd, Harry thought. The strange way she spoke English, with that funny accent, often muddling up words or putting them the wrong way round in a sentence. She looked wealthy, Armani sunglasses perched on her head, but there were little things that didn't make sense – like the fact that her nails were bitten right down, and her poor table manners. And he was sure he'd seen a flash of a tattoo on her arm.

In fact, he mused, as she gnawed on a marinated tiger prawn, there was lots about her that he couldn't figure out. For a start, she was clueless. Of that Harry was certain. He'd been spouting bullshit at her for over an hour and she hadn't challenged him once. In fact, he reckoned that if he told her to buy any kind of stock, then that's what she would do.

What kind of idiot must her father have been to leave his daughter the fortune he had? Surely if he was going to leave his only child a multi-millionairess, he might have prepared her better. Taught her about money, perhaps, and how it worked.

But then he pictured the sterile, privileged life in Tokyo that she'd described to him, and how she'd always dreamed of travelling to London and Paris, and he couldn't help feeling a bit sorry for her.

He had to admit that in her own warped way, she'd been very flattering to Harry all night. She'd told him she'd met someone who knew Cole Menzies, which is how she'd been introduced, and how grateful she was that he'd come to meet her. And of how Cole couldn't have sung his praises highly enough.

Yet the more she talked, the more it made Harry realize that he should have extricated himself sooner from his arrangement with Cole. This girl had expectations he couldn't possibly fulfil, and the more she said, the more trapped he felt.

Harry stole one more look at his watch. He wished Kim would damn well hurry up and finish her food so he could get out of here. Dulcie would be waiting. Lovely Dulcie. Dulcie who would make him feel good again. Who would make him laugh. Dulcie who had asked *him* for a date. She'd clearly forgiven him about that night with LaMay. Not that she'd believed LaMay had been there.

He realized that his heart was already beating in anticipation. That despite everything that had happened with LaMay, the Russian girls and even Bella, Dulcie had never been far from his thoughts. And now the thought of seeing her again made his pulse race.

Everyone deserved a second chance, didn't they? Well, this would be Dulcie's. If he'd been in her position, he'd have been just as sceptical. Tonight he was going to tell her what he'd discovered: that he had the power to make all his dreams come true, and all hers too, if she chose. She wouldn't be able to resist him then.

'Why you look at watch all the time?' Kim said, interrupting his thoughts, her chopsticks paused halfway to her mouth.

'I'm sorry,' Harry said, forcing himself to return his attention to his dinner guest. He shot her his most charming smile.

Kim nodded and, catching the eye of the waiter, asked for the bill.

Knowing he was entertaining Kim on the bank's behalf, Harry reached into his Gucci leather jacket and put his credit card down on the small silver tray the waiter provided. But a few moments later, when the waiter came with the credit machine, Harry's card wouldn't work. Neither would three others. And he was clean out of cash.

He felt saliva flood his mouth as his last card didn't work. He'd been so busy flitting around from party to party and eating the food on Cole's yacht that he'd hardly paid any attention to his financial affairs. But obviously all his accounts were over-drawn and the cards had been stopped. And now he remembered the overdue loan repayment on his mortgage, the Internet betting site he owed money to . . . The list went on. Sweat prickled the back of his neck. Why hadn't he thought of sorting it all out before? He was such a damn idiot.

This was embarrassing, he thought, smiling lamely at Kim, who insisted on paying the bill.

'Where are we going now?' she asked, as she shrugged on her jacket. She smiled at him then, flashing her slightly stained crooked teeth. Why hadn't she seen an orthodontist if she was loaded?

We? There was no we. Harry had already explained that he was meeting someone.

'I'm afraid—'

'I come with you,' she said, as if it were already a done deal.

Harry shifted uncomfortably, not sure how to play this. Why couldn't she just back off? It wasn't as if they were friends. Right now he wanted to see Dulcie alone. Did she have no concept that he had a private life? *Jesus*.

'I like to see what you do,' she continued, looking directly at him. Her eyes were cold. Calculating. 'I have car. We drive. Together.'

Harry realized he was hardly in a position to refuse her offer. He had the key to the most fabulous luxury, but ironically, right now he wouldn't be able to get cash out to hail a cab and time was running out. He needed to get to Shoreditch. And now he owed her for buying dinner.

Reluctantly he followed Kim outside to her smart four-by-four and gave the address to the driver.

He found it easy to give a running commentary about the

sights of London through the tinted window of Kim's car and she leaned forward, taking it all in, as eager as a child, but his mind was still racing as they drove through the city. How was he going to explain Kim Lee to Dulcie? He'd have to tell her that he'd been promoted and that she was a client, but it would hardly be a great start to their reunion.

It was already a quarter to eleven and he was late. Dulcie might think he wasn't coming.

Kim's driver turned into the warren of backstreets beyond Liverpool Street, but as the neighbourhood grew ever more shabby, Harry started to become uneasy. When the car stopped outside a seedy-looking club in a backstreet of Shoreditch, he asked to re-examine the scrap of paper he'd given the driver. The bar had a sign of a naked lady above the door. A large bouncer stood outside.

This couldn't be right, could it? He'd assumed from the address that Dulcie wanted to meet him at some trendy East End private members' club. But this place? This was the sleazy bar Nick Grundy and his boys used to come to. He was sure of it.

He realized that all of his assumptions might have been wrong. While he'd been living the high life, Dulcie's life might have taken an equally dramatic turn . . . but for the worse. What if she'd lost her job at the Savoy? Jesus, had she become a lap dancer to get that ticket to South America?

No, surely not. Dulcie wouldn't do that.

Kim was getting out of the car and Harry quickly followed. A camera flashed. He was shocked to see that Kim had just taken his photograph. She took another one of the pink neon sign and the bouncer, who scowled at Harry and wagged his fat finger in disapproval.

'Please, no, Kim, don't. You'll get us into trouble,' he said, putting his hand out to stop her, while apologizing to the bouncer.

'Why don't you go?' he said, trying to usher her back towards the car. She couldn't come in the bar with him. Cole would be horrified that he'd brought her here. But Kim broke away from him. 'This is clearly a mistake. Let me just sort this out—'

'You friend? She exotic dancer?' Kim asked, wriggling out of his grasp and walking right up to the door. She clearly had no intention of leaving.

She smiled at the bouncer, who looked along the street and then opened the black door for her. 'We have bars like this in Tokyo,' she said, as Harry caught up.

'Jesus,' he murmured, quickly following her.

Inside, the music was loud, heavy bass throbbing out. Several semi-naked girls swirled round the poles on the stage. He felt his erection springing to attention. Kim nodded her head in time to the music, already heading down the steps towards the bar.

Harry stared at the girls writhing and crouching round the poles in their high heels, their hands in their hair, feigning sultry desire. They were doing a damn good job of making it look real, Harry thought. He'd find Dulcie and discover what the hell she was doing in a place like this before he got too distracted. But then he remembered that he had no credit cards that worked. He was relying on Miss Investment for drinks.

Half an hour later there was still no sign of Dulcie, and to Harry's surprise, Kim seemed to be enjoying herself. She kept buying him drinks, but Harry was feeling increasingly disorientated and weird, his vision cutting in and out, the music throbbing uncomfortably in his veins.

He couldn't help feeling disappointed too. Dulcie hadn't shown up yet. And the longer she didn't, the more certain he felt that she wasn't coming. So why had she left a message being so specific about meeting here? It didn't make sense.

He went to the gents' and did another fat line of coke, expecting it to wake him up and get his clarity back, but it only seemed to make things worse.

He staggered over to the bar and waited for the girl to serve him, rummaging in his pocket for some change.

'Your friend the Japanese girl left,' the busty blonde said, full of smiles. 'She's left money for you to have a good time. You can have anything you want.' She winked, her meaning clear.

No way. Kim Lee had left. And she'd left having paid the bar bill. Maybe she wasn't so bad after all, he thought. Well, fuck Dulcie. If she wasn't going to bother showing up, then he was damn well going to enjoy himself.

'I want a magnum of champagne,' Harry slurred. Now he was free of Kim, he could do what he wanted. 'And bring me girls.'

He rubbed his eyes, trying to focus, but his vision was jagged, like cut-up pictures.

What had been in that drink to make him feel so pissed? Usually they watered stuff down in these places, but he could barely stand upright.

'There is someone who wants to see you out in the back room,' a stripper whispered, escorting him from the bar. Her sweaty breasts pressed up against him, her saccharine perfume choking him.

Harry stumbled as she led him towards a padded red leather door in the corner.

'Is Dulcie here?' he slurred. What was wrong with his

speech? He could hardly get the words out. It was as if his tongue were made of glue. 'Dulcie?'

There was a large booth beyond the padded door, and the waitress gave him a gentle, friendly shove towards a red velvet couch, the throbbing bass of the music making him feel like his own head was an amplifier. And then, on the other side of the booth, another small door opened and there were girls, five of them, swaying and giggling towards him. Two sat down either side of him, pressing their limbs against his legs. Another stood on the small raised platform. She pressed a button and a silver pole rose from the floor. She writhed suggestively in time to the music.

'Hello,' Harry slurred as the other girl sat next to a girl on his right. She had colossal breasts, straining to get out of her bra. She leaned over the other girl towards Harry and it was all he could do not to bury his face in her soft cleavage.

Another waitress appeared through the doorway with a magnum of champagne and the girls clapped and laughed as she popped open the bottle, tipping the spilling froth into Harry's mouth. He choked and laughed. Then he was aware of someone else in the doorway and was blinded by the flash of a camera.

'No,' he slurred, waving his arms. 'No photos.'

Then he saw to his horror that it was Kim.

What was she doing here? The girl behind the bar . . . she'd told him Kim had left.

'But you funny,' Kim told him. She waved to the girls, who pushed back Harry in his seat. They pouted and posed around him as Kim snapped away.

Harry felt a momentary flash of panic. She was Cole's client. He was supposed to be showing her a good time. Not *this*. She certainly couldn't be forming a very healthy impression of him. And if she reported all this back to Cole . . .

But then, Kim seemed to be enjoying herself too, laughing and directing the girls. If they minded being photographed, they didn't object. In fact, they seemed keen to pose for her.

'Seriously, enough,' Harry said, but he was laughing and groaning as the girls petted and stroked him. They swarmed around him and he felt his shirt being unbuttoned. Music and alcohol strobed, his vision blurring.

One of the girls stood on the banquette above him. She swayed over him in her skimpy thong, the tiniest patch of black silk covering her vulva. He could see the smooth inside of her legs. He felt his erection swelling, yet he knew he couldn't move. He glanced over at the two girls next to him, and as they looked him straight in the eye, one of them swiped aside the fabric of the big-busted girl's bra and then, still looking at Harry, flicked her tongue over the girl's dusky-pink nipple.

'Oh Jesus,' Harry moaned.

He no longer cared if Kim was taking photos. She was probably a dyke who could get off on these pictures later. And perhaps this was the kind of thing she was used to, coming from Japan. Maybe she went to places like this in Tokyo all the time.

The dancer squatted over him; her crotch was just millimetres away from his throbbing cock.

He felt himself relaxing, all thoughts of Dulcie forgotten.

CHAPTER THIRTY-ONE

Julia sat at the desk watching the swirls of dust sparkle in the sunny classroom, a smile on her face, as the rowdy class fought around her. She seemed to have taken leave of her senses and could only focus on one thought: Christian. Christian in her apartment. Right now. In her bed. Christian's face when he'd told her that he loved her too.

It had felt – it *still* felt – amazing. So amazing she wanted to dance and twirl across the desks. Because this was the real thing. There was no doubt in her mind.

She heard a loud shout and looked up to see Maria coming into the classroom wearing cut-off jeans, her checked shirt tied up. Reluctantly, the kids simmered down and took their places, the room filling with the sound of scraping chairs. Maria eyeballed Julia as she marched towards her desk at the front of her class and dumped her bag on a spare chair.

'You still ill? You don't look ill.'

Julia shook her head, amazed that Maria seemed to be so in control. Maybe the assertiveness training course that Maria had been on in Julia's place had been educational after all.

'Tell me where you were,' Maria said. 'And don't bullshit. I know you weren't ill.'

'Oh, all right, then. I went away . . .' Julia said, her joy spilling over, 'with the man – with Christian – you know, from the train.'

'You sly old dog,' Maria said, her face breaking into a wide grin.

But just as Julia was starting to describe what had happened, Senhora Azevedo poked her head round the classroom door and frowned at all the noise. 'Julia, can I have a word? Now.'

'She doesn't know, does she?' Julia panicked.

'No, your sickbed performance had us all fooled. You should be an actress, girl.'

But a few minutes later, as Julia entered the office and was instructed to sit on the headmistress's couch, her good spirits evaporated.

Senhora Azevedo looked at her briefly, then back at some papers in her hands. 'I'll get to the point,' she said, pacing in front of Julia. 'I have applied for more funds from the local authority,' she said. 'After the grant they gave to the school.'

'Oh?' Julia said, not sure where this was leading.

'I was sent on quite a wild goose chase between departments, but it appears there was no lottery between all the schools. Someone *did* apply on your behalf for a grant behind my back.' She looked over the top of her glasses down at Julia. 'So it appears you lied to me.'

'Please. I can explain—'

Senhora Azevedo held up her hand. She hadn't finished. 'Can you? Because then I called your home yesterday and I spoke to a' – she studied her papers – 'Mr Marcello Pires.'

'Oh God,' Julia whispered to herself. What had Marcello told her boss? He was furious that she'd moved out and had left him alone to be responsible for Fredo. He'd accused her of concealing things from him and changing into someone he no longer recognized. Buying a new television for the apartment had helped, but Marcello was still behaving strangely towards her. She'd had to tell him she was going away for a few days, to make sure that he'd cover her visits to Vovo at the hospital.

'He said you'd gone on a small *vacation*' – her look and tone betrayed her horror at Julia's deceit – 'and that you were no longer living at the home address we have for you.'

Julia felt herself withering in the headmistress's glare. She'd been so fearful of being exposed as a liar, but now that she had, she felt even worse than she'd imagined. A wave of shame hit her as she tried to think of a way to explain herself.

As the headmistress waited for an answer, Julia's mind whirred frantically, but there was nothing for it. She'd have to come clean and tell the truth. She wasn't a bad person, she reasoned. If Senhora Azevedo knew the truth, then she'd forgive her, wouldn't she? She'd see that Julia had always acted with the best possible motives.

So, haltingly, she began. She told Senhora Azevedo about finding the wallet. About how she'd met a stranger who'd told her that she'd been selected to receive a key that would help with whatever she wanted, but that all she'd ever wanted was to give the kids some new horizons. So she'd made a request for the school trip.

'You expect me to believe this rubbish?' Senhora Azevedo said, shaking her head. 'I know you have a vivid imagination, Julia, but of all the low excuses—'

'It's the truth.'

'So where is this magic key of yours?'

'I . . . I don't have it.' Julia stalled, remembering her key spinning into the spray of the falls, glinting in the sunlight, like a final wink. She'd thought such a spontaneous, liberating gesture would make her feel free, but now, as her boss stared at her open mouthed, she tried to remember the conviction she'd felt at that moment. The surety that it had been the right thing to do. That she would be better off without the key. That without it, she could live her life better. That she could be honest and true to herself, without feeling that someone was watching her from a distance and judging her.

But instead she felt herself sinking in quicksand. She'd been an utter fool. She should never have thrown away the key. What had she been thinking?

'I have standards to uphold. Of loyalty and honesty, Julia. You obviously feel this school is somehow beneath you and you have let me and the children down. I don't think I can have someone like you on my staff any longer. Not when there's a list of willing, dedicated teachers queuing up to take your place.'

Julia was shaking as she left the school for the last time on her moped, negotiating the potholed road through the rain. Maria hadn't been able to believe that Julia had been dismissed so quickly. She'd had no time to say goodbye to the kids, only making Maria promise, through her tears, to be sure she watered the orchids and looked out for Eduardo.

Above her, storm clouds rumbled, but Julia hardly noticed that she was soaked to the skin. The further away from school she got, the more miserable she felt. She'd told Senhora Azevedo the truth, but it had backfired. And she could understand why. Her story did sound far-fetched and too good to be true. She'd have been better off if she'd told her that she'd won the lottery, like Julia had told Vovo. At least she might have been believed.

What if Christian had the same reaction when she told him

about the key? What if he didn't believe how she'd got her apartment, and all these clothes, not to mention Vovo's private hospital treatment? She couldn't bear for him to think of her as a liar too.

Because now that she didn't have the key to prove the truth, why would he believe her? Again she pictured it spinning away from her into the spray of the falls. At the time she'd felt elated, thrilled that she'd made such a bold decision, but now she wished she could take that moment back. The key wasn't responsible for her guilt and shame . . . *she* was. Nobody had forced her to use it. It had been her choice all along.

And now, with no income, and no key, how was she going to be able to afford to live? And what if the hospital came after her for Vovo's medical bills? She wouldn't be able to get another job straight away, and even if she did apply, what kind of reference would Senhora Azevedo give her now?

All the excitement she'd felt about introducing Christian to her grandmother later now felt tarnished. She'd thought throwing away the key would bring her closer to telling the truth – living the truth – but it had only done the opposite. She'd have to lie even more now, not only to Christian. What would her grandmother say if she knew Julia had been fired from her teaching job? After all that hard work . . . the struggle through college and now she'd blown it.

She braced herself, wiping away her tears and turning her key in her apartment door, expecting to find Christian waiting for her. But as she opened the door, she knew straight away that he wasn't there. That he'd gone.

There was an envelope pushed underneath her door and Julia pulled it open.

'*My darling Julia – I've gone away*,' the note read. She

realized that this was the first time she'd ever seen Christian's handwriting. '*I'm sorry I didn't have a chance to explain. I'll be gone for a week — two at the most. I'll explain when I get back. I love you.*'

Two weeks.

Julia let out an anguished sob. Two weeks. That felt like forever. Because there had hardly been two minutes that she hadn't thought about him, spoken to him, touched him . . .

And now he'd gone.

More deep, heart-rending sobs came and she steadied herself on the kitchen counter, staring at the note, willing it not to be true. She gazed at the view from the window, at the dark grey sky through the slashes of rain on the glass. The palm trees on the beach were bent over in the wind.

Why had Christian gone away? What did his note mean? How could he just leave for two weeks?

Had it been anything to do with that man he'd bumped into at the bar of the hotel? That old colleague? Christian had looked pale and worried when she'd joined him at the bar after her spa treatment, although he'd told her he was fine. Then, when she'd woken up in the middle of the night, he'd been staring out of the window into the darkness, lost in thought.

Why had he gone without any kind of explanation or warning? It felt as if he had run away. But why would he do that when things were going so well? Julia couldn't figure it out, but alone in the apartment, her worst fear swamped her: he'd gone because she'd told him she loved him. She'd pushed things too hard. All the security she'd felt when she'd been with him vanished now he'd gone.

Alone in the strange, soulless apartment, she felt cut off from everyone and everything she loved. Without her job, without

Christian, her world seemed unbearably empty. She couldn't even call Nat. Because Nat would be furious when she found out Julia had thrown away her key. But then, Nat had never understood the conflict Julia had felt about it. She'd just seen it as an opportunity.

Why, oh, why couldn't the key have gone to someone like Nat instead? Why Julia?

She still felt wobbly when she took a tram to the hospital a few hours later. The rain hadn't eased and she had to dodge past puddles with her umbrella. As she walked through the sliding glass doors with her soggy flowers for Vovo, she remembered the first time she'd come here in the private ambulance. That night she'd met the man who had given her the key. And all the lies she'd told since.

Julia chatted to the nurse, swapping pleasantries, and she made her excuses for not coming earlier. To her surprise, the nurse told her that Vovo already had a visitor and Julia braced herself for seeing Marcello, although the only reason she'd come to visit Vovo at this hour was because she was sure he'd be watching football on the TV with Fredo. It was just as well Christian wasn't with her.

She felt her heart racing as she pushed open the door to Vovo's room and saw a familiar figure standing by the bed. It was Ricardo. Her brother.

'Riccy. Oh my God. What are you doing here?' Her voice sounded shrill as she put down the flowers on the chair by the bed.

Her estranged brother's handsome good looks had hardened somehow into something flinty and cold. He looked rough too. He'd always taken good care of himself and his appearance, but his jeans were dirty, and when she hugged him, he smelt of stale sweat.

His hug was unfriendly and he all but pushed her away. She covered up her panic by trying to make conversation. If Riccy was in one of his black moods, then there would be trouble.

'When did you get here? Have you seen Fredo? He'll be happy to see you.'

Riccy pulled a nonchalant shrug. He didn't care about Fredo. He never had and he never would, but at least he was here, she told herself. At least he'd bothered to come and see Vovo.

'So tell me, Julia,' he said, his eyes narrowing suspiciously, 'how did you manage to afford all this?'

Julia pressed her lips together. She took Vovo's hand and squeezed it, but the old woman didn't move. She looked in a deep, troubled sleep. Julia couldn't believe how much frailer she seemed than when she'd seen her last week. Had Riccy done something to upset her?

As Julia stared at her grandmother, she felt her brother's eyes boring into her and her skin prickled. Now she remembered the Riccy of old. How mean he could be. How avaricious. Had he fallen for the excuse she'd given Marcello – that Vovo had won the lottery? If he had, then he was undoubtedly here to claim his share. She braced herself for trying to bluff her way out of the fact that there was no money left.

She was saved by Doctor Sanchez, who pushed open the door.

'Ah, Julia,' he said with a smile. She remembered how attractive she'd found him when she'd first met him. Since then she'd fallen in love with Christian and now she couldn't imagine finding anyone else attractive. 'How nice to see you again. I'm glad you're here.'

He looked enquiringly at Riccy.

'This is my brother, Ricardo,' Julia said.

'Would it be OK to talk about your grandmother?' Doctor Sanchez asked her.

'I'm her next of kin. Why wouldn't it be?' Riccy said. His tone alarmed both Julia and the doctor, who cleared his throat and looked down at his clipboard.

'You'll see that we've given Consuela a mild sedative,' he said. 'I'm afraid I had to break some bad news to her.'

'Bad news?' Julia asked, stepping towards him. She felt sick with guilt. She should have been here by Vovo's side.

'We did some routine blood tests that have revealed why your grandmother hasn't been responding to her surgery as well as we'd hoped.'

'What's the bottom line, Doctor?' Riccy snapped. Julia bristled at her brother's rude tone. He had no idea what Doctor Sanchez had done for Vovo. How he'd saved her life.

'Your grandmother is suffering from a rare blood disease.'

'What kind of disease? Can you treat her?' Julia asked.

'Not at this stage. The disease is too advanced and she's very weak.'

'You're saying that she's going to die?' Riccy said.

Julia felt her eyes welling with tears, but at the same time she felt furious with Riccy for being so blunt. For sounding so uncaring.

'I'm afraid, that yes, that is looking likely.'

'How long?' Julia asked, swallowing back tears.

'Days at the very most.'

Julia felt a sob escape her. 'Days?'

'I'm sorry, Julia. We did the best we could. The heart surgery was a success, but none of us figured on this kind of complication.'

Julia nodded and went to Vovo's side, staring down at her face through a blur of tears. She hardly noticed that the doctor had gone until the door shut.

'Oh, cut the bullshit,' Ricardo snapped. 'Just give me my share of the money. From her win.' He glanced at Vovo. So he *had* fallen for the lottery explanation after all. 'I need it. And I need it fast.'

Julia backed away from him, all her illusions shattering. Of course he wasn't here because he cared about Vovo. He just wanted money. 'I can't . . . I don't have any money.'

'Oh great,' he said, throwing up his arms. 'So you've fucked us all over. Me and Marcello.'

'No, I haven't. I—'

'So you took her money,' he interrupted her. 'You paid for this fancy hospital, but then you spent all the rest on yourself. On your fancy clothes and your fancy apartment.'

He knew about her apartment?

'It's not like that,' she began to protest, but one look at his face and she knew it was useless. He was furious. And he really did believe she owed him money. 'Vovo, she only won enough for the hospital. Everything else . . . I got myself.'

'I don't believe you.'

'But it's the truth.'

'Seriously, cut the crap, Julia,' he told her, his tone cold and menacing. 'You'd better find some money fast. Because you owe us.'

'What do you mean, "us"? You and Marcello? I don't owe you anything,' she said, trying to keep her voice strong. How dare he talk to her like this when the doctor had just told them that Vovo was going to die? Fury reared up in her. She'd kept his family together all this time. 'If you haven't noticed, I've paid for *everything*. And *I'm* the one who has looked after your son—'

He sneered at her, throwing up his hand to cut her off, and she saw that he wasn't going to listen to her. He didn't care about Fredo. And he wasn't ever going to thank her for holding their family together, while he came and went as he chose.

There was a beat of silence as she battled with enraged tears. She didn't want to break down in front of him. He'd love that. He'd love to see her being weak.

'She took you in, you know,' Riccy said, staring down at Vovo.

Julia was so surprised her tears stalled. His voice was sad.

'What?' Julia asked, confused. She followed his gaze to Vovo's sleeping face, horrified by the look of contempt in his eyes. He wasn't sad. There was another emotion going on – something that she didn't understand.

'She took us both in,' Julia corrected him.

'They weren't your parents,' Riccy said, his wrist jiggling nervously. 'Haven't you got it yet?'

He twirled his finger by his temple as if she were mad. Julia clenched her fists together to stop them shaking.

'Stop it,' she managed, but her voice felt fragile. She felt terrified of where he was going with this.

'So you really are going to play the innocent,' he said, adding with a sarcastic laugh, 'Still? After all this time?'

Riccy strutted away from her and back again. He faced her from the other side of Consuela's bed.

'These guys in this picture?' he said, pointing to the

photograph of Julia's parents that she'd had reframed and had brought to Vovo's bedside to remind her of home. 'They were *my parents*,' he said. 'Just mine. I was their only son.' He stared down at Vovo. 'I was her flesh and blood, but she took you in too. And she always preferred you. Always.'

'What?' Julia felt sick.

'You were the reason we had to stay in the favela. To lie low. To never be official. She could have done so much, but she backed away from every opportunity. To keep you hidden.' He looked down at Consuela, a look of disgust on his face. 'A woman like that . . . she had so much intelligence, but she chose to be a cleaner.'

'Stop it!' Julia shouted, putting her hands up to her ears. 'Don't you dare say these things. Don't you dare.'

He stepped to the other side of the bed and put his hand round Julia's throat. 'Shut up. Shut up. It's the truth, you stupid bitch. Everything she ever told you was a lie.'

She stared at him with wide eyes, seeing the truth . . . the fury in his, seeing for the first time the magnitude of the resentment he carried inside him. He let her go and she gasped, staggering away. This couldn't be happening. What he was saying, it couldn't be true . . .

'We all played along for her. Even Marcello. That fool.'

Julia closed her eyes for a moment, her mind spinning. What he was saying . . . if it was true . . . then it would rewrite her entire family history. Vovo couldn't possibly have lied to her, could she?

Her brain refused to believe it. And yet . . . yet something tugged at her conscience. Now that she looked at Ricardo, she could see how little they resembled each other. And something else . . . another memory . . . one she'd never been able to pin down . . . one that she'd always thought of as a dream. A swimming pool and a woman who was crying, kissing her and saying goodbye. And a little girl with blonde hair.

And Vovo – when she'd had her heart attack, she'd tried to say something about Julia's mother, as if she had some kind of secret to get off her chest . . .

Julia stared over at Vovo, tears pooling in her eyes.

'I wouldn't ask her anything. She can't help you now. She can't protect her darling Julia any longer.'

'No, oh God, no,' Julia sobbed.

'So you'd better give me what I need, or I'll tell that fancy boyfriend of yours exactly where you came from.'

'What?' Julia stared up at him through her tears, panic clutching her insides.

'You think I don't know about your blond lover boy?'

She saw him relishing the power to hurt her with these words.

'Oh, yeah, I can't wait to tell him the truth about who you really are.'

CHAPTER THIRTY-TWO

'Scooter Black's office,' Scooter heard. She smiled as she walked downstairs and saw Lin, her new assistant, coming through the front door of her Bel Air mansion, a cell phone tucked between her shoulder and ear, her arms full of paper bags of groceries.

Scooter did have a new office in Brody Myers' production company, where she usually worked in the mornings, but since she'd moved here after leaving Cannes and things had got more serious between her and Dallas, there were a couple of paparazzi-types hanging out in the studio parking lot and she preferred to work at home rather than risk being caught on camera.

Besides, since she'd asked the key for somewhere to live and the agent had given her the keys to this house, she hardly wanted to leave it. Bette Davis used to own the lovely wisteria-covered period mansion and had thrown parties round the famous pool in the palm-fringed garden in the 1940s. Hollywood legends had graced these rooms and corridors for decades and Scooter loved every inch of it.

She hurried over and grabbed two bulging bags from Lin, thinking how much easier life would be once the new house-keeper and chef started next week and she and Lin wouldn't even have to shop for groceries any more. She could see how quickly she could become cut off from the real world living this kind of life, but hell, after the two years she'd had since Dean left, she deserved a bit of pampering. She couldn't deny that it felt wonderful.

Lin put her hand over the phone and whispered, 'Dallas's agent. You still on for lunchtime?'

'Sure.'

Scooter watched Lin, realizing that she wasn't yet experienced enough in the business to realize the magnitude of lunch with John Cross. But it hardly mattered. Lin was cute and eager, and of all the assistants she'd interviewed she was the only one who was genuinely honest. The only one who hadn't been sycophantic or hadn't name-dropped. She didn't want to be an actress or a producer anytime soon. She just needed a job.

She handed Scooter the pile of mail from beneath her arm and Scooter flicked through the envelopes, spotting several glossy invitations to charity galas. It seemed that everyone wanted Scooter at their party these days. Especially if she came with Dallas.

Lin rang off. 'You're meeting him at one at the Gallery,' she said.

'OK,' Scooter said with a grin.

She didn't know what today's meeting would be about, but Dallas had just got the lead in the big-budget Spielberg production and it was still unsure who was to be the leading lady. Was that why he'd insisted on this meeting with his agent?

Dallas wasn't very keen on the idea of her co-producing Brody Myers' film, but that was to do with the fact that Brody had caught a cold on his last five projects in a row and they'd been flops. Dallas was protective enough not to want Scooter to be associated with his sixth if it also tanked. Besides, Dallas seemed determined for Scooter not to give up on her dream of being an actress, and he'd clearly convinced his agent of the same thing.

But even so, would John Cross *really* take Scooter on as a client? If he did, then she'd get to see a casting agent. And then, maybe then, she'd be able to audition for a part in Dallas's movie. It was such a long shot she told herself not to get excited. But even being just a step closer to being considered for the kind of part that would make her globally famous felt more intoxicating than any drug Scooter had ever taken.

She told herself to keep her feet on the ground. Nothing had happened yet.

'I'm going for a swim,' Scooter told Lin. She loved the outdoor pool. She loved the feeling of pushing off underwater and swimming a whole length before coming up. Dallas had told her yesterday that she was like a dolphin. 'You want to join me?'

'What, me?'

'Yes, you.' Scooter stared at her. She was determined never to be a snobby, pushy boss. If Lin was going to be working in her home, then Scooter was going to make her feel like she was welcome. 'You can swim, can't you?'

'I'd love to. It's so hot out there.'

The doorbell rang, making them both jump.

Lin raised her eyebrows. 'What d'you think? More flowers?'

Scooter opened the door. In front of her was a bouquet of bubblegum-pink hydrangeas.

'Oh my,' she gushed, accepting them from the flower guy, who was hidden from view behind them.

She took them inside as Lin tipped the guy and laughed about the probability of him being back in the morning.

'Are you getting the message yet that Dallas Laney kinda likes you?' Lin said.

Scooter laughed, looking for the card.

Good luck with John today xxx

'Three kisses,' she told Lin.

Scooter bit her lip, delighted with the flowers and the card. She knew this was all a game. Of course she was attracted to Dallas, especially after all the fun they'd had at her party in France. But she was deliberately keeping him at arm's length until she was sure he wouldn't run away. Besides, what could be more exciting than to be sent a bouquet of fresh flowers every day from the world's sexiest man?

Scooter was still smiling as she drove insanely fast along the coast road in her brand-new red convertible Lexus to meet John Cross at the Gallery, feeling the sun on her face, the ocean sparkling in the distance.

She looked down at her pale blue Armani skirt and funky wedges. She hoped she looked the part and not overly groomed, but she hadn't been able to resist the outfit. Her shopping session with top celebrity stylist Cheri Masterson last week had been one of the most illuminating days of her life. She'd asked the key for someone to give her shopping advice in LA and Cheri had turned up on her doorstep offering her services.

Cheri had given a brutal appraisal of Scooter's wardrobe, culling half her outfits as entirely unsuitable, before whisking her off on a tour of exclusive boutiques in search of a 'vital capsule wardrobe', as Cheri had put it. Scooter hadn't paid for a thing. In fact, Cheri had made it clear that the shops positively fell over themselves to welcome Cheri and her handful of exclusive clients. 'Darling, they don't call me "the Cherry-Picker" for nothing,' she'd said with a wink, as she'd signed for the items. When Cheri had shown her how to put all the outfits together, for the first time it had felt as if Scooter had finally understood how to dress. She would never look back.

Today the dream was just getting better and better.

Dubbed for the fifth year in a row the best restaurant in California, and known to be the biggest celebrity haunt in Beverly Hills, Scooter felt self-conscious as she walked from the sidewalk to the steps of the Gallery. The art gallery to one side that showcased some of the best modern artists in the world had been eclipsed by the restaurant, which was always packed out, even when an art show wasn't on.

John Cross was waiting for her. She recognized him from all the online pictures of him at various awards ceremonies. He had a bald head and distinctive thick black-rimmed glasses, and had the casual, scruffy style of only the very successful in Tinsel Town.

'It's a pleasure to meet you, Miss Black,' he said, kissing her cheek. He smelt of expensive cologne. 'I've been hearing great things about you.'

'Scooter. Please, call me Scooter.'

'Have you been here before?'

Scooter shook her head, looking at the large open-plan restaurant beyond. It was simple and yet elegant, with beautiful long white tablecloths and black chairs beneath a stunning modern glass chandelier. The ornate woodwork was all painted white, with large doors along one side opening onto a flower-filled patio, where the tables were said to be blessed with Hollywood magic.

'The squid salad is to die for,' he said, waiting patiently in line. Scooter could see the maître d' greeting Justin Timberlake

up ahead. Oh, and wasn't that Anne Hathaway? In fact . . .
everywhere she turned, she saw faces she recognized.

Then she remembered that she was somebody now too. She
was lunching with John Cross.

They arrived at the podium and the waitress's eyes sparked
with recognition. She stood up straighter, flashing her perfectly
capped teeth. Her eyes gave Scooter a look of awed respect.
For a second Scooter longed to blurt out that until a couple of
months ago, she'd been a waitress too. Not somewhere like this,
but at a grotty diner in Brooklyn. She wanted to tell the girl that
dreams really could come true.

'Hi,' John said, smiling. 'We have a table for two.'

But now, as the girl looked down at the ledger, her smile
vanished.

'I'm afraid, Mr Cross, that I don't quite . . .' She trailed out
in a quiet voice, flipping over the pages. Colour rose in her
cheeks.

'Well, this is embarrassing.' John laughed to Scooter. 'I'm
going to murder my assistant.' A man now appeared at the girl's
side. He had perfect hair and teeth. 'Leon, there seems to be a
problem,' John said.

Scooter could see the tips of Leon's ears had gone pink, and
a rash rose at his neck.

'Mr Cross, sir, let me see,' he said. His English had a heavy
French accent.

He looked down at the ledger and back up again, flipping
over several pages. Scooter could feel the people behind them
becoming impatient.

'I'm sorry . . . Oh dear. Who made the reservation?'

'My assistant, Lucy. Weeks ago. She confirmed this morning.'
John's tone had lost its friendly edge.

'We have no reservation for you. Not today. Or anytime this week.'

'But . . . but . . . come on, Leon. Surely you can fit us in?' John leaned forward towards the podium, acutely aware of the people behind them and heads in the restaurant turning.

'I'd love to, really I would, but I'm afraid we're completely fully booked today. Totally. If I could possibly fit you in, I would.'

'You have got to be kidding me.' John turned away, his face a mask of fury. He was clearly a man who was not used to being turned down. He looked at Scooter, his casual demeanour now completely ruffled.

Scooter put her arm on his and smiled. 'Let me try.'

She walked to the podium and discreetly put her key down on the open ledger so that Leon could see it. She shielded her action from John.

'Might this help?' she whispered.

He paused for a moment, then looked up. As their eyes met, Scooter knew that somehow the magical key had changed everything.

'Give me two minutes,' he said. 'I'll set another table up for you on the patio. I'm very sorry for all the confusion. Lunch will, of course, be on the house. And I think we have some rather good sauvignon blanc that Mr Cross likes.'

Scooter felt triumphant as they walked to their table out in the sunny courtyard.

'How did you manage that?' John asked in a low voice.

Scooter shrugged. She didn't want to tell him about the key. She was enjoying the moment of power too much. The fact that he'd assumed she was clearly so well connected she could get a table where he couldn't had put their lunch on an entirely different footing. She could hear the other diners murmuring about them as Scooter and John sat down at the newly laid table.

John chose wine and water, and the conversation flowed easily. She told him about her recent work with Brody Myers and how she'd met Dallas. She told him, too, about how she'd always wanted to be an actress and how Miranda had told her she'd missed the boat.

'We'll be having words about that,' he assured her.

They ate squid salad, and she told him how much she was enjoying her new house and how she loved swimming in the pool. He didn't ask her about how she was able to afford it. She'd noticed the rich never asked such indiscreet questions. When Dallas – in a roundabout way – had asked her how she'd been able to procure such a real-estate gold mine, she'd hinted at old family money and he'd asked no further questions. She'd almost told him about the key, but had decided she'd wait until she knew him better. But now, when John asked her about her family, Scooter realized she didn't want to lie to him.

'My mom, she was so weak,' Scooter said, with a sigh. She pushed her knife and fork together and dabbed her mouth with the napkin. 'I mean, you know you see in movies the typical trailer-trash mom? Well, that was her. Only worse. She drank and smoked herself stupid and then let a whole succession of assholes cross the threshold, sure each time that they'd be "the one". I guess at heart she was a romantic.'

John listened and she could tell he wasn't judging her. 'What about your dad?'

'Who knows?' Scooter told him, amazed that she was opening up like this to a virtual stranger. 'He was some kind European art expert who my mom fell hook, line and sinker for.

She always loved him. She probably still does. Despite the fact that he promised her the world and then took off back to Europe as soon as he heard she was pregnant with me. She never heard from him again. She always told me that he was a good guy, that he'd look out for me, that one day he'd come for me, but you know, it's just horse shit.'

John laughed. 'That's very honest of you. You seem remarkably balanced given all of that.'

Scooter shrugged. 'I haven't always been, but sometimes you just have to move forward. You make your own luck, you know.'

'And what about love?' John asked. 'Are you a romantic, like your mom?'

Scooter grinned over her wine glass. 'Hell, yeah.'

Suddenly, John's phone buzzed in his pocket. He took it out and looked at the screen.

'Excuse me. I've got to take this . . . Larry, hi,' he said, getting up and raising his finger to tell her he'd only be a moment, an apologetic look on his face as he walked away. 'Did you get hold of Geoff? . . . Yeah, yeah, I'm here now.'

He apologized again as he walked out towards the front of the restaurant, but Scooter didn't mind. She liked being in the dappled courtyard, soaking up the ambiance. She wondered if she was doing OK. Whether she'd been wrong to open up to him the way she had. *Just be yourself.* That's what the key had told her. And so far it had worked. She hoped it would work today. She liked being here. Being part of this world. Being a player.

And then she saw something that made her good mood pop. Her ex-boyfriend Dean was walking across the restaurant towards her. Dean . . . with his faded jeans and floppy hair. He hadn't changed a bit. She felt her insides melt with familiar hormones.

He stopped at her table and shuffled in his cowboy boots, looping his thumb in his belt the way he always had.

'Looks like we both eat a bit swankier these days,' he said by way of introduction, with his lopsided smile.

'Dean, what are you doing here?' Scooter rearranged the napkin on her lap.

'I'm here with my new music agent. Funny how we seem to cross paths.'

'Do we?' she asked, trying to inject as much sarcasm into her voice as possible. 'Only, I thought I hadn't seen you since you walked out on me two years ago.'

Twenty months, three weeks and two days, to be precise, she now realized, but she didn't say it. She wished the butterflies would stop.

Dean bit his lip, obviously wrong-footed by her reaction to seeing him.

'You were in Cannes when I was there,' he said, as if this backed up his point about their paths crossing. 'So I heard.'

She bet he'd heard.

'Yeah,' Dean said. He shifted feet. 'You had quite a party. So they said.'

So they said. She remembered now how much she'd wanted to take revenge on him. To throw a party and deliberately snub him. But now everything had changed. *She*'d changed. Back then she'd only been able to define herself as *not* being with Dean. How obsessed she'd been about the fact his life had moved on, while hers had stayed the same, by how left behind and rejected she felt. But now . . . now everything was different. She felt empowered in a way that would be impossible to explain to him.

She was aware of the other diners watching Dean standing by her table.

'Man, you look good,' he said, shaking his head. The slow smile, the one she'd always adored. 'I hear you're doing good.'

'That makes two of us,' Scooter said, keeping her tone brusque and polite, but despite herself, she couldn't stop staring at him. His face was so familiar. The face she'd kissed thousands of times. 'I hear "Find Me" all the time,' she said pointedly. The song she'd practically written. And he knew it.

'Oh, that. You know . . . it just sort of happened,' he said, bashfully rubbing the side of his face. But he wasn't fooling her.

Because it hadn't 'just sort of happened'. The first opportunity he'd had to grasp at success and he'd seized it, treading on Scooter to grab on. The same as Mona had.

It was his naked ambition that had caused their relationship to end, she realized now, not any failing on her part. The fact that he now perceived her to be successful and that this somehow made them equals made her furious. *How dare he?*

She would never be like Dean and Mona. She would have success on her own terms, by being nice and being honest and treating people with respect. She wasn't going to start treading on people. And she would surround herself with people who were the same. Like Dallas.

Because she hadn't realized until right at this moment, seeing Dean, that it was truly over. That it was safe to let someone else into her heart.

It was the key, she realized. The key had set her free. The key had made the rest of her life possible. Without Dean.

'You know, we should catch up sometime,' he said, staring into her eyes.

Did he honestly think that he could work his old magic on her? Scooter thought, staring back and feeling strength surging through her. No. It wouldn't work. Not now.

She saw that John Cross was walking back to the table with another man. She stared at Dean.

'You'll have to go, Dean,' she told him.

'I'd like you to meet Geoff,' John said, arriving breathlessly at the table and introducing a man he'd brought with him. He was in a green shirt and was in his sixties. He looked as if he'd been racing here: sweat was popping on his brow. He dabbed his forehead with a napkin.

John looked excited, as if this was some sort of coup. 'Geoff Maynard, Scooter Black.'

That was Geoff Maynard of Maynard Lee? Possibly the most powerful casting agent in the world?

John stared confusedly at Dean, waiting for an explanation.

'Oh, this is Dean, someone I used to know,' Scooter said.

She saw the surprise register on Dean's face. The shock that she'd referred to him the way she had, that she was being dismissive. She watched him nod to Geoff and John, knowing they weren't interested in him either.

'Good to see you again, Scooter,' Dean said. 'See you around.'

He walked away from the table and Geoff winked at Scooter.

'An old admirer?' Geoff asked with a chuckle as Dean walked back into the restaurant. She knew from the slope of Dean's shoulders how dejected he felt.

'Something like that,' Scooter said, feeling a mixture of emotions churn inside her.

'What do you think?' John asked Geoff, and Scooter realized that they were both appraising her. 'This is the girl I told you about.'

Geoff's eyes didn't leave Scooter's face. 'You know he's

hauled me out of a meeting to get here? Told me he was lunching with the hottest girl in town, and, you know . . . he's not wrong.'

John grinned next to him, raising his eyebrows at Scooter.

'I was just thinking about Steve's conundrum over his leading lady,' John said to Geoff.

'Well, I don't think there's a conundrum any more, do you? I think we've just found her. Now pull me up a chair and let's get some champagne open. We've got business to discuss.'

CHAPTER THIRTY-THREE

Harry didn't have any idea where he was when he surfaced from the deepest sleep. Deep-down black-oil sleep. But as he swam through the fog, he was aware that his head felt as if it were in a vice. Then the smell overpowered him. Of stale vomit. As he coughed, the taste of it made him gag, bringing him fully round.

He was in his apartment on the floor of the sitting room and he was still fully clothed. A mess of cocaine remnants and an empty whisky bottle littered the glass table just above his head. He dragged himself up onto the sofa.

'What the fuck . . . ?' he muttered.

He'd had low times, but never before had he felt this bad. He buried his face in his hands. Then he got to his feet and headed for the shower. The water was only lukewarm, but it didn't matter. He stripped off and stepped into the water, his head pounding.

His cock hurt. He noticed it straight away as the water hit it and he looked down to see that the end of it was red and swollen; his balls, too, were purple and bruised. What the hell had happened?

He thrust his face into the stream of water, hoping it would wash away the bleariness so he could remember what had happened last night, but it remained a blank. A terrifying blank.

He remembered the restaurant, the Japanese girl . . . Yes . . . Kim. But after that? Where had they gone? Somewhere in a car . . .

And then nothing. As if his memory had been entirely erased. He soaped his body, but his mind was in overdrive, veering on panic.

He snarled to himself, cursing as soap got in his eye.

Christ, he felt bad.

When the home phone started to ring again, he groaned. That was the second time he'd heard it ring. Why wasn't the answer machine working? And then he remembered unplugging it. Well, at least he remembered something, he thought.

The phone stopped. The silence, only broken by the hiss of the shower, felt like a relief. Then the ringing started again.

'Goddamn it,' he shouted, slipping in the shower as he ran to answer the phone.

'For fuck's sake, Harry, where have you been?'

'Dulcie?' Harry recognized her voice.

'You have no idea how many times I've rung you. I even came to your apartment last night, but you weren't there.'

'Hang on,' Harry said, trying to focus. Why did she sound so upset? 'I don't understand.'

'Are you OK?'

'To be honest, no, I'm not.'

Harry sat down with a thump as Dulcie started talking. About a Japanese girl who'd come to see her at work. At the Savoy.

'She was weird. With mixed-up English. She had black eyes. Scary-looking.'

Kim. It could only be Kim. But how had Kim found Dulcie?

Harry felt his heart racing.

'She scared me. She really scared me,' Dulcie said. 'She told me that she knew which way I took the bus home. That I walked through the dark stairwell to my flat. That she'd be waiting for me and she'd cut me. She showed me a knife and scars on her arms. She told me she'd do that to my face. That if I went to the police, she'd just do it worse. But if I did as she said, she'd leave me alone.'

'Oh God. Oh, Dulcie.' Harry could hear the anguish in her voice.

'She made me call you and leave a message. To say that I wanted to meet you.'

The message. The memory clunked into place. Dulcie's message to meet him at the club.

The club.

Jesus.

A flashing, blinding strobe of memory snippets made Harry gasp. Christ, what had happened at that club? How had he got home? He couldn't remember anything.

And where the fuck was his key?

He ran to the bathroom and searched his trouser pockets, panic making his skin prickle, but they were empty.

'I don't know what's happened or what you've done, Harry . . .'

'I haven't done anything. She . . . she . . . was a contact of Cole's. She tricked me . . .'

Harry felt terror and fury rising up in him in a way he'd not felt since the day he'd kept his trading position open.

Where was that bitch Kim Lee?

Just at that moment his mobile started ringing, and apologizing to Dulcie and telling her he'd call right back, he answered.

'This is Sir Menzies' office. Putting you through,' a familiar voice said. It must be Alice. How strange that she hadn't addressed Harry directly.

Harry swallowed hard.

'You're fired,' Cole barked. Harry had never heard such disgust in someone's voice. 'Never contact me again. After all I've done for you.' The bitterness and scorn in the Texan's voice made Harry breathless for a moment. Then the line was dead.

Harry called straight back and got Alice. 'What's going on?' He couldn't keep the panic out of his voice.

'I suggest you turn on the TV,' she said.

Harry tripped over himself as he turned round in a circle, his eyes scanning the detritus of the room for the TV remote, his heart and his head pounding. At last he found it under a cushion and pressed it at the television.

'This is yet another example of the terrible lack of discipline in our financial organizations,' he heard, seeing a news reporter standing outside a familiar-looking building. And then he realized . . . it was America Bank. And in that instant Harry knew that Cole must have found out what he'd done. To Nick Grundy and the rest of the team and all the lies he'd told . . .

He stared at the TV.

He had no idea what had happened, but that Japanese bitch Kim had something to do with it. She'd set him up. Worse. She'd deliberately set out to destroy him.

And now he retched . . . the strippers, the naked girls flashing into his mind, along with Kim's camera and, more terrifyingly, a fleeting snippet of memory. No more easy to cling on to than a wisp of smoke, yet he chased it nevertheless and found . . . his words . . . *and I got away with it* . . . coming out of his mouth as he laughed. But he couldn't remember anything else.

Did that mean that he'd told her? He'd told her everything . . . ?

Shaking, Harry pulled on his jeans and a jumper. He flung open his wardrobe and grabbed his overnight bag, thumping it down on the bed. He would go away. He'd get to the airport and disappear. He ripped down a few pairs of trousers from his wardrobe, then gave up. His hands were trembling too much. There was no point in packing anything. He'd buy new stuff wherever he went.

He checked the drawer in the hall for his passport, wrenching open the rest of the drawers to look for cash. There was none.

But worse than all of that was that he didn't have his key. His precious key. Where the hell was it?

The strippers. They must have taken it from him, he thought, forcing himself to think logically. He would have to get there somehow. Get over to Shoreditch and get his key back. Then he could disappear . . .

But just then the TV in the sitting room caught his eye. He saw a swarm of reporters in a familiar-looking housing estate.

That was Gina's house. The reporters were outside his sister's house.

'Oh, no. Oh Lord, no,' Harry whispered.

He watched the front door open and his sister step out. She was wearing a shabby coat, which she pulled around her as she walked down the short gravel path next to the scruffy lawn. She looked distressed and nervous and so much older than he remembered, but as he watched her glance nervously at the cameras and then down at the paper shaking in her hands, he remembered that this was Gina. His big sister. The one who'd stood up to bullies in the park. The one who'd been goalie for him even in the rain, so that he could practise football. The one who made giant Sunday lunches and laughed with all her kids. Gina. His Gina.

'Harry had a bright start, but since he went to London . . .' she began, her voice shaking, her Yorkshire accent so pronounced. 'He was given every opportunity by our parents, but he were . . . he was always greedy. I'm not surprised that this has happened and that he's lied and cheated.'

If she'd punched him, Harry couldn't have felt the impact of her words with any greater intensity.

'You haven't had any contact with your brother?' a reporter shouted.

'He's been too selfish to call home. We've been worried about him, as he left work and hasn't been back to his apartment, and his mobile phone hasn't been working. My mother was so worried it has had a serious effect on her health. This can't have come at a worse time.'

'Do you have a message for your brother?'

Gina looked straight into the camera. She had deep grey smudges under her eyes. 'Yes. You brought this on yourself and have brought shame to your family.'

He watched as she dabbed the corner of her eyes, then walked quickly back into her home.

Harry stood, his lips wobbling, as he took an intake of raggedy breath.

He grabbed his bag and his keys and ran to the lift in his apartment building, then not waiting for it, bolted down the stairs. He had to get away. He had to disappear.

He raced out of his building, his head down.

And then it happened.

With a yell, a wall of people with flashing cameras stampeded towards him. Caught like a rabbit in headlights, he put his elbows up over his face, fear enveloping him as his ears filled with a barrage of questions. And above it all, a police siren.

He watched a police Range Rover with blacked-out windows pull up on the kerb. Even before it had stopped, a plain-clothed officer was out, another following from the other side.

'Harry Cassidy, I'm arresting you on charges of fraud. Anything you say may be used in evidence against you,' the policeman said, wrenching Harry's arm away from his face.

There was a strobe of camera flashes as he stumbled forward, being pushed through the crowd on either side.

Harry felt the police officer's hand on the top of his head, pushing him down inside the police car, as the TV cameras and photographers jostled to get better shots of him.

Harry shook as he sat in the back of the police car. It drove off, through the scrum of press, the siren blaring.

'Yep. Picked him up,' he heard the police officer say into the radio, looking at Harry in the mirror and glancing down at the seat beside him. And that's when Harry saw the picture on the front of the *Sun*. Of him surrounded by strippers. The headline screaming, 'Corrupt-Trader Carnage.'

CHAPTER THIRTY-FOUR

Malene, Christian's sister-in-law, tugged the thick woollen hat over Christian's brow and then rubbed the top of his head with her knuckles like he was one of her kids. He was sitting on a swing chair on the back porch of his brother Kenneth's house. The stars twinkled above the eaves of the wooden house, the tree-covered hills a dark shadow against the indigo sky.

'There – wear that if you two are going to insist on sitting out here,' she said. 'Besides, it will cover up that filthy tan of yours,' she added, grinning at Kenneth. 'We don't like it.'

Christian laughed. Malene had always treated him like a kid brother – the same as Kenneth always had. Even though he hadn't seen them for years, nothing had changed. Except his nephews, who were unrecognizable, they'd grown up so much.

But Kenneth and Malene were the same as they'd always been and Christian was delighted to see that, if anything, the connection between them had only grown. He'd felt nothing but welcomed and cherished since he'd arrived from the airport earlier. For the first time since he'd seen Dan at Iguazu Falls, he felt himself relaxing a bit.

He'd wanted to call Kenneth from Iguazu, to question him straight away about the key and whether he'd sent it to Christian and why. But Kenneth lived way out here without a phone, and after everything that had happened since the falls, his only choice had been to come in person.

The door creaked as Malene pushed back inside the wooden house, the warm glow and the sound of the children helping in the kitchen coming outside, then cutting off as the door shut.

Christian breathed in the cold air of the black Norwegian night. He remembered how he'd felt in Africa when he'd been captured by the colonel. When it had been *this* he'd thought of. The deep sadness that he'd never see home again. But then he'd been freed and he'd put it out of his mind.

Except that he wasn't free, he remembered.

'Good to be home?' Kenneth asked, misinterpreting Christian's sigh as one of satisfaction.

How could he tell his brother that it felt so good to be back, but this place no longer felt like home in a proper sense? It no longer felt like the place he belonged. How could it when Julia was on the other side of the world?

'She seems well,' Christian told his brother, changing the subject and nodding towards the door Malene had gone through.

Kenneth pulled the zip of his grey fleece up and then stoked the outdoor fire. Now that Christian looked more closely, he saw that his brother had in fact aged – deep lines around his eyes.

'She is. She's wonderful. More wonderful every day. So, have you found yourself a woman?' Kenneth asked, pouring the strong home-made vodka into some small glasses and handing one to Christian.

'I think so.'

'You think so?' Kenneth smiled. 'I may not have seen you for a while, little brother, but I know a man in love.'

They raised their glasses and drank, and then, warmed by

the alcohol and his brother's sympathetic ear, Christian told Kenneth about seeing Julia on the railway and how he'd felt that day, going to the statue above Rio. How he'd been there because he'd promised their mother that he'd go and see the view, like she'd always wanted to do. And how it had felt as if Fate – or maybe some kind of spiritual intervention by their mother – had deliberately brought him and Julia together. He told him about their date and how they'd stayed holed up in her apartment and how wonderful it had been at the falls.

He stopped there. He didn't tell him about Dan, and the terrible shock he'd had. Or the terror he felt now he knew he was being trailed by the CIA. He didn't tell his brother the fact that unless he got another key for the colonel, Adid had promised that he'd step up his 'activity' in the region and kill hundreds of innocent children.

He didn't tell Kenneth that he'd done everything he could to get another key, but even the CIA's best guy had completely failed to hack the key's interface to discover who was behind it. With time running out, it had made them more determined than ever for Christian to find out this vital information for himself.

He remembered Dan's parting words as he'd given Christian back his key.

'She's a pretty girl,' Dan had said, referring to Julia. 'It would be awful if she got caught up in all of this.'

The thought of losing Julia was one thing, but the idea that she may be harmed because of him chilled Christian to his core. It was that fact that had given him the courage to leave without saying goodbye, although it had almost broken his heart to do so.

He thought now of her finding the note in her apartment.

How could she possibly understand how much she meant to him, and what an idiot he felt for not telling her the truth?

'Make sure you're not rushing into anything. You hardly know the girl,' Kenneth said.

Christian shrugged, appreciating his brother's concern but knowing it was useless. 'But somehow I just *know*.'

Kenneth laughed. 'And maybe you do. Love is a mysterious thing. Who am I to argue?'

Christian nodded and drained his vodka.

'So if you're in love, why do you look so worried? Why the sudden visit? We'd have liked to have met Julia,' Kenneth said.

Christian looked into the fire. He longed to tell his brother all about the key, about Africa and the colonel. He wished he could offload all his anxieties and fears, but he couldn't. He'd been sworn to secrecy by Dan.

So Christian bluffed, telling Kenneth that he was still anxious about the things he'd seen in Africa. And once he'd started chatting about the Afri-Aid work, it wasn't long before he was able to drop in the question he was here to ask.

'So, Ken, I forgot to mention before. Did you send me a package a while ago?' he asked, trying to sound like it was no big deal. 'When I was in Africa?'

'Some letters perhaps. Malene was contacted by the post office. They had a load of mail for you and your mailbox was full. She sent it on, I think.'

He'd been sure it had been Kenneth's writing on the padded envelope, though maybe it had been Malene's. But if she had sent the package on to him in Africa, it didn't make sense. There had been no other mail from the post office. Just the key.

'You didn't send me something? You didn't send me a key?'

'A key?' Kenneth asked, looking bemused. 'What kind of key? A key to what?'

Christian saw that his brother clearly had no idea what he was talking about and he shook his head. 'It's sort of important,' Christian said, wondering if this would jog his memory.

'Malene?' Kenneth called, and a moment later the door creaked open and Malene poked her head out. Kenneth asked her about the mail she'd sent to Christian.

'There were ten letters or so,' she told him. 'Mostly from your father. I addressed the envelope to the Afri-Aid headquarters in Nairobi, like you said. Is everything OK?' she asked, looking between Christian and Kenneth.

'There wasn't a key?'

Malene frowned. 'There was one letter that had been hand-delivered to you. It came in a chunky envelope. It just had your name on. It might have been a key, or something bulky like that. I put that in a separate envelope, to the same address.'

Christian's heart flared with hope. That must be it. 'You don't know who sent it?'

'No. The post office said it had been hand-delivered. That's when they contacted me, because it wouldn't fit in your postbox.'

'You didn't open it?'

'Of course not. It was addressed to you.'

So who *had* delivered the key? Where had it come from? Why had it been delivered by hand? Who would have known his post office address in Norway? He would go to the post office tomorrow and ask them if they knew more.

'What's all this about?' Kenneth asked. 'Christian?'

'Sorry,' Christian replied, realizing he hadn't been following a word his brother had been saying. 'It's nothing. Really.'

'How long are you staying this time?' Kenneth asked. 'We

were thinking of going up to the cabin if you want to come. The kids would love it.'

Christian shook his head. 'I can't stay long. I have another job,' he lied. He hadn't been able to bring himself to tell Kenneth that he'd been fired. Only that he was going on a new assignment and had been taking a break in between.

When would the lies stop? he wondered. When would he be free of this terrible mess?

'Well, whatever you do, you must go and see Dad,' Kenneth said, in that big-brother tone that Christian remembered so well.

'Of course.'

CHAPTER THIRTY-FIVE

The brightly neon-lit Ginza entertainment district in Tokyo was busy tonight. The air was hot and humid, filled with the heavy aroma of fried street food and car fumes. Music blared from the bars and competed with the cries of the street traders, who called out the bargain prices of fake designer watches and handbags to passers-by.

Kamiko scooted out of the way as an old-fashioned American silver Lincoln car came out of an underground garage and slipped into the traffic. She'd done her research coming here and she wondered whether the car belonged to a gang member. Whether she'd meet a bona fide member of the Yakuza now that she was heading to an address that was right in the heartland of their criminal territory. She felt a frisson of nervous excitement.

After her success in London, she felt confident. Nothing could faze her. Not now. No one was beyond her reach.

Since she'd arrived from London, Kamiko had been sleeping off her jetlag in a modern hotel near the airport and had been basking in the success she felt.

It had been so easy to bring Harry down. It had been glorious to see the headlines in the newspapers and her pictures from the strip club as she'd caught her flight out from Heathrow.

Harry Cassidy had deserved it. He'd been a sitting duck. A greedy, vain liar. Spiking his drink had really made him talk. She'd got the Rohypnol from Tom, the guy who worked on the reception desk at the hostel. It hadn't been much, just enough to disorientate Harry.

It had been with the help of Caroline, the stripper, that Kamiko had procured Harry's key. And now she had his key, he was well and truly out of the game. So that only left Scooter, Christian and Julia, and Kamiko was already forming her plan about how to take them out too.

For the first time since she'd woken up to find Tiko and Susi had stolen her key, Kamiko started to feel she was back on top. And in with a chance.

She had to admit that it helped to be on home soil once more. To speak the language and to fit in. Now that she'd collected more cash from the reserves she'd left in the station, she was going to find her uncle Murushi. If everything went well, she planned to show him the necklace she'd taken from Martha Faust's safe.

She stopped outside the pachinko parlour and stared at the scribbled directions on the piece of paper in her hand. When she'd called the number she had for her uncle yesterday, nothing had happened for ages and then a man had answered. When she'd asked for her uncle, the phone had gone dead.

She'd called back and had left her name and explained that she was Murushi's niece. She'd been asked to call back in half an hour. When she'd rung back, she'd been given an address and told to come here tonight at six.

Now, she pushed through the glass doors and headed into the brightly lit parlour, the noise of the clanking machines assaulting her ears. She hadn't played the game for years, although her stepmother had always been an addict. The slot machine sent a tiny chrome ball flying through a vertical maze, like a pinball machine. It was a mindless game, and the rows of dull-faced men sitting on the brown stools in front of the clattering machines only confirmed her opinion.

She wondered now whether the man who had arranged the appointment was the man at the far end of the pachinko machines. He rose as she approached. He was wearing a shiny black suit, had pointy-toed shoes and longish pomaded hair. He didn't smile. She noticed that his little finger was heavily bandaged and she felt a dart of fear. Such mutilation was a trademark of the gangs.

Kamiko fought down her nerves, strode confidently towards him across the shiny lino floor and gave her name. The man looked her up and down. She wondered whether he was going to frisk her. He reached for the beige phone on the wall beside him, picked it up and pressed a button.

A few moments later a woman appeared through the door behind him. She was wearing a smart cocktail dress and she nodded for Kamiko to follow. Away from the racket of the pachinko machines, she heard the soft strains of the Beatles being performed on a koto, a traditional Japanese banjo. It reminded her of the music in the sushi factory and she tensed as she followed the slowly sashaying woman up the deep red carpeted stairs.

At the top of the dark staircase was another door, which was opened from inside as they approached. Kamiko walked through it into a club and the woman pointed to a far booth where a man sat, looking at a laptop. In between, scattered on the thick carpet, were several groups of men at tables, playing cards. The room was silent as she crossed it.

The man at the laptop stood and nodded for her to follow through a door and she felt the hairs on the back of her neck standing up. Why this subterfuge? Where *was* her uncle?

He led her up three more flights of stairs. At the top, they stepped through a doorway outside onto a walkway between the buildings. Kamiko could see the road far below. Across the street, the walkway terminated in a black door next to a giant brightly lit hoarding of a woman's face.

Kamiko walked across, looking back over her shoulder at the man, who was now talking on a mobile phone. He waved her forward. The wind was strong up here, whistling between the buildings and blowing her hair across her face. The walkway swayed slightly and she wondered whether it might collapse and plunge her down to the street below. What was this? Was she walking into some kind of trap?

Before she got to the door, it clicked open automatically. She stepped into the dark space beyond, seeing the bright red dot of a camera swing round.

'Come up the stairs,' she heard a voice say. It sounded like it belonged to an old man.

She saw rough metal stairs leading upwards.

She emerged into a large warehouse-like room with high brick walls. As she walked forwards, overhead striplights flickered on. Below them, large, long wooden benches hinted that it might once have been used for some kind of industry. But whatever industry it was, it was certainly secret.

A man was walking towards her from the far end. He was hunched forward and it wasn't until he was much closer that she saw that he had a scruffy white beard.

When they were close, he stood upright and she saw that he

wasn't as old as she'd thought – no more than in his early sixties. His eyes were magnified by thick round-lensed glasses.

The man's wrinkled hand came towards her. Ridged blue veins stood proud from the paper-thin skin. He smelt bad. His teeth were brown, although several were missing at the front. He reminded her of a snake.

'You are my uncle? Uncle Murushi?'

'So, you are here, little Kamiko,' he said, smiling. 'You look exactly like your mother.' He nodded and patted her shoulder, staring intently at her. 'Kamiko, Kamiko. All grown up.' He shook his head. 'Where does the time go? Come, come.'

She followed him and he stopped at the far end of the room, turning out lights and plunging them into darkness.

He pushed another door open and Kamiko followed him into the room beyond, where a television blared. He muted it and walked to a small cabinet in the corner, where he filled a kettle. As he did, his mobile rang and he talked rapidly into it, tutting. Kamiko stared around the sparse room, looking at the small cot behind the curtain. Sheets of newspapers were glued to the walls. She saw another curtained cubicle and smelt a sharp tang of stale urine.

Her uncle had clearly fallen on hard times. So much for him being a diamond dealer. She'd hoped he would be rich, but now she saw that the truth was very different.

He fussed over making tea and it took a while for Kamiko to broach the subject of their family connection again.

Murushi smiled a brown-toothed smiled. 'Your mother, Nora . . . she was so much like you. And you were her pride and joy.'

This was news to Kamiko. She could barely remember her mother.

'She never spoke of her family.'

'She wasn't allowed to. Your father made her disown us,' Murushi said harshly.

'Why?'

'Before the gang took over, I was a rich man. People came from all over the world to see me. You see these rooms? Once, this was just the entrance hall to the palace above. It is a fancy apartment block now, but then it was my home, filled with beautiful furniture and books.'

Could he be telling the truth? Kamiko wondered.

'I had a talent, you see. I could make one thing turn completely into another,' he said, producing a small origami butterfly in his hand as if he'd conjured it from thin air. Kamiko gasped, then smiled as he handed the yellow paper to her. 'I was a forger of some of the greatest artworks. I've heard that some of my work is still on show at the Louvre.' He chuckled.

As he spoke, Kamiko felt herself warming to her uncle, and when he brought out pictures of her as a baby in an album, Kamiko felt a new bitterness rising up in her and all the un-answered questions crowded into her head. She'd had a family. All this time. There was her mother, with her brother and their parents. And Murushi as a young man, dandy in a 1960s suit.

'Your mother, she made a bad choice marrying Nozaki.' He put his hand on her shoulder. 'We bailed out his father, you know. The factory was going under, so as a favour to your mother, we financed him back on his feet. Your father owed us . . . certain obligations . . . but he did not fulfil them.'

Kamiko felt a picture she'd only guessed at slipping into place. 'We?' she asked.

'My son – your cousin – joined the gurentai. I couldn't stop him. You can't stop your children doing anything, and in fairness, I didn't mind. For a long time his protection helped my business. Because there was a business here, my little Kamiko. A good business. And for a while the Yakuza had my back.'

All this had been going on in her family all this time? Kamiko was stunned by the news. Her cousin had been a gangster. A gurentai, no less. A Yakuza hoodlum, in charge of a protection racket. And all the while she'd been living in Kadoma in that dull house. All that time Shikego had abused her. Taken away the childhood of a grieving child. She'd have been safer here, even if it had been the centre of gangland. Her uncle would have protected her.

'Your mother tried to come back several times, but' – he shrugged – 'your father . . . he always came for her. I think he'd tried to brainwash her. He thought he could escape his debt. He was wrong.'

Kamiko showed him the note she'd found in Shikego's wedding suit.

'So, this is why you are here.' He nodded, looking at the note as if lost in memories. 'Do you want money from me, child? Is that what you want?' he asked, chuckling at her. 'You are fifteen years too late, I'm afraid. I gave this note to your stepmother to give to your father on their wedding day. I went to him, you see, to appeal to let me have you. I lost my son, you understand. He was killed in the line of his business, so you were all I had left. You, little Kamiko, are my only family. I thought that if Nozaki had a new wife, then she wouldn't want you so much. I promised your mother, you see, that if anything should ever happen to her, then I would take care of you.'

Kamiko stared at the old man, an unfamiliar sensation rising up in her. She saw his eyes welling with tears as he patted her hand.

For a second she was tempted to rail at him. To tell him that he should have tried harder to keep that promise. He should never have trusted her father or Shikego. Her mother's instincts to run back to him had been right. She knew Kamiko would need protecting and she'd entrusted her brother to help. But he hadn't.

Looking at him now, though, she saw that he'd suffered a lifetime of regret already. Chastising him would not make it better. Now that she was here, she felt a sense of responsibility. As if she in some way belonged to him.

'Did you give her a diamond? Shikego?'

'Yes. I did. I gave her the diamond that ruined me.' He sighed heavily. 'She took it to the police, you see, telling them I was involved in extortion. That I was trying to buy a child. I think she must have hoped that I would be arrested and that your father would be left in peace and be free of his debt.'

Kamiko stared at him. All this drama had been because of *her*?

'What happened? Did they arrest you?' Kamiko asked, wondering if he'd been in jail.

Murushi shook his head. 'No. Worse. The police came, but they didn't arrest me. They were more corrupt than the Yakuza. At least there was an honour code with the Yakuza. Not so with the police. Once I was in their sights, they made me turn the profits from my business over to them. They took the rest of my diamonds . . . and they shared them out among themselves.'

He waved his hand as if the mess had made a bad smell – even now.

'Everything I'd ever worked for . . . my reputation . . . it all went, once people realized I was owned by the Yakuza *and* the

police. I never made money again. Not real money. People . . .
they went elsewhere for the kind of expertise I could offer.'

'What did the Yakuza say – about the police!' Kamiko
asked, struggling to understand.

'They had a lot to say. But they came to an arrangement
further up the chain. For years now the Yakuza have used me to
pay off the police in various scams. And I am trapped here, doing
their bidding.'

Kamiko's head was reeling with the revelation. Shikego had
done that to her uncle? She'd deliberately turned him in to the
police. She felt a fresh surge of hatred rising up in her. That bitch
had deliberately ruined so many people's lives.

Well, one thing was for sure – when Kamiko won this game,
when she got rich, she would do whatever it took to make
Shikego suffer.

'Come. Enough of the past. You don't wish to hear an old
man complaining. You must be hungry,' her uncle declared.

He changed his slippers and she followed him through a
warren of deserted corridors and down more flights of stairs.
Eventually, they came to some double doors in an alley. Across
the alley and past the bins, her uncle slipped into the back of
a restaurant.

The kitchens were busy, chefs shouting above the hiss of
frying food. The hot air was filled with the aroma of delicious-
smelling dumplings.

Before long they were seated at a small round table at the
very back of the kitchen. Her uncle was clearly a regular here.
She watched him laughing with one of the chefs and he introduced her.

'He talks about you all the time,' the chef told Kamiko, as

a waiter brought over a bowl of stir-fried vegetables. 'He always said you would come.'

Kamiko blushed, amazed. She felt her uncle beaming next to her. And as they chatted away, him telling her stories of her mother, she started to feel that in some way she had made the old man happy. That he'd been waiting all these years for her to find him. The fact that he'd loved her from afar moved her in a way that nothing had ever before.

Soon he asked her why she was in Tokyo and Kamiko found herself opening up about Susi and Tiko. It felt good to confide in him. It felt good that he, too, was horrified that she'd been drugged and robbed.

'Do you know how I could find these people?' she asked, showing him the pictures she had taken on her camera and had printed.

Her uncle nodded slowly, taking the copies of the pictures from her. 'This, I can do for you.'

He whispered to a chef, who passed a message on to a waiter. Soon the man Kamiko had seen in the pachinko parlour, in the shiny black suit and a bandage over his finger, came in.

Her uncle introduced him as Shou. She watched as her uncle gave him the photos and clarified the names of Tiko and Susi, then despatched him. He may be stuck in between the Yakuza and the police, but her uncle did have some authority, she realized. And probably more of a clue where to start looking for them than Lisa, the private detective in London, who'd drawn a complete blank.

'You think he'll be able to find them?' she asked.

'He knows people who can,' her uncle said. 'But what did they steal?'

'Something that I need back,' she said.

Kamiko was touched by his concern for her. Nobody had ever cared what happened to her before.

'Something valuable?'

'Very,' she replied. And then she told him. She told him about getting the key. And how Tiko and Susi had taken it from her. Her uncle listened, his face clouding.

'Who gave you this key?'

'I don't know. I don't know who is behind it. Only that it is some sort of test. It's a game. I'm sure of it. But once I get my key back, then I can help you,' she told him. 'I can help you like you once tried to help my mother. We can move you out of here. You can be rich again.'

'Oh, Kamiko.' He patted her hand again. 'You are a sweet girl to think of your old uncle.'

'And there's something else,' she said, smiling, enjoying this sensation of making him happy. She waited until she was sure they were alone and the chefs were distracted. 'I've got this.'

She reached into her jacket and pulled out the diamond necklace that she'd taken from Martha Faust's safe. It glinted in the bright kitchen lights.

'Can you tell me how much this is worth?'

Her uncle took an audible gasp, his eyes wide as he looked at the necklace. She watched him turning it over in his hand in the shadow of the table.

'But it's . . . it's impossible . . .' he whispered. He clearly recognized it. 'Where did you get this?' he asked, his voice clear, as if he were a much younger, sharper man.

'I . . . I . . .' Kamiko stumbled, unsure of the sudden change in mood.

'Does anyone know you have it?'

'No. Only you. I thought—'

'Tell me, child, and tell me honestly . . . is this necklace in any way connected to the key you were given?'

Kamiko nodded. Because it was connected. It belonged to Martha Faust. But her uncle clearly saw a connection she had not made.

Murushi took a sharp intake of breath, then nodded. Kamiko thought she saw a smile on his lips.

'Take this necklace away and hide it. Hide it well. And never tell anyone you have shown me.' His voice was urgent.

CHAPTER THIRTY-SIX

It was harder to visit his father than Christian had expected. The weather had closed in and the Gisund Bridge, which connected the mainland to the island of Senja, was temporarily closed. He sat in the traffic queue, drumming his fingers on the steering wheel of his hire car, the soporific political talk show on the radio giving him a headache. The post office had had no answers. They couldn't even remember the package that had been delivered by hand for Christian, and they barely remembered Marlene either.

Now he'd been guilt-tripped into going to see his father, when all he wanted to do was to turn round and drive back to the airport. He was so conscious of time ticking, so aware he still had no answers. But then, Kenneth would tell his father how close Christian had been. He couldn't justify leaving without seeing his father once.

Tired and frustrated, he booked into a travel motel late that night. He was back in his native land, but he couldn't seem to connect with it. Other people made him feel even more lonely. He lay in the dark, looking at the shadows on the walls, thinking of Julia. He ached to call her, to hear her voice, but until he'd sorted out this mess and got Dan off his back, he didn't want to risk putting her in any danger. Besides, she'd ask too many questions. And he had no answers.

He thought of that day at the falls and how beautiful she'd looked. How she'd told him that she'd fallen in love with him. How she wanted to be honest. And he'd told her the same thing. But even that had been a lie. Not the loving her part – of that he was sure – but he hadn't been honest with her. About the key. About what had happened. About what he'd promised to the colonel.

The very thought of what that maniac might do – what Christian knew he would do – was sickening. And those children's deaths would be on Christian's head. How could he ever explain that to Julia?

But he knew he had to try. What if he explained everything to her? If he could just share this with her, then maybe, just maybe she'd be able to help him. He knew it was a long shot, but he simply couldn't bear this heartache any longer.

In the dead of night he logged on to the key. He would book flights back to Rio for the day after tomorrow. He couldn't stand to be away any longer.

But just after he'd put in his request for the ticket to be available for him at the airport, a message popped up on the screen.

The next time you allow a hacker to use this portal to try and discover who I am will be the last time your key works.

Christian stared at the message, his heart thumping. The key *knew*. The key knew that someone more experienced than Christian had tried to get behind the interface. To find out who was behind the key. Christian quickly typed a reply.

But I had no choice. I have to find another key just like this one for someone else.

Do not attempt this. The key will not allow it.

The key was monitoring him. He stared at the screen, feeling paranoia creeping across him like a rush. Was someone watching him now?

Who are you? he typed.

The key wishes you a pleasant journey.

And that was it. The key would not answer any more questions. Oz would not reveal himself and would not be found.

What he did know was that whoever the CIA's guy was, he had annoyed the person behind the key. They did not want to be found. Not yet, at least.

He was glad when the sun came up and he could finally stop his mind whirring round and round.

The fog had cleared and the bridge had reopened, and as Christian drove across to Senja, he was amazed, as he always was, by the beauty of the landscape – the sky pink and purple against the snowy peaks in the distance, the water stretching in all directions like a silver mirror.

His father's church was in a traditional village community in the far Troll, and as Christian drove along the empty coast road, he noticed a red fishing boat slicing through the water, a flock of seagulls behind it. The air was bitingly cold and fresh, the tang of woodsmoke on the breeze.

His father's simple whitewashed church was on a small jut of land, the mossy banks either side of it leading down to the shingle shore. Above, the bare cliffs were jagged, like knuckles threatening the sea. Further out, around the rocks, the sea shimmered in a patchwork of jewel colours from emerald green to sapphire blue to deep onyx, where Christian had seen whales basking the last time he was here. A long time ago, he realized. Before he'd gone to Africa. When he'd still been an innocent young man, determined to do his bit to change the world. How different he was now.

The ground was icy and the air bitterly cold as Christian knocked on the flaked wooden door of his father's cottage. He stamped to try and keep the circulation going in his feet, wondering how his father survived out here. Wondering, too, how his father would react to his sudden visit.

'Oh, it's you,' Teis Erickson said, as he opened the cottage door. His face was weathered, his glasses taped together with sticky tape. His grey fingerless gloves couldn't hide the swollen joints in his hands. 'Well, make yourself useful,' he continued, waving a gnarled finger at his son. 'You can bring in the logs.'

After he'd stacked the logs by the fire in the cottage, Christian finally had the chance to take in his surroundings and was shocked to see that his father was living in squalor. Although he'd aged, it had not diminished his energy. Christian hardly had a chance to speak to him before he announced that he was off to see an elderly parishioner and would be back later.

Bristling at his father's lack of affection, Christian found himself muttering as he started to clean up the small cottage. Resent coursed through him. It was irrational, he knew. Other people looked after their families with kindness and patience, but Christian felt only fury that his father had marooned himself somewhere so far away, and clearly refused to get help or look after himself properly. How could Christian have so easily saved so many lives and helped so many people, but found it almost impossible to help his own father with any of the same grace?

Alone in his father's house, all he could think about was that he had twenty-four hours to work out his next move, but he was stumped. He couldn't risk anyone hacking the key again. But who was this person behind it? Who was typing those messages? Why wouldn't they reveal themselves? Where would this all end?

He was still musing over it when his father came in. Christian was kneeling by the fire, building it up with logs.

'Don't use all those,' his father said anxiously.

Christian turned to see his father taking off his hat. His blond hair had gone white and was thin on his crown. He was frowning. He didn't comment on the changes Christian had made to the cottage, or that a stew was cooking on the freshly cleaned stove.

'But it's cold.'

'It's wasteful. That's what it is.'

Christian bit his tongue, annoyed by his father's frugal ways. He watched his father hang the brass church key on the hook by the door. Then he sat down in his leather chair by the fire. His knees cracked loudly.

'You need looking after,' Christian said.

His father chuckled. 'Don't you worry yourself, son.'

Christian busied himself, blowing the leather bellows on the fire. As it got going, they chatted for a while, about his father's crumbling church, the state of the economy and the problems with the local fishing industry. The outlook around here seemed bleak, Christian thought. Or maybe it was just age that had made his father hunker down, shutting out the outside world, preparing for the worst, as if the end of days was nearly here.

'Dad, what would you do if someone said you could have whatever you wanted. Money, luxury . . . anything. Would you take it?' he asked, warming his freezing hands on the fire.

'No. I doubt it. I knew a rich man once. He wanted to help me,' his father said. 'He came to see me.'

'Who?'

'Just a guy I helped once. He wanted me to have his money.'

'Why didn't you take it?'

'Because I didn't want his charity. Because I'm fine as I am.'

'But you're not fine. You live like a monk.'

Christian imagined a rich parishioner wanting to leave their wealth to Teis Erickson and his father refusing on the grounds of some warped religious ethic. It made him feel angry that he was so belligerent. That he'd always been so belligerent and stubborn. But then he remembered how suspicious he'd been of his key. Perhaps he was more like his father than he realized.

'Don't look like that. I have my comforts. And I'm closer to God this way.' His father gave him a look and started to fill his pipe.

Christian shook his head. He'd never understand his father's faith.

'It's funny, isn't it, that we named you Christian and yet you turned out to be the one who didn't believe in God?' his father said, striking a match and putting it to the tobacco.

'I do believe—' Christian began, but stopped himself. Having a theological argument with his father would end badly. It always did. The last argument they'd had, before he'd gone to Africa, had resulted in them hardly speaking. Christian found himself tied up in knots whenever he spoke about his beliefs to his father. He couldn't articulate the conflict he felt.

'I'm glad if you do,' his father said cautiously. 'Because living a faithless life is no kind of life to live.'

'I have faith. Maybe not in the same things that you have faith in, but it's faith nevertheless.'

Because he did have faith, didn't he? He had faith in him and Julia. In the love he felt. In the fact that they were meant to be together. He thought of them sitting in the sun-filled church in Rio and how happy and content he'd felt by her side.

They huddled round the fire, eating the stew Christian had cooked, and with a full belly, his father finally relaxed and thanked Christian for coming. Just this small morsel of affection was enough to make him glad he'd bothered to come. At least here, at the far tip of the world, Christian felt momentarily safe. The cursed key and all the trouble it had brought couldn't touch him up here.

Even so, Christian was still thinking about the rich parishioner as he served up seconds of the stew and poured himself another glass of wine. The fire smoked and he coughed.

'I wish you'd taken the money from that man,' Christian told him. 'You could do with having your chimney fixed. Not to mention the church roof. And you could take a break. Go and see Kenneth and Malene and the kids. Let them look after you for a while.'

'I can't leave. Besides, I'm fine.'

'But you're not.'

'And you think someone else's money will fix all my problems? Pah,' his father answered. 'I don't want that on my conscience.'

Christian shook his head, amazed by his father's conviction. He noticed his father staring at him.

'Why are you smiling? Because you don't think I know what it's like to have a conscience? Well, let me tell you, son, I do. My guilty conscience is what split your mother and me apart.'

This was news to Christian. When they'd split up, he'd always thought it had been because his religious duties clashed with her free spirit. But now he realized that it must have been something else.

'What happened?' he asked. 'Did you . . . did you have an affair?'

'No.' His father shook his head. 'No, nothing like that.'

'Then what?'

'I helped someone once, someone I met when I was working in prison, and I don't know . . . maybe I shouldn't have done. Your mother certainly didn't think I should have.'

'Then why did you?'

'She didn't understand that I'd seen the spirit of the man. She believed the newspapers. She thought he was a killer. Or at least was capable of killing. She hadn't seen what I'd seen, or heard his confession. I believed him to be innocent.'

Christian sat down opposite his father, astonished by this revelation. Astonished that this quiet, pious man had done such a thing.

'So what did you do?'

'He was a prisoner. A lifer. I helped him to escape from jail.'

Christian dropped the metal ladle, which clattered onto the stone flagstones. 'You did what?'

His father shook his head. 'It was a long time ago. I had been expecting to take my secret to the grave, but your mother, she always saw right through me. She could tell I was troubled, and when I told her why, she threatened to turn me in. If she had, I would have been thrown out of the Church. We fought over it . . . and eventually said too many things that couldn't be unsaid. And . . .' Christian saw the emotion was still as raw as it had ever been. His father gave a shuddering sigh and continued, 'And she left me. She never forgave me.'

'Was that the rich man who came to see you? Who said he'd help you?'

His father nodded. 'Yes. He had all the money in the world.

All he wanted to do was help me for helping him. He was a good man, you see.'

As Christian stared at his father in the dim firelight, the steam from the stew rising, his father talking about an infamous prisoner, long ago, he felt a new kind of realization stirring in him. And as the wind howled outside, Christian knew that he might be at the far end of the world, but he might just have discovered the key to it all.

And it brought no comfort. No comfort at all.

CHAPTER THIRTY-SEVEN

On the thirty-third floor of the downtown hotel, Kamiko was dreaming about level nine of *Death Con 3* when the hotel phone by her bed rang loudly. She jerked into consciousness, picking up the grey receiver. It was still dark outside. Not even dawn.

'The good news is that your friends are in Tokyo,' her uncle said, not greeting her. His tone was hushed and hurried.

Kamiko sat up in bed, remembering how they'd parted last night. How strange he'd been about the necklace. How he'd told her to take it and hide it – that nobody must ever see it. But he'd been excited too, as if he were hatching a plan. He'd told her that it was vital that she got her key back.

So now he'd come good on his promise to find Tiko and Susi.

'They are in the penthouse of the Falcon Hotel. Shou, whom you met yesterday, has a key card to get into their room. He is on his way to collect you. I have given him a package for you,' her uncle continued in a rush. 'Do not open it until you are alone. And be careful.'

'And then I will come to you,' Kamiko said, her mind racing.

There was a pause. Her uncle's voice sounded strange. 'No. You cannot.'

'But I told you. With the key, we can—'

'Shh. These walls have ears, little Kamiko,' he whispered, then rang off.

Kamiko was still fretting over her uncle's call half an hour later, as she crossed the deserted road outside the hotel and got into the black Mitsubishi. Shou sat in the front. He looked at her in the rear-view mirror. She saw his bandaged finger on the steering wheel.

Was this a trick? What if the Yakuza or the police had interrogated her uncle? What if they'd got to Tiko and Susi first and had taken her key? What if they now took it to use themselves? But maybe it wouldn't work.

These walls have ears, little Kamiko. Her uncle's last words to her in a hushed whisper seemed to imply that he'd had to tell other people about the key – or they'd found out.

Or maybe he was warning her. He'd told her that he had to walk an exhausting line between the police's demands and the Yakuza's. Maybe he meant his apartment wasn't safe for her to come to again. She thought about how far he'd fallen and how much she hoped finding the key would help him.

'My uncle said you have a package for me?'

Shou looked at her in the rear-view mirror, his eyes flicking sideways, and she saw that there was an envelope in the back-seat pocket behind him. She picked up the envelope and slipped it inside her jacket. It felt heavy.

At the Falcon Hotel, they parked round the corner, then slipped in through the goods entrance. Unseen by any staff, they travelled in silence in the lift. Kamiko noticed that Shou now had black leather gloves on and was wearing shades. They walked together silently along the carpeted corridor, past the vases of fake flowers. At the end room, Shou nodded and handed her the key card to the penthouse suite. Then he reached into his jacket and took out a pistol with a silencer screwed on the end. He offered it to her and Kamiko felt her heart racing as she took it.

She remembered the last time she'd held a gun – the one in Martha Faust's study. The one that had killed her. But that had been an accident. And this felt . . . It felt right.

She slid the plastic card into the door. She liked the weight of the gun in her hand. The power it made her feel. Tiko and Susi would not ignore her now. They could not overpower her. She relished the thought of having this final revenge.

There was a small click and she turned the handle.

The door of the hotel room swished quietly against the thick carpet. Inside it, what should have been a sanctuary of mini-malist calm was a shocking mess. There were the remains of a raucous party. Kamiko tiptoed through the debris.

Tiko and Susi were asleep together in the giant bed, covered in a dove-grey duvet. Susi had a mask over her eyes. A pink vibrator was on the table next to the bed with an open bottle of lubricant.

Kamiko moved to Tiko's side of the bed. She picked up the expensive watch and cast her eye over the discarded designer clothes on the floor. She saw his body tense beneath the sheets.

'How sweet you look,' Kamiko said, standing over Tiko.

He gasped, fully awake now. He nudged Susi, who scram-bled backwards on the bed, pushing back her eye mask and pulling the duvet over her chest.

'No,' Kamiko said, waving the gun at the duvet, 'don't cover yourself up. You were going to show me, when you left me. Remember?'

She saw Susi's eyes widen with fear. She should be afraid, Kamiko thought, enjoying this delicious moment.

'Do it,' she shouted.

Panic flashed in Susi's eyes. Kamiko felt a sharp thrill as Susi pushed down the sheets to reveal her breasts. They were just as perfect as Kamiko had imagined they would be.

How annoying it was that she and Tiko had been so greedy. The three of them could have had fun together all along, but they'd cut her off. Discarded her. Like she meant nothing.

'Kamiko,' Tiko said, 'let me explain.'

'What is there to explain? You're a thief and a liar. All you have to do is give me back my key,' she said. 'That's all.'

Tiko got out of bed now, his cock flaccid. He ran to his suit and searched in the pocket. He held out the key to Kamiko; his hands were shaking. 'There. There it is. Take it.'

She felt a flush of relief run through her as she took the silver key from him and opened it. It still looked pristine and new. And now it was back in her possession.

'I presume you've been having fun, have you?' Kamiko asked, pointing the gun between them, enjoying the look of fear on their faces. 'Pretending to be me. I mean, I take it that's what you have been doing, right? You knew my security log-in?'

Tiko threw a panicky look in Susi's direction. She let out a whimper and shrank beneath the cover.

'Uh-uh,' Kamiko warned. *She* was in charge here. *She* would say when Susi could cover up.

'I can tell you. I can tell you who's behind all of this,' Tiko whispered frantically. 'I will tell you everything if you let us go. If you don't do anything to us . . .'

Kamiko thought for a moment, noticing the terrified look he flashed Susi. 'Go on . . .' she said.

'We only found out last night. We had a party and we asked the key for supplies even though it hadn't been working, and—'

'Hadn't been working?' Kamiko asked. This was news.

'Tiko, don't. Don't say anything,' Susi hissed. 'You promised.'

'And the thing is, it spoke to us. The key. It answered. On screen. It told us it knew we weren't you. That the key was meant only for you, which is why it had stopped working for us. So that can only mean one thing . . .'

'What?' Kamiko asked, gratified that the key was loyal to her. That *she* had been chosen for the game.

'There's a handler. Someone who's been watching. Someone who's been tracking it. Maybe it sends out a signal to someone who knows where we are. Where we are right now.'

Kamiko stared at the key in her hand. Could it be true? Was someone watching them right now?

'There was a message. On the key,' Tiko continued, panicking. 'A number to call. So we could arrange to give back the key.'

'What number?'

'Don't say anything. Make her go away,' Susi cried.

'The number is in my phone.' He glanced down. Kamiko saw the bulge in the inside pocket of the jacket on the floor.

She stooped down and took the phone from his pocket.

'Find it,' she said, handing the phone to him. His hands trembled as he took it and pressed a few buttons. He handed it back to Kamiko.

She pretended there was no signal and walked out of the hotel room. Her knees were shaking. She had her key back. And Tiko's phone. And the number of the person behind her key.

Shou stood in the corridor. Kamiko gave him back the gun. 'Thank you,' she said.

'What now?' he asked.

What now? It was a good question. She'd left Tiko and Susi inside, but she didn't want to go back in there and confront them again. She was alarmed at the feeling of power the gun had given her. How easy it would have been to use it. How satisfying it would be to make them pay for their greediness. How she wouldn't have felt anything other than triumph. She heard them behind the door. Hushed, frantic whispers. They were up and getting dressed, ready to run.

'Shall I finish the job?' he asked.

She nodded, hardly giving herself time to think. *Yes*. She *did* want the job to be finished. They deserved to be punished.

He opened the door with the key card. There was silence; then she heard a muffled scream. A moment later there were two pops of the silenced gun.

She felt an almost ecstatic thrill run through her.

She wished now that she'd had the nerve to finish the job herself. She would next time.

Without even waiting for Shou, she dialled the number on Tiko's phone.

'Hello—' the voice said, sounding surprised.

'This is Kamiko Nozaki,' she interrupted. 'I have retrieved my key from Tiko. You will meet me at the bar on the first floor of the departures terminal at the airport in one hour.'

She'd find out once and for all what this was about. She'd make the handler talk. She'd find out who was behind this. Who he worked for.

She'd find out how to win.

August 2000

It was hot in Spain, that was for sure, Mack thought, as he parked the van round the bend in the lane in a shady lay-by. The sun was high in the sky, and now, in mid-August, it had scorched the land to dust.

It had taken months for Mack to track down Voss, as he'd always suspected it might. There'd been rumours, of course, about the wealthy recluse in the hills, but finding the exact location had taken time.

He thought of Tobias and wondered how he was getting on in his new yacht down at the coast. He'd wanted to come today with Mack, but Mack had insisted that this was something he had to do alone. But he knew his friend was concerned for his safety. He'd made him swear that he'd come back alive tonight – with his family. And Mack had promised.

Now the moment he'd been waiting for – for fifteen torturously long years – was finally here. He looked in the rear-view mirror, pulled the cap down low on his head, grabbed the metal toolbox from the seat beside him and stepped out into the wall of heat.

From the outside, it would have been difficult to tell that a millionaire's mansion was hidden behind the long row of tall pine trees that ran the length of the bumpy lane. It certainly was an isolated spot to build on, Mack thought. Ten miles in from the coast in the barren, rocky mountains and miles from the nearest village. Voss sure must have wanted to keep himself to himself here. But that would have been easy with Mack's family to entertain him.

He felt a familiar burn of pure hatred pumping in his blood as he locked the van. Tara had just been a baby, Mark only two, when Voss had raided Mack's Edinburgh home that night long ago. The night he'd forced Mack to agree to planning the train robbery.

Kate had been terrified, he remembered. As had he. But what choice had he had other than to cooperate, when Voss had threatened his family? It had felt as if the Devil himself had invaded their home.

But it had got worse. Because Voss had seemed to take an extra-special interest in Mack's precious family unit. The last time Mack had seen them had been in the South of France, just before the robbery, when Voss had beaten up Mack in front of them. He'd told Mack to cooperate fully with the plan or else he'd never see his family again. The last time he'd seen Kate she'd had tears pouring down her face, Voss's fat arm round her shoulder.

But Voss had had no intention of letting Mack see them again. Right from the start. That's why he'd framed Mack for the train robbery. Because he knew Mack would never give Voss up as long as he had Kate, Tara and Mark.

That bastard had deliberately stolen his family. He'd taken away the one thing Mack had cherished above everything else.

Well, now he was about to claim them back.

Still, the thought of the imminent reunion made him jittery with nerves. Tara would be almost grown-up by now, he thought, remembering how he'd drawn her birthday cards in jail, and written hundreds of letters that he'd never sent, not knowing where to send them.

Or Mark. His little Mark would be a man now. The same as Barry's son. Had he played football too? Had he had any kind of childhood? Mack wondered, dreading the damage he'd find. Or maybe he'd stood up to Voss already. Maybe he'd got his mother and sister to safety? But if he had, then surely they would have all visited him in jail. He thought of those long days. How he'd prayed for a sign. Any sign from them. That they'd escaped. But he knew deep down that Voss would never have let them out of his sight.

Most of all, his heart thumped now for Kate. His poor darling Kate. What must it have been like living here all these years, in isolation with that monster? She liked cities – buses and shops and people. He remembered how happy they'd been in that little flat in Edinburgh, when they'd first moved in as newly-weds. She hadn't minded the cold. Misty October drizzle – he remembered her telling him once – was her favourite weather.

Did Kate still cherish all those memories in her heart as fondly as he did? he wondered. Now he was so close to meeting her again, to rescuing her, as he'd always longed to do, he felt a moment of panic. He'd been so strong in his conviction for all these years. In the bond they shared that could not be broken – by time, by distance and, most of all, by Voss. That was the promise they'd made to one another.

And yet . . . now that he was so close, doubts he'd never let himself express before plagued him.

Would she have forgotten Mack? Or their promises to each other? Might the faith that had kept him alive have dwindled and perished in her?

What if . . . ? He felt his mind touch on his worst fear, like dipping his toe in scalding water. What if she didn't want him back? What if Voss had corrupted her and she was no longer his princess, waiting to be rescued?

He heard the plaintiff bleat of a goat up on one of the hills, bringing him back to the present. He forced himself to focus. He walked quickly along the shadow of the tall pine trees, then crouched silently near the last corner, before the curve of the trees and the road swept round to the front of the mansion, with its huge steel gates.

He and Tobias had studied this place in detail over the last month. They'd hired a helicopter to take aerial shots, so they knew how well Voss had protected himself: with cameras all round the property and a round-the-clock armed guard on the gate. His level of paranoia was quite impressive. He must still be running some kind of business out of here – drugs most likely, Tobias had thought.

It had immediately been clear that a straight break-in wouldn't work. Until Tobias, thinking laterally, had come up with a plan. They'd found the boss of the local electricity company and had befriended him, posing as local agents, and had given him a complimentary yacht for the day. Clearly open to a bribe, it hadn't been long before Tobias had found out how and where to get access to the plans of the electricity grid up here.

Now, Mack knew that if he could just get to the grey power box that was situated between the walls, just along the line of trees, he could open it with the special key, get inside and cut the power supply to the security cameras.

Inhaling and exhaling to prepare himself, he strolled casually round the corner towards the box, pulling the electrician's cap down low over his face. Softly whistling, he crouched down next to the metal box and opened it. Behind a thick spiderweb was a tangle of wires and Mack set to work, sweat pouring down his brow.

Then, suddenly, he heard the metal gates clanking and opening a metre or so, then footsteps. Someone was approaching – as he knew they would. Mack's heart raced as he prepared his Spanish explanation.

'Hey, you!'

He turned to see a thickset guy in a vest with a pistol tucked in his red shorts jutting his chin out at him. He was chewing gum, his mirrored shades glinting in the sun, reflecting Mack crouched low in his grey boiler suit.

Mack spoke Spanish, flashing his identity card from the electricity company. The guy seemed to be appeased, and a second later when his phone beeped, he turned away to look at it, walking back towards the gates.

Mack snipped the final wire, glancing through the trees and seeing a red light go out on the camera above the gate.

Bingo.

Standing straight, he grabbed the crowbar from the metal toolbox, adjusting his grip round the hot metal. In two steps he was right behind the guy, who was texting on his phone.

Do it, he told himself, seeing the thickset neck of the guy. Don't think about it. This is your only chance.

Mack took the swing. The phone clattered to the ground and the guy staggered. Mack helped him, lowering him onto the grass in between the trees.

In a second Mack had taken his pistol and, deciding that it was better than his own, quickly walked towards the gates.

He felt his heart pounding as he slipped through the metal gates and into the courtyard, ready for more guards, but the guard box was empty.

A couple of large palms drooped over a central fountain, which was dry. A gold cherub, which should have spouted water, pursed its tarnished lips at Mack as he tiptoed past. Hot, shiny tiles stretched in every direction to the artificial beds of wiry bright green grass, the outbuildings of the mansion rising in bright pink gaudy plaster blocks. All the shutters were closed, the heavy heat shrill with cicadas, as loud as a burglar alarm.

Mack strained his ears for signs of people, for voices, but there was no one around.

He ran quickly across the tiles to the archway, pressing his back against the wall. A gecko slithered behind the metal cover of a wall light. He carefully and slowly cocked the pistol. He stared up at the security camera above him, praying that it too was on the circuit he'd disabled and he wasn't being monitored.

The house beyond was a modern mansion with fancy pillars holding up a porchway. A big four-by-four was parked outside the front door. Mack scoured the house, seeing six more security cameras. He ran in his limping gait fast and low across the gravel and hid behind the car.

The front door of the house was open, and as he peeked through the car windows, he saw a marble hallway lined with gold-framed paintings leading to the back of the house, where he could see the edge of a pool. He heard voices in the house and ducked down. Could that be Kate? Was she in there? His heart hammered. It took everything he had not to run to her.

He waited. The voices faded. Then he was up, into the porch

and through into the hall. Rooms and corridors stretched off in both directions. A fancy stairway with a long glass chandelier curled away to the right. Had his children slid down that banister? Was this the place they considered home?

Mack stepped through the wooden and glass doorway into the backyard, where a large, rectangular pool seemed unfeasibly blue in the bright sun.

Voss was lying on a sunlounger at the far end of the pool under a large white umbrella. His conker-brown stomach domed above him. A paperback was splayed out on top of it, rising up and down with his sleeping breath.

Mack strode as quickly as he could along the side of the pool, his gun stretched out before him, his shadow crossing the closed white shutters of the pool-side doors like a ghost.

He stopped. Staring down at Voss. The man who had haunted every dream and most of his waking thoughts for over a decade. It took all this strength not to blow his brains out. But he had to be patient. He had to find out the truth.

Voss stirred, lifting up his sunglasses and squinting into the sun.

'Where are they? Where are my family?' Mack demanded.

If Voss was shocked that Mack was pointing a gun at him, he didn't show it. He didn't move from his reclining position.

'Where are they?' he repeated.

Mack saw a figure then, coming out of another wing of the house on the other side of the pool. Hackett. He was dressed in shorts and a T-shirt. His eyes widened with shock.

Voss shuffled up the lounger and put his veiny feet on the ground. His revolting stomach bulged over his yellow shorts. He reached for the cigar in the ashtray on the small table next to him.

'Well, well, well. Blow me down. Mack Moncrief.'

Mack pointed the gun at Voss's head. 'Where is Kate? And the kids?'

Voss chuckled a low, menacing chuckle. 'You came back for them. This is all very touching.'

'Where are they?'

'She never gave up on you, you know. Old Katy.'

Mack swallowed. Why was he talking about Kate in the past tense?

'Where is she?'

Voss put the cigar in his mouth and puffed on it for a moment, before inspecting the end. It had gone out. He put the cigar down.

'You know, she was the most beautiful woman I'd ever seen. Classy. Classic. I wanted her right from the first moment I realized she was yours. I always wanted a family, see. I got everything else, but a wife and kids . . .'

'They're mine. They weren't yours to steal.'

Voss chuckled again. 'True. But then, I can steal anything I want. You proved that.'

'Kate is *my* wife.'

'She was. A long time ago. Then she was mine.' He looked up at Mack, his watery eyes black and evil. 'She was mine *every day*.'

Mack felt dread make his knees weak. Hatred reared up in him.

'Was?' he managed.

Voss shrugged. 'Things don't last forever. Not even your jail sentence, apparently.'

For a moment hope reared in Mack's heart. Had she gone?

Had she escaped Voss? Then he met Voss's eye and saw the truth. No one escaped this evil man.

Mack felt the gun trembling in his hand. He'd been such a stupid fool. What had he expected? That his family would be here? Waiting for him? That Voss would hand them over?

Suddenly, without warning, Voss pounced, barrelling upwards from the sunlounger, catching Mack unawares as he shoved his massive bulk into him.

Mack staggered backwards, dropping the gun. As he tried to regain his balance, Hackett came from nowhere, through a side door, punching Mack hard in the guts. But Mack was fast to recover. Desperate now, he pushed Voss away and smashed his elbow into Hackett's chin. Then he grabbed Hackett by the throat and, with a primeval yell of fury, forced him backwards, lifting his feet off the ground. Mack shoved him hard into the edge of the door he'd just come through. Hackett's head cracked loudly, the force of the blow shocking them both.

Mack let go like he'd been burned. Hackett slumped to the floor. Mack wasn't sure if he was dead. He was certainly unconscious.

Voss made a frustrated growl, reaching for Hackett's gun, but Mack was quicker, kicking it out of the way, through the doorway.

'Where are they?' Mack snarled. 'Where are my family? Where is Tara?'

'Oh, Tara. My little princess,' Voss said. His sneer made Mack's blood run cold. 'She wasn't as keen as her mother. But then she was only little. I liked her that way. She was about ripe at eleven, see. She had a very tight—'

The shot rang out, echoing off the concrete walls and silencing the cicadas.

Voss flew backwards, the bullet almost dead centre in his forehead. He landed flat on his back, his head in the pool.

Mack stared in the direction of the shot, which had just missed him but had hit Voss. A maid was standing in the darkened hallway, holding Hackett's gun. Her lip trembled, but her eyes didn't leave Voss. They blazed with hatred. In the silence that followed, she didn't drop the gun.

Mack walked towards her. She was in her forties and was pretty with dark hair scraped back into a ponytail. 'Are you . . . are you OK?' Mack asked cautiously.

His heart was pounding hard. He pressed his hand on the gun and she lowered it, letting it go. It clattered to the floor.

She nodded. 'He was a pig.' She spoke with a Spanish accent.

They both looked towards Voss. Blood was seeping from his head into the pool, mixing with the water. The silence felt deafening.

She spat, then wiped her mouth with the back of her hand. She looked up at Mack and their eyes met. And he knew that she recognized him, although she was a stranger to him. A stranger now bound to him by Voss's murder.

'Now go. You must go,' the maid pleaded, coming back to Mack. 'He has people everywhere. If you go now, they will never find out you were here.'

'I can't go,' Mack exclaimed. 'I can't just leave you. If you hadn't shot him, I would have tried my best to.'

'His people will find me, but I can save you.' The maid's eyes looked up at Mack.

'I have come for my family. I'm—'

'I know who you are, Mack,' the woman said, touching his arm. 'They had pictures of you under their pillows. Kate talked about you endlessly, and you were a hero to Tara. She always talked about her daddy coming for her.' She let out a choked sob. 'I always told her you would.'

Mack reached out and the woman fell into his embrace. She shook in his arms. Then she pulled away. He grasped her by the shoulders.

Mack stared at the woman. He'd been through his own torture in jail, but it had been nothing compared to what his family had suffered. Nothing at all. And here was this brave woman prepared to risk her life for him.

'What is your name?'

'My name is Helena Montez. I have worked here since they came. Kate and the kids.'

'Please tell me it's not too late for Tara and Mark too,' Mack said, trying to stave off the grief that threatened to overwhelm him. The horror of Voss's unspoken words rattling around his brain, too horrifying for him to focus on. 'Tell me what happened.'

'They are gone, Mack. All of them. I'm so sorry. He killed them all.'

'Please, God, no.'

He felt the hope that had kept him alive all these years crumbling.

'He wanted them to be his family, but he knew they were only pretending,' she said quietly. 'That they all loathed him. He killed Kate three years ago. He beat her up so badly after an argument she never recovered. And then he honed in on Tara. None of us could protect her. It was a living hell here. Eventually, she took an overdose of pills. Voss was furious.'

Mack felt his heart detonating like an abandoned building.

'And Mark?' He forced out the words, but he could barely speak.

'He was the first to go. Seven years ago. He was still a boy.

He ran. He was brave. It broke Kate when they brought his body back. That's what I mean. Voss blamed hyenas, but that wasn't what ripped him apart. Voss has people everywhere.'

Mack let out a sob. It was all he could do not to wail with grief. They had gone. They'd all gone. And now he had nothing.

'You have to go. You have to go now,' the woman insisted, pulling him away, along the corridor.

Mack looked behind him at Voss and Hackett. She couldn't be serious. He couldn't just leave.

'Wait. Stop. How can I? How can I leave you here?'

'I know his people. I can invent a cover story, until it's safe. There will be more people back here soon. Any minute.'

He realized now how intent she was, how scared. If Voss had done those unspeakable things to his family, then what would his men do to Mack? And this woman seemed sure she could protect him.

He followed her as she took him through the empty house. She unlocked a back gate in the wall between the fir trees. A lane ran upwards into the olive grove, the gnarled trees shimmering in the heat, against the vivid blue sky.

'Go,' she told him.

'But how can I help you?' he said, terrified of leaving her, unable to put a foot onto the path ahead.

'Tara and my daughter, they used to play,' she said.

'Used to?'

The woman nodded and closed her eyes, as if it were torture to remember. 'When I realized . . . when I realized what was going on here and what he was going to do to Tara, I got my daughter out of Spain, although it broke my heart. I sent her away when she was tiny, before Voss got hold of her too. I tried to do the same for Tara. I promise you I tried.'

Mack stared at Helena, realizing that she, too, had felt unspeakable pain.

'Just promise me that you will find my daughter, Julia, and help her. I sent her to my friend Consuela Pires in Rio de Janeiro, where Voss couldn't find her. Just promise me that and I will be happy.'

'I promise.'

Helena nodded, tears brimming in her eyes. She leaned up and kissed Mack's cheek. 'Now go. Leave here and never, ever come back.'

CHAPTER THIRTY-EIGHT

Kamiko squinted in the bright Californian sunshine on the doorstep of the grand mansion. She waited for a few moments, then rang the doorbell again. She could hear the chime echoing in the hallway beyond.

She glanced back along the bougainvillea-lined driveway to where the pink and white flower van was parked on the pavement outside. She thought of the delivery guy she'd tied up in the back of it. In such an exclusive neighbourhood as this, where all the houses were gated, there was little chance that their fracas had been seen on the road. Fortunately, when she'd put the pad of chloroform over his face, he had fallen backwards into the rear of the van and she'd bundled his feet in quickly and locked up.

Uncle Murushi's parting gift of a set of poisons had certainly come in handy. She felt confident and strong. He was behind her all the way, he'd said in his letter. She just had to focus on the job ahead.

'Coming,' she heard a woman calling from inside. Then a moment later Scooter Black answered the door.

She had a radiance about her that Kamiko hadn't expected. Her teeth were very white, her eyes bright green. In the photo she'd taken from Martha Faust's safe, she hadn't expected Scooter Black to look so . . . present. She'd expected a flighty, grungy actress, but Scooter had a joyfulness about her that threw Kamiko.

She was wearing a very pretty floaty silk robe, her long hair loose around her shoulders. Despite wearing no make-up, she exuded a kind of glamorous beauty that made her look lit up from within.

'Where's the usual flower guy?' Scooter asked, seeing that Kamiko was holding a bouquet of roses.

'He away today. Here,' Kamiko said, handing over the flowers.

Scooter smiled and glanced at Kamiko. 'I never get bored of them,' she confided, 'although this is just getting so over the top!' She laughed again.

She was about to close the door, but Kamiko stood her ground and Scooter remembered herself, smiling before disappearing for a moment and then coming back with a twenty-dollar-bill tip. She thrust it into Kamiko's hand.

'Thank you,' Kamiko said, not sure what to do with the money. Scooter was already turning away. 'When I saw it was this address, this house, I asked for flower job.' Kamiko put her hand on the door.

'Oh?'

'I old friend of Lin's . . .'

It was a gamble. The weakest part of her plan. She hoped Scooter would fall for it.

Scooter smiled and nodded. 'Oh, OK. I'll tell her you stopped by.'

Kamiko doubted it. Sweet little Lin wouldn't be coming back to work anytime soon. Not after Kamiko had called her pretending to be from the Japanese Consulate and had suggested that she cease working for Scooter until she could provide a valid visa that conformed to the new criteria that Lin had clearly never heard of. That was unless she wanted her famous boss to hit the headlines.

'She here?' Kamiko continued, in her most innocent voice.

'Not yet. She should have been here by now, though.'

'I wait?' Kamiko insisted. 'I arrange flowers?'

Scooter Black paused for a moment, then smiled. 'Sure. You know, come in. I'm so overrun with flowers, if you could sort them out, that'd be great.'

The actress sure had done well for herself, Kamiko thought, as she walked into the small utility room off the grand hallway and dumped the roses roughly in the sink. Scooter must have been keeping her handler busy with requests, like Xen had been for Tiko and Susi. Although Scooter clearly had more sense and ambition.

Kamiko thought back to her meeting a few days ago with Xen at the airport. He was a nervous-looking guy who'd explained to Kamiko how horrified he'd been when he'd discovered that it had been Tiko using her key and not Kamiko.

He looked stylish and wealthy, Kamiko noticed. Like a college graduate. But he had a nerdy vibe to him that appealed to her. In different circumstances, they might have been friends. 'I didn't realize at first,' he said, in a lowered voice. 'I assumed it was you signing in.'

'What did they request?' Kamiko asked.

'Nothing that big. Tickets to concerts. Hotel rooms. A couple of flights. Then drugs. That's when I realized and stopped it working for them.'

'Who are you working for?' Kamiko demanded. 'Who is financing this key?'

Xen shrugged. 'I send an email report once a week to a guy called Robert. He was the guy who employed me, but I know he's working for someone else. I don't know who.'

'Do you know where Robert is based?'

'All over the place. He's in LA mostly, I think. But I know there's a handler in London and one in Brazil. You know, Robert is pretty strict about keeping this all discreet. I don't know how you feel about it, but I'd rather he didn't find out that there was a mistake over your key. I don't think they'd like it if they knew we'd met. It's against the rules.'

Kamiko smiled and nodded. *So there were rules.* 'Sure. But how did you find me? I mean, at first? In the game?'

Xen smiled. 'I work for them. The game company. That's my day job. It's highly illegal to decrypt users' information, but in your case I made an exception.'

Kamiko nodded, impressed. 'Do you know why I have been chosen?'

'No. But you're not alone. There's a handful of others with the same key. But all of you are so lucky. I mean, what I wouldn't give for unlimited luxury.'

Xen had tried to sound jovial, but Kamiko knew he was scared. He'd be even more scared she realized now once the police found Tiko and Susi's bodies and made the link back to him.

'I suggest you go away for a while. I won't be needing you,' she said.

'Where are you going?'

'Away. You can book me a round-the-world open ticket.'

She got her key out of her pocket and smiled. She took some

of the tissue and wrappers that had got caught on it and put them in the ashtray on the table.

'Do I need to log on, or maybe you could just book it for me here and now?'

Xen nodded nervously. 'I guess I can do that.'

He took a smart phone from his jacket. 'Where do you want to go first?'

So she told him she'd always wanted to go to Hollywood, and before she knew it, she was on a flight to Los Angeles. First class.

Once she'd arrived in LA, Kamiko had booked into the swanky hotel in Wiltshire Boulevard that Xen had reserved for her and set about her mission to find Scooter. It had been easy. The celebrity gossip sites were full of speculative articles about the new girl on the block.

A bit more digging and Kamiko had found a celebrity tour site. On the bus yesterday, she'd driven around the neighbourhood with fat tourists as the tour guide had pointed out the homes of the rich and famous. They'd stopped across the street from Bette Davis's old house – the place that it was reported Scooter Black had moved to. That's when she'd seen the delivery van and the guy with the bouquet of pink flowers. The passengers on the bus had been buzzing with speculation about whether the flowers might be from Dallas Laney.

As they cooed with the vicarious thrill of their proximity to a celebrity life, Kamiko had felt scorn for both them and Scooter filling her heart. Scooter Black hadn't come by all this fame and fortune through luck or talent. She'd got it all through the key. And Kamiko was going to put a stop to it right away. Scooter'd got herself way ahead in the game, but she wasn't going to win it. Oh, no.

Now, she heard voices on the stairs and opened the door a fraction to look out into the hallway.

'Hey, baby,' she heard a man say. He had dark hair and was doing up the buttons on his shirt as he jogged down the peach-carpeted staircase. 'I am so late. I ran that bath for you. I just wish I could stay and share it with you.'

Kamiko felt a dart of shock. That man was Dallas Laney. That famous movie actor. She'd seen him in a movie on the plane from London to Tokyo. The woman in the next seat had recommended the film to Kamiko, saying he was 'to die for'.

But he was here. Right here. With Scooter Black. The rumours on the tour bus were true, then.

She watched as Scooter wrapped her arms round his neck and kissed him. He grabbed her bottom, pressing him against her, like he wanted to have sex.

'Don't.' Scooter giggled, pulling away and glancing over in Kamiko's direction. Kamiko quickly slid back from the crack in the door. 'There's a girl in there.'

'Who is she?'

'She's a friend of Lin's. She's come to sort out the flowers. The flowers you sent me.' She laughed, playfully hitting his chest.

'Just trying to woo the lady,' he said.

'Well, it worked. Enough already.'

They kissed again.

'I'll call you later. We'll talk through the script.'

'OK. See you, co-star.'

'See ya. Don't go getting into any trouble.' He put his finger on her nose and then kissed her again affectionately.

'As if I would.'

Scooter leaned back against the door, her eyes shining.

Then, with a laugh to herself, she pushed off the door and ran up the grand staircase, her silk robe flying out behind her like butterfly wings. A moment later Kamiko heard running water and Scooter singing.

Leaving the utility room, Kamiko crept silently up the stairs and towards the source of the singing. She walked into a huge, sun-filled bedroom, with a rose-pink carpet and large four-poster bed. Flowers were in every vase and filled the room with scent.

A door on the far side of the room was open and Kamiko walked towards it, peering in through the crack.

Scooter was relaxing back in a deep bath, which was in the middle of a sumptuous bathroom, raised on three carpeted steps. French windows were open onto a balcony that overlooked the manicured garden beyond. It looked like something from a magazine shoot.

She had cucumber slices over her eyes, but even alone, Scooter had a smile on her face.

Kamiko slid inside the door into the fragrant steam, her trainers sinking into the soft carpet. This would be even easier than she thought, she realized, stepping closer and seeing Scooter's pale nipples poking through the oily surface of the water, which was scattered with rose petals.

Still, she cursed herself for forgetting the chloroform spray that was in the flower spritzer downstairs. Perhaps she should go back for it.

'Lin? Lin, is that you?' Scooter sat up in the bath, taking the cucumber slices from her eyes.

She gasped when she saw Kamiko standing in the bathroom.

'What are you doing?' she cried, covering her chest. 'Get out. Get out!'

'He know about your key?' Kamiko asked, stepping closer, realizing she'd have to act quickly. Now.

Scooter put her hand to her neck, her eyes widening. 'How do you know about that?'

'I know you are cheat. That someone else pays for all this.' She nodded up at the gilt-framed mirrors around the bathroom walls. 'Do you know there's a guy who sits on a computer all day waiting for your requests? He gets paid to do that.'

'How do you know? How do you know all of this?' Scooter said, backing away from her in the bath.

'Because I have a key too.'

'You?' Scooter asked, shocked.

Kamiko nodded. 'You see, it's a game. Someone is playing with us.'

'A game?'

'Yes. The key is a game. And unfortunately for you, you just lost.'

Scooter backed further away. Kamiko liked the power the look of fear in the actress's eyes gave her.

'Whatever this is, we can work it out.'

'Where is your key?'

'It's in there. In the drawer by my bed. Take it if you want. Please don't hurt me.'

But Kamiko knew that Scooter realized it was already too late to beg. She screamed as Kamiko lunged at her.

Kamiko put her hands round Scooter's neck, plunging her head under the water. Scooter flailed wildly and it took all of Kamiko's strength to hold on, kneeling on the edge of the bath, her arms wet. Scooter was thrashing, her legs kicking.

Kamiko felt sweat breaking out on her forehead, terror rearing up in her. This was supposed to be easy, but Scooter was strong. Her arms clawed at Kamiko's face and she had to duck out of the way. For a moment Scooter was up above the surface, gasping in breath, her eyes bulging as they met with Kamiko's.

But Kamiko was more sure than ever now. She had to get rid of Scooter. Now she'd started, she had to finish this. Growling with effort, she squeezed as hard as she could, pressing Scooter down in the water.

Scooter flailed some more and then, quite suddenly, she stopped.

Just like that. She stopped. Her body went completely still and floppy. Kamiko let go of her neck, stepping back and staring down into the water. Scooter's head was under the water, her eyes open, her red hair swirling around her in the rose petals.

Kamiko stumbled back, falling down the steps, gasping for breath. She could hear the birds singing outside in the garden. She waited for what felt like ages, trembling, until her breath returned to normal. Then she stood, her knees shaking. She breathed out, catching sight of herself in the mirror. Her eyes blazed with triumph. She'd done it. She'd taken Scooter Black out of the game.

It hadn't exactly been easy, but it had been less traumatic than she suspected. But then, she'd heard that drowning was one of the quickest ways to go.

Scooter was motionless in the bath. Kamiko took one more peek at her, just to check that she was dead. Then she backed out of the bathroom. She was running out of time. She had to get out of here. She'd calculated it would take her just over an hour to drive to Los Angeles International Airport in the flower van.

Then she would catch her flight to Rio.

As she closed the bathroom door, she didn't see the bubble escape from Scooter's nose in the bath.

CHAPTER THIRTY-NINE

'You've got a visitor,' the policeman said, sliding across the mesh guard on Harry's cell door. 'Move it.'

Harry stumbled out of his cell and along to the interview room, wondering whether he was in for another visit from Marcus Weeks, his lawyer, who'd told him that his case was going to be almost impossible to win. Especially without any evidence of his 'so-called' key. Weeks claimed he'd checked with the key organization in Zurich, who had heard of Sir Cole Menzies, of course, but had never heard of Harry Cassidy. Or issued him with a key. His lawyer clearly thought Harry had lied about the whole thing.

Meanwhile, almost daily, the news was focused on Harry's illegal open trade. How he'd cost ten other traders their jobs. Not to mention the bank's cover-up and the flagrant breaking of the financial regulator's rules that had brought the whole banking industry into the media spotlight. The scandal was not going away.

The magistrate had set the bail ludicrously high for Harry's own good, he'd told him. Being in the protection of the police was far better than being on the outside while there was such a media frenzy going on. It seemed to Harry that he had been made a scapegoat for every evil practice in the City.

It was impossible, Harry thought, refusing to get his hopes up, that his parents would have been able to raise the bail, even if they'd received the letter that he'd written and begged Marcus to send to them, explaining everything.

Just the thought of what his parents would have to do in order to get the money together made all his shame multiply. But what choice did he have other than to beg them? Being held here indefinitely in police custody was a living hell. It might as well be jail.

The trial – when it was finally scheduled – would be a joke. Marcus Weeks had made that clear enough. He'd strongly advised Harry against bringing his story about the key into the case, or even thinking about incriminating Sir Cole Menzies in any way. Cole had friends in very, very high places, who could make life very uncomfortable for Harry, if they so chose. Including having a direct bearing on the length of his sentence.

Which meant that Harry was going to be a lamb to the slaughter. Jail was where he was heading, for sure, and everyone was keen to tell him how much worse it was going to be than this, though Harry wasn't sure how that was possible.

He braced himself for the visitor, dreading seeing Marcus Weeks and his disapproving face again. Dreading to hear more bad news.

But when he went into the visitors' room, he looked up to see his father waiting for him at the table. His chest tightened.

'Oh, Dad, Dad, you came,' Harry said, a sob rising in his voice as he walked towards his father.

Ever since he'd seen Gina on the television on the day of his arrest, Harry had been living in black despair. Yes, he'd been a fool. Yes, he'd told lies, taken drugs and got himself into trouble. But the worst thing by far was letting down his family. It was the thought of them cutting him off forever that had hurt the most.

But now, here was his dad. There was a chink of light after all.

He stared at Barry Cassidy, the man who had once thought his son was the best thing on the planet.

'I'm sorry,' he whispered, sniffing loudly. 'Oh, Dad, I'm so sorry.'

'I know you are,' his father said. He patted Harry on the shoulder. Harry had never seen his father look so emotional, or so old. He should be retiring soon, and Harry should have been the son who took him on golf weekends and spoilt his old man. Not this. Not being forced into a grim trek to the other side of the country to see a son behind bars.

Harry wiped his eyes as they both sat down. 'How's Mum?'

His father shook his head. 'She's not good.'

'But she'll get better, right?'

Again Barry shook his head. 'It's cancer, son. And it's everywhere. She's being very brave, but we're not sure how long she's got.'

Harry put his elbows on the scuffed Formica table and buried his head in his hands, trying to control his tears in front of his father, but it was almost impossible. He wanted to cry like a baby. His mum had cancer. And now Harry might never see her alive again.

'Does she know . . . ?' he began. 'Does she know about me?'

Barry Cassidy gave an exasperated laugh. 'Everyone in the whole world knows about you,' he said.

Harry wiped away his tears. His father's look told him

everything and he realized how his father's life must have been turned upside down by what his son had done. He imagined him trying to brave it through football training in the recreation ground with all the parents whispering and pointing at him. The good man of the community ruined by his greedy offspring.

'I wish I could go back,' he told his father. 'I wish I'd just . . . I'm so, so sorry, Dad . . .' He trailed off. How could he explain to his father the mountain of regret he felt? His father, who'd never had to feel remorse so overwhelming it felt like it might crush him.

'I'm here because I need to hear it from you,' his father said. 'And don't you dare try and bullshit me. Just tell me the truth. What the hell happened? I want you to explain everything you wrote in that letter.'

Harry took a deep, shuddering breath as he met his father's frank gaze.

'OK, I'll tell you everything, but you won't believe me, Dad. Nobody believes my story, but it's true.'

So out it came in a tumbling jumble of words. About how Nick Grundy had bullied him at work and how he'd made a stupid decision to show off and keep his trade open against the rules. About how he'd only wanted to be accepted and to be included. And then how he'd gone to see Dulcie and a guy had beaten him up because he was jealous. He told him how much he'd wanted to impress Dulcie and how she'd had to take him to hospital and then back to her flat.

He told his dad about waking up the next morning and the panic he'd felt and then how he'd been sent the key and how he'd ignored it, thinking it had been an apology present from Guy. But then, with nothing to lose, how he'd gone to see Sir

Cole Menzies and how his lie had spiralled so quickly out of control. How he'd started to question where the key might be from, but just assumed someone wanted him to have it. How he'd been arrogant enough to think he'd been chosen for some sort of elite club.

'It was like magic. All I had to do was name my desire and it happened. I thought I was special. I thought . . .' He trailed off, seeing his father's deep frown.

What a deluded fool he'd been. He buried his head in his hands again. There had never been anything special about him.

'I fucked up, Dad,' Harry said, tears threatening to choke him again. 'I fucked up, and now they're going to pin everything on me, and yes, the truth is that I did tell a lie, but I didn't mean any of this to happen.'

'But the club, the girls, those pictures . . .'

'Yes, I was there. Those pictures are all real, but the Japanese girl who set me up . . . I think she drugged me. When I woke up, I couldn't remember anything.'

'Your mother . . . she's so upset.'

'I know. I know how bad it looks, Dad, but I wasn't trying to hurt anyone. I thought I was there to see Dulcie. I hoped . . .' Harry felt his voice cracking. He'd never see Dulcie ever again. 'People like Nick Grundy, he always went to clubs like that with his posse of boys, but the irony is, I never did. I just tried to work hard and get ahead. Until that day. Until I kept the trade open. And now I'll be in here until I'm old and useless. And I hate it. I'm frightened all the time and I can't sleep—'

'Pull yourself together,' his father interrupted, his voice urgent. 'You've got to hold it together, OK?'

Harry nodded, forcing down his fear.

'I've been in many jails in my time and let me tell you this is a walk in the park compared to them. I've seen men tormented by much worse demons than yours and having to be braver.'

Harry felt humbled. He knew his father was right. He knew he had to man up. He didn't deserve his father's sympathy. Not after what he'd done.

'You got greedy and scared, but you didn't kill anyone,' his father pointed out. 'And the truth is, this is my fault,' his dad said, bowing his head.

'Jesus, Dad. How can it be *your* fault?'

'I spoilt you. I never really knew the meaning of that phrase . . . to spoil someone, but that's what I did. I gave you too much. Not that it was much, but I made you believe you could have whatever you wanted. And that's how you spoil a child.'

Harry couldn't bear that his dad was taking all this on his shoulders. That's what he'd always done.

And that's when Harry felt something switch inside him. It was as if all his self-pity had been shut down and in its place was a steely determination to bear the hand that Fate had dealt him. As he looked at the bowed head of his father, he knew that however great this ordeal was, he'd survive it and one day be the kind of man his father would be proud of.

Barry Cassidy sighed and wrung his hands together. He looked deeply troubled. 'And there's another reason . . .'

What was he talking about? Harry was confused. He could see his father was struggling.

There was a knock on the door and the policeman opened the glass-panelled door. An older man walked in. He was in his seventies and was wearing a shirt, tie and green jumper under his jacket, despite the heat of the room. He carried a battered leather briefcase.

'It's good to see you again, Chief,' the young policeman said, with a friendly smile to the man.

'Looks like you couldn't keep me away, after all,' the man said.

The man looked at Harry's father and nodded to him, before squeezing his arm. Then he looked at Harry. His eyes were friendly, his face kind.

'Hello, Harry,' he said. 'My name is Chief Inspector Andy Harris. We've got some things to discuss.'

'What things? What's going on?' Harry asked, looking between his father and Chief Inspector Harris.

'You didn't tell him, Barry?' Harris checked.

'No, not yet,' his father said, hanging his head.

'Ah.' The inspector gave Harry a long look. 'Well, son, your father showed me your letter.'

'He did?'

Why hadn't his father mentioned this before? His father didn't meet his eye, but stared down into his hands.

'I've managed to arrange for you to be granted bail. But I need you to sign some paperwork first because there's conditions.'

Harry surged with relief so powerful he felt faint. He was getting out of here. His father had fixed it after all.

'In fact, there's a good chance we might be able to make this whole nasty business go away, if you agree to cooperate and help us solve a very old case.'

'Anything. I'll tell you everything I know,' Harry said.

'Have you ever heard of the great train robbery of 1985?' the inspector said, opening his briefcase and taking out a huge bundle of papers wrapped in a plastic band and putting them on the desk. They landed with a thud.

CHAPTER FORTY

Way up over the canopy of trees in the Amazon rainforest, a pair of eagles soared. Mack Moncrief stood by the circular window of his mansion looking out over the treetops at them. There was no other building as far as the eye could see, just miles and miles of jungle. And in the far, far distance, a dark blue strip of sea.

He thought of Tobias and how much he'd loved sailing out there. What a pity it was that his old friend couldn't be here now. There hadn't been a day in the last six months that he hadn't grieved for Tobias, after he'd died of an unexpected heart attack.

But then, Tobias had gone in the way he would have wanted to. He'd always believed in living life to the full. He'd never given up wine, or smoking, or women. Not even right at the end. He'd been with his latest lover, Maria, on board his yacht when he'd had a sudden heart attack.

Mack wondered now whether Tobias would have enjoyed the last few months of his plan coming to fruition, or whether he'd have found them as stressful as Mack had. Perhaps the best part of this whole thing was always going to have been the planning.

Because that is what Tobias had loved best. Working out a strategy, coming up with a plan. And this had been his greatest brainchild ever. Tobias had been working on this key idea ever since he'd skied with his old lover Martha in Switzerland ten years ago and she'd got the top job at the marketing organization in Zurich. Boy, that sure seems like a long time ago now, Mack thought wistfully.

At least Tobias hadn't lived to hear the news that Martha had died in terrible circumstances – a burglar breaking into the beautiful cabin retreat Mack had had commissioned and built for her.

But the greatest shame was that he hadn't lived to meet his daughter, Scooter. How much it would have pleased Tobias that she, perhaps more than all the others, had benefited so hugely from her father's brainchild. How the key had made all her dreams come true.

'Mack,' Robert said, bringing him back to the present, 'are you OK?'

Mack turned slowly to see that Robert had poured him a stiff Scotch.

Mack walked with his stick past the white designer couches and took the glass from him. The blond Californian had been an integral part of the team from the start. Both Mack and Tobias trusted him completely. Mack knew it was good of Robert to leave his wife and kids and come here at his request.

Mack paused and took a long sip of his Scotch. 'You know, Robert, I asked you here because I think it's time. Time we brought them all together.'

'You're sure?'

'Yes. I think it's time we finished what we started. Send them all a message and arrange to bring them here.'

*

After Robert had gone to the office, Mack stared again out of the window, surveying the incredible view. He looked at his own reflection in the glass. He was old now, with white hair, and although he dressed in fine designer shirts and lived in this beautiful house, inside he still felt like a rough Scot from Edinburgh.

When had this started? he wondered. When had his destiny changed to the crazy course it had? How could it be that the shy lad from Scotland had ended up here? Had it been when he joined the army? When he'd defused his first bomb? Or after that, when he'd retired from the army and taken that security job in Edinburgh?

No. It was none of those things, he reflected. Those were all choices that followed on in a straight line from the Mack of old. What had changed him, and thrown his life so radically off balance, was simple. His fate had been sealed by one man: Alan Voss.

And now, as he took another slug of whisky, he remembered that day. That day he'd finally confronted his nemesis in Spain. Every second of it was etched on his mind as if it were yesterday. And he remembered, too, the feelings that had overwhelmed him afterwards. Of sheer fury and grief. But he'd had no one to direct it at except himself.

For weeks afterwards he felt impotent with rage. He should have torn Voss apart himself, limb from limb. While he had the chance. The fact that he'd been denied vengeance made him burn inside.

As he floated on the sea in Tobias's yacht, staying away from shore, he felt a kind of wretchedness that he couldn't shake. He felt ashamed of leaving Helena in Voss's mansion. But then, she'd been so insistent and he'd been so shaken with grief that he'd just followed her commands.

He'd begged time and again for Tobias to take him back, but Tobias refused. Mack was to wait. To sit it out. Until they could be sure the coast was clear. Helena had her reasons for acting the way she had, he'd reasoned.

But Mack constantly worried about what had become of Helena. Had she really been able to cover up what had happened in the mansion without implicating herself? She'd certainly been terrified of Voss's 'people', whoever they were.

Mack's brain would go round and round in a loop, back to the beginning, to his incandescent rage that Voss had kept Kate and his children prisoners. The fact he'd guarded them so jealously, making them pretend to be his family, made him feel weak with sadness. His jail sentence had been a holiday by comparison. At least he'd been able to keep himself to himself, and his dreams intact.

The days and nights now bore a new kind of torture for Mack. He had so few details about what had actually happened to his family from Helena, but as he brooded on them, the facts that he did know grew and blossomed like monsters in his imagination. Voss raping Kate 'every day'. He couldn't shake the thought – seeing it as if it were a movie in his mind.

He could imagine her face, her eyes flickering closed in disgust as Voss, with his fat belly, mounted her. And Tara too. His baby. Her childhood taken by that monster and then her innocence.

And brave Mark, running to safety. Mack's heart went out to his son. He'd have known the risks, but he'd done what Mack would have done. He'd tried.

Mack couldn't shake the storm of emotions that raged in his head until he thought he might drown with grief. He was richer than he could ever imagine being – and yet he couldn't help feeling that without his family, without the prize he'd yearned for for so long, what was the point? What was the point of even being alive when he had no one with whom to share his journey? No one, that was, apart from Tobias.

At least his old cellmate hadn't deserted him. In fact, Tobias did everything he could to try and cheer Mack up. But Tobias had always been better than Mack at life. Mack watched him from the wings, but the more Tobias partied and tried to enjoy their new-found riches, the emptier Mack felt.

In the end it had been Mack who'd insisted that they move away from Europe. He wanted a clean start. And he'd started to obsess about Helena's daughter, Julia, and his promise to find her.

And that's when he'd come to Rio.

He'd fallen in love with South America straight away. He liked being somewhere where there were troubles he could fix. He liked starting again, with a new identity.

The first thing he had done was to buy a huge tract of land in the rainforest when he heard developers were going to burn it down. He employed a young designer to design him this eco-house, way out in the wild, where he could watch the eagles soar.

He set up a hospital and a vaccination clinic, all in Kate's name. With every child that came through the door and was given a life-saving injection, he felt a tiny chink of light had blotted out the evil darkness of Voss's shadow.

To remember Mark, he founded a school and paid for teachers to come. When one boy showed promise, he arranged for a football coach to come from Rio and helped the boy to live his dream. That boy had just been picked for the national side.

The community loved him; the children thanked him for the chance he'd given them. Over the years the more involved Mack got, the more he started to remember what it was like to live again.

And all the while, in anonymous bank accounts around the world, the investments from the diamond money grew and grew, as if Fortune had realized its mistake and was finally making up for lost time. Mack watched his computers as the numbers spiralled upwards. Until his fortune was vast. A fortune that someone could use to change the world.

A fortune the authorities would still take away, if they found out his true identity.

So the burden of where it would go, or what would happen to his money when he'd gone, started to rankle him. He didn't want to give it away to a charity that would squander it. He wanted it to go to someone who would carry on his mission, to blot out the evil that had befallen his life by bringing light and life to those in need.

But who would carry on such a mission?

Time and again he'd pondered on his conundrum. The irony that he was rich beyond measure when he was old and increasingly infirm was not lost on him. If only he'd had all this when he'd been young. When he'd still had time to look after his family and make the right choices. It had been a thought that had obsessed him. Until Tobias had been skiing with his old lover Martha and had come back and told him about the key.

Mack turned away from the window now, as Robert came back in.

'I know Christian is on his way back to Rio, and Kamiko will get her message next time she logs on. There's a message waiting for Scooter too, but I can't find Julia. Or, for that matter, Thomaz,' he said, looking at his mobile phone.

Mack didn't like his tone. It was unlike the Californian to

be ruffled. Mack frowned. Thomaz was Christian's handler, but he was Julia's too. And she was the key-holder Mack cared about the most.

It had been Julia who had been his starting point for the whole key idea. He'd watched her from afar all these years, trying to find a way to help. But the one time he'd confronted Consuela, she'd been terrified and had sent him away.

She'd told him that Julia was hers now. That he must never interfere with her family. That if he did, she'd tell the police.

So he'd kept his distance and bided his time. It felt good to be paying Consuela's hospital bills. To have finally found a way to help anonymously. It felt good, too, that Julia had moved to a decent apartment at last. He felt sure the key had changed her life in a positive way, although she hadn't requested anything for a while. Just as quickly as she'd started to turn her life around, she'd stopped asking the key for anything. And then the signal from her key had gone and not Thomaz, Mack or Robert had been able to track her down. Thomaz had been working round the clock trying to find out what was going on.

'He's offline, and there's no answer from his phone,' Robert said, holding the mobile to his ear.

'That's unlike him,' Mack said, concerned now. 'Where could Thomaz be? I don't know, but without him, we have no way of getting in touch with Julia.'

Mack frowned. He needed Julia here. He needed her, along with Christian, Scooter and Kamiko. He needed them all to hear the final decision he'd made.

CHAPTER FORTY-ONE

Julia coughed, the dust of the tiny basement filling her lungs. She could see weak light through the thick glass panel in the ceiling above. She tried to wriggle her hands again, but they were still bound tight to the bench. She heard the distant sound of the mobile phone ringing again.

She tried to shuffle the bench across the floor, but there wasn't much space. Sweat trickled down her back. Her throat was parched.

How long had she been in here? Minutes? Hours? Days?

All she remembered was the woman coming to her apartment. When the door buzzer had rung, Julia had, for one second, hoped it might be Christian.

Her heart was pounding as she ran to answer the door. But a Japanese woman was standing in the doorway. She had on high heels that looked uncomfortable, and straight checked trousers with a leather jacket.

'Who are you?' Julia demanded, looking the skinny woman up and down.

'Hello, Julia. My name is Kim. You come with me,' she said, flicking her eyes along the corridor as if someone were waiting. Her accent was strange. She had dark eyes – almost black – and an intensity about her that Julia found unnerving. How did she know her name?

'What?'

'I have information about your key.'

She knew about the key? Julia felt the colour rising in her cheeks.

'But I don't have a key,' Julia said. 'Not any more.'

The woman didn't seem to understand. 'You have to come now. Everything will be explained.'

'I can't,' Julia said. God knew she'd wanted her key back ever since she'd thrown it away, especially since Riccy had threatened her, but right now was the worst possible timing.

'My grandmother,' she explained, fighting down the tears that were so close to the surface all the time. 'My grandmother has died and it is her funeral today,' she said, throwing out her arms as if to explain her black dress and veil. 'I must leave to go to the funeral. I have no time. You will have to come back later.'

'This will not take long,' the woman said. 'You will come with me in the car. I will drive you to wherever you need to go after.'

Seeing that the woman wasn't going to go away, Julia reluctantly agreed. A free lift would be handy, now that she was wearing her high black heels.

But as they left the apartment block and got into the smart cab with blacked-out windows, Julia's mind went into overdrive. Where could this strange Japanese girl be taking her? Because she was more of a girl than a woman, Julia now realized.

What was all this about? Was she part of the key organization? Were they Japanese? If so, how on earth had they contacted Julia? Why had she been selected?

She had a whole head full of unanswered questions, but time

was running out. She couldn't miss Vovo's funeral. But the woman stayed silent, ignoring Julia's protests, telling her they were nearly there.

As the car finally arrived at a small house in a suburb she didn't recognize, Julia knew straight away that she'd made a mistake. Someone who bestowed luxury and paid for hospital bills and apartments didn't live in a place like this. A place that was miles away from where she was supposed to be *right now*.

She could see the back of the Cristo Redentor way off in the distance, behind a tree-covered hill, and she tried to get her bearings. She looked at that statue often, as it was a constant reminder of Christian, but right now she wasn't thinking about Christian, she was only thinking that she was miles away from where she should be.

This was one of the southern suburbs and was affluent by Rio's standards, but still, the small houses were crowded together, surrounded by myrtle trees and climbing vines. She looked along the street to see a ragtag row of empty roof decks with trellises and plastic furniture. All the windows had closed white shutters. Most people who lived here would be at work. To her horror, she watched as the Japanese woman paid the cab driver and it drove quickly away.

'Wait,' she protested, 'I need the car. You promised it would take me on. I have to be somewhere.'

But the woman ignored her. Julia rushed after her, following her up the narrow path to the white door of the house, which she unlocked with a key.

Inside, it was dark, the windows blacked out with blinds.

The living room and kitchen were filled with computers. Whoever resided here was a serious geek. And it stank. It smelt terrible. Of chemicals.

And that's when Julia saw photographs of herself on the wall.

'What is this? What's going on?' she cried, but the Japanese woman grabbed her from behind and put something over her nose.

It must have been some sort of drug, because the next thing she knew, Julia had woken up in a tiny room she assumed must be a basement, tied to this bench.

Now, she suppressed a sob of anguish, as she thought about Vovo's funeral going on at this very minute, imagining the church, the meagre flowers she'd organized. The handful of mourners, all cursing Julia for not turning up. What if they thought she'd stayed away deliberately? That she'd taken the family rift Riccy had instigated to heart and was protesting with her absence.

It was all too much to bear. What if no one was missing her at all?

The last week had been the worst of her life. She'd stayed with Vovo, sitting at her bedside, holding her hand, praying for her to wake up. Begging her to tell her the truth: that Riccy had been lying. That those awful things he'd said couldn't be true.

But then Marcello had come with Fredo, and the second he'd walked in, she'd known that what Riccy had said was true. They *had* all lied to Julia. Whatever hold Vovo had had over them to keep her secret, Ricardo had broken it.

She'd been so upset that she and Marcello had hardly spoken. There was a distance that she couldn't bear to broach with words. It had been so painful watching Fredo saying goodbye to Vovo, but she hadn't been able to comfort him. He seemed to be distant from her too, as if they'd all closed ranks.

She felt tears rolling down her cheeks now, remembering it

all, wishing she'd handled it differently. Wishing she'd shared her grief. Wishing she'd told them that whatever relation Vovo had been, she had been the only one Julia had ever known. Her rock. The woman who'd believed in her and supported her to make a better life for herself. She wished, too, that she hadn't lied about the key, or let them think that Vovo had won the lottery and that she'd used the money for herself.

She tried her hands again, her wrists already chaffing and burning. What if that crazy Japanese woman didn't come back? What if she left her here to die of dehydration? What then?

A wave of panic made her breath catch.

She thought of Christian, seeing his smiling face so clearly in her mind's eye. What if she never saw him again? That's if he ever came back from wherever he'd gone. Which he would if he really loved her – like he'd promised he did.

She cursed herself for lying to him, too. If he'd only known about the key, then she might not have ended up in this mess. He might have persuaded her not to throw it away.

And everything would have been different.

But most of all she wished that she'd followed her gut instinct right from the start. She wished that she had never set eyes on the key, or taken the money in the wallet. She wished she'd had the sense to realize how dangerous it would be in her life. How it would turn everything upside down and make a liar of her.

Because the key had ruined her life. And by the time she'd got rid of it, it had been too late. The damage had been done. Whoever was behind it was warped. Evil. Manipulative. If she ever, ever had the chance to find out who they were—

A scraping sound made her look up and gasp, hope flaring

in her chest. The door to the basement opened. Sunlight illuminated the thick dust in the cramped space.

'You two. Get to know each other,' the Japanese girl said, pushing a man into the basement. As he moved, Julia saw that the Japanese woman was tying his hands behind his back, too.

Julia recognized the man who had given her the key by the *theatro* all that time ago. His face was grim as his eyes locked with hers. The weird Japanese woman followed him down the stairs and pushed him on the bench next to Julia. She wrapped the rope quickly and tightly round the legs of the bench.

'Wait, please,' Julia begged the woman, but she said nothing. 'Please, please don't go. I need water.'

But the Japanese woman walked out. She seemed preoccupied. They heard a chair being pulled across the doorway.

'Oh shit,' the man said. 'She got you.'

'What the hell is happening? Why am I here? Who is that crazy woman?'

It took all of Julia's effort to remain calm. The man winced again. He was clearly in pain.

'Kamiko is another key-holder. She came to Rio, and Xen, her handler, said that I could help her out.'

'Xen? Who is Xen? Who is Kamiko? Jesus, what is all this about?' Julia asked him, her voice frantic. 'What the hell is a handler?'

The man hung his head. 'My name is Thomaz. And all I know is that a man from California called Robert employed me. I was paid – paid incredibly well – to find you and give you the key. Although, it was so difficult to get your attention I had to break my cover to give it to you in person.'

'But why? Why was I given a key? What is all this about?'

'All I know is that it was to track you and I had to be on

call twenty-four seven. I had to get you anything you wanted. Once a week I had to send an email to an encrypted address outlining what you'd done, where you'd been, what you'd asked for. And that's it. That's all I know. Really, I'm as much in the dark as you.'

Julia thought about how much she'd questioned the key, how strongly she'd distrusted it. She now realized the huge level of subterfuge behind it.

'But who? Who would want me to have all this?'

Thomaz shrugged. 'I don't know. But you are very lucky.'

'Lucky? How do you call this lucky?' Julia cried, staring at him. Thomaz looked away. She felt a new kind of terror sweep over her. Thomaz was the contact for the key. The only possible way she was going to get out of here. And he was being held captive too.

'I know there are only a few of you – key-holders, that is. All around the world. And Kamiko is one of them.'

'So how did she find me?'

He groaned. 'She told me that she wanted to meet you. She logged on to the key and told me that she knew I was a handler in Rio. I don't know how she knew about you, but she knew your name and that you were a teacher. I assumed you must have known about her. She was very charming and said it would all be OK, that the people above knew all about it. So I typed back the details of your apartment.'

Julia let out a frustrated wail of despair. 'How could you?'

'How was I supposed to know she was crazy? She seemed so sincere. But then she logged on again. She said she had information for me. About you. About your key. I gave her this address. When I came back, she was waiting for me. She hit me . . .' He winced again.

Julia felt sorry for him. She could tell he was in pain, and just as confused as her that he'd been tricked by Kamiko. But still, this was his fault.

Now the door opened. Kamiko came back in with a bottle of water. She walked down the steps and put it to Julia's lips. Julia drank greedily. Kamiko didn't offer any to Thomaz.

'So what did Julia get?' the girl, Kamiko, asked, nodding her head towards Julia. 'With her key?'

Thomaz glanced nervously at Julia and then back to Kamiko. 'An apartment. Hospital care for her grandmother. Nothing extravagant.'

Kamiko brought out a gun from behind her back.

She had a gun. The crazy woman had a *gun*.

Julia felt sick with fear. She tried to shuffle backwards in the chair, but she was trapped.

'Harry was the worst, I think,' Kamiko said. 'Or perhaps Scooter. She got a lot. More than she deserved. But now there are just three of us left in the game. You, me and Christian Erickson.'

For a second Julia didn't think she'd heard her correctly. Her head whipped round and she stared at Thomaz. Now a new kind of terror made her brain clear.

'Christian?' she whispered.

Christian was a key-holder? He was mixed up in all of this? It couldn't be true.

'Please, Kamiko. You've had your share too. I'm sure you have,' Thomaz said.

'No, I haven't. That's just the thing. What about Christian?' Kamiko demanded. 'Do you know about him? What did he get?'

'I don't know exactly. But not very much,' Thomaz stumbled. 'Not as much as he could have. I organized a trip to Iguazu Falls for him, a helicopter and a hotel.'

Julia stared at him, her heart pounding like horse's hooves. 'You? You arranged that?'

'You didn't know? I thought you knew. I thought he must have told you,' Thomaz said, looking confused. 'I thought that was why you were together.'

'Oh, you know Christian?' Kamiko asked. She walked towards Julia. 'That's clever, you two working together.'

'I'm not working with him,' Julia gasped. What was going on? What was happening? 'I didn't even know he had a key. Please let me go. We can work this out.'

'There's nothing to work out. The game is over. Because I know who is behind the key. I know he has been testing us, to see who he will leave his fortune to. And now he has called us together to deliver the prize. And I am going there now. What a shame you won't be going too.'

'Let us go,' Thomaz shouted.

'Shut up,' Kamiko snarled, turning the gun on him. Then she pulled the trigger. Julia screamed, watching as Thomaz looked down at his chest and the horrific gunshot wound, then at her.

Julia was trembling all over as Kamiko pointed the gun at her.

'I say goodbye to Christian. For you,' she said, 'before I kill him too. He was the last on my list.'

And then she pulled the trigger again.

CHAPTER FORTY-TWO

The jeep rocked along the bumpy road, and Christian stared out of the window. It had only been a short drive from the small landing strip in the jungle, but now, as the jeep slowed, he realized they'd arrived at their destination. He stared upwards at the curiously shaped building. It was mostly made of glass and wood, and stretched high up into the sky. A round room was right at the top, like a spaceship, overlooking the surrounding jungle. The sun glinted off the glass windows.

And yet it would be almost impossible to see – even from the air, he concluded. Right in the heart of the jungle, it was miles away from the nearest town, let alone city. All he knew was that it had been a four-hour flight from Rio.

For how many hours had he been on the go? he wondered. He was too full of adrenalin to feel tired, but he realized that it must have been days since he'd slept properly. He had crossed several time zones since leaving his father's house and arriving back in Rio.

Dan had met him off the plane, taking him to a large corporate hotel to meet the team of five who'd now gathered.

Christian had been exhausted. He'd wanted nothing more than to see Julia. It had been unbearable to be in the same city and not be able to contact her, but Dan and his team had been very clear: Christian's number-one priority was to get another key. Time was running out. He would be able to contact Julia after that.

Which is when Christian had cracked and told them what he'd discovered. About his father's link to Mack Moncrief. He'd handed over the correspondence he'd read on the plane from Norway, even though it had pained him to do so, knowing it meant he was implicating his father in a crime. But he'd felt he'd had no choice.

He watched as Dan and his team read Teis's belligerent insistence that he wanted nothing to do with Mack's stolen money. From Mack's letters back, it was clear that Teis had told him about how proud he was of Christian working as a doctor in Africa. And that his father had sent photos too.

'He sent Mack a picture of me in my first boat,' Christian had told Dan. 'That's why he used that question in my security set-up. How else would he have known that I even had a boat? Let alone that it had been orange?'

Then there had been the last communication from Mack, insisting that he would find a way to pay back the enormous debt he owed Teis, whatever it took. That he had heeded Teis's words. That his life had been good. That he'd done everything he could to blot out the evil that had befallen him.

'I should just confront him,' Christian had told Dan, rubbing his face, as the team in the background frantically made calls to do background checks on Mack Moncrief. 'Tell him what I know. That I know it's him.'

But it seemed that Mack Moncrief had beaten him to it. As soon as he'd logged on to the key's page, a message had flashed up.

It is time to meet. A plane will be waiting at Rio Airport at 8 a.m. A car will be waiting for you.

And that was how he had come to be here. Delirious through lack of sleep, Christian was about to confront the man who was responsible for his parents' separation, for him losing his job and for the terror of the past couple of weeks. He just wanted it to be over. He wanted to be free, to be with Julia.

Now he stared at Robert – the American guy who'd picked Christian up in a jeep from where the small plane had landed and who now held open the door.

He was in his mid-thirties and had an athletic build. He had close-shaven strawberry-blond hair and trendy silver glasses. In his crisp white shirt and khaki shorts, he looked dependable and trustworthy, and he'd been very charming and friendly so far, and had seemed to know such a lot about Christian that it had been difficult not to warm to him. Robert had chatted on the short drive, telling him about his kids back in America and his wife. How he'd been a top programmer at MIT, but had been offered a job that had been difficult to refuse.

'What Mack's done is amazing,' he told Christian now, with a smile. 'You'll see.'

Christian refused to believe it. Moncrief was a thief. He had to keep his distance. He was not being sucked in to his PR machine in the form of Robert. This was wrong. Everything about it was wrong.

He couldn't forget that he was being monitored. Dan and his team had made Christian wear a wire under his shirt, just in case anything went wrong. Although looking about him now, Christian doubted they'd be able to pick up a signal from somewhere this remote.

'What is this place?' Christian asked, noticing the roads

stretching off in either direction. He could see a large, well-tended field and a set of sprawling modern-looking white buildings. In the other direction, there were small houses. Kids walked along the road in school uniform. They turned and waved at Robert, who waved back.

'It's a hospital. People come from all over the Amazon Basin to get treated here. It is a centre of excellence, but a very well-kept secret. The government doesn't like people to know about it,' Robert said. 'And the school is down there.'

Then, just overhead, another small plane swooped down over the trees towards the landing strip.

'Your host has other guests arriving today,' Robert said. 'Come in. Please. You are welcome.'

Christian was shown inside and he followed Robert into an elevator, which took him up inside the building to the enormous room at the top. The doors of the elevator opened and Robert patted Christian on the shoulder, gesturing for him to step out onto the white carpet. Robert walked quickly to the other side of the room and through a set of white double doors. Christian saw a room beyond with desks full of computers.

Left alone and still feeling confused, Christian took a further step into the room. The low coffee table in front of him was covered in glossy hardback books; the walls, too, were filled with books and ornaments. Mack Moncrief was clearly a very cultured man.

But it was the panoramic view that really took his breath away. It was so astonishing that for a moment Christian couldn't move. Being in the room was like flying across the sky.

Mack Moncrief was standing by the window. He looked older and more groomed than he did in the pictures Christian had seen on the Internet, but he guessed those images were twenty-five years out of date, when Mack had been a notorious inmate. Now, the elderly man before him, the man his father had called a friend, looked tanned and in good health, apart from the fact that he was leaning on a stick.

'Ah, Christian. Come and see my eagles,' Moncrief said, gesturing for Christian to join him at the window. He smiled like they were old friends. Not strangers. Or even enemies.

Christian walked across the white carpet, disarmed at the lack of formal introduction, but relieved, too, that he didn't have to speak. He felt too overwhelmed.

'I trust your journey was comfortable?' Moncrief said, smiling. 'That plane ride over the jungle is quite something, isn't it?'

'I don't want to be here,' Christian told him. 'I came to tell you that I don't want you in my life. Whatever this is . . . why ever it is that you've chosen me, I don't want anything to do with the key. The key you gave me.' He was surprised with the force with which he'd spoken. That he'd blurted it all out.

'I'm sorry to hear that,' Mack said. He sounded genuinely hurt.

'What you did . . . it destroyed my family. My mother and father.'

'Did Teis tell you that?' Mack asked, surprised, looking into Christian's eyes.

Christian's fury stalled. All his father had said was that Mack was an innocent man in his eyes. And that he'd had to escape to save his family. That if their roles had been reversed, then Teis, too, would have tried to escape. That he respected him. That he would call him a friend. That as a chaplain, he knew a good soul when he saw one. And that Mack would have helped him in the same way. He'd have bet his life on it.

Even so, all the way here Christian had built Moncrief up in his head to be a monster. A kind of evil manipulator, a man with a crazed power complex. But now he saw that he was quite different to how he'd imagined.

'I meant to cause no harm,' Moncrief said. 'You must know by now that your father helped me more than I can possibly say. I wanted to help him back.'

'Then help *him*,' Christian snapped. 'Not me. He needs help. I can live without anything from you.'

'Why are you so angry?' Mack asked.

'Because you have no idea what I've been through,' Christian said, the pressure of the past few days threatening to overwhelm him. 'You have no right to play God with my life,' Christian told him. 'No right at all.'

'I am not trying to play God, Christian. Only find someone I can trust.'

Well, he couldn't trust him, Christian thought wryly to himself, wondering which CIA satellite was picking up this conversation.

'And I asked you . . . I asked you for another key, one that I need badly, and you refused.'

'The keys are not for others. Just for the ones I have chosen,' Mack said reasonably. 'I could not risk bringing others into this. You must understand.'

'But—'

'Has getting the key really been that bad? Truly?' Mack asked. His eyes searched out Christian's again. 'Didn't you use it to go to Iguazu Falls? I'm glad you did that. It's such a wonderful place.'

Christian swallowed hard, feeling conflicting emotions raging inside him. Mack was right. Getting the key hadn't been that bad.

It had saved his life, for a start. And maybe without the key setting off the chain of events it had, he'd have never met Julia.

But at the same time he could see now that Moncrief was intractable. If Christian was going to get another key for the colonel, then he was going the wrong way about it.

Mack turned and looked at the view. 'All I ever wanted, Christian, was to be free. I was raised to believe that a hard day's work equals honest pay and that a man should live within his means. I'd seen generations of my family be that way and they were happy. Aye . . .' He paused. 'That was the way to live. Everyone knew their place.'

Christian stared at him, baffled. If he felt like that, then why not give all his wealth away?

'So go and live like that.'

'I can't live like anything other than this. Don't you see? I have swapped one kind of prison for another. I can't go home to Scotland.'

Because he was a criminal. A wanted man.

'But I have been happy here. I have done many things of which I'm proud,' he continued. 'I just wanted to pay back the people who had helped me to survive.'

'What if they don't want paying back . . . ? My father doesn't.'

'People often don't know what they want. Until they are given vision.'

Christian followed Mack's gaze out to the horizon. He could see how from up here, high up in the canopy, rich and omniscient, he had struck on such a plan like the key. But it didn't work. Not in the real world.

'And, of course, I needed a way to find my successor,' he said with a smile.

Christian was astonished. He'd said it so flippantly, but he saw that Moncrief was serious. He'd used the key to test Christian? To find out whether he was a worthy heir? And heir to what? To his vast fortune? To this house, even? Is that what he meant?

Had he passed the test?

He felt his mind spiralling, but he had to focus. Do what he was here to do.

'If you really want to help me, then you can,' he told Moncrief. 'I promised a key to another man. A man in Africa. A terrorist who kills and maims, who won't stop unless he gets a key too. If I can just get him a key, then he can be tracked—'

'By who?' Moncrief asked, clearly upset by Christian's suggestion. 'Who would track him? Why would you involve me in this?'

Christian looked away. He couldn't answer. He couldn't bring himself to tell Mack that he had brought the CIA to his door. That now they knew who he was, it was very probable that his assets would be frozen pending an investigation. That every penny he'd ever made would now need to be accounted for. That if he was found guilty of any sort of fraud, then he would be going straight back to jail.

'Mack,' Robert interrupted, coming out through a doorway across the room. Beyond it, Mack could see another man standing by the computer screens. 'Can I have a word? Xen is here.'

'Excuse me a minute,' Mack said. 'Have you found Julia?' he asked, as he walked towards Robert.

'Julia,' Christian interrupted, running after him. 'Did you just say, "Julia"?'

It couldn't possibly be *his* Julia they were talking about?

'Yes, Julia Pires,' Mack said. 'She's another key-holder, but unfortunately we can't find her.'

CHAPTER FORTY-THREE

Kamiko stood by the door in the stairwell and darted her head up to look through the glass. She saw Mack Moncrief walking into the computer-filled room to talk to Xen and she swore.

She'd seen Xen arrive just now. She'd been with a driver, who had picked her up from the landing strip. He was Brazilian and had a friendly smile, but spoke hardly any English. He'd driven straight up to the curious tower-house and shown her into the lift, coming inside for a moment to press the button for the top floor.

But just as the doors had been closing, she'd seen a jeep pull up and Xen had got out, talking rapidly into a phone.

She'd pressed the button for the floor below, stepping out of the elevator on another floor that seemed to be full of empty bedrooms. She'd found a stairwell and, taking out her gun, had tiptoed up the stairs. Now she'd found the doorway to the office, but Xen had beaten her to it.

If he was here, then it must mean he'd found out about Tiko and Susi.

She was close, so close, Kamiko thought, feeling her veins flood with adrenalin; she could not afford for Xen to blow it now.

Through the glass she watched the men talking. There was Xen and a blond guy, who had a frown on his face, as well as Mack Moncrief.

That was him. That old guy. She was sure of it. He was the man who owed everything to Uncle Murushi. The man who would be nothing, who would not even *be* in this tower without Kamiko's family.

And now another guy came in from the other room. It was Christian Erickson. She recognized him from his photo. He'd been summoned too.

She saw everyone freeze as another plane roared overhead.

She contemplated her options, trying to think quickly. She was not going to have the prize snatched from her by Christian. Not after everything that had happened.

She thought of the letter Murushi had given her, along with the gun and the pot of chloroform. How he'd told her that he'd converted Mack Moncrief's stolen diamonds and given him untraceable dollars in return.

It was Murushi who'd figured out the key. He'd told her that Mack must have picked her because of her connection to him. He'd told her, too, that Mack was vastly wealthy. That if the key was a game, then he'd devised it in order to find an heir. That whatever she did Kamiko must claim the prize. Claim what was theirs.

She thought about Julia in Rio. She was a weak idiot. She didn't deserve anything. No, this was between her and Christian. And she would win. Whatever his connection to Mack Moncrief, hers was greater.

She pushed her foot against the bottom of the door, opening it a fraction so that she could hear what they were saying.

'I came straight away,' Xen was saying. 'As soon as I realized.

She's here. She's coming up in the lift now. You have to work out what you're going to do. But she's definitely the one who attacked Scooter in LA.'

'But she's OK, right?' Mack asked, looking ashen.

'She's fine. Shaken but fine. Her flight is delayed, but she'll be here later.'

Kamiko bit her lip. It couldn't be true. Scooter was alive? But Kamiko had drowned her in the bath. She'd been dead . . .

But Xen was still talking. And now Kamiko's heart really started to pound.

'Hold on – you're saying that these other two people who stole Kamiko's key, Tiko and Susi . . . they're dead?' the blond guy said.

'Yes, they were both found dead in their hotel room. But that's not all,' Xen said. 'She left some rubbish on the table in the airport when we met. I found a receipt from a coffee shop in Zurich. I remembered when you called, Robert, you told me about Mack's friend Martha Faust being murdered. I did some research. The receipt was for the day before her death.'

'Kamiko was in Zurich? Then she must have met with Martha,' Moncrief said. Kamiko could see his face. How shocked he looked.

'She must have known about the others. She must have found out from Martha,' the blond guy, Robert, said.

Kamiko didn't give herself time to think. She burst through the door, her gun outstretched. She was not going to leave without a fight. She was going to win this. No matter what.

'Kamiko,' Xen said, jumping backwards when he saw her gun.

'You will transfer all the money to me,' she said, advancing towards the old guy. Moncrief.

'Please put the gun down,' Moncrief said, holding up his hands. 'Please, Kamiko, this is a misunderstanding.'

'No. You transfer all money to me. I am winner.'

'There's no game,' Moncrief said.

'Just give the money to her. If that's what she wants,' Christian said, advancing forward towards her. 'Where is Julia?' he then asked. 'If you know about the others, then where is she?'

Kamiko stepped closer. She put the gun against Mack's head.

'Stop,' the other guy, Robert, commanded. 'Please. Stop.'

'Transfer the money to me. To my account. Here.' She slapped down a piece of paper on the desk with the details of the account Murushi had given her.

'I can't, Kamiko. It doesn't work like that. The money is in bonds,' Mack said. His voice trembled.

'The prize is your fortune. I work it out. I am not stupid.'

'Where is Julia?' Christian repeated, and Kamiko saw the surprise on Mack Moncrief's face. And confusion too.

'You see, you don't know everything,' she told him. 'He and Julia, they are together. They are lovers.'

'How do you know that?' Christian asked.

'I found out when I met Thomaz.'

'You've met Thomaz?' Robert asked.

'He with Julia. He's dead by now.'

'What have you done? What have you done?' Christian gasped.

'You will transfer all the money to my account now. If you don't, you'll never see Julia again.'

'Just do it,' Christian shouted. 'Do whatever she wants.'

Mack stared at Robert. Then he rattled some keys on a computer keyboard, consulting the paper Kamiko had given him.

She smiled as she looked at the computer screen. The transfer was taking place.

It had worked. She'd won.

Suddenly, there was a deafeningly loud noise and the sound of a large helicopter close by, descending on the building.

Now another man appeared through the door behind Christian. He had dark hair.

'Mack Moncrief, I am Dan Gilbert from the CIA,' he said.

Then she heard another voice. 'Miss, drop your weapon.'

There was a man approaching through the door with a gun, dressed in camouflage clothes.

Kamiko fired her gun at him, then ran backwards into the stairwell, her heart thumping. She heard footsteps pounding up the stairs from below. She ran upwards towards the roof, bursting out a moment later onto the flat space. The whir of the helicopter rotors just above made her hair fly around her head in a frenzy.

But there was someone behind her.

'Where is she?' Christian shouted. 'What have you done to Julia?'

'She'll be dead by now,' Kamiko shouted back.

'Stop. Just stop.'

Christian ran towards her, but Kamiko stepped back. He wasn't going to catch her. She would get away.

She had the money. She'd won. She and Murushi would be free forever.

She ran across the roof to another hatch further across, but suddenly the helicopter dipped down lower; the wind from the rotors began pushing her back towards the edge of the roof. She couldn't keep upright.

She flailed out her arm for Christian to catch her, but she couldn't reach.

Then she lost her footing altogether. She was on her stomach being pushed to the edge of the roof by the wind. She couldn't hold on. She screamed for Christian to help, but he couldn't reach her. Her fingernails scrabbled across the roof of the tower.

And then she was falling . . .

CHAPTER FORTY-FOUR

As he waited outside the ornate building in Rio in the sunshine, Christian stared over the wrought-iron balcony at the gravel path below, seeing a black twig. For a second a flash of memory made him see Kamiko's body lying on the ground outside Mack Moncrief's house when she'd fallen from the tower. Her black hair splayed out around her, her legs bent, her eyes closed. He'd known instantly that she was dead.

He remembered, too, the mayhem afterwards. The blur of action. Dan being there with his team. Mack being injured from Kamiko's gunshot wound, and in the chaos, Christian and Robert starting the search for Julia.

They so nearly hadn't made it. An hour later and it would have been too late. It had been Christian who'd found her in the basement of Thomaz's house behind the door with the chair against it.

He'd never forget how she'd been – delirious with dehydration, barely conscious, Thomaz's dead body slumped against her. He'd taken the wire cutters he'd found in the kitchen and cut her hands free, but her wrists had been congealed with blood where she'd struggled. He remembered how she'd fallen into his arms and he'd held her tight, so relieved he'd found her. And as he'd shouted for Robert to call an ambulance, how he'd begged her to stay with him, how he'd promised that if she only stayed alive, then he'd never, ever let her go.

'Hey,' he heard a voice say now.

He turned to see Julia coming out of the door of the Spanish Embassy. She had a big grin on her face and a bounce in her step, in her red sandals and pretty yellow dress. His heart skipped, seeing her face.

She was carrying a sheaf of papers, which she was trying to order and get back into her folder. He could tell right away that her appointment had been a success, as they both hoped it would be.

She was on her way to being reunited with her mother, Helena. Christian only hoped that the meeting would be as wonderful as Julia had built it up to be.

It had been a big shock to them both hearing the whole of Mack's story. Christian and Julia had visited him in hospital after she'd been given the all-clear herself. She'd been desperate to find out her own connection to the great train robber, after hearing about Christian's ordeal. Julia had been furious that she'd been taken hostage by Kamiko and Christian had assumed that she was going to be furious with Mack, too. She held him directly responsible for Thomaz's death.

But Mack was more sorry than Julia had realized. That was clear. He'd been deeply shaken by what Kamiko had done, by the devastation she'd left in her wake. What a terribly troubled soul she'd been.

Christian and Julia had listened as Mack started from the beginning and told them his own story. Christian had even started to feel sorry for him, understanding for the first time how his father must have felt all those years ago. He too now knew in his heart that Mack was a good man. That he had tried so hard to make the most of a life blighted by tragedy.

Julia had been in tears by the time Mack had revealed his enormous debt to Julia's mother. How she'd saved her from Voss. How she'd sent Julia to safety with Consuela and how, despite his repeated efforts, Consuela had stopped Mack from contacting her. That the whole idea for the key had come from wanting Julia to unlock the door to a better future for herself.

Ever since that day Julia had been on a mission to find her mother, and Christian had helped her. They'd found a possible address in Spain, but Julia wanted to meet her mother in person. It had been a complicated process, sorting her out a passport and now a visa.

'They say they'll process my visa application right away,' she told Christian. 'Then we can book flights.'

She grabbed hold of his arm and smiled. He leaned in and kissed her. 'That's wonderful,' he said.

She pulled a face at him. 'Don't look so stressed,' she told him. 'It's over now.'

Christian nodded. He was stressed, for several reasons.

It was true it would be over by now. Under duress, Mack had provided a key for the colonel, which Christian had sent out to Africa with Dan, along with a handwritten letter. It had made him feel wretched to fulfil his promise to Colonel Adid, to write so sycophantically and apologetically, but in the end it had been the only way he could save the lives of the innocent children the colonel had threatened. And now the CIA were in the process of tracking the colonel through the key. Last night Dan had emailed Christian to say that the mission had been a success.

Christian felt sad for Mack. Because despite all his good intentions, the key had ultimately been Mack Moncrief's downfall. The CIA had only just begun their investigation, while the investigation into the train robbery had been reopened in Europe. Mack was under arrest, and his assets had been frozen. The vast fortune he was planning on bequeathing to Kamiko, Julia, Harry, Scooter or even himself would now vanish into the legal system, in lawyers' fees and tax arrears.

It was a shame that the hospital and the school would have to close, Christian thought, remembering the brief glimpse he'd had of the small piece of Paradise Mack Moncrief had created deep in the jungle. Maybe one day, when all of this had calmed down, Christian would take Julia there and show her what might have been.

But that wasn't the reason he was stressed. Not today. He fingered the small box in his pocket. He'd had the diamond from his key set into a silver ring and he planned to give it to Julia and ask her the question to which he hoped she'd say yes.

Julia held hands with Christian as they walked towards the cafe, watching the birds flitting between the trees. She delighted in feeling the sun on her face, Christian's hand in hers. It was the first time since Christian had rescued her that she'd started to feel normal. She thought so often of poor Thomaz and each time she did, she said a little prayer for his soul. Of all Kamiko's innocent victims, he'd been the worst. She only hoped that in time she would be able to put the whole horrible ordeal behind her.

'Where is this place we're going to?' Christian asked.

'Confeitaria Colombo. Just over here. It's near where Vovo used to work. In these offices. She always wanted to come here. So we are going for afternoon tea,' she told him. 'Nat is bringing Fredo along in a while and you can finally meet them both.'

It was the first of many ways in which she would honour her grandmother's memory and build bridges with her family.

Learning what Consuela Pires had done – that she'd taken in her friend's child and hidden her from danger – had been a shocking and humbling revelation to Julia and one that she was still getting her head around.

For the first time she could understand why Ricardo had felt the resentment he had towards her, why Consuela had kept the family as she had. But these were all rifts she hoped to heal in time. For now, all that she cared about was that she and Christian had each other and that she was alive.

She pushed through the doorway of the cafe, delighting in the opulent chandeliers and the mirrored walls steeped in history, thinking of how much Vovo would have loved coming in here, how much she regretted not arranging it while she was alive. How many more small kindnesses she could have bestowed on her dearest grandmother.

From now on she would never put off something she wanted to do, she vowed. If she'd learned anything, it was that time went by too fast. That there was no point in planning for the future, or mourning the past. That life was for living right here and now. And nobody was ever, ever going to mess around with her destiny again.

In the back of the blacked-out car, Mack Moncrief took his binoculars and watched Christian and Julia chatting and laughing in the corner booth of the fancy cafe. Of all the consequences of the key, he had never imagined that they would find each other, but it made his heart glad that they had. And that they had both survived Kamiko and her terrible plan. It had been obvious, he now realized, that they'd been together. He should have guessed when they'd tracked Christian and Julia to Iguazu at the same time and then Julia had thrown her key away.

He still couldn't believe she'd done that. It touched him deeply that when it came down to it, neither Christian nor Julia had genuinely wanted his money, only their freedom. In that respect, they were both like him. Both his rightful successors.

Scooter, of course, had already benefited from her legacy. When they'd finally met, in all the chaos after Kamiko's outburst, Mack had hardly had a chance to talk to her before he'd been whisked away. But he knew she'd be OK. She hardly needed his help now: she was so successful in her own right. He heard she was going to star in a huge movie next year. He hoped he'd get to a cinema somewhere in the world to see that.

He'd planned for so long to leave his fortune to his five successors, but after what had happened, he doubted there would be a penny left to his name. However, he had been prudent enough to take out an insurance plan. When the lawyers came to read Consuela's will, Julia would be in for a shock: Consuela's estate was worth a small fortune.

He'd known Julia from afar for so long that he hoped that she'd use the money to school Fredo properly and to find her mother, as she planned to. And when she did, Helena would realize Mack had come good on his word. He pictured the two of them reunited and felt a pang of bittersweet sorrow that he would not be there to witness it.

But for now Mack was on the move again. He'd escaped from the hospital last night. It had been easy to evade one guard and bribe another. Now that Chief Inspector Harris was on his way to Rio and Harry was a free man, Mack saw no need to hang around and face more questions. He would not give the inspector the satisfaction of having the final word.

Thanks to Martha's diamond necklace, he'd be able to finance himself wherever he went. Those diamonds had saved him a second time round. Robert had found the necklace in Kamiko's backpack, which she'd left in the corridor by his office, along with her camera. All the evidence they'd needed of how corrupted Kamiko had really been. How badly the key had gone wrong in her hands.

There were always going to be greedy people in the world, Mack concluded. Avarice had a way of poisoning people like Kamiko, but even so, might she have followed a different path if he hadn't intruded in her life? His intention had only been good, his only thought to help her, but his intervention had caused untold harm. And for that he felt truly sorry.

But looking at Christian and Julia now, he took some small comfort. Because seeing them joining hands across the table, united and happy, proved what he'd known all along about life: that the key to it all . . . is love.

BC	4/14